D1571343

Dark Days
Troubled Times

1st Edition

By Matthew D. Mark

Dark Days, Troubled Times

Library of Congress Control Number : Applied For

46600 Vineyard
Shelby Township MI 48317

ISBN Info:
Soft Cover 3rd Edition: 978-0-9890045-5-8
E-Book: 978-0-9890045-6-5

The dedication of a book pales in comparison to the dedication people show to each other. Through a serious family illness, I have learned a truer meaning of the word dedication.

Watching two people dedicated to surviving, to keeping a family together, and more importantly, dedicated to loving each other, I have found the truest meaning of the word. Mom and Dad, this is for you.

Love always,

Matthew

Acknowledgements:

I have to thank each and every person who encouraged me to continue the story from Dark Days Rough Roads. The overwhelming support from family, friends, and most importantly, the readers that gave me the inspiration to finish is greatly appreciated.

As I have said before, I could not have completed this second book in the series without my life experiences and the contributions from those I know. In one aspect this time was a little different.

A member of my family was dealt a serious illness during the writing of this book. Strangers came to the aid of our loved one. They prayed for us, hoped for us, cried with us, and they stood by our sides to help us.

They did this not because it was their jobs, but because they were human beings doing what we should always be striving to do. Caring for one another, no matter what differences we may have, no matter what our beliefs are, what country we hail from, or economic class we live in.

I thank each and every member of the emergency services and the medical professionals. From the doctors and nurses all the way down to the support staff who not only bring a hot cup of coffee, but also offer a smile and hope. You are all unsung heroes. Thank you.

Kayla, I love you kiddo. Dez, you're still alright even though you broke my rifle. Kathleen and Michelle, thank you again for the first editing. Kim, with WWO, thank you for the additional editing support. Lacey O'Connor, you provided another great cover. Thank you.

Preface:

A new cold war is upon us. We hear more cries from North Korea. Other countries are rapidly advancing their militaries and nuclear might. There are even more strained Middle Eastern relations.

Tornado's, floods, mudslides, hurricanes and multiples of natural disasters continue to happen on a daily basis around the country. These take days, weeks, months and years to recover from.

There also exists a larger problem. Our own country is dividing itself over race, religion, politics, and economics. This division can ruin our country and the foundation on which it stands.

The rights of the people, as individuals, are being challenged. What will happen if these individuals fight back? Will it be martial law? Will it be rioting? Will it be a revolution? A civil war? As modern as our country is, yes, it could happen. We see it around the world daily.

No matter what you believe may or may not happen, wouldn't it be nice to have a couple weeks worth of food and water on hand just in case? Something to get you by, to give you hope, to help you survive? Even in the most simple of events, it can make a difference.

The internet is full of useful tips and ideas on how to prepare for a week, a month, a year, or a lifetime. Give yourself a chance to beat the odds in an emergency. Just hope, we never need it.

Table of Contents

Chapter 1

Roger Haliday sat at the table drinking his cup of coffee and talking to his daughter, Kayla. The past two months had taken them on quite a journey. In a short period of time they had gone from a very normal life to fighting for their lives in what had amounted to a small civil war.

Now they would have to piece together the news they were hearing daily on the ham radio and try to figure out what caused the EMP, what was happening across the country, who was on which side, and more importantly, which side they would be on. They were not sure if the fight would reach their retreat or not.

They had endured their fair share of fighting the past several weeks and didn't care to endure any more. Winter was here and the next few months meant that a lot of people would be battling the cold weather in addition to battling the lack of food, water, and security of the lives they once had.

Unfortunately for most people, the next few months would mean life or death. The current population of the country would easily be halved as people froze or starved to death. Freezing to death would actually be better than starving to death. Going to sleep on a cold night and never waking up would be more humane than wasting away day by day.

Nobody had heard of any government help anywhere as far as camps or food distribution networks were concerned. No one really had any faith in them, regardless. You were talking about a government that took days to respond to smaller regional emergencies like hurricanes.

With somewhere near 75 percent of the country being essentially in the Stone Age with no technology, no power, no running vehicles, and no food or supplies, it only made sense they would be overwhelmed. There was no way they could have been prepared for such a large magnitude event as this. The sad thing was, the government knew the possibility existed.

The reasons behind the EMP were still unknown, but the simple fact was it could have been anything; it could have been North Korea who had seemingly gotten a grip on controlling missile launches and satellites; it could have been China, knowing they would never see a return on the U.S. debt they held. Taking the country and its vast resources would settle the debt in their eyes.

Conspiracy theorists pitted the government against a rogue group of anti-government individuals, the military against the government—a group calling themselves the Constitutional Restoration Army—and on and on. The EMP for that matter could have been caused by Mother Nature herself. The fact was simple: it could happen and it did.

Haliday heard a shot and jumped up right away. Everyone else in the house started running, grabbing their rifles and getting ready. The rifle report was close so he knew it had to be from somewhere close to the cabin. He ran over to the ham radio, but no one was there. He keyed the mic and spoke into it. "Kevin, what's going on out there?"

Kevin replied, "I got a deer, Uncle Roger. It just walked right into the field."

"Well, maybe a little heads-up before you fire a shot would be nice. We're all in here ready to fight," Haliday told him.

Haliday looked around and focused on Randy. He told Randy to go outside and send Kevin in.

Randy could tell by Haliday's tone of voice that he wasn't very happy. Randy put his boots on, grabbed his jacket and a rifle and went outside.

In just a few minutes Kevin came in. "What's going on, Uncle Roger?"

Haliday answered him. "We have rules for discharging firearms around here. You need to let us know if you're taking a shot for hunting. We all jumped up not knowing what to expect. You have to understand, things are much different these days."

Kevin kind of looked down. "Sorry, everyone. I just got excited. It's my first deer."

Alan, Haliday's brother, said, "Apology accepted. Let's go. I'll help you gut it and dress it out."

They got ready to go back outside and Haliday stepped out onto the porch. He looked through some binoculars toward the field at the dead deer. It was definitely a buck and had quite a nice rack on it. Looked like a 10-point.

Alan and Kevin came out and Haliday stopped them. "Kevin, I'm just a little uptight. We still have no idea what we are in for. Now getting back to the business at hand, nice shot, Kevin."

Haliday walked back inside to see that everyone else was already getting settled back down. They kept two people on security detail at all times, which reminded him that someone was supposed to be sitting at the ham and taking notes. He wanted to know who.

Haliday walked over to the dry erase board and looked at the roster. He looked at the ham station and saw Dawn sitting there. He walked over to her and looked down.

She just looked at him sheepishly. "I had to use the bathroom," she said.

Haliday said, "OK, here's what we are going to do. We are going to keep a portable on the desk at all times and if someone needs to go squirt or squat, they take it with. That way no radio traffic from the outside sentry gets missed. Go ahead and leave a note on the table and I'll pass it along to the others as well."

Haliday went over to the dry erase board and jotted a note down there, too. He also wrote down that he wanted the outside watch to start using the crow's nest on top of the cabin. This would give them some protection from the wind and they could use the small chiminea up there for heat.

He walked back over to the table and grabbed his coffee. He poured it into a small pot and placed it on the wood burner to heat it up.

As simple of a foodstuff that coffee was, there was no more wasting food for any reason. Every little bit of food went to use in one manner or another. Everything was rationed out in order to stretch their supplies.

They had completed an inventory of food stores and determined that they could make it almost three years based on what they had. This of course included any crops they would raise. The deer and any other game they could hunt would stretch their stores even further. He even had the guys get the ice fishing gear ready. Every little bit helped.

When he thought of how unprepared most of the country was, it actually saddened him. It was not just the idea of an EMP; there were so many possibilities for something going wrong in the country that it didn't make sense that people didn't prepare for an emergency. Anything could have happened.

You could watch on TV any one of the shows that were about preppers or survivalists or whatever you wanted to call them, and you could call them nut jobs or whackos all you wanted, but the thing was that they were much better off than most people right now. Oh sure, some of the scenarios portrayed were way off base, but regardless, they had stocks of supplies.

They could sit there and tell people about the New Madrid Fault, the Yellowstone Volcano, EMPs, nuclear war, oil emergencies, financial collapse or even alien invasion, but the fact remained that they had supplies that most people would kill for right now. That was exactly what was happening in a lot of areas right at this moment.

Haliday had previously made contact with an older man named Adam close to where Alan lived. He was able to put Alan in touch with Haliday and they communicated almost daily on the ham radio. Adam was basically on the outskirts of Detroit and had a pulse on the events transpiring there.

Adam had mentioned that gangs had formed and other people were cutting them down in the streets to protect anything they had and to keep their families safe. This had started to happen after just a couple of weeks. After the last month however, the gangs and their goals took on a whole new meaning.

Adam had told Haliday that the surviving gangs were well equipped now and moved in larger packs. They would encounter resistance and based on how severe the resistance was they would either move on to another target or decimate the home they were attacking. They singled out the smaller groups or individual families.

They moved from house to house and would steal or kill without any remorse. Once they left a home there was nothing of use left in it. They would rape women, they would kill anyone who interfered, and they took everything the people had. Sometimes they would stay a night or two and move on the next day.

Haliday had asked Adam how he managed to avoid the gangs. Adam told him that he had close to 30 people in the house and all carrying AR15s to keep them safe.

They had placed barbed wire and traps around the house and a large sign that said "Enter on your own free will, or die on ours." The gang took a couple of potshots at the house, but soon figured out it was better to leave them alone.

The neighbors close by got lucky as the gang skipped a few houses. However, not many were as lucky. Adam said they fought the instinct to rush out there and help but it would have been suicide. Haliday told him he understood. He told Adam that you had to pick your battles carefully in that environment.

People just didn't get it these days. Not having anything to protect you with was downright dangerous. As these gangs were moving along the cities, too many people were finding this out the hard way.

They were just *sheeple*, as Haliday called them, awaiting the slaughter. The gangs didn't care about laws or how they got their firearms—they had them and that's all that mattered.

Food was another story. The government preached a two-week supply. The current event was far past two weeks, but that time period might have allowed people to group together for defense and safety. It might have made a difference for at least some of the people.

Kayla walked up and Haliday set down his coffee cup. She sat down across the table and looked at him. "Looks like you have something on your mind, Dad," she said.

Haliday took a sip of his coffee and looked over at her. This kid had been through so much lately he didn't want to ruin her day. He replied, "I'm just going through things in my head, trying to make sure we are all ready for spring and planting in the fields. I'm trying to come up with a few more gizmos to help keep us all safer."

"What kind of trouble you expect? You think we'll have any problems?" she wondered.

He looked at her and smiled, then said, "You know me, always thinking ahead."

Haliday walked over to the ham and sat down next to Dawn. He turned on the portable and called Rob. Rob had taken over the governing of the Bad Axe area after removal of the rogue militia group there. Since they had regained control of the small airport and also the area in general, things were not as bad.

The benefit to the area was that it wasn't prone to people forming gangs and going rogue because of the rural layout of the area. After defeating the warlord-like militia, people respected the authority of Rob and the group.

Rob asked him if it was okay to meet and Haliday told him it would not be a problem. He told him to bring Brad, who was now the area's Defense Coalition Commander.

Spring would be here in a few short months and they needed to be ready and they had questions to ask. Haliday told them to bring him 50 pounds of corn and ten pounds of sugar to trade. Rob told him okay, but didn't ask why.

Haliday keyed the mic again and asked, "Mike, you guys on right now?" There was no immediate answer but just as he was about to turn off the portable, he heard a voice.

"Roger, this is Mark. Mike is busy. Sorry it took a moment, I had to dry my hands. I was on kitchen duty. How can I help you?"

Haliday said, "The guys are coming by tomorrow at noon to talk a bit and I'd like you here if possible."

"That's fine, I'll be there. I have some things going on here we need to talk about. We might need to make some changes," Mark said.

"Sounds good," Haliday said. "We'll have an early dinner and send some back with you."

He wondered what was going on. They were about 20 miles away, but without a lot of running vehicles and then gas being at a premium, it was a little too far for comfort.

They were also closer to a more heavily populated area, which could be the reason. Maybe it was time for them to move on over to Haliday's cabin or the vacant house across the street.

Haliday had already started running through the logistics of that possibility. The food stocks would immediately be reduced to about a two and a half year supply. The rest was incidental. Food and water were the important things.

He did not know what Mark's group had to bring and how that would balance out, but he knew they did have some stores. Whether they stayed at the cabin or the house across the street would determine wood use for heating.

Haliday looked over at the woodpile outside. The pile was under a 20-by-20-foot car port with tarped sides to keep moisture out. They had 20 full cords of wood stacked high, which was plenty of wood for the large wood burner they used for heat and cooking.

This would actually last them almost two years. Next spring and summer, however, he would have the group stocking more, so it would be well-seasoned by the time it would be needed.

Haliday let everyone know that they would have visitors tomorrow. They planned to cook up the deer that Kevin had shot and smoke the rest into jerky. Some basics like mashed potatoes, some mixed vegetables, and biscuits would round out the meal. It'd be nice to see some fresh faces as well.

Kayla walked over to Haliday and said, "So, are Mom and Mike coming too or just Mark?"

"It's just Mark tomorrow, sweetheart. I think they need the security over there from the way things sound. But, I also think we may need to change that and get them over here," Haliday replied.

Moving them over would be a fairly large task by itself. They did have the two trucks and trailers, but then Mark also had livestock. Haliday thought to himself a bit and came up with an idea. They would have them pre-pack everything and then stage the animals in a pen. They should only have to make two trips.

One trip would be for food and clothing. For the second trip they would have to find some horse trailers or something similar and use those for the livestock.

They would have to plan it out carefully and make sure they had security details in place to make the move safely. Food, firearms, and supplies were prized targets for thieves and thugs.

Rich, Haliday's father, came over and sat down across the table from him. He poured them both a fresh cup of coffee. Alan came over and sat down as well. They all talked about the move.

Haliday was going to be insistent that it get accomplished now regardless of what Mark thought. When the snow and cold hit heavy it would be too hard.

Haliday looked at Alan. "Hey, you get that deer cleaned and dressed out already?"

Alan said, "Sure did; with the two of us working and that wonder knife you have, it was pretty easy."

Haliday asked him, "What do you mean, wonder knife?"

"That Alaskan thing, the Ulu. That thing works great on game," Alan remarked.

Haliday hadn't really thought about it before. He received it as a gift and never thought it would be used. It was one of those simple tools that people would have to rely on these days. No more plugging in an electric knife any time soon. No modern conveniences.

Dinner was over and everyone was settling in for the evening. Haliday volunteered to take a double shift on the ham. He took some notes, scanned through frequencies, and listened to what was going on in the world. He flipped over to one frequency in Florida and chatted a few minutes with a guy.

"Hey, Blake, come here," Haliday called out to his daughter's like-aged friend.

Blake came over. "What ya need, Mr. Haliday?"

"Well, I have some good news for you. The *Caribbean Star* has been located. It docked in Belize and everyone on board is safe and sound," Haliday told him.

"Do they know anything else?" Blake asked.

"The Belizean government is keeping everyone there for now; they are giving them food and shelter. They will be setting up some type of communications in the future for people to contact family," Haliday said.

Blake was relieved and it showed. His mother and grandmother had been on a cruise when the event had occurred. The ship they were on was the one that was now in Belize. Kayla walked over and put her hand on his shoulder and told him that was good news.

Blake said, "I agree. I can't wait to talk to her and let her know I'm all right."

Everyone else settled into bed and Haliday finished out his shift. He marinated the venison so it would be ready to cook in the morning then climbed in bed himself. He would sometimes lay there for hours going over all of the information he had heard and try to decipher it all. So far, he trusted no one, and would not admit to anyone that he had no idea what the hell was going on in the rest of the country right now.

When he had more information and when things were more apparent, he would give them his opinion. They could then sit down as a group and figure out if they would even be involved or how it would impact them. Things could go down in so many different ways, and it was too early to say right now.

Morning came and they all ate a light breakfast consisting of Cream of Wheat, toast with jelly, and coffee or juice. Everyone reviewed their tasks for the day. Most were menial and consisted of stock rotation, wood stocking, cleaning, and other small things. They were just meant to help keep people busy and avoid cabin fever.

Haliday had marinated the venison the night before. This morning he lit up the smoker and placed some in to cook for dinner. By the time Rob and Mark got there and they finished talking, dinner would be ready. For security purposes, Haliday would save most of the discussion with Mark until after Rob had left.

With the town supplies being limited and people in the outer areas growing desperate themselves, it was important not to let others see their supplies for fear of an attack. Haliday made sure everything was hidden. Appearances would show Haliday's group to be only a bit better off than most. That was one of the reasons for having the deer for dinner and not the stocked meat.

Haliday walked the property and made sure everything was in good order. He double checked to make sure nothing was out of place. He walked over to the pole barn. Next to it he shifted a barrel around that hid a small cover in the ground. They had a small 500-gallon tank buried. It was full of treated gas.

Haliday then walked back to the cabin and went inside. He had everyone check around to make sure nothing technological other than the ham radio could be seen. They wouldn't let anyone in the basement. People would freak out seeing the TV, stereo, and computers. They had gone through so much trouble to keep them safe from the EMP. They'd all want that tie to civilization.

Haliday was sitting at the kitchen table when he heard a vehicle approaching. He stood up and went to the door. Mark was the first one to arrive. He came inside and greeted everyone. They all talked a few minutes, but mostly they were curious to know how Mark's wife Lisa was. Mark had told them all she was healing really well and was quite mobile now. That was good news.

About 15 minutes later they heard another vehicle approach. This one had Rob and Brad in it. The two of them came up to the door, where they where greeted. After the brief hellos, they all went to the front of the cabin and took a seat. Bev, Haliday's mom, had made a fresh pot of coffee and brought in cups for everyone.

Rob looked at Haliday and said, "I brought the corn and sugar you asked for. What the hell you need it for?"

Haliday smiled. "I have a small still. I'm going to brew up some good old-fashioned moonshine. I'll give you a little food for the corn and sugar. I'm going to bottle the shine and trade it for what we need."

"That's not a half-bad idea," Rob said.

Haliday said, "Yep, you'd be surprised at how handy alcohol will be. My brew will be a little like apple pie. Some apple juice added and a little cinnamon. I have some liquor on hand, but not a lot, and nothing I'm going to trade away."

Of course that, too, was being deceitful; Haliday's group probably had about 50 bottles of various liquors stored. However, it made sense to make it, bottle it, and save the good stuff for later. He always joked around and said it was for one big welcome back to civilization party.

Haliday said, "OK, gents, let's cut to the chase. What's on the agenda for today?"

Rob spoke and said, "We are losing a lot of people in the area. Not everyone is rationing food and not many are coming in from the outskirts. We don't know what to do."

"Listen, guys," Haliday said, "it's not going to be pretty. Not everyone is going to make it. A lot will die; there's just no way around it. Until spring comes around and you can start getting crops in the ground, food will be scarce. It'll be the end of summer before the crops produce anything anyway."

Brad looked over at Haliday and said, "How many people do you think will die before spring?"

"You can probably count on half. It will be six months in April since the power went out," Haliday answered.

Rob shook his head. No one there really wanted to think about it. It wasn't really the rest of the people they were worried about; it was the fact that they were thinking about themselves and their families. The odds were not very good.

"What about by the end of summer?" Rob asked.

Everyone went silent and waited for the answer.

"I'm not too sure, but by the time it comes around to reap those crops, I would say we will be lucky if fifteen to twenty percent of us are still alive. I'd say maybe ten to fifteen might make it, to be more honest," Haliday said.

Everybody sat there silent for almost five minutes. It seemed like hours before anyone spoke. Haliday could only imagine what they were all thinking. Mark knew how it was, but neither Rob nor Brad, just two months ago, would have thought they would be sitting there discussing this.

Rob looked at Haliday. "What the hell do we do, Roger? Isn't anyone going to help us? I mean, the government has to be taking action somehow. Maybe we just aren't hearing about it."

Haliday had probably heard more news than anyone else there and shared his information with the group. He flat out told them that as far as he knew nobody was going to be helping anyone until somebody took a foothold in running the country. It was still unclear who the hell was doing what.

He went on to explain that he had hoped that Canada and some others would offer aid, but that posed a new set of problems. How would they move the supplies and who would distribute them? If it was the United Nations, they were all screwed. That might be why the borders were kept intact, to keep armies from using the opportunity to take the U.S. by force.

Fortunately for a lot of people who had guns, it made survival right now a lot easier. They were able to protect themselves and their families and do so efficiently. The more you had the better. The standard capacity magazines were barely enough.

There were instances where someone protecting their home would use dozens of magazines and hundreds of rounds within ten or fifteen minutes. Taking time for reloading was a luxury some people could not afford.

The country had over 300 million firearms. Nobody in their right mind would invade a country with that many armed citizens. Even with the population decline due to the EMP, the U.S. would still be a formidable fighting force that would be near impossible to overcome. If it was our own government, the same would apply.

Everyone sitting there right now knew all too well after the past two months exactly just how important it was to be well armed. Practically everyone in the room would be dead right now if wasn't for that very reason. No one in the room would ever contest that fact.

Haliday looked around again. "Look," he said, "it's going to be a natural triage process. The sick and elderly will go first and then the next group will be those who can't live off the land or offer anything in trade for food. Some will rebel and try and take supplies and more people will die. In the end, it will be those with either skills or preparation."

"What do you think our chances are?" asked Rob.

"I don't really know guys. I wish I did," Haliday said.

Mark looked at Rob and Brad. He said, "You guys need to band together now. You need to consolidate your resources into groups. Like we told you guys at the airport, everything needs to be rationed out. You need to have strict rations. Keep the Defense Coalition Group strong and ready, too."

Haliday suggested they set up some area kitchens for group meals and distribution of food. With so many people being spread out and no modes of transportation other than the few vehicles they had running there was no way to go door to door and try and feed everyone.

"You might want to try and condense people into the town and surrounding areas to make it easier," Haliday said.

Rob asked, "You think that's a good idea?"

Haliday said, "Strength in numbers, Rob, strength in numbers."

They spent the next hour talking about some defensive plans for the area and running through some different scenarios. They didn't talk about the recent events with the firefights at the cabin and the airport. The wounds were still too fresh. They just left that conversation for another day.

Dinner was ready by then and they all sat down to eat. The deer tasted great and there was plenty to feed everyone. The leftover food was packaged up for Mark, Brad, and Rob to take home with them. Brief goodbyes, and Rob and Brad headed back to their homes.

Mark and Haliday sat down again and Kayla and a few others joined them. Haliday didn't waste another minute; he wanted to make sure Mark got on the road and back home well before it got dark out.

"You guys ready to make the move here?" Haliday asked.

Mark answered, "I think it's a good idea. We are starting to get quite a few wanderers around and it's just a matter of time before we meet a group that we can't handle."

Haliday asked them if they wanted to move into the cabin with them or one of the nearby houses recently vacated. For security purposes he suggested they move into the cabin for the winter, and then they could move over to one of the houses in the spring.

They talked about the options for a few minutes and decided the cabin was the best one for now. They could rearrange the equipment in the outbuildings and use one for the livestock. That way they could keep an eye on them without worrying about a cow or something going missing in the middle of the night.

Next, they talked about how soon Mark's group could be ready to move and then set up a timetable. It was going to be as quick as possible, just as Haliday had originally thought. Locate the trailers for the livestock. Load up the cargo trailers first and make one trip, then a second trip for livestock.

The plan was to do it all in one day. With everyone doing their share they could pull it off. They would take a slightly different route the second time. This would alleviate the ambush concerns.

Plenty of security would be on hand. Moving the food and firearms was priority. Mark had told them they had enough supplies for about a year for the six of them. That was welcome news. The livestock was a bonus. They would breed them for food. Haliday smiled.

"What are you smiling about, Dad?" Kayla asked.

Haliday answered back, "Fresh eggs. I can't wait."

Mark took the food packed up for him and his group and took off. The next day they would be packing up, and the day after that they would be making the move.

No one else knew and that's the way they wanted to keep it. That's why they had waited until Rob and Brad left before discussing it. There was always a chance others listened in on their own hams.

Mark made it home okay, walked in, and placed the food on the table. As he looked around he remembered growing up on the small farm as a child. His parents had inherited the land and moved to the Michigan thumb area to leave the city life.

He told his mom to go ahead and put it on the stove to heat it. Mike and Linda set the table and made some tea. They all sat down and ate while Mark filled them on the plan. They all agreed it was in their best interest.

When morning came, Mark got everyone up and ready to pack. He walked out to the fields with his father, Bill, and gathered all of the livestock so they could put them in the pens instead of trying to round them up the next day. Bill came across one of the cows lying down and the closer he got, the more he knew something was wrong.

"Hey, Mark, heads up. We had company and they might be close by!" Bill yelled.

Mark had his AR15 with him and he raised it to the low ready position. He started to scan the area, checking for people who might be nearby. He slowly approached Bill, who had now drawn his own pistol and was looking around as well.

"Damn," said Mark. "We needed that cow. I'm surprised they didn't take more."

The cow had been killed, and whoever did it had crudely butchered it. They took maybe 10 percent of the useful meat and that was it. Mark and Bill looked around and saw three different sets of footprints. The kill and tracks were fresh. Mark told Bill to go get the tractor and a skid to haul the cow in.

While Bill headed into the barn, Mark stayed with the cow and crouched down low. He constantly scanned the area for movement. With the kill being this fresh he wasn't sure that the people would not be coming back for more. The sooner they got this out of there the better.

Bill pulled up with the old tractor and a small skid. The skid was basically a trailer without wheels, using skids instead. They winched the cow onto the skid and took it back to the barn. Bill's wife, Linda, and Mike's wife, also named Linda, came out to help.

The men got the cow hung and they prepped it for a quick butchering. They went back to getting the livestock and the house packed up while the two Lindas butchered the cow. They packed it in butchers wrap and placed as much of it in coolers as possible. The weather was 30 degrees out, so it all kept cold.

Throughout the day, they packed up everything that would be going and got everything staged. They went over the list they had made and triple checked everything. They locked up the windows and then sat down for dinner. Bill's wife Linda snapped.

She said, "I can't believe someone would do this to this country. It's pure madness. Who the hell could do this to people?"

"Hey, we're all emotional here," Bill said. "Let's just take it a step at a time."

Linda was still sitting there stewing.

Mike went outside to have a cigarette. He didn't have many left. Bill had a stash of tobacco and rolled his own. Soon enough they would be completely out.

Mike looked off toward the woods. "Hey, Mark, come here," he said.

"What's going on, Mike?" Mark asked as he walked out onto the porch.

Mike turned and looked at him. "Don't be too conspicuous, but look over my shoulder toward the woods. I think we have company."

"Looks that way," Mark said, casually glancing that way. "I wonder how many there are. I can see one for sure. I bet it's the guys who killed the cow."

Mike said, "You saw three sets of tracks, so we know there are at least three."

"Yeah, so we can count on more, probably double that at a minimum," Mark said.

They went inside and talked about it a bit more. Mark went over to the ham radio and called Haliday. He told him what had happened and that they were being watched.

Haliday told Mark to keep someone posted for security all night and stay on schedule. Haliday gave him a few more instructions and then signed off.

At his own cabin, Haliday then briefed his group on the plan for the following morning.

Chapter 2

It was about an hour and a half before daylight when the group left Haliday's cabin. Rich, Bev, Karen, David, Nancy, Diana, and the younger kids would all stay behind. The rest of the group, Alan, Kevin, Blake, Kayla, Randy, Dawn, Sarah, and Matthew, were on the way to help move.

No sooner had they left with their caravan of vehicles and trailers when Mark called them. "We have trouble here. Two guys tried to break into the barn about half an hour ago and we fired some shots. They ran off and yelled that they'd be back," he told Kayla when she answered.

"We're on our way. We have an ETA of about twenty more minutes. Make sure the gate is unlocked," she said.

The group sped up a bit in order to make it there. As soon as they reached Mark's group, they pulled through the gate and positioned the vehicles and trailers in order to get everything loaded up as quickly as they could. Everyone except Mark, Mike, Bill, and Alan, who were standing security, got busy loading. Haliday was staying behind.

It took them about two hours to get everything loaded up. Except for the livestock, they were good to go. The trucks pulled out and headed back to Haliday's cabin. The plan was simple: They would drop the trailers at the cabin; on the way back they would pick up the livestock trailers and then get the animals and the rest of the folks.

Blake and Kayla stayed behind to help with security. They had spotted the guys who had intruded earlier in the woods and weren't sure whether or not they would try something. Two extra guns right now was not a bad idea. Blake and Kayla waited patiently for the return of the others.

From out in the woods, three figures appeared. They moved slowly toward the house. Mike yelled out and told them to stop. The figures stopped, but started yelling back—they wanted the beef. When Mike told them they had taken enough, they said they wanted the cow they killed, and a few more.

Bill originally had 10 and now had only nine. He had about 30 chickens, which was good. He had two horses and a couple of goats. There was no way he was going to give them more cows.

Mark called out next. "You guys better get the hell out of here before a shit storm comes your way!"

"Well, buddy, you ain't dealing with no damn amateurs here," the guy said. "We know how to get what we want!"

Mark gave them one more warning. "Listen, guys, we don't need the hassle. You don't need the hassle. Back off now!"

Over in the woods, one man was kneeling down and had taken aim on Mark and Mike. He was waiting for his signal from his cohort in the field. Once he got that signal he would fire on their targets, Mark's guys, and provide cover fire for his group so they could either retreat or advance.

The man in the field raised his hand and flipped off Mark and Mike. Before he could lower his arm, the man kneeling in the woods dropped to the ground as the inside of his chest exploded out through his back.

Haliday had seen him move his finger to the trigger and knew it was game time. He then shifted slightly and fired at the guy in the field, hitting him in the elbow and taking the man's lower arm completely off. Haliday loved the Barrett that he had re-appropriated from the now defunct Bad Axe militia.

The guys in the field all dropped down.

Mike and Mark retreated as Blake and Kayla provided cover fire for them.

Two of the guys started low crawling back toward the woods.

Haliday took aim on the third guy trying to crawl back. He kind of chuckled to himself. He thought, *Hey, Dad, its like Vegas; there's your one-armed bandit.* He fired one more shot and the man stopped moving.

A few shots rang out from the woods.

Haliday shifted again and scanned the tree line. The guys low crawling back were easy picking, but the people in the woods were the current threat. He finished off the big mouth in the field, figuring he was the group's leader.

Mark and Mike had made it to safe cover. They assumed coverage on that side of the house while Blake and Kayla moved to the other side to keep watch. Bill and both Lindas grabbed rifles and made their way toward the back of the house. They ducked down behind some wood stacked up on the back porch.

Lisa was inside, staying nice and low. She was healing okay from the last fight at Haliday's cabin. She could not afford to get hurt again. She called on the radio and let the guys know that they were under fire. This was going to put a damper in their plans. The livestock was too valuable to leave behind and they were trying to make a plan to pull it off.

Outside, Haliday spotted movement in the trees. The man was moving toward a side road. It looked like he planned to try and flank them. Haliday spotted a second person almost 10 yards behind the first guy. He scanned the area again and came up with four more definite aggressors plus the two low crawlers who got up and ran back into the woods.

Haliday keyed the mic on his radio. "I count at least eight people left. Two are moving to flank on the north side of the house. I have those guys handled. You guys watch for the rest."

The ETA for the trailers was 10 more minutes. Haliday could not let the two people make it to the north side. He watched them carefully. They paused toward the edge of the woods. The first one was using the trees as cover and was doing a good job at staying concealed.

The second person was not as careful. This person stopped, almost in complete view. Haliday could see a rifle in their hands. Haliday took aim and the person turned. Haliday looked right into their eyes through the scope even though they could not see him. It was a woman.

As his heartbeat settled, he pulled the trigger and she went down. No doubt she had felt the round and died almost before she heard the shot. The first man dropped down real low.

Mark called Haliday. "Damn, man, you pissed someone off big time. The guy is out there screaming his head off."

Haliday could not let it bother him. Anyone with a gun firing on his family and friends was a threat. That meant anyone regardless of gender. They could not afford to play God by determining what targets might or might not be a threat. If they had guns and were firing, they were equally capable of killing as they were capable of being killed.

Haliday watched the first guy move a bit more. There were very few shots being fired right now. He kept watching. He heard vehicles in the background and called them. "You guys coming in?"

Kevin said, "Yeah, we're about half a mile out."

"Pull in and swing around quickly," Haliday said. "The hostiles are on the north and east sides, so make sure you don't get out on those sides. Take your cues from Mark."

"Understood, Uncle Roger," Kevin responded.

The vehicles pulled in quickly and looped around, staging themselves next to each other. Mark and Mike laid down suppressing fire so they could back the trailers up by the livestock barn. They paused when the guys got out of the trucks. It was going to take some skill and luck to get this done.

Haliday watched carefully; his target was still well-hidden. He took a gamble and fired a shot into the tree the guy was hiding behind. He saw the guy move and lay prone behind the tree, but he didn't have a good enough angle to fire another shot. He told the guys he was watching this man and that they had to watch the rest.

The group rushed toward the back of the trailers. When they got there, they looked around. It was fairly safe and they were confident they would be able to load the animals without any trouble. Alan went to the back of the barn to cover them from there.

There he found a window and took a quick peek out. He was met by a couple of wild shots and ducked back down. Instinctively he touched his cheek where he had been grazed by a bullet a few weeks earlier. He wasn't interested in having a matching scar on the other cheek, or worse.

He looked around a bit and spotted a hole in the wall. It looked like someone had been in a hurry backing up the tractor and the rear hitch had gone through the wall. This wasn't optimal, but it would have to do.

He picked up a nearby shovel and held it over the hole. No shots were fired. He rested it on the ground and waited a few seconds. He did this one more time and again no shots were fired. That was a good sign. The aggressors were only watching the doors and windows.

Bill and his wife Linda, along with Mike's wife, also named Linda, made it out to the barn to help load the animals. They moved quickly to get the livestock all into the trailers.

The trailers would be loaded past capacity, but under the circumstances it was more than acceptable. They would move slow and didn't have far to go. Besides, the trucks would be using everything they had as well.

Bill would be taking the tractor and hay trailer, which was loaded up with all of the feed. With the heavy trailers and slow moving trucks he would be able to keep up without any problems.

Over in the woods, there were six people left, not including the one Haliday was watching. They kept taking pot shots at the barn and house to make it hard on the group. They were hungry and taking a lot of chances.

Next up was getting the coolers loaded. The cow had been butchered enough to get everything to fit in the coolers and they had a couple of boxes of meat that had been wrapped in butchers paper.

They had gotten lucky that they had the butchers' paper. Bill had always butchered his own cows and so always had some lying around. This was all moved to the trailer the tractor was pulling.

Everything was loaded up now and the animals were all in the trailers. The chickens had been put in cardboard boxes with hay for warmth. They tied these up on the roofs of the trucks. That was the last of it. They were ready to move out.

Haliday kept his eye on the man over on the north side, hoping he would show himself. This guy could cause a serious problem when the group moved out. Haliday waited patiently.

Mark gave a quick whistle to signal it was time to move out. He had Blake, Kayla, and Randy assist him with suppressing fire as the rest mounted the vehicles and got ready to pull out.

The vehicles were all started. Haliday told them to hurry it up. He saw movement and suspected that the people in the woods were ready to make a move.

The Tahoe pulled out first, and indeed it moved slow, but not as slowly as the Cherokee. The driveway had a slight incline and the Cherokee struggled with it. Last to pull out was Bill on the tractor.

Bill's wife Linda yelled out to stop. Alan hit the brakes. She got out of the vehicle and started heading toward a small brass and copper lawn ornament shaped like a cat that her mother had gotten for her as a child.

She would accompany her mother to the local farmers market on the week-ends. A man there would make the lawn ornaments for his customers. On his display wall was mounted the one of the cat.

It was a simple, but rugged ornament. Each week-end her mother would set aside a small amount of change. One week-end her mother surprised her with the lawn ornament as a gift. It meant the world to her.

Haliday keyed the mic and told them to get moving.

The firing from the woods increased when the aggressors saw the vehicles stop.

Mark, Blake, and Kayla were near the tractor and returned fire.

Bill's wife was only feet from the Tahoe when she fell to the ground. Bill gunned the tractor and pulled up next to her. He jumped down and ran over to her. Mark did as well.

Haliday saw her drop and swung the Barrett toward the woods the best he could. He fired several shots in hopes of splintering trees around the men to let them know they were in the line of fire.

Kayla and Blake took aim and concentrated their fire in that area as they moved slowly toward the gate. Mark and Bill picked up Linda and placed her on the hay trailer. Bill jumped up and Mark climbed on the tractor.

Haliday swung back around and saw the man on the north side taking aim at the group. The man fired a couple of shots, striking the vehicle, but no one was hit.

Haliday had taken a bead on him just below his nose and fired just as the man was ready to fire again. The man fell backwards behind the tree and Haliday knew he was down for good. He then swung back toward the woods.

The vehicles were moving out as fast as they could. They cleared the gate and everyone was back on board and moving out now. Haliday searched the woods, but it looked like the men had given up.

The trucks made their turn and Haliday got his gear together and waited to be picked up. He moved to the edge of the road and was squatting down low when he heard the noise.

Off by the north side of the property he saw a vehicle rapidly approaching. It looked like two people were standing in the back seat of a convertible and were holding guns.

He keyed his mic, but didn't need to say anything. Blake and Kayla, who had jumped on the hay trailer, started firing at vehicle.

Haliday knelt down and lifted the Barrett and bipod. It was actually fairly difficult to shoulder. He had three rounds ready to go. As the car bounced along, he noticed it looked like a late sixties Mustang. The driver and three passengers were inside. The two rear passengers were sitting on the rear of the back seat.

33

They were firing wildly toward the small convoy, but were still a distance away so the shots were not accurate. A couple of the chicken boxes took hits and there were a few random hits on the Cherokee as well.

Haliday could not get a very clear shot on the Mustang's occupants. He lowered the rifle a bit and fired into the grill. He fired again and then one more time. The front of the vehicle erupted in a cloud of steam. The rear passengers ducked down as the vehicle started to slow.

The tractor had pulled up alongside Haliday and he jumped on. He loaded the Barrett, but didn't fire. Blake and Kayla emptied a magazine each toward the Mustang as they continued on.

Haliday put the Barrett down. His shoulder was killing him. Three shots from the Barrett while shouldered were just insane. He would definitely be bruising up with that one.

He looked down at Linda as Bill hovered over her. She was still holding that lawn ornament. He moved over to her and took a look, then rolled her over and saw a pool of blood. It wasn't good at all.

He grabbed a bandage and reached under her coat and placed it against the wound. It was off center of her heart. He thought it may have hit her Aorta. He grabbed another bandage and pressed it against the first. He slowly lowered her back down.

Bill looked up at him. He had tears in his eyes. He knew the same thing Haliday did. The round had hit something major and there was nothing they could do. His wife wasn't going to make it to Haliday's cabin.

Mark kept looking back while trying to drive the tractor until Haliday signaled him to stop. Mark ran back and jumped up on the trailer. Haliday took over behind the wheel.

Haliday keyed the radio and told the other two trucks to slow a bit more but watch for trouble. He told them Linda was injured extremely badly. Everyone in all three vehicles was silent. No one had expected to lose anyone.

Bill was now on one side of Linda and Mark on the other. They held her hands and talked to her. She was slowly starting to go in and out of consciousness. It would now only be a matter of minutes before she would die.

They still had about 15 miles to go to reach Haliday's cabin. Everyone was on high alert. Haliday called ahead and told them to ready a cot on the first floor for Linda and to get medical supplies ready.

He knew it was fruitless, but he had to go through the motions—not just for Bill and Mark, but for everyone. This was going to be their first casualty since the country went dark.

In the larger picture, there had been Erik who had died in the elevator the first couple of days, but no one in Haliday's group really knew what happened to him or saw him trapped. This with Linda was indeed going to be different. This would not sit well with anyone.

After just another five minutes Haliday looked backed. Bill had his head lying on Linda, and Mark had his hand on Bill's back. She was still gripping the lawn ornament and Haliday hoped that she had gone in peace.

Another 40 minutes and they were pulling in the gate of Haliday's property. He told Bev to have Sarah take the kids down into the basement and keep them occupied down there for awhile.

They came to a stop and Haliday barked out some orders for everyone. He walked back to the trailer and had Alan help move Linda to the cabin. They got inside and laid her down on a cot that was prepared for her.

Bev and Karen walked over and started to pull out some medical supplies. Mark grabbed Bev's arm and said, "Thank you."

Bev and everyone stepped back to let Mark, Bill, Mike, his wife Linda and Lisa gather around.

Haliday had now sent everyone else outside or downstairs to get out of their way. Bev and Karen waited nearby and Rich went outside to supervise. Haliday pulled out a bottle of whiskey.

He poured a couple of fingers and tossed a pill inside. He mixed it up and set it aside. Knowing Bill as he did he figured a quick drink would help calm him a bit and the sleeping pill would put him out for a bit.

They sat next to Linda for about an hour. Karen and Bev helped clean her up. Bill did indeed drink the whiskey and shortly afterwards fell asleep in a chair nearby.

Haliday went out to the pole barn and started up the old backhoe he had commandeered from the neighbors. He grabbed Blake and Randy and they went to the back of the property near the wood line. Haliday picked out a spot in the corner.

After digging the grave he went back to the cabin. He went inside and Alan helped him move Linda to the trailer. Haliday walked outside with them and looked over at Mark and said, "Go ahead and stay here. I'll come back up for you in a bit."

"Thank you, Roger," Mark replied.

"It's the least I can do," said Haliday.

They took Linda down and buried her. They did the best they could, making the grave as presentable as possible. Haliday took the lawn ornament and forced it into the ground as a marker. They all went back up to the cabin.

Bill was stirring in his chair. Everyone had cleaned up and taken the cot down so it was not as obvious. Mark and Lisa walked over and sat down by Bill and held his hand. They sat for a few minutes.

Haliday had everyone get together and they all walked down to the grave. Kayla, Blake, Kevin, and Randy all kept watchful eyes on the area. Everyone gathered around in a semi-circle.

When all was quiet, Haliday pulled out a Bible. This was different than with Lance and his family. This would take a few more delicate words. He had marked the pages only two weeks ago. Almost as if he knew he would need them. He read the passages aloud to his mournful listeners.

Fifteen minutes later he had finished. Mark, Lisa, Bill, Mike, and Mike's wife, now the sole Linda, stayed behind as the rest went back to the cabin. They stayed out there about half an hour before working their way back in. It had started to snow.

It was the first part of December and this was the real first snow of the year. No one expected it. No one could, there was no way to tell the weather forecast. The ground started to whiten.

Inside, everyone was sitting around. They had skipped lunch and it was now late afternoon. Bev, Karen, Dawn, and Nancy just prepared a bunch of sandwiches and snacks and set them out for whoever got hungry.

Bill excused himself and went to bed. Lisa was not too far behind. Mark came over and sat down next to Haliday. "I'm sorry, Roger," he said. "We put everyone in danger."

Haliday said, "Listen, I'm sorry about your mom, Mark, but you needed our help and that's what we're here for."

"I know," said Mark, "but look what happened."

"Mark, those guys would have moved in on you sooner or later and who knows what would have happened," Haliday said.

Rich joined them and sat down. He looked at both of them.

Haliday got up to get a cup of coffee.

Rich glanced at Mark. "I'm sorry about your mom, but Roger is right. If it's getting that bad out there, they could have gotten all of you."

"I just keep thinking I should have been able to do something," Mark said.

"There's nothing you could have done," Rich told him. "You were outnumbered. It would have gotten worse. It is getting worse. People are beyond desperate now."

"I guess you're right," Mark said.

Rich said, "Go get some rest; take as much time as you need."

Mark got up and joined Lisa in bed. They had been through a lot. There was no telling what else was going on out there; twenty miles away, but they were also twenty miles closer to a more populated area. They hoped it didn't get much closer.

The watch schedule was set and everyone settled in for the night. Before going to bed, Haliday called Rob and filled him in on what had happened. He flipped through a couple more frequencies and listened in.

Things were getting really bad out there now.

Chapter 3

Breakfast was quiet, but that was to be expected. It was a Wednesday morning and the kids would be taken downstairs for some schooling and kept out of the way for the day while everything else was settled.

The original plan when Mark and the others moved over was changed. They were going to keep the animals at the neighbors' place, but security would be too hard. That brought up another point; they would need to add a third person on security detail.

It seemed liked the more populated areas of Port Huron and Imlay City were getting desperate now. The people were moving out in search of food. They probably thought the farms had plenty and it looked like they aimed to take it.

Mark walked over and sat down next to Haliday at the kitchen table. "Good morning," he said.

"Good morning Mark," Haliday replied. He wasn't about to ask the obviously stupid question of how he was doing. He'd just lost his mother and it was apparent how he was doing.

"Anything on the ham radio last night?" he asked.

Haliday said, "Not really. I talked with Adam a few minutes. Detroit is a complete war zone from what he said. No one is safe going outside. People are raiding each other's houses, stealing whatever they can, and killing senselessly. It sounds real bad."

"I think we can expect quite a bit more of activity around here," Mark told him. "I noticed the past week a lot of activity around the farm and should have gotten out of there sooner."

Mark lowered his head; he blamed himself for his mother's death. In all actuality, someone there was bound to die, though. They simply did not have the manpower for adequate security. If people were on the move this far out, they mean business.

Bill came down the stairs and sat down next to Mark. Bev walked over and set down some breakfast and Karen came over and gave him a cup of coffee. Bev returned with a plate for Mark as well.

Bill quietly picked at his breakfast and sipped his coffee. Mark ate his breakfast slowly. More than likely he was doing it just to stay and keep his father company.

Haliday looked at Mark. "I'll catch up with you later." He then got up and went over to the ham station and sat down next to Blake.

"Anything going on, Blake?" he asked.

"Yeah, actually there is," he said. "I was about to call you over."

Haliday looked a little perplexed. "What is it?" he said.

Blake handed him the headphones and Haliday put them on. He sat there and listened for almost 10 minutes. He started writing down notes.

Blake wrangled up another pair of headphones and plugged them into the portable ham and dialed into the same frequency. He sat there and listened also.

Haliday looked at Blake and Blake just looked right back at him. Neither of them knew what to make of what they were hearing. It almost sounded unbelievable.

After about another 10 minutes Haliday took the headphones off and looked around. He was wondering whether or not he should tell anyone. He turned to Blake and put his finger to his lips for Blake to keep quiet.

Haliday got up walked over to the stove and grabbed a cup of coffee. He looked over at Alan and Rich and motioned for them to follow. They went up toward the front of the cabin by the fireplace and sat down.

Haliday looked over at Mark who had finally just finished eating. Mark got up and walked over, sensing that whatever was being discussed was important. He would want to be in the loop.

Alan asked, "What's going on? What did you hear?"

"I'm not sure. I don't really know what to make of it," Haliday answered back.

Rich said, "Well, it has to be something. Maybe we can help figure it out."

"I'll lend a hand as well," Mark said.

Haliday explained to them what he had heard. Camp Grayling had been secured from the start. It was a National Guard base with an airfield that was used mostly for annual training. They had quite a wide array of ranges and equipment there.

They were able to host practically any unit, including fighter wings. With 147,000 acres, they had plenty of space for an aerial gunnery range for air to ground practice. That was nothing compared to the best thing they had going for them.

They had a MATES, which was a Maneuver and Training Equipment Site. This unit had over 500 tracked vehicles in place for training and that included roughly 70 M1 tanks. Units could move in and practice without having to truck their own equipment in. There were also hundreds of wheeled vehicles. How much of the equipment was running was the magic question though.

Haliday had picked up bits of information that alluded to parts being brought in. There was no telling what type of equipment would be running or how soon. However, they also wondered what it was going to be used for.

Haliday wasn't able to pick up much more information than that. That was about all that the local ham operator Dennis could provide. He had been broadcasting this openly for others to hear.

No other information was available because he said no one came off the base or talked to anyone and no one was allowed in.

Through previous conversations, Haliday had learned that Dennis had worked in a rather odd industry. He had started a small fatality cleaning company for crime scenes and also did removal services for funeral homes. He had worked almost 20 hours a day for close to 10 years. He had saved his money and moved his family out of the suburbs toward the Grayling area.

It was he, his wife Kelly, and their two teenage sons, Jake and Gage. Dennis and Kelly both worked at a local lumberyard to pay utility bills and buy food since their land and house was paid off. Haliday knew he would be keeping in touch with him.

Haliday looked around after relaying what he knew. "What do you guys think?"

"Maybe they are prepping a FEMA camp," said Alan.

Rich said, "No. They are up to something else. The camp would be operating and they would be using people as labor to help them."

"I have an idea," said Mark. "Maybe it's a stronghold for the state."

Haliday looked at him. "That's what I'm thinking. If you think about it, it's central for the lower peninsula and far enough from all the BS going on for them to start operations."

"What kind of operations?" asked Rich.

Haliday went on to explain his point of view. He figured that the military was setting up camp to start securing the state. They were getting ready to take control of the area. He said, "If they are doing the same thing at Selfridge and over at Fort Custer in Battle Creek, then they would pretty much be able to lock down Michigan and gain control."

The question that was lingering in their minds was what *kind* of control. Were they operating on their own? Were they under Federal control? Or were they part of this Constitution Restoration Army they kept hearing about?

Nobody was able to get straight answers on what the hell was going on around the country, Haliday determined. They just knew the borders were secured by the military and that the three factions seemed to be at war with each other.

The men sat and talked about different scenarios for a while. They came up with all kinds of conspiracies, but left them at that. They did make a point of getting as much information off the ham radio as they could, however. They wanted to see if the stronghold theory was correct. That would mean checking in on Fort Custer and Selfridge Air National Guard base.

They thought about trying to make contact, but that idea quickly died out. They wanted to remain anonymous in case they were targeted for any reason. All they needed was to be hunted down by the military.

Actually, they didn't want anyone to know who they were. That reminded Haliday of something. He would need to contact Rob and make sure they kept a low profile and kept things quiet about Haliday's group.

This little project would keep them busy, which was important. Other than the manual labor of keeping the cabin running, they needed the mental exercise as well. It was a little brain food to keep them sane.

They all agreed to keep this quiet until they had more information; this way nobody jumped to conclusions and nobody fed off anyone else's causing paranoia.

With that settled Haliday got up and walked over to Blake, who was at the kitchen table. He told him to keep notes on anything he heard but not to tell anyone else. He made sure Blake understood the need to keep this under wraps for now. Blake understood completely.

Haliday looked at the clock. They had been sitting there for almost three hours talking about it all. He heard the kids coming up the steps from the basement. It was lunch time for them. None of them looked very happy.

Elizabeth, the youngest at four, was frowning heavily. Sarah, her mother, asked her what was wrong.

Elizabeth said, "I don't like this school stuff."

Sarah said, "Honey, it's very important that you learn what Aunt Nancy is teaching you."

"I don't want to learn."

"Sweetheart, don't you want to be smart?"

"No, never."

"Why not?"

"Aunt Nancy is going to make me be hungry."

"She wouldn't do that."

"Aunt Nancy said she would give me two apples, and then take one, and then she asked me what I would have left."

Everyone burst into laughter; little Elizabeth was taking the math lesson too literal. Maybe Nancy would have to scale back a bit on the lessons.

The kids sat down and got themselves ready for lunch. It would just be peanut butter and jelly sandwiches and some milk, fresh from a bucket of powder. It was gourmet compared to what some people around the country were eating.

Haliday walked over to the whiteboard and changed the assignments around a little. He took Blake's name and placed him on the ham more often. He penciled himself in as well.

Bev walked up and asked what he was up to.

"Not much, Mom, just having the guys work on a little project for me," he answered.

She looked a little miffed. She didn't like secrets being kept from her.

The adults usually skipped lunch and at best just grabbed a light snack. Being sedentary in the winter, they didn't need as much energy. They did, however, keep limber and exercise on equipment downstairs to keep up their strength.

Haliday called Randy and Kevin over. He spoke to them quietly for a few minutes. They nodded and then left. They put on their jackets and boots and went outside to take care of a chore they were given.

When they got outside they went over to the pole barn and grabbed some gear. They loaded it in the back of the four-wheeler and went down to Linda's grave. They paced off a 20-by-20-foot area.

They hand dug some holes with a post hole digger and dropped four-by-four posts in it. They backfilled the holes and tamped them down as best as they could. They put some eye bolts in and strung some thin wire and cloth tape for a makeshift fence.

Hopefully, this would keep the livestock off of the area. Haliday had them section off a bigger area just in case more graves would need to be dug. It would also serve as a reminder to folks to pay attention to what was going on, lest they end up there, too.

Dawn, Mike, and Linda all went outside and together they got the livestock settled. Bill came outside and went down to the grave with Lisa and Mark. Bill then came back up and went back into the cabin with Lisa.

Mark came over and asked if he could help.

"You know how to build a chicken coop?" Mike asked.

"I can give it a try," Mark answered.

Mike said, "OK, let's go see what we can scrounge up around the neighbor's house."

They commandeered the four-wheeler and went to see what they could find. There were three houses close by, but all of them were empty, so Haliday had told them they were fair game.

It took them almost eight trips, but they managed to gather up the materials they needed. Kevin and Randy helped as well. They went to work and in about four hours the chickens had a new home.

It was a basic shed design with feeder area and roosting and nesting areas. It would hold about a dozen and a half chickens, but after the encounter at the farm, the original dozen was reduced to 10 plus a rooster. Plenty of room if they managed to incubate some eggs to hatch.

Outside they penned off an area for the chickens to roam. They actually had some chicken wire. Around the pen and inside of it they placed some stakes and used twine to create a grid. They used lids from cans and attached them to the twine in spots.

Although it was not foolproof, the design's intent should keep away any large predator birds. The twine grid and can lids would make it hard for large birds of prey to swoop in and steal a chicken if they were intent on trying. Any ground predators would be shot by the security patrol outside.

This would give them some fresh eggs to use and what a treat that would be. Haliday was licking his chops at the thought of a simple fried egg sandwich. It was amazing what people took for granted these days.

The two birds that had gotten shot in the boxes were going to be dinner tonight. Fresh fried chicken. Everyone would get a piece and what was left would go into a soup. No waste at all.

Everyone went inside and got cleaned up for dinner. Those on security had to wait their turn, but their plates would be nice and warm when they were ready.

Haliday allowed snacks while on duty but not full meals. That took away from their concentration. With things heating up to the south of them it was only prudent.

The meal was a good one. Chicken, mashed potatoes, green beans, and cornbread. Complete with some iced tea. They cooked up some TVP chicken nuggets that the kids ate. They didn't know the difference. They thought it was just like the fast food chains. Elizabeth thought they were better.

With a few vegetarians in the cabin, Karen, Dawn, and Diana, everyone actually got two pieces of chicken and there wasn't any left for soup. Max the dog shared the bones with the cats.

After dinner most of the adults settled by the fireplace. Diana, Dawn's sister, took the kids downstairs to watch a movie. Rich joined them along with Karen and Bev.

Diana's collarbone was healing up rather well and since chores were still out of the question she did what she could to keep the kids entertained. She usually watched movies and playing games with them.

Bill joined the group around the fireplace for about an hour. He just sat quietly as everyone talked, but it was a good sign that he was starting to come around. He even chuckled a bit as stories were told.

Haliday told them about a time he and another guy scared the crap out of a fellow soldier while on a field exercise. Haliday had taken his 1911 .45 caliber pistol and rigged it. He then took a 5.56 mm blank and wrapped duct tape around the cartridge and slipped it into the 1911. He let the slide rack forward and holstered it.

He had approached his friend, Bob, and said, "Where's my MRE?"

Bob had said, "I ate it; get over it."

"You bastard. That was my lunch!" Haliday had yelled back.

They had kept arguing back and forth, and Ricky, their friend, kept egging both of them on.

Haliday had pulled his 1911 pistol and stood back about 10 feet from Bob.

Bob had said, "Go ahead. You don't have any live rounds."

"They're called alibi rounds you dumbass," Haliday had said.

Haliday then pulled the trigger and the blank went off. Bob dropped to the ground and Ricky about crapped his pants. He ran off running and screaming.

Ricky returned moments later with the platoon leader and platoon sergeant, who found both Haliday and Bob sitting there eating MREs like nothing had happened.

Ricky had been stuck cleaning out the Mermite cans from dinner that night. These were insulated metal cans used to transport hot and cold foods from the mess halls to the field. He hated the two of them for doing that to him.

Haliday related to his cabin audience another story about an operation held in the Sinai in the mid-eighties. They had taken their weekly dose of anti-malaria meds and it usually gave the guys the squirts. Not a very appealing side-effect.

The bathroom they had was fairly unique. It was nothing but a large pit dug into the ground about 100 yards from a tent city. They laid planks over it, put boxes down with holes cut into them, and mounted plastic toilet seats on them.

They had posts stuck in the ground with 42-inch-wide white cloth strung around them as walls. It was as funny as could be. You'd be sitting there and armored vehicles would just roll by. No room for vanity there.

One evening they needed to go to the bathroom and drew straws to see who would drive the Jeep. One hundred yards walking with squeezed cheeks was just a bit too hard. They set up Ricky to make sure he drew the short straw.

The M151s, old school Jeeps, were still in use as the Humvees were just being introduced. Everyone got on board and Ricky got behind the driver's seat very carefully. They were ready to go, quite literally.

Ricky had one foot on the gas and one on the clutch. The clutches had quite a long throw and when he released that clutch and his legs spread apart it was all over. The seat on that Jeep was ruined forever. They called him Squirts after that and he hated it.

Everyone sat around by the cabin fire, mostly reflecting on days gone by. Haliday thought through his past, wondering if he was satisfied with how things had turned out. Kayla walked up to him, and he knew it had.

Mark looked at Haliday. "Any regrets while you were in?" he asked.

"I did a lot of stupid things, in retrospect," Haliday answered.

"Like what?"

Haliday explained about a booby-trap that had gone bad. They had taken a can of blank ammo and poked the tips out of each round and dumped the powder in the ammo can. They put a booby-trap simulator in it and tamped down a bunch of paper.

Next they bent the lid enough for the trip wire to run through. The ammo can was placed under the backseat of one of the observers for the field training exercise. The trip wire was tied off.

This O-4, a major, got in with his driver and they took off. It was like a small bomb. The backseat, which wasn't really secured, went flying out of the Jeep and both occupants had singe marks on the back of their BDUs.

Haliday had never run so fast in his life carrying a full gear load and his M60 machine gun. He sweated that out for days. Plenty of questions were asked, but nobody but he and Bob knew.

Haliday had filed that bit of information away. It might come in handy in case they needed to build some more toys to fend off any invaders. He got up, walked over to the ham station, and wrote a few notes down.

The kids, Matthew, Elizabeth, and Theresa, were now in bed. Everyone else slowly filtered that way as well. The last of the group left by the fire was Haliday, his brother David, and Mark.

Mark turned to David. "How's the leg doing?" he asked.

"It's sore, but I'm doing a lot better," David answered.

Mark asked, "You able to get around OK?"

"Yeah. I won't be running any marathons, but I'll survive."

David had taken a leg shot and it was fairly bothersome. Both Haliday and Mark were thinking the same thing: If they have to move quickly on foot, David wasn't going to make it.

Add Rich, Bev, and Karen, all in their early and mid-seventies, and they had four who would not be very mobile. This wasn't counting the kids, ages, four, nine, and twelve. They would need to make some contingency plans for them.

Haliday didn't say it aloud, but he was wondering if he shouldn't have brought some more people into the group. It wouldn't have hurt to have a few more ex-military or survival-minded folks on board.

He couldn't complain, though. Everyone had been put through the paces lately and they had proved their worth. They managed to survive some hellacious firefights with nothing but some injuries until now.

The problem with having a group that was too large was two-fold. Logistics were one concern. The food and supplies needed would be hard to adequately stock and control.

The most important aspect was the OPSEC, the Operational Security. Too many people would start blabbing and you would end up with an entire neighborhood looking for food and safety.

Everyone got up and started heading toward the upstairs to go to bed when Randy waved Haliday over.

"Uncle Roger, Dawn is in the crow's nest and needs you up there."

Haliday answered, "OK, tell her I'll be up in a couple of minutes."

"She said hurry."

Haliday bolted up the steps and then up the small ladder to the crows nest. This looked ornamental on the cabin, but served as an observation post and firing position. It was just high enough to see the surroundings, and with the leaves off the trees, the view was pretty far.

"What's going on?" he asked when he reached Dawn.

She pointed and said, "Look to the south."

"Damn," he said. "How long have they been there?"

"I saw the lights about ten minutes ago, but wasn't sure what they were. They moved closer and closer, though, and I know now what they are."

Haliday told her to keep watching, and he went downstairs and stopped Mark and Alan. "We have a few vehicles a couple of miles south of us, not sure what kind."

Alan asked, "They heading this way?"

"I'm not sure, but we need to post some extra people on tonight," Haliday said.

"I'll take the first couple of hours," Mark said.

Alan said, "I'll get some sleep and take over after that."

"OK, wake me when you're done and I'll take over until morning," Haliday said.

Haliday went back up and watched for a while with Dawn. When he came back down, Mark had his winter gear on. He asked Haliday if he saw anything.

"Looks like they stopped. They haven't moved in a bit and might be bedding down for the night," Haliday told him.

Mark nodded.

Haliday walked around the cabin and checked the AR15s and magazine loads. He did a double check of the shotguns as well. Mark had taken Haliday's M24 sniper rifle up with him.

Haliday didn't wake anybody up, but made sure that each person being relieved from their detail passed the information on. He didn't want to alarm everybody just yet.

He lay in bed and dozed on and off but didn't really sleep. He kept running different ideas through his head. It was only a couple of months past the EMP strike and he was already tired.

Chapter 4

Haliday wondered what was happening around Michigan. He wondered how bad things were in and around Detroit and in other populated areas. There was no way of telling—he could only imagine. Little did he know.

*****

The couple was in their early seventies. The man had put in over 40 years as a woodshop teacher at the local high school. The woman had worked various jobs here and there to help when money was tight.

The move to the rural area after he had served in the early Vietnam War was just what he needed. He desired to avoid city life and the rural area had suited him just fine. They had a home built and they still lived there.

It was a small five-acre plot, but it provided plenty of land to garden on and to raise a few small animals. They relied heavily on their own skills to provide for themselves. Other than the occasional nods from neighbors they didn't engage in many social activities.

When the EMP had hit they didn't have to change their lifestyle that much. They had always stored what they ate, and ate what they stored. They were frugal and canned most foods.

The lack of electricity now was a nuisance, but other than powering the furnace and refrigerator, they hadn't used much power before the event. Rarely did they watch television. They didn't have a computer or cell phone. They had no children and no close family nearby. The man's name was Steve and his wife's name was Peggy.

Steve walked outside of their modest home to grab some more wood for the fireplace. He was returning from the woodpile when he heard vehicles approaching the house. He set the wheelbarrow down and hurried toward the house. The vehicles were now stopped in front of it and he could hear shouts.

As he approached he saw a couple of old pickup trucks, a couple old Chevys and an old Dodge Dart. There were younger people spewing out of them, walking around the yard and up onto his porch.

Most of them were in their twenties or early thirties. One guy spotted Steve and yelled out, "Hey Lenny! We have an old man here!"

Nearby, Lenny responded, "Big deal."

Steve looked around nervously. A few of the people gathered around him and started taunting him. He didn't like the looks of the group that had invaded. He yelled loudly, "Peggy, lock the doors!"

A man named Vince walked up and grabbed Steve's shoulders. "That ain't gonna do you any good, old man." He then pushed Steve down to the ground.

Steve fought to get back up and started moving toward the porch. The front door of the house opened and Peggy stepped out onto the porch. She fired a round from a double-barreled shotgun into the air.

"Get out of here, you hoodlums!" she yelled. She fired the second shot into the air as well.

Steve had almost made it to the porch when the thugs fired at him. He fell onto the steps.

Peggy tried to open the shotgun and reload it but she was cut down with a couple of shots from Lenny's pistol. She crawled over to Steve and grabbed his hand.

Steve was laying there looking into Peggy's eyes. She returned the gaze and told him she loved him.

"I love you, too," he said. They both just laid there on the porch as their lives slowly faded away.

The thugs walked right over them and made almost a dozen trips walking in and out of the house, removing all food and items of value. The older couple was helpless.

The house had now been emptied in less than half an hour. The thugs lit some of the curtains and furniture on fire and then left. They returned to their vehicles with their stolen goods and pulled away from the burning house.

Steve and Peggy had already slipped away, still holding each others' hands as they became engulfed in the flames from the small house they had called home.

*****

The apartment was small but it was all that they could afford. Tim had been laid-off from work for almost a year when his benefits ran out. He took a job as an assistant manager at a local burger franchise.

Tim's wife Andrea was working in a small accounting firm as an administrative assistant. She had never really held a job, but after Tim lost his job as an engineer, things had spiraled downwards.

The loss of his large salary was a surprise. He had been told all along not to worry. He went to work one day to find everything at his desk had been packed up in a box. He was escorted to the door by security.

With their two daughters in college nearby they decided to forego luxury and do what they could to help keep them in school. They sold their house, their cars, and most of their personal belongings.

The jobs and apartment allowed them to keep their daughters in school and still make ends meet. It was almost embarrassing, and many of their friends seemed to shun them and their lower standard of living.

Andrea was a prudent shopper. She took advantage of coupons, weekly sales, dented cans, and tried to save money anywhere she could. She prided herself on her pantry, which was fairly well stocked.

When the EMP had occurred the family was completely separated. Both daughters were at school and Andrea and Tim were at work. The daughters shared a car and drove to school together. Andrea dropped Tim off at work and then went to work as well. She would pick him up at the end of his shifts.

When it was evident that the power was not returning, Tim and Andrea made it home within a few hours. Their daughters Kate and Wendy made it home after almost 10 hours.

For the first couple of weeks they did what everyone else was doing. Waiting for help to arrive. Tim had a sense it was far more serious, though. He put them on a strict daily ration.

They were subsisting more than they were living. Water was found from a small stream near the back of the complex. They piled blankets on top of blankets to keep warm.

The fireplace was lit only to boil water and heat up food. There was very little wood to burn. Tim would venture out to look for wood and bring home what he could. The only problem with that was everyone else was doing the same thing.

Tim started to bring home deadfall from around the small creek. The colder the weather got outside the more warmth they needed. He had tried some small branches from trees that were still alive but they didn't burn very well.

Several weeks had passed by now. Everyone except Andrea was out gathering wood. She was at home trying to plan out the rations. There was not much left at all. They might make another two weeks and that would be it.

Tim heard it first. He walked toward the road. The girls started walking toward the road as well. He could see the camouflage on the Humvee.

Kate said, "Dad, it's the Army."

They started waving at the Humvee. Tim then saw the vehicles behind it. He shouted at the girls to run. They stood there for a moment, not understanding why he told them to run.

"Run, girls! Go hide!" Tim said.

The girls did their best to run as the vehicles approached. The thugs inside jumped out of the Humvee. Tim tried to stop them. The thugs beat him severely.

Four of the thugs ran after the girls. The girls were weak and couldn't run very fast. The thugs caught them almost immediately. The more they resisted, the more they were beaten. The thugs dragged them back to the vehicles.

Tim was lying on the ground, beaten and bloody. The thugs left him there for dead. The girls screamed as they were bound and put into the vehicles. They stared at their father as the vehicles drove away.

Tim was helpless. There was nothing he could do. He had fought the best he could and had hoped the girls had enough time to get away. He laid there crying.

Tim managed to work his way home. A couple of people had passed by but no one stopped to help. It took him almost two hours to make his way back to the apartment.

Once he got inside he explained to Andrea what had happened. She helped clean him up and they both cried through the night. They knew they would probably never see their daughters again.

*****

Jimmy had lived on the streets for almost four years now. He was accustomed to sleeping in odd places and eating whatever he could find in order to live. He knew the city better than most.

He was in his mid-forties and looked like he had seen better days. He had on an old, ragged desert camo field coat pulled over multiple shirts and a sweater.

Jimmy had graduated from high school and entered the Army. He never seemed to find his niche. He seemed to always find trouble. After Desert Storm he became more of a problem.

After numerous Article 15s—Disciplinary Actions—he was ready to get out. One day in the motor pool he simply snapped. He picked up a wrench and went after a fellow soldier. With one hit the soldier was out cold.

After months of treatment and test after test, he was diagnosed with PTSD, post traumatic stress disorder. He was given a general discharge and left the service. This was the start of his downfall.

After years of fighting for medical benefits and a change in his status to a medical discharge, he gave up on everyone and everything. He spent year after year moving from one town to another, working one small job after another.

Usually he would get in some type of trouble and would just pack up and leave. He continued this for years. Jimmy had basically disappeared from society. Society had given up on him as well. Until he landed in Detroit.

Jimmy walked into a soup kitchen one day. He wasn't bothered at all. He received his food and went and ate in private. This became his routine almost daily.

After almost three months a priest sat down next to him one day at the table. Nothing was said between the two of them. The priest himself had a meager meal that he enjoyed next to Jimmy.

When the priest had finished his meal he rose from his seat. He placed a small pocket Bible next to Jimmy. Noticing the camo jacket and dog tags around Jimmy's neck, he said, "Thank you for your service, son."

The priest walked away.

Jimmy had a tear in his eye. He had no family to speak of. He had a hard time making friends during his time in service. This was the first person who had ever thanked him.

Jimmy picked up the small Bible and placed it in his pocket. He kept it there for weeks. He never took it out to read it until one lonely night. He would read it again and again.

Over time he started to socialize more with the staff and priests at the kitchen. One day he helped fix their car. After that he would help around the kitchen fixing things for small amounts of money.

He became quite well known in the neighborhood. They nicknamed him Jimmy Fixit. People would have him help fix their cars. They needed almost as much charity as Jimmy did.

It was small things, like alternators, water pumps, battery changes, etc. They would give him what they could afford. He would buy himself some extra food, but most trips he made were to a small pawn shop.

Jimmy had a small cart that he wheeled with him everywhere that he went. Inside was a variety of odd tools. Nothing matched, but it was good enough to help him do his job.

He had found a purpose in life. He treasured what he had. He was happy and continued to live this style of life. It was what he had chosen and it suited him just fine.

He walked over to the soup kitchen, as usual. There was no line today. He walked up to the door that was open. He went inside and looked around. There had not been anyone there in weeks. The food had run out.

Still, it was a place he found peace. He would sit and think about the past several years and the conversations he had had with several of the priests and other homeless people.

They had come from all walks of life. There were office workers, finance managers, teachers, engineers, ex-military, and all types of others. He lived life through their stories. He always listened, regardless of how mundane the conversation was.

Jimmy got up and went to an abandoned building nearby. He went inside and walked by another man who was lying next to a barrel that had a fire inside. Jimmy locked up his cart and placed a blanket near the barrel.

There was plenty of office furniture, papers and more to burn. Most people had fled the inner city in search of food and safety. Wandering gangs, thugs and others did not bother homeless people. They assumed they didn't have anything to offer anyway.

Each night Jimmy when closed his eyes he would say a prayer. It was simple but effective. He thanked his Lord for allowing him to live another day. He would close his eyes and go to sleep, not knowing what the next day would bring, never knowing if he would wake up or not.

59

Before Jimmy drifted off to sleep this night he made a decision. He, too, would move to another city. He would seek refuge further north. The city was becoming more barren. It was becoming too dangerous.

*****

The group of thugs had started out as just a few people. They preyed on the weak and the elderly that were around them. They took what they wanted from them. Few of their victims could fight back.

Most of the thugs had either been gang members, hung out with gangs, were criminals of one type or another or just followed trouble. Very few if any had contributed to society in any respectful manner.

Once they started to encounter resistance they figured out quickly that there was more power in numbers. They slowly added to their ranks to build the group's numbers. At almost 35 strong they were a formidable force.

If anyone in the group showed signs of weakness they were forced out. That practically meant certain death. The group knew that to survive they had to be strong. To stay strong they had to eat. To eat meant taking what they needed, by force if they had to.

They started near the middle of the city. As food ran out they started to venture outward. Once they were able to secure some running vehicles it made their task easier. They could cover more ground.

They moved further outward until they stopped in a small city. The area seemed ripe for their activities. They would find an unsuspecting home and attack it.

This was their method time and time again. They had no regard for the rights of others. They didn't care who they hurt or even who they killed.

As time went on, they developed a taste for the power that their crimes gave them. They became more brazen and took more risks. They wanted to rule their area.

They came to enjoy raping, beating, killing, stealing, and raising hell. It was their new way of life. Party all night, commit crimes all day.

Eventually they had taken everything they had and settled into a small trailer park. They took over the clubhouse and moved in some beds and furniture. This became their home. They would prey on anyone and everyone.

*****

The apartment building was one of the city's oldest. It was built in the late twenties and had been remodeled three times since being built. It consisted of a loft and studio apartments.

The building had 20 floors. The ground floor was mostly small retail stores. The rest were homes to an eclectic group of people. On the eighteenth floor was a younger couple who was prepared.

When the EMP hit, they rallied almost half of the neighbors together. The rest of the neighbors either left or avoided them. As time progressed, they all understood the importance of sticking together. In the first week of the event they had gathered every available container they could find. They used these to store as much water as they could.

The group had taken measures to secure the apartment building. Unfortunately, the retail stores were all stripped within days. The group managed to secure the window gates and board up the openings that were not gated.

When society's civility had all but ended, they found themselves trapped inside. Going out into the city was suicide. Letting anyone in the building was suicide. They fought off gangs as long as they could.

One day a large gang of almost 50 people tried to force their way in. Gunfire had erupted as the gang continually attempted to enter. The invaders knew that there had to be food inside and they wanted it.

After several hours the gang lit the first floor on fire. The residents were unable to put out the fire as it climbed each floor. Those who left the building to avoid the fire were beaten or shot.

The fire climbed each floor. Eventually the entire building became an inferno. This scene was repeated in multiple buildings, in multiple cities across the affected areas of the country.

*****

Selfridge Air National Guard Base was a flurry of activity. They had secured the perimeter with the troops they had available. A lot of the National Guard and reserve troops that made it there had helped secure the small base just outside of Detroit.

The small base had served a variety of purposes throughout its history. Its current tenant was the 127th Wing, comprised of three different groups, being the Air Mobility Flying KC-135 Stratotankers for refueling, Air Combat Flying A10 Thunderbolts, and a Special Air Operations Command weather flight.

The base also hosted a huge variety of smaller units from all branches of the services, Coast Guard, DHS, and state and federal government. Right now everyone had joined forces for their upcoming mission.

Equipment was being brought in on a daily basis. This included aircraft, vehicles, support equipment, parts, and more military personnel. The base was growing quickly as far its population was concerned.

Civilians had previously attempted to gain access to the base but had been convinced it was a bad idea. There were skirmishes and shots fired, but surprisingly, there were no casualties. The goal was to keep the installation intact, not kill civilians.

It was a tough job for the troops on the base. These were their countrymen. These were humans much like them and their own families. If the mission was to succeed, they had to remain calm and, unfortunately, cold right now.

Sergeant Edwards, an active duty MP, had flown in just a few days prior. He was assigned to work with First Lieutenant Crothall, who was in the reserves and worked in military intelligence.

Their job focus here though was quite different. They were placed here to help assist in stabilizing the area and preparing it for the upcoming mission

Chapter 5

The coffee smelled good so Haliday decided to climb out of bed early and go grab a cup. It was 5:30 in the morning and he was only 30 minutes early for his shift. He had slept in his clothes so he didn't have to waste time getting dressed.

He wandered down the steps and walked up to the wood burner stove and grabbed the coffee pot. He poured a cup and added some powdered creamer and sugar. He sat down and looked around and noticed Nancy.

"Anything happen last night?" he asked.

Nancy said, "No, nothing at all."

"Who's up in the crow's nest?"

"Alan is," she replied.

Haliday looked over at the ham station and saw Randy sitting there writing notes. Haliday got up and walked over and looked down at the notes. As he went to grab them, Randy slapped his hand away; he was still writing something.

Haliday told him to bring them up to the crow's nest when he was done. Haliday grabbed his coat and a few pieces of wood and went up into the crow's nest. He tossed a log into the chiminea.

"Good morning," he said as he met Alan.

"Good morning," Alan replied. "Nothing at all last night."

Haliday said, "That's good, but I still wonder who they are."

It was still dark out and he couldn't see anything over to the south where they had seen some lights last night. He contemplated a recon mission, but decided not to at this point.

Alan went back into the cabin and then went to bed. His wife Nancy was just finishing making breakfast and setting it out downstairs. Sarah was awake and joined her to help. By the time they were done setting the table and double checking everything, everyone else had filtered down from upstairs.

Bill spoke up first. "Anything going on? Find out anything?"

Not everyone knew about the lights yet, or exactly what he referred to and that sparked some questions. As they had passed on the information through the night, and some of the folks didn't have to pull any shifts, they had missed out on the info.

Mark asked everyone to be quiet and then he explained everything about last night's events. He really didn't have any information and couldn't answer the questions. Eventually they all just sat quietly and ate.

Randy went up to the crow's nest. "Uncle Roger," he said, "this is what I heard this morning."

"What ya got?" Haliday asked.

Randy went on to explain that he had heard about troop movements over at Selfridge Air National Guard Base. No tanks or heavy armor were reported; just light wheeled vehicles and troops.

The troops were acting just like the Grayling group and not saying anything to anyone. One thing caught Haliday's attention, however; there were reports of helicopters. That put Haliday's group within easy reach.

"OK, go get some sleep. Good job," Haliday said.

Randy left and Haliday kept scanning the area and double checking the south. The sun was starting to rise and this would make it easier as he would be able to use the binoculars.

Another hour passed and there was still no sign of movement. No vehicles or larger groups of people moving that he could see. This was bad news as far as he was concerned. He didn't like it at all.

Mark came up and joined him. They just looked at each other. It was almost as if they knew what each other was thinking and the things they left unsaid, they both knew. Since they were veterans, they had shared a certain brotherhood, and experience sometimes filled in the gaps.

"They're rogue, hoodlums, scum—whatever you want to call them," Haliday said after the lengthy silence.

"That's what I was thinking," Mark said. "Most people under these circumstances would be up and moving already. Trying to find food, supplies, even just survive."

Mark was right. Under the circumstances, these people would have gone to bed early and risen early. No clocks, no lights or anything; it was just natural.

The thinking here was bandits or someone moving along and stopping to party along the way. Getting high, drunk or whatever; they were more than likely sleeping in right now. It was almost 10 a.m. before they saw movement.

The only thing Haliday and Mark could really see were four vehicles moving. They couldn't even really tell what kind. Haliday called downstairs and told them that he wanted everyone close to a firearm.

He added that he wanted volunteers to stand watch outside with rifles and be ready for action. He told Kevin, Blake, and Dawn to dress warm.

"So much for volunteering," Kevin said.

"Well, let's change it to volun-told," Haliday added.

He got a wry grin in response.

Haliday looked back up and saw a plume of smoke. This smoke started to thicken and darken the sky around the house where the people had obviously been staying.

He knew the area and figured the house was about three miles away. Working in their favor was the fact that the roads didn't run completely straight through for easy traveling. They would have to make a lot of turns to reach Haliday's cabin.

This would place a good 40 houses between him and this group. Depending on what they were up to, this might not be enough. He called for Mark.

Mark came up to the crow's nest and his attention was immediately drawn to the smoke.

"Mark, grab the maps and let's see what we can do to help ourselves."

"What exactly do you have in mind?"

"Well, if you look at the roads leading here, you'll see it's not a straight path, right?"

"Yeah, I see that, but I'm still not understanding," Mark said.

"Take a closer look, Mark."

He did. "Oh, damn, I see what you mean."

"We just need to get out there fast before they get close enough to hear what we're doing."

Mark looked at the maps and studied their own position. He made a mental note of the locations they needed to get to and then went downstairs.

Once he got there he called everyone into the front of the cabin and explained what was going on. He sent Rich up to the crow's nest to relieve Haliday. Within moments Haliday came down and they finished up the plan.

Haliday said that Blake and Kevin would make the trip with Mark and himself. This would serve as a preliminary assault team in hopes of staving off the group making their way toward them if they ended up coming this way.

Alan, Randy, Dawn, Kayla, Nancy, Sarah, Rich, Bev, Karen, and Bill would all be staying behind to defend the cabin. They were the main defensive force for the property.

Diana, David, and Lisa would take the children and hide. This took the injured and kids out of the equation. And they would only be used as a last resort, but the effectiveness they could provide was not a lot at the moment.

The ham went off and it was Rob and Brad over in Bad Axe. They conveyed that they had been in touch with a few folks outside of the area and had some information they thought was related to the group of bandits coming in.

The group numbered around twenty. Their ages consisted of mostly between 25 and 30. They were quite an ethnic mix and were all known in Imlay City as the worst in the area.

While they were not really a formal gang, it seemed they had all lived together in a few apartments in the city. The cops always had run-ins with them for various crimes.

Although most of the problems were drug and alcohol related, they had quite a mix of other charges within the group. Theft was the most prevalent; however, they also had some domestic violence charges and aggravated assault charges on their records.

The reports Rob and Brad had heard were not pleasant at all. The group would find soft targets to pillage and burn as they moved along. If they encountered too much resistance they moved on. The lack of law enforcement had emboldened them.

Rob and Brad asked Haliday what they should do. Haliday told them to do nothing; just prepare the town for the bandits' arrival if they should make it that far. Haliday didn't expect that to happen.

Chances were the gang had gotten run out of Imlay City and were preying on the lone survivors in the rural areas on their way north. It was one thing to take on a group of people in a city, but it was another to attack single homes and families.

Haliday got his crew packed up. They loaded up a Jeep and got the two bikes ready. It was a chilly 30 degrees outside and snow flurries peppered through the air. They needed to accomplish as much as they could before any serious amount of snow hit the ground.

If the snow stuck, and they got any significant coverage, they would end up leaving tracks. You didn't have to be an expert to spot the tracks and figure out what was going on. Haliday's group was almost ready to go.

Bill, Karen, and Dawn started to bring in the horses and livestock. Rich and Bev were trying to round up the chickens. Haliday looked at them and started laughing.

"What's so funny?" Rich asked.

Haliday said, "You two, trying to round up the chickens in the pen."

"Hey, we're in our seventies you know."

"Yeah, but you might have better luck if you tried it without licking your chops there, Colonel Sanders."

"Don't you have some place to go, Roger?"

Haliday walked over and gave him a hug. Bev came over and told him to be careful. Haliday waved Kayla over and she walked up slowly.

"I'm getting tired of these goodbyes, Dad." She hugged him and he kissed her forehead.

Haliday and his team took off.

First stop was south of them. They approached a house that looked like it was still occupied. Haliday made his way slowly toward it while Mark covered him. A man opened the door and walked out onto the porch.

He was early fifties and looked gruff. He had a shotgun in his hands, but didn't point it at Haliday. "What you want?" he said.

"Listen, we just wanted to let you know some bad folks might be coming this way," Haliday said. "You might want to be careful and protect yourself."

"Well, what you guys have planned?" the man asked.

"Sir, we plan to reroute them by blocking their way and trying to stop them if we have to."

"I appreciate it. Me and Ma will take care and hide if they come this way."

"OK; we're blocking the road down the way. Not sure when they will get here, if they even do."

"Well, thank you kindly. Good luck."

Haliday and his team mounted the vehicles and took off just a bit further down the road. They came to some woods and jumped out. Haliday grabbed a chainsaw out of the Jeep. He walked toward the trees and started cutting.

The trees were selected for their size. He dropped them at various angles across the road and tried to get them to land on top of each other. He dropped three from each side.

This effectively blocked the road, and if you didn't have a four-by-four or bike, you weren't getting around them. He placed one of his homemade spike strips in the only area anyone could pass through and covered it up.

It took them another three hours to hit five more spots. The only place they used spike strips were the other two roads closest to the cabin. This would deter vehicles from coming down these roads.

There was one problem, though; with these roads being blocked, people would then assume it was to protect something good. It still bought Haliday's group time though. He'd rather fight people assaulting them on foot rather than in vehicles.

The rest of the gear they would set up when they had a better idea of which direction the bandits were heading. Haliday called the cabin and checked in. He told them he had nothing to report and they told him the group seemed to be stopped at another house. They were still too far away to really make out any details.

Still too close for comfort.

Haliday asked Mark what he thought about coming up from behind and trying to check them out. Mark wasn't thrilled with the idea, but thought it couldn't hurt.

Haliday said he would do it. He took off on his bike and made a five-mile loop and ended up at the house that had been burning earlier. It was merely smoldering now.

Haliday walked up and looked around. He looked into the ashes and didn't see much. As far as he could tell, there weren't any bodies in the burned building. The gang had probably burned it for the hell of it.

He called Mark and told him what he had found, then pulled out his binoculars and looked down the road. About a half of a mile down, he saw the group at another house. He watched for a few minutes.

He wanted to get closer but knew better. He could see people going in and out of the house, putting stuff in their vehicles. He could see two old pickup trucks, an old Chevy of some sort, and an old Dodge Dart.

Haliday watched a little longer and saw them carry a couple of gas cans to one of the trucks. As he watched, they took another one and start dumping it all over the outside of the house. Looked like nothing but thugs burning down houses after stealing from them or staying the night.

He was about to get back on his bike when he heard a single shot. He ducked low and looked toward the group. He saw two women kneeling down on the ground over a body. His radio went off.

"Roger, you OK?" Mark asked.

"Yeah, I'm fine. I think they shot someone in the house they just looted," Haliday replied.

"Any idea why or anything?" asked Mark.

"No clue. I'm too far away to make out any details," Haliday said.

"Head back this way and we'll regroup toward the cabin, Mark said.

Haliday said, "No, I'm going to give it a few minutes."

The house started to burn and he watched the group leave. They went across the street and checked on another house, but left after just a few minutes. It appeared to be empty and not have anything they wanted.

The homes here were located on one acre sized parcels. The distance between the houses was almost one hundred yards. The time it took the group to move to the next home gave Haliday a few moments to think.

He watched them reach the end of the road and make a right turn. He got on his bike and rode down to the burning house. Out in the driveway were a woman and her daughter who appeared to be around ten years old. They were still kneeling down by a man who Haliday assumed to be the husband and father.

He walked up and they did not notice he was there. He knelt down and felt the man's pulse. This startled them and they backed away. Haliday told them he was here to help. He told them he would not hurt them, but they were still cautious.

Haliday checked the man on the ground once more. He was dead. He placed the mans arms over his chest. He stood up and looked at the house, which was burning quite a bit now. The ham went off again.

"Dad, we see another house burning," Kayla said.

He answered, "Yeah, I know."

He told Kayla to keep an eye on the vehicles. He went across the street and checked the house out. It was empty. It looked like an older couple had lived there, but it didn't look like they had been there recently.

The tables were very dusty and the furniture was covered with sheets. More than likely the owners were snow birds. They were probably in Florida or Arizona for the winter. He really didn't care.

The cupboards had been opened, along with the closets and cabinet drawers. The looters had checked to see what they could find, but it didn't look like there was anything to take.

Haliday went down the stairs into the basement and looked around. The gang had been down there, too, but everything looked fairly untouched. He spotted a small door under the steps.

He opened it up and looked inside. There was a small shelf unit inside and what looked to be around three or four dozen jars of canned foods. They were dusty and had probably been there and forgotten about long ago.

He could safely assume that was probably why the looters didn't take them. They probably thought the stored food was spoiled. He grabbed a jar of green beans and popped it open. He sniffed the jar then reached in and grabbed one out. He took a small bite. It was still good.

Haliday went back upstairs and crossed back over the road. He walked up to the lady and her daughter. He said, "Ma'am, anything I can do here?"

"All he did was try and stop them from taking our food."

71

Haliday looked at her and said, "I can understand him trying to protect you and your daughter."

"They're animals," she said miserably.

"That's true. Times like this can bring out the worst in people. They'll do whatever they can to survive. That includes killing people for food."

"What are we supposed to do?"

"The house across the street is empty. There're about forty quart jars of canned vegetables and fruit under the stairs."

"It's not ours."

"Lady, move into the house and use the food."

He explained that the couple who lived there was probably never coming back or at least not any time soon. She and her daughter could use the food and make it a few more weeks. Hopefully by that time help would arrive. The absent owners had wood cut and she and her daughter could heat the home with the fireplace enough to keep warm.

"What if they come back?" she asked.

Haliday looked at her. "Don't worry about that. They won't."

Haliday climbed back on his bike and took off. A few moments later he met up with Mark, Kevin, and Blake just a few miles away and filled them in on what had happened. As he expected, they were all as mad as he was.

They took up a position by one of their roadblocks that were only about a mile from their cabin. They quickly got to work and started setting up the ambush site.

The first thing Haliday did was set up a small portable hunting blind off in the woods. He lit a portable propane heater to warm it up. Kevin walked over to him.

He said, "Uncle Roger, we're only a mile away from the cabin. Why don't we stay there?"

"While that may seem like an easy idea, the way we have the blockades set up it's not a smart idea."

"I don't understand."

"We need to be as quick as possible or the ambush will not work."

"But why don't we fight them off like we did the militia?"

Haliday went on to explain. "The blockade here is the most likely one to stop the group. This is the best ambush site. The cabin is still far enough away to stay hidden."

If the bandits did come down this way, by the time they were spotted and people put into motion they would be too close to the cabin already. Trying to fend off another group with the injured they had was a bad idea.

The other fact was if the gang had seen a few of the other blockades and no one was around, they would assume the same thing here.

"Kevin, I don't think we're dealing with a group of Einsteins here," Haliday said. "The only theory of relativity they know is probably how inbred their relatives are."

They took a quick break and ate some dinner. The light was fading quickly now and the snow flurries from earlier in the morning were back. The ground started to whiten with snow.

They finished up what they needed to do and double checked everything. The Jeep and the bikes were camouflaged and everything looked untouched. They went over their plan one more time.

Kayla called on the radio. "You guys almost done?" she asked. "Your flashlights are sticking out like sore thumbs in the snow."

"We're just waiting now," Haliday said.

*****

The group of thugs had stopped at a few more houses along the way. Each one they went into they found pretty much the same thing—they were empty and there was nothing of value to steal and no food.

There were two more houses they were going to check. At the first house they approached they didn't even make it halfway down the driveway. They were fired upon immediately by the homeowners. They returned fire and backed out as fast as they could.

Three families had joined their resources to try and make it through the aftermath of the crippling event. They were not about to give up a single item. Haliday had stopped at this house earlier, too.

The second house the gang approached they were met with almost the same result. More shots were exchanged and they left this one, too. It only proved Haliday's theory. They were preying on the weak only.

The thugs stopped for a bit and talked over their plans. It was getting late. They would have to stop and stay somewhere for the night. They sat there at the intersection.

The self-appointed leader was Lenny. He was about six-foot-tall and 200 pounds. Two months ago he had been 25 pounds heavier. He told the group they would head west.

"I don't know about that. What about the roadblock down there?" another man asked.

Lenny said, "Listen, I'm tired of these roadblocks. Let's just go around it. I'm ready to party."

"I'm with Lenny," a woman in their midst said. "Let's go have some fun; it's too cold out here for bullshit anyway."

The group got back in their cars and approached the roadblock. They got out and took a look to see how easy it would be to get around it.

This was the last mistake they would make.

Chapter 6

Lenny was the first to get out and look around. Moments later the rest of the group got out.

Lenny said, "Let's see if we can move any of these trees and get outta here." The snow was starting to fall more heavily now.

He looked around and reached into the car. He grabbed a handheld spotlight and swept the area. He called his buddy over. "Hey, Vince, grab your rifle and come here."

Vince walked over. He was around five-foot ten inches tall and carried a healthy 150 pounds and was of African-American and Mexican lineage. "What you want, man?"

"Go over there and check that out. It looks funny, dude," Lenny said, pointing to a bucket in the middle of the road.

"Aw, hell no, brother. I ain't that damn dumb."

"Take someone with ya."

"No way, man. Ain't none of us that dumb."

Lenny nearly spat out, "You damn wussy."

Everyone started to gather around. They all started mumbling about the cold and the snow. They wanted to get to a house and warm up and party. They didn't want to stay out there arguing about anything.

Unknown to them and out of sight, Mark slowly pulled a thin cable that was about 1/32 inches in diameter. Behind the gang's vehicles on the road, two of Haliday's spike strips slid across the road. If it hadn't been for the snow, the thugs might have heard them dragging on the pavement.

A girl walked up. She had a small frame, with short hair that was at one time been spiked and multi-colored. She was maybe 100 pounds, around five feet tall. "Come on guys," she said, shivering and antsy. "Let's go."

Lenny said, "None of these chicken-shits wanna go over there and check that shit out."

She said, "I'll go." She hopped over the logs and walked over to the small bucket in the middle of the road. There was a piece of paper on it with a rock on top.

"You chicken-shits let a ho show you up," Lenny said.

Vince said, "She's yo bitch. If she wanna be bad, that's her choice, Jack."

Form his hiding spot in the woods, Haliday cringed; he hated listening to people talk like that. He remembered at work attending a cultural diversity class. 'You have to respect other individuals' cultural differences,' he'd been told. "Show me the culture that used ho, bitch, dis, dat and the like and I'll respect it," he had told the instructor.

It was nothing more than a butchering of the English language, Haliday had always said. Kids were not held accountable in school these days. The educational levels in the country were becoming embarrassing. Basic math and English skills were defunct.

The girl crossed back over the logs and walked over to Lenny and handed him the note. He opened it up and looked at it. He turned it sideways, then back upright.

The girl grabbed it back from him and read it aloud. "'This area is closed off and you are not welcome. Leave immediately. Do not attempt to gain entry. You will be fired upon.'"

Lenny grabbed the note back and looked at it like it was going to change or something. He mumbled under his breath and looked around. The rest of the thugs all started looking around and brought out their own weapons.

Lenny held his pistol out sideways like a good old gangster wannabe. He said, "Bullshit, man; you people ain't nothing." He squeezed off a few rounds and a couple of the others did as well. They all just fired blindly.

Haliday yelled, "Last chance to leave!"

Lenny fired at the voice, and that was it.

Haliday yanked a small cable. From each end of the log barricade there erupted five shotgun shells filled with double aught buck.

In a matter of seconds a total of 10 shells dispersed 90 pellets. The pellets all flew out in a small array, similar to a claymore mine with the exception of Haliday's gadget having much fewer pellets.

"Fun for the whole gang," Haliday thought.

It was an easy rig to set up. He'd mounted five short pieces of pipe designed to hold the shells to hold the shells in place. The threaded cap on the back had a hole in its back. These pipes had very slight angles to disperse the pellets over a wider area. He had inserted a small, thin piece of rubber between the cap and shell with a heavy pin in the middle to serve as a firing mechanism. The weight was hinged and came down on the pins, causing the shells to fire.

This gadget could be mounted on a vehicle, house—the logs, in this case—or anywhere else solid because of the recoil. They were 12-gauge flare launchers, for all practical purposes, although the ATF was not out enforcing laws at the moment.

They would have come in handy during the militia's assault on Haliday's cabin. It was after that when he decided he needed to increase his firepower against larger advancing groups. The devices were incredibly effective.

The thugs at the front of the group took the majority of the pellets. Two of them dropped immediately. Vince had gotten hit in the abdomen, chest, and neck and he was down for good.

Lenny got lucky and had been hit in the leg only. His girlfriend got hit in both legs and screamed in pain. Four others also received hits, their injuries diverse. They consisted of legs, abdomens, arms, necks, and even a head injury. They didn't know what hit them.

Lenny yelled at them to fire, but they didn't really know where to fire so they hesitated.

The thugs were all yelling at each other and scrambling to try and get in the vehicles. One guy and his girlfriend jumped in the old Dart and gunned it in reverse. The rear tires caught the spike strip and deflated immediately.

They continued to drive in reverse to get away from the barricade. The rims simply slipped on the now flattened rubber. The car stopped moving. The two jumped out and ran away, leaving everything behind.

The rest of the thugs continued to rush toward the remaining three vehicles. Lenny paused to fire his pistol at Haliday's previous position, but Haliday had moved.

Haliday took aim and fired five rounds into Lenny.

Mark and Blake had moved in from the side where they had waited. They took a few shots and put out the tires on the pickup trucks. When the thugs fired on them, they started firing back.

Haliday and Kevin were on the other side. They had arranged themselves so they would not get caught in crossfire. They had taken positions so that each of the two groups firing toward the thugs would almost form a V-shape.

Kayla called on the radio. "You guys need any help?"

Haliday responded, "No, we're good, but call Rob and tell him to have Chuck come out here first thing in the morning with the Deuce for prisoners."

A couple more of the thugs ran back down the road. After this, the rest of them figured out hiding behind the vehicles was safer for them. They moved toward the back of the three that were left.

Haliday and Kevin stayed in place and Mark and Blake moved down a bit in order to take up a better vantage point. They fired a few rounds to let the thugs know they were no longer safe.

Haliday shouted out to them, "You guys done playing roving warlords or you want us to finish playing fish in a barrel?"

There was dead silence.

Haliday had Mark fire a few rounds to make his point. A couple minutes passed and Haliday shouted over to them again. "Last chance before we just open up entirely!"

"OK, OK, we give, man! God damn, chill!" someone called out.

"One by one, come out and stand in front of the Chevy," Haliday said.

"How we know you ain't gonna pop us, man?"

"Because you'd be dead already."

"You promise us, man?"

"You want an engagement ring and a kiss?" Haliday said. "Get moving now!" he added.

The thugs all came up to the front of the Chevy. Haliday took a quick count. Four had run away, three were dead, five were wounded, and five were untouched. Three were missing.

"There're three more of you out there!" Haliday shouted. He waited a few minutes. "OK, we're firing again!"

"Wait! Wait!"

A female came out with her hands raised. This still left two people out there somewhere.

Haliday called Mark and asked him if he saw anyone. Mark told him no. They would have to check the vehicles closely before proceeding.

Haliday grouped all of the thugs close together. Blake covered him while he searched them for weapons. He found an odd pocket knife, but that was it.

"Listen," he said, "you guys stay put or he opens fire." He motioned toward Blake.

He moved over to the vehicles and called Kevin over. They started moving slowly down the line of vehicles, checking each one while Mark watched carefully.

They got down to the end vehicle and finished up. Somehow two of the thugs had managed to get away. There was no telling when that had happened. Haliday needed to make sure they were not out in the woods waiting for the chance to fire on them.

Haliday's team moved the thugs away from the vehicles and across the log barricades. The thugs had to help each other across. Haliday had them sit down on one of the logs on one side. Three out of the five wounded were not going to make it to the morning.

Haliday built a small fire and let them stand or sit around it. His crew backed off and kept watch, not wanting to be illuminated by the fire. They took turns going into the deer blind to warm up.

Morning arrived and they heard the Deuce coming down the road. The snow had accrued to about an inch and a half and that was all. As the daylight started to light the area, they looked around.

There was blood splattered all over the place and on the ground. The bright red against the white snow made it look even more horrifying.

The Deuce pulled up. Brad, who was the head of the area's defensive coalition, jumped down with Chuck, who was handling the law enforcement for the area.

"Damn," Brad said, looking around. "You guys were busy last night."

Haliday said, "We have some who got away. You mind taking care of these while we do a quick search of the area?"

"No, not at all, go ahead."

"OK, back in a few minutes."

Haliday's crew went over to the vehicles. They found a blood trail and started to follow it. It led into the woods north of the ambush site. There were two sets of footprints. They were not sure if both had been hit. It looked like just one.

About 100 yards in they came across the body of a man slumped against a tree. There was no telling how long he had been dead. They looked around and saw the second set of prints.

"You want to follow them?" Haliday asked.

"Let's go another hundred yards," Mark said.

"OK. You feel giddy, so you take point."

"Gee, thanks."

Mark moved out and they started tracking the person. They had moved about 50 yards further in when a shot rang out. All four of them dropped. Two more shots fired at them.

Haliday and Blake moved to the left flank and worked their way toward the person. Blake saw her first. It was a woman around 30 years old, her long, blonde hair in a ponytail, wearing a light spring jacket, with piercings all over her face. She looked over toward Blake.

Blake fired his rifle with a single shot to her chest. She dropped the pistol she had been using. Haliday called to Mark and told him they were going to move in to check her out.

They approached with rifles at the ready and walked up on her. There was no rise and fall of her chest; she wasn't breathing. Haliday slung his rifle on his back and Blake and he grabbed her and they carried her to the spot where the first body had been found.

Mark called Chuck. "We have two; one DOA and one now dead. What you want us to do with the bodies?"

Chuck said, "If you can bring them out that would be great. If not, just leave them."

"Let's go," Haliday said. "I'm not hauling them out."

They walked back to where Brad and Chuck were. Chuck looked at the group of prisoners. "These are the looters and thieves?"

"Murderers, too," Haliday added.

"We didn't kill no one," one of the thugs piped up belligerently.

Haliday walked over to him. "I saw the man at the last house you burned down. Don't lie. It isn't going to help."

"Well, too bad. They ain't no law now."

Haliday stepped closer and planted his boot right in the man's groin. The man dropped down to the ground. Haliday placed his boot on the man's shoulder, knocked him over, and stood over the guy.

"Listen, puke, you may not think so, but I guarantee you there is," he said. "You just wait and see how it all shakes down during your trial."

The man looked at Haliday and spit on his boots. Haliday was tempted to kick him again but didn't. He walked over to Chuck. "Chuck, if you want the other two bodies you'll have to have these guys drag them out."

"I'm just going to leave them out there," Chuck said.

"Good idea."

"Hey, man, that ain't cool," the smartass said.

"You are more than welcome to go in and bring them out," Haliday told him. "Come on, let's go. Pick a friend to help."

The guy didn't say anything.

"I thought as much, you piece of garbage," Mark said.

It didn't shock anyone there. Not only was the group of thugs running around without the rule of law, or so they thought, but even after everything they'd done they still wanted society to take care of them.

Haliday heard a second Deuce coming up. He looked over at Chuck with concern.

Chuck said, "Sorry, should have warned ya. We got the second one running now."

The Deuce pulled up and Rob, the acting head of government, got out along with someone Haliday did not know.

Rob's two sons got out as well and they all walked up and shook hands with Haliday and his men. The new man was introduced as Hunter.

"What's the plan?" Rob asked.

Haliday said, "You guys take the prisoners, try them, and administer whatever sentence you give them."

Rob looked away and said, "Yeah, that's what I thought."

"Right now concentrate on getting them back and then getting these vehicles back on the road," Haliday said.

"What about the food and stuff?" Rob asked.

Haliday answered, "I'm going to take some to a woman and her daughter whose husband they killed and house they burned down."

"Sounds fair enough. We'll try to distribute the rest through the community."

"I'll take a couple guns for the lady, too. You can have the rest."

"You want anything vehicle-wise?"

Haliday shook his head. "No, use them all."

Haliday's crew went through the vehicles and put together a small amount of food. He grabbed a shotgun and 9mm along with some ammo. They loaded it in the Jeep.

He told Mark and Kevin to take it back to the lady and then come back to help them pack up the ambush gear. He gave them directions and Mark and Kevin took off.

They got to the house in about 10 minutes. Once they got there they noticed the fireplace burning. With a quick look they also saw a mound of rocks across the street. With the hard frozen ground it was the best they could do to bury the man without the use of a tractor.

Mark and Kevin unloaded the items from the Jeep. Kevin had actually had the foresight to grab some of the clothes to give the woman and her daughter. No one came to the door when they knocked, so Mark yelled through the door that the stuff on the porch was for them.

They didn't expect a response, so they just left and went back to the ambush site. They were about half a mile away when they heard shots being fired. Mark gunned the Jeep.

*****

At the ambush site the smartass thug had rushed Hunter. His hands had been zip-tied in front of him and when he got a moment he grabbed Hunter's pistol and shot him. He then spun around and took aim at Brad. One of the other thugs rushed Rob at almost the same time.

Haliday and Blake had just arrived when it happened. They dropped the gear from the blind and came running. As soon as they saw what was happening they started firing at the thugs. There was quite a struggle and it was confusing at first.

Brad was close enough and managed to grab the pistol, which discharged next to his ear, blowing out his ear drum. He stepped back at the same time Haliday dropped the thug.

During the struggle one of Rob's sons was hit in the arm. Blake was able to drop the second thug before he could get any more shots off. The rest of the thugs just dropped to the ground after that.

Mark was speeding up the road and stopped about 100 yards away. "What the hell is going on?" he called to Haliday.

"A couple of the thugs rushed them," Haliday said. "We have two more dead thugs and we lost one man from the town along with an injury."

"Is it safe to come in?"

"Yeah, come on in."

"OK, be there in a minute."

Mark and Kevin pulled up. Haliday had them help change the prisoners zip ties to behind their backs. They thought it would be easier to load them in the Deuce with their hands in front. That proved to be a deadly mistake.

The prisoners and injured were loaded in one Deuce, the other one they used for the supplies and food. Once loaded they took off right away and headed back to town.

Haliday's crew loaded up their gear and took off, too. In five minutes they were back at their cabin. They pulled up and put the vehicles and gear away and then went inside the cabin.

Bev sent them all straight to the bathroom to change. They were covered in dirt and some had blood on them. Lisa and Dawn brought them some fresh clothes and then they took turns taking quick showers.

After they emerged from the bathroom they went in and sat at the dining table. They answered questions for about an hour as they explained what happened to the others. The looks on their faces pretty much summed up their feelings.

They were at the point now where desperation had really set in. People were dying from hunger and they were looking for food and supplies to help them survive. They didn't care where it came from and would do anything.

The criminal element was taking full advantage of no law and order in society. The only thing people could rely on was their personal firearms. Some people would never stand a chance. They didn't have food, firearms or supplies.

These were troubled times.

Chapter 7

It had been a few days since the thugs had come their way when Rob called and told Haliday they had tried the survivors. There were only a few left alive; the injured had died. They still had the prisoners locked in the local jail.

Even though they were hesitant to sentence any of them to death, they also knew they would consume valuable resources. They all agreed to wait a few days to make that decision.

Haliday called Adam on the ham radio. Adam was just outside of Detroit with his group where they had bugged in. They had enough people to keep themselves safe. That was their plan and it was working.

One of the benefits of staying in touch with Adam was the information he could provide on what was going on in the city. Haliday was interested in what condition it was in, such as answering questions about how many are dead, food sources, any help being offered, etc.

"Hey, Adam," Haliday said.

"Roger, I heard you guys had some trouble a couple of nights ago," Adam replied.

"A little bit. How did you know?"

"Oh, you're famous on the Michigan airwaves."

"Are you serious?"

"No, we just tuned in to your frequency last night."

"You're a funny man, Adam."

Haliday went about the business at hand and asked Adam what the current situation was around him. Even though it would be close to three months before Haliday returned to check it out, he wanted to know.

Adam told Haliday his group had went out to check the neighborhood. They only ventured about three miles away, which was all they needed. Things were bad.

Adam told him the group stopped by a house of a friend just a mile away. The house was open and when the group went inside they found the whole family dead. The bodies were strewn all over the house, appearing to have been raided.

The man had been an attorney. Everything was always perfect in his house, his office, everywhere. He suffered a severe case of obsessive compulsive disorder.

Whenever Adam had brought up subtle hints about preparing for emergencies he could tell the attorney thought he was a nut job. One day Adam flat out told him that FEMA suggested certain precautions.

Adam had said, "He told me FEMA stands for Friggin' Egotistical Morons Association, people who run around crying about the sky falling."

"No offense to you or your friend," Haliday said, "but I think the clouds of Mother Nature snuffed him out."

"No offense taken, Roger."

"Adam, you hear anything about the troops in the area?"

"Probably the same thing you did."

"I have a friend named Bruce over by Fort Custer in Battle Creek."

"He tell you anything?" Adam asked.

"I haven't been able to get in touch with him lately."

"You think he's OK?"

"He has a very small group. It's just his family, his father, and his mother in-law."

"Doesn't sound very good."

"He has a very small place out in no man's land," Haliday said. "Might be something different going on."

"OK, talk to later. I'll let you know if anything changes."

*****

Bruce was feeding the wood burner some more logs. The trailer was easy to heat because of its small size. He had purchased it years ago and prepped it for the permanent location where it now sat.

Bruce and his family sat on only 20 acres, but it was smack in the middle of some heavy woods. There was really nothing but hunting shacks around. Moving the 32-foot travel trailer in was a nightmare. He had to actually cut trees down to get it in place.

The path was cut in a zigzag so it could not be easily spotted by hunters passing by. Even having the land marked "No Trespassing" didn't stop some hunters from crossing the land. Most observed the request, but a few never bothered to follow the rules.

Once the trailer was in place, he put supports under it and flattened the wheels. He insulated and closed off the bottom and ran a sewer line to a makeshift septic field. The field was small, but worked under the circumstances.

He had a 55-gallon steel drum buried in the ground acting as the tank. He had a few small PVC pipes for liquid runoff going into a small tile field. When the drum became filled with sludge, he could add some diesel and burn it off.

Without the constant running of showers and with water conservation, it was all they needed. There were a total of six of them. Their security was staying put and out of sight. It wasn't ideal, but it worked.

Bruce sat down by the ham radio and made a few calls himself. He was trying to raise Roger Haliday, but had lost the frequency list he once had. His radio didn't have it programmed in. He didn't want someone to get a hold of the radio and have all the frequencies in it already.

His wife, Alexi, had spilled some coffee on the list and decided placing it on top of the wood burner to dry was a good idea. Once it ignited after drying out it was gone in an instant. Bruce wished he had laminated the thing.

His main storage for his preps was a cinderblock shed he built with a steel door and thin concrete roof. It was a mere eight-by-eight-foot in size, but held plenty.

On the outside he used old planks, half-assed framed around it, making it look antiquated. Since his trailer was 25 years old it blended just fine. Looked like an old hunter's camp. Both shed and trailer were painted to blend in.

Inside the trailer he had stripped out the bedroom and put in bunks to save space. The rest was gutted and small furniture placed inside; nothing but a kitchen table, some cabinets, a couch, and chair.

Six people in an 8-by-32 was cramped quarters, but was far better than their homes in Livonia, which was just outside of Detroit. He didn't count on his home being there when he got back.

His house there was an older bungalow-style home with far too many windows and was impossible to secure. The homes had nothing but driveways separating them—worse than Roger Haliday's brother's home in Canton.

Bruce spent about 30 minutes trying different radio frequencies. He would try one, wait, and flip to another. He had remembered most of it, but the last part of it left about 2,000 possibilities. He'd find it sooner or later.

He heard a noise and stopped to listen. It was getting closer.

Thump, thump, thump.

He hadn't heard that in quite some time. It was the distinct sound of a Huey. He stepped outside to take a look.

He listened carefully and zeroed in on it. When he was in the service he had trained as a crew chief in the helicopters. He watched carefully and saw it coming straight for his camp.

He looked to the roof of his trailer; he could see the smoke of the wood burner rising effortlessly into the air. While people might not spot him from the ground, anyone from the air surely could.

He stood there as it approached. It seemed to be slowing down. The more he watched it, the more he realized that it *was* slowing down. It came up on station over him and then circled a couple of times. It was very low now, maybe a hundred feet off the deck.

The pilot turned the bird sideways and the crew chief inside looked down at Bruce through the opened side door. The crew chief pointed to him and then gave him a thumbs-up sign. Bruce returned the thumbs-up.

The crew chief reached into the bird.

Bruce was sweating a bit; he didn't know what to expect. The crew chief dropped a small canister to the ground. The bird then arced and rose back into the air and moved on.

Bruce ran over to the canister and picked it up. It was bright orange and hard plastic and resembled a big medicinal capsule. It was maybe five or six inches in diameter and a foot long. He took it back to the trailer where his group, consisting of his mother in-law, father, wife, and two daughters were waiting.

"Open it up," Alexi said.

Bruce hesitated. "What if it blows up?"

"Oh for goodness sake," she said. "Open the dang thing."

"I'm still not sure."

"Then give it to me."

"No, no, I'll open it."

Bruce slowly unscrewed the cap. He tilted the capsule and spilled the contents out onto the table. It was an odd mix of components that appeared to have been packaged just for this event.

The first thing he grabbed was a pack of some type of food bars. They had foreign writing on them, but someone had placed a plain white label on them explaining they were high calorie food bars and to eat one a day.

The next item was an emergency blanket. There were some matches inside, a small compass, a signal mirror, whistle, water purification tablets, tape, a few other small items, and a small map. There was an odd piece of thin cloth, bright orange in color.

There were also a couple pieces of paper, and the kicker was a very small radio with ear buds. It had a sticker with the station it should be tuned in to written on it.

They all looked at each other.

Bruce put the ear buds in and turned the radio on. He sat there and listened to it while Alexi read the papers. It was very strange, and they looked at each other at the same exact moment. They could still hear the Huey off in the distance.

*****

Karen walked into the cabin from outside and called over to where Haliday was sitting.

"Hey, Roger, you better come out here," she said.

"What's going on?" he asked, looking to her.

"This is something you have to see."

"OK, let me grab my rifle."

"You won't need it."

He looked puzzled. He stood up and walked over to the door, grabbing his jacket on the way. They walked outside and saw Dawn, Alan, David, Blake, and Kayla all standing there rifles at the ready.

They were all staring toward the south. Haliday followed their attention and saw it as well. He couldn't make out what type of bird it was. It looked like an OH58 Kiowa, a military scout and observation helicopter.

It seemed to be circling something. Haliday strained to look and then yelled up to the crow's nest. Kevin was up there and Haliday asked him if he could see anything from his elevation.

"I can't see anything, Uncle Roger," he called down. "It's too far away."

"Nothing at all?" Haliday asked.

"Well, it looks like there might be another one a little further away and closer to the ground."

"OK, keep an eye on them." Haliday looked at the others. They were all still staring to the south. He walked up behind them and yelled "Boo!"

They all jumped, then turned and looked at him.

"Pay attention," he said. "You all sat there staring at the thing and no one was keeping watch elsewhere."

Haliday went back into the cabin and over to the ham. He called Rob. He reached Rob's son, who told him Rob was out in the pole barn. Haliday waited while the boy ran out to fetch Rob.

Karen came back inside and met Haliday at the ham. "What do you think they are doing?"

"I don't know," he said. "Could be a lot of things. Where's everyone else?"

"They're afraid to come in after getting yelled at."

"Go out and get them. Tell them it's OK."

Karen went out and got everyone and they filtered back into the cabin. They had all been outside doing one thing or another. Haliday told them no matter what was going on, they needed to pay attention at all times.

Kayla piped up first. "What ya think, Dad?"

Haliday said, "My guess is recon."

"Why is that?"

"Well, that looked like an OH58, which is an observation platform."

She nodded. "What about the big ball on top?"

"It's an MMS, a mast-mounted sight."

"Yeah, that sounds like observing."

The ham crackled and it was Rob. Haliday went on to explain to Rob what they had seen. He also told him he didn't know what to expect. It could mean anything.

Rob sounded optimistic, of course. He said it was probably help on the way and then asked Haliday if there was a way to contact them. Haliday went on to explain it wasn't such a good idea right now.

"I don't understand," Rob said.

"It's like this, Rob," Haliday said. "If they are here to help, then they will seek us out."

"But why not tell them who we are and where we are?"

"Would you rather *know* they were here to help and then contact them, or would you rather take a chance and have them put a hellfire up your ass?"

"I guess I would rather wait."

"We'll know soon enough Rob."

"You deal with the prisoners yet?" Haliday added.

"No, not yet."

"Why not?"

"People wanted to wait since it was so close to Christmas."

"So, you walk up say, Merry Christmas, we got you a bullet."

There was silence. Haliday knew it was a tough decision, but keeping murderers around didn't make any sense. He thought maybe he should go into town and handle it himself.

"OK, Rob, you guys do what you need to," he said, ending the conversation. He got up and walked over to the kitchen and looked out the window. Now he saw it.

He heard the loud rush of the single powerful engine as the F-16 flew over. The horses outside reared up and then started running around. The cows were startled as well.

This jet had come over at just around 500 feet off the deck. Kevin called down from the crow's nest.

Haliday went up to see what the ruckus was all about. Once he got up there another one buzzed by. This one was not as close. He watched for a little bit as they did a few circles and flew over the airport in the distance. They turned back around and headed south. Haliday decided that more than likely they were out of Selfridge.

Everyone was abuzz now. Everyone was talking about all of the possibilities and what might be happening. They were all excited over the recent events of the past 15 minutes.

Haliday let them enjoy the excitement as it raised their spirits and most of all their hopes. He had to admit himself that it was pretty spectacular. Maybe things were not as bad as they all thought.

*****

Bruce said it first. "You have to be kidding me?"

"Considering it's all we've got right now I don't think so.," Alexi answered. Bruce's dad took the papers out of her hand and started to read them.

When he was done he looked around. Alexi's mom didn't bother to read it; she simply asked, "What's going on?"

Bruce picked up the papers. He said, "The message on the radio is the same as this." He then went on to explain what he heard and what the paper said.

The Constitution Restoration Army was a small radical faction in which members was actually part of the government, military, and big business. They had attempted a coup using a combination of military and civilian assets.

A large series of EMPs had been setoff using both nuclear warheads at higher altitudes and a newer technology from specialized EMP missiles that were far more advanced than anyone originally thought. The effects were grossly miscalculated. There was more damage than they had intended.

During the initial struggle for power a large number of top level government leaders were either assassinated or had abandoned their positions; just a small fraction survived. The President had not survived. Most of his cabinet had not survived either.

The Secretary of Defense was currently running the country and was using the military to stabilize the borders and the remainder of the government. The CRA had managed to create a huge amount of confusion.

The CRA was essentially eliminated and only a few small resisting groups remained. These were subsequently being eliminated as well. The ruling government was still being recognized worldwide.

The military was taking up positions across the affected areas of the country. They would be moving in troops and equipment over the next few weeks as equipment became available.

Once the troops' bases were secured and checks of their assigned regions were made, they would start to distribute as much aid as they could. They were honestly not sure how much that would be.

Foreign governments had all offered assistance in various forms, from fuel and equipment to food and even troops. The level of aid from these countries had not yet been determined.

One of the biggest slaps in the face was the U.N. They had basically came out and said that if they could not bring in troops and control the country until full order was restored they would not provide any aid of any type.

The Secretary of Defense, who was now the acting president, immediately denied that option and then threatened to fully withdraw from the U.N. He went as far as to say that any U.N. troops setting foot on U.S. soil without an invitation would be fired upon. It would be considered to be an act of war.

Not following in the footsteps of the U.N. were multiple countries pledging their support outside of any U.N. resolutions or plans. The U.N. was now a mess, with little direction.

That in itself was hard to digest. Bruce and his family couldn't believe it. That pretty much meant everything that they heard was true in some effect, except that it was now a fractured government leading a fractured nation.

The next part of it was horrifying. It was two months after the event and all estimates were that 60 to 70 percent of the population was now dead with many on the brink of dying.

They expected another five to ten percent to die off before aid could be delivered consistently enough to stabilize the areas. It was a massive logistical nightmare to get aid delivered.

In typical government fashion, it was suggested that in the interim anyone with adequate supplies should open their homes and supplies to help those who were in need.

Bruce laughed at that.

Sure, give away everything you have based on what the government is telling you. Then when they don't come through you're that much closer to dying off yourself. That wasn't going to happen, he thought. Not yet, at least.

Everyone was advised to avoid heavily populated areas. These were under control of gangs and other criminal elements. The largest cities were the worst. It would be suicide to enter them. Of course, it didn't say how that would be handled.

*****

With a hunch, Haliday went downstairs and grabbed a small radio that he had pulled out of his Faraday box. He went back upstairs and turned it on. Slowly he thumbed through the frequencies.

He stopped when he heard it—the same pre-recorded message that Bruce in his neck of the woods had heard. Haliday turned it up as loud as he could so everyone else could hear it. They all sat there and listened to it a few times.

After it started to repeat itself a fourth time Haliday turned it off.

"Why did you turn it off?" Sarah asked.

"What else did you expect?" Haliday said. "Top Forty with Casey Kasem?"

Everyone burst into laughter except for Sarah, who didn't find it too funny.

She walked away mad and said, "Uncle Roger, you can be such an ass."

The message gave them all a whole lot of things to think about now. It answered a whole lot of questions, and on the other hand, it raised a whole new set of questions. Haliday called Rob and told him what he had heard.

Chapter 8

The previous day had been quite uplifting for the group. Everyone was still in a good mood. They were moving about the cabin a little more enthusiastically. It was good to see.

Haliday said he was making a trip to Bad Axe to see Rob. He asked if anybody wanted to go. Practically everyone raised their hands; they wanted to get out and see something different than the cabin.

He took Kayla, Dawn, and David with him. The kids wanted to go, but he was not going to put them at risk yet. They members leaving got dressed and grabbed their gear.

They piled into the Tahoe and took off and were in Bad Axe in about 20 minutes. They pulled into town and up to the City Hall next to the jail. They all got out and looked around.

There wasn't anybody around. It was desolate. It was strange to see even a small town empty like this. Rob and Brad stepped out of the jail. They all greeted each other and then walked back inside.

Haliday came back outside with Brad and they jumped in the Tahoe and drove a few minutes away. Haliday pulled into a small strip mall and stopped in front of a hobby store.

The door was broken and Haliday walked in and looked around. He spotted what he was looking for. He grabbed the boxes and then a bunch of batteries and went back to the truck. The place had been looted, but not much had been taken. No one wanted the stuff. They drove back to see Rob.

Haliday and Brad walked in and set the boxes down.

Rob looked at them. "Are you serious?"

"Absolutely. Give it a try," Haliday replied.

Rob cracked open a box and about 30 minutes later he was tuning the frequency of the small little AM radio kit. It was one of those old hobby kits anyone could buy.

These looked like they had sat on the shelf for years. They were solder-free and meant for young kids. There had been seven of them on the hobby store shelf.

Rob tuned in and found the station. "I can't believe this still works."

"There isn't anything to them," Haliday said.

"Put these together, guys," Rob said.

Rob's people all grabbed a box and started putting them together. All but one worked, so they had six working AM radios. They would try and distribute these as best as they could.

Haliday walked next door to the police department. There was a man sitting there guarding the prisoners. Haliday looked to the cells. There were only five people left; three men and two women.

"Where's the rest?" he asked.

"This is all that lived," answered the man.

"What are you guys feeding them?" asked Haliday.

"Corn and soy nuts," the man replied.

"Sounds appetizing. What about you guys?" Haliday said.

"We have a bit more, but not much variety; trying to make it last," the man said.

"Well, hang in there," Haliday said.

Haliday walked next door to the city hall. Chuck, who had assumed the law enforcement duties for the area, was there now. Haliday asked Rob how they were all set for food.

"Not bad, I guess," Rob answered.

"You guys have enough to get through the winter?" Haliday asked.

"Pretty much. With not a lot of people around it's lasting longer than we thought it would."

"I guess that's good, "Haliday replied. "Good thing this is farm country and you guys had that co-op."

"Roger, you hear those jets yesterday?"

"Sure did."

"What do think they are up to?"

"Low level recon," Haliday told him.

"What do you mean?"

"They are getting a good idea of what's going on around here."

"For what?"

"Before they move any troops into this area they need to make sure it's OK and they know what to expect."

"Ah, I got it now."

"You have the radios," Haliday said. "Tune into the ham frequency they are giving out, but still remain cautious."

They said goodbye and Haliday and his crew started back on their way home.

Haliday stopped at an intersection and paused as he listened to Alan telling him they had seen the helicopters again. They were to the south again, but closer today.

A mile down to the left was another intersection. Haliday thought he caught a vehicle in the corner of his eye. He turned suddenly but didn't see anything. Maybe his imagination was playing tricks on him.

He paused for a moment. He was going to go check out the intersection and see if there was a vehicle, but decided to just head home instead.

*****

Bruce was back at his ham and slowly flipping through the frequencies again. He was marking them off on a list as he progressed through them. Same sentence each time.

"Roger, it's Bruce. You there?"

"Roger who?" a voice said.

"I'm not going to give up a last name," he answered back.

"Then we don't know a Roger."

Bruce marked an asterisk next to this frequency. He would try it again later to see if he could reach Roger Haliday directly. He was fairly sure this had been the one.

*****

Haliday pulled into his driveway. He was getting out of the Tahoe with everyone else when he heard the helicopter. He slightly raised his rifle. Everyone else did, too. Almost everyone inside the cabin came out.

The Huey was about 200 yards out and came to a halt. Haliday eyed it carefully. He wasn't surprised it was a Huey instead of a Blackhawk; fewer modern electronics and they still had tons of them around, especially overseas.

The pilot looked toward Haliday and the people on the ground. He moved the bird left and right to check out the property.

Haliday noticed a couple of door gunners and that was it. No rocket pods mounted on it.

The Huey inched closer and canted to the side.

Haliday could see the door gunner motioning for them to drop their weapons. Haliday gave them the finger. "I think they'll get the point," he told everyone else.

The bird just sat there for a few more minutes. The gunner motioned again and Haliday shook his head no in an exaggerated motion so they understood. He had no idea what these guys were up to.

Haliday heard a second bird approach. He yelled at everyone to drop their weapons and raise their arms up high. Just about

150 yards off over the middle of the field was an AH1, a Cobra gunship helicopter.

The pilot made a concerted effort to let them see the 20mm chain gun sweeping back and forth. The Huey moved in closer and set down at the intersection near Haliday's cabin. A couple of soldiers got out and approached.

"Do not move," Haliday told everyone.

"I think I just crapped my pants," Bev said.

"Well, you can change later," he told her.

He knew she was kidding, though. They all waited as the soldiers approached them. One of them, a sergeant, asked who was in charge.

"I am," said Haliday.

"You can put your arms down, folks. Just don't go for any weapons," the sergeant said.

"And miss out on my chance to dance with the Cobra?" Haliday said.

"How many are in your group?"

Haliday looked around. "Too many."

"Look, sir, I don't have time to play games."

"Neither do I, Sergeant."

"What's that supposed to mean?"

"I'll tell you exactly what it means, Sergeant," Haliday said. "Get down to business. What do you want?"

"You think you're in a position to demand that?"

"Look, junior, I have a fifty caliber Barrett on your man in that Cobra over there, with armor piercing rounds. I have a three-oh-eight on you."

"Take it easy, sir, easy."

"Easy, my ass. We don't want to die and you don't want to lose assets. Are we clear?"

"OK, we're clear. Let's try this again."

Haliday noticed the Cobra slowly drifting backwards. Mark was off in the woods with the Barrett, Alan with the M24—no match for the Cobra or guns on the Huey, but at least they could make things interesting for a brief moment. That was just a fleeting thought. Haliday knew better.

The Cobra had backed off several hundred yards now. Haliday looked at the sergeant. "They can leave, or you can tell them to take up station even further away, at least fifteen hundred yards."

The sergeant relayed the message.

"Now, let's get back to business. Sergeant, what do you want?"

The sergeant started to tell him about what was going on and Haliday stopped him. He told him they knew all about it. He wanted to know what they wanted here, at Haliday's cabin.

The sergeant didn't really know how to take this encounter. He looked around at Haliday and the rest of them. Next he looked back at his own guys. He walked over to the Huey and retrieved one of the capsules. He made his way back to Haliday and handed it to him. "You're a pretty brazen man taking on the military, sir."

"Not really," Haliday said. "I just know when someone's blowing smoke up my rear and posturing." He handed the capsule back to the sergeant. "When I need a suppository for a T-Rex I'll let you know."

The sergeant started to speak and Haliday cut him off. "Sergeant," he said, "we're OK here. Your help is needed elsewhere."

The sergeant looked at the other three homes in the area.

"They're empty," Haliday said.

The sergeant just gave a quick nod to acknowledge him; he turned around then went back to the Huey.

The engine puffed a bit of black smoke and the helicopter started to spool up. Once the RPMs hit peak, the pitch of the engine changed as the pilot applied collective and the bird lifted off.

It continued to lift into the air. The pilot applied a small amount of left pedal torque and the nose started to point west. The pilot maneuvered the cyclic and as it flew off to the west, the Cobra moved off with it.

Mike walked up. "Why in the hell do you continue to screw around with the military?"

"I don't," Haliday said, "but I'm not going to sit here and play sheeple with them either. Let's see what's going on first."

*****

Chuck walked out to his Bronco and climbed in. He was going to deliver the little radios to a few of the others. He started the vehicle and put it in drive. He was ready to pull out when one of the men on jail watch ran over.

"You mind if I catch a ride?" the man said.

"Jump on in, Barry," Chuck said.

The jail watch crews took turns. They would spend 48 hours in the jail and then 48 hours at home. Inside the jail they took turns sleeping. Barry was ready to go home.

They were about three miles outside of town when Chuck saw a vehicle pulled off to the side of the road. He slowed down and then came to a stop. He looked around at the asphalt road, and surrounding woods, and waited. Everything looked normal.

Chuck had not seen this vehicle before. It was an old Dodge. He had no idea who it was. The hood was up and the engine was steaming. It looked like it had overheated. He looked over at Barry. "Let's check it out."

They moved up closer until they were about 30 yards away. They could see a man and woman looking at the engine. It looked like there was a younger child in the vehicle, too.

The guy looked up when Chuck neared and said, "Hey there."

"What seems to be wrong?" Chuck asked.

"I think it overheated."

"Where're you folks from?"

"We came from Port Huron."

"What brings you up this way?"

"Same as everyone else; we're looking for food."

Chuck explained to them that they didn't have anything up there. He told them that their best bet was to head back to Port

105

Huron to look for help. The child in the back of the vehicle got out.

He was only about twelve years old. He walked over to his father and said he was hungry. His father told him to get back in the car. The boy protested and the father told him to go get back in the car and watch his sister.

Barry walked over to the side of the car. He opened the door and looked inside. As soon as he saw a woman lying on the rear seat he started to move backwards.

The blast from the shotgun was loud and Barry took the entire group of pellets to his chest. He stumbled backwards and fell to the ground. Chuck spun around, but it was too late.

The man had taken a belt with the end looped through the buckle and dropped it over Chuck's head. He pulled the end of the belt tightly as Chuck struggled to break free.

Chuck reached down and grabbed for his pistol. The man forced Chuck down to the ground and took the pistol from his hand. He aimed the barrel at Chuck's back and pulled the trigger three times.

Chuck lay on the cold, wet pavement gasping for air. Blood trickled from his mouth. A larger puddle formed under his body. After a few short moments he stopped breathing.

The man called out for the woman to get out of the car. She climbed out and looked at both Barry and Chuck. The young boy just stood there. It had been a well-planned trap.

They had opened the hood of the car and as soon as they heard a vehicle, they turned the engine off and took their places. They had taken a small water bottle and poked a small hole in it. They'd placed it on the engine and as the water drops fell onto the manifold it created steam. Looked just like an overheating engine.

They transferred everything from the ratty old Dodge into Chuck's Bronco. They searched Barry's body and then Chuck. Satisfied that they had gathered anything worthwhile, they climbed in the Bronco and took off.

One of the women followed in the Dodge. They headed back south. They figured they would be able to keep the Bronco and trade the old Dodge for food. They had committed the act as if they had done it a hundred times before.

*****

Haliday was sitting down with Nancy, Dawn, and Diana. They were going over the layout for the spring planting. Dawn had a large variety of seeds stored for planting. They didn't see any harm in getting the crops laid out early.

Rich came over and whispered in Haliday's ear. Haliday stood up and walked over to the ham. He sat down and put the earphones on. "Go ahead, Rob," he said.

Rob answered, "Roger, we have some terrible news."

"What is it, Rob?"

"Chuck and Barry are dead."

Haliday paused for a minute. He had just seen both of these guys just a few hours ago. He tried to figure out what could have gone wrong in so little time. "Rob, what happened?"

"They were murdered in cold blood."

"Tell me what you know, Rob."

Rob explained that Chuck and Barry had left. When Chuck didn't check in they got worried. They took the route to Barry's house to look for them. They came across their bodies lying in the roadway.

Haliday had to process this for a minute. Now he knew it wasn't his mind playing tricks on him: he had seen a car. Maybe a split second earlier and he would have positively identified it.

He was angry with himself. He should have said something on the radio. He also wondered how Chuck managed to get ambushed. He'd find out soon enough.

"Rob, I'm sorry," he said.

"Is this ever going to end?"

"Not any time soon," Haliday answered. "We are at the stage where primal instinct has kicked in."

"What are we supposed to do?"

Haliday told him the same thing he did before. "You guys need to move in groups. You need to be careful. You need to

107

watch around every corner. You need to move into homes where you can provide security for each other."

Rob mentioned the military again. Haliday had to explain to him that there were simply too many areas and too many people for the military to play law enforcement. Rob just wasn't getting the picture.

Rob said he was going to try to contact them anyway. Haliday told him to go ahead and see for himself. He was a little miffed at Rob and cut it short.

Another voice cut through, one Haliday wasn't expecting.

"Roger, it's Bruce. You out there?"

Haliday answered back. "Hey, Bruce. What the hell happened to you?"

"It's a short story involving coffee, a frequency list, a stove, and some ashes."

"OK, so having a backup was something you planned for the future?"

"I know, I know; three and four copies spread out in case something happened."

"What's the word over by you?"

"We got a small care package from Fort Custer."

Haliday nearly laughed. "The dino enema?"

"Yeah, you got one too?"

"They tried but we sent them on their way politely."

"What do you make of it?"

Haliday explained his thoughts. He told Bruce he thought they were trying to get aid stations set up and then would slowly start to restore normalcy around the bases.

He said they probably hoped to build support around the bases and as they expanded the areas would grow together. Smaller pockets of trouble would eventually be snuffed out.

This would leave the rest of society to rebuild what they could. With the help of other countries they could get the country back on the grid in a few years, or at least a good portion of it.

The bad thing about it was the limited resources. There was no telling what would happen between now and then. He filled Bruce in on the recent events.

Bruce agreed. The worst was yet to come.

Chapter 9

Haliday called Rob and said he was going to come by and see him. This time he only took Mark with him. They didn't want to leave the security of the cabin too thin. The killing of Chuck and Barry had them on edge.

They loaded up their gear and rifles and took off. They took a slightly different route to town. They would start to alternate their routes for security purposes in case they were followed or anyone was gathering intelligence on them.

When they pulled up to the city hall complex a woman came out and told them Rob was over at the airport. They had taken the prisoners there.

"Why did they do that?" Haliday asked.

"The military told them to," she answered.

"They what?"

"The military told them to," she said. "Rob talked to them last night."

Haliday and Mark got in the Jeep and took off for the airport. It was only a few miles away and they were there in just over five minutes. The pulled in through the gate as two of the townspeople motioned them through and then waved at them.

They pulled up to the administration building and went inside. Rob and Brad were already there. Haliday and Mark walked over to them and made their greetings.

"Sorry to hear about Chuck and the other guy," Haliday said.

"Thank you," Rob answered.

"It must have been an ambush or some kind of setup for sure," Brad added.

Rob said, "We buried them this morning."

Haliday and Mark looked around. "Where are the prisoners?" Haliday asked.

Rob said, "We have them in the building the militia kept the other prisoners in."

Mark looked at Haliday and both of them walked outside. They looked toward the south and saw four helicopters coming their way. The first one closed in but then stopped. It was an OH58 Kiowa. It took a few flights around the small airport and then backed off.

Two more helicopters came in. These were Hueys. Haliday and Mark both saw the Cobra gunship move in as well. This one did not get as close. The two Hueys came in and landed.

Haliday recognized the sergeant from the previous day and noticed a first lieutenant walking over with him. *At least it's not a butter bar*, Haliday thought to himself.

The soldiers paused and surveyed the area. There were burn marks on the ground, bullet holes in the buildings, burnt out vehicles and blood splatters. After a couple of minutes they approached Haliday.

The lieutenant spoke first. "What the hell happened here?"

Rob pointed at Haliday. "He did."

The sergeant looked over at Haliday and nodded. Haliday returned the greeting with an exaggerated Queen of England wave and goofy smile.

The lieutenant looked over at the sergeant. "I see what you mean."

He then looked over at Haliday and extended his hand. "I'm Lieutenant Crothall."

Haliday shook the kid's hand. This guy was maybe 28 years old tops. He had brown hair, was 180 pounds, maybe six-foot-tall, with an average build, not overly muscular.

"How can we help you, Lieutenant?" Haliday said.

"I didn't catch your name," the lieutenant answered back.

"I didn't give it."

"Well, it would be nice to know who…"

Haliday cut him off. "Like I told the sergeant yesterday, I don't have time for BS."

"Sir, I just wanted to know who we were dealing with," the lieutenant said.

"I realize that, and so do I," Haliday shot back.

"I introduced myself."

"OK, I have a name, that's it."

"We're the U.S. Army, sir."

"Lieutenant, I mean no offense, but I have no idea what the hell is going on in the country. I used to be in the military and know that not everything is always what it appears to be, so please bear with us."

"Fair enough. Can we go talk somewhere?"

"Follow us, Lieutenant, and if you want to call off the fast movers on station over the water feel free to do so."

Two F-16s had been circling over to the east and over the lake waiting for the go ahead to come in and wreak havoc if given the signal. No one except Haliday and Mark had noticed them, not even Brad.

The lieutenant made a call on the radio and the two F-16s roared off. Haliday told him they could have the Kiowa and Cobra land if they wanted to, but the lieutenant said they would move on and recon the area some more. Haliday took that instead to mean the lieutenant didn't trust them that much; they would be staying close.

They all walked over to the admin building.

"Some major crap went down here, huh?" the lieutenant remarked.

Haliday gave him a 10-minute synopsis of what had transpired with the militia group. He wouldn't have said anything, but trusted the lieutenant based on the fact that he had called off the F-16s and other two helicopters. Haliday knew they were still close though.

They all gathered around a table in the admin building and Rob grabbed a pot of coffee. Since most of the food and supplies were here from when the militia commandeered them all, Rob and Brad decided to move everything they could here.

This would consolidate their operations and allow them to more adequately secure everything except the co-op. They would work on moving the grain and supplies from the co-op to this location as soon as they could locate trucks to move the trailers.

Rob started to bombard the lieutenant with a ton of questions that he couldn't answer or wasn't going to answer. The lieutenant had to ask him to slow down.

This actually angered Rob a bit. "You guys are the military and supposed to be here helping and so far I don't see you guys doing anything."

"It's not as easy as you think, sir," the lieutenant responded.

"You guys have tanks, helicopters, truck's, everything you need."

"Listen, sir, it isn't that easy; we have a lot of problems, too, you know."

The lieutenant went on to explain the sequence of events in a little more detail. He explained that once things started going sour for the CRA they started to backtrack and try to change the plan. They used their military connections to direct the military under the guise of them helping the country during the situation. They were able to direct a fair amount of troop movement before it was discovered what had truly transpired.

Once they were discovered and the battle for power grew, the military members of the CRA, if not arrested, left their posts to

114

run and hide. This left the remaining military personnel in disarray until they could regain a chain of command.

During that course of events a lot of members of the military who were not really fully informed abandoned their posts for a variety of reasons. Some members thought it was a coup attempt and did not want to partake. Many thought it was an actual EMP from a foreign government and they fled to take care of their families. A few more thought it was an attempt by the government itself to disarm the people, extend martial law and rule under an emperor. Regardless, the effect was the same.

Rob would not give up, though. He insisted that the lieutenant and the military were not taking enough action.

The lieutenant finally told him like it was. "Listen," he said, "we have a ragtag of people that are fighting off citizens like you, fighting off an attempt by foreign governments to get a stronghold in here, and odd factions still trying to takeover the government in some areas."

Rob sat and there and shook his head. He mumbled a little bit as he listened to Mark and Haliday who asked a few questions. Brad just sat and listened.

"What exactly is it you want us to do, Lieutenant?" Haliday asked.

"We need people like you to handle things appropriately," the lieutenant said.

"What would that be?" asked Rob.

"Well, by the looks of it, Mr. Haliday here already knows the answer to that question."

Haliday noted that they knew his name. "We need to police the community, eliminate the threats to ourselves, and help the military. We need to make sure we have open supply channels and pray that the good people can prevail over the scum."

Everyone looked around at each other. It seemed simple, but they knew it wouldn't be that easy.

The lieutenant went on to explain that there was not a lot of support they would be able to give people right now. He explained that they were still bringing in equipment and parts from around the world in order to set up relief channels and help

115

get things back to normal. "We have troops around the country that are being overrun by citizens as soon as they leave the bases. So far we have decided to lock them down until we can make contact with people like you guys.

"We need to make sure that the aid gets properly distributed," he emphasized. "We need to make sure people are reorganizing and not just looking for handouts. It's vital we commit to rebuilding."

"So you want us to take care of the criminals?" Haliday said.

The lieutenant said, "Yes, we want you to be the law keepers."

Haliday laughed and said, "Law keepers? You watched too many episodes of *Defiance*?"

"That's not what I meant. What I mean is you guys set up your law enforcement and we will back your authority," the lieutenant said. He asked for the names of the prisoners.

Rob handed him the list of names. The lieutenant wrote down all five names on a piece of paper and asked Rob to sign it. Rob looked it over briefly and signed it.

They walked out to the small building and the lieutenant had a few guys round up the prisoners. They double checked to make sure they were properly restrained and then loaded them in a helicopter.

Haliday and Mark talked to the lieutenant and sergeant alone for a bit. They all shook hands and then Mark and Haliday backed off. The helicopters spooled up and then took off.

Haliday had kept a keen eye on a soldier sitting in the helicopter. He had noticed the soldier had a few file folders that he tucked into a case before the helicopter left.

He made an assumption that the folders contained information on him. Exactly what type of information it was though was another question.

With the technology that had existed before the EMP, it could be anything. Most likely it was from military records, tax records, and who knows what else.

With everything that had happened in the area and Haliday's involvement, it was only natural to understand they worked up a file full of intel on him. He was none too happy about that thought.

Rob walked over to Mark and Haliday. "At least those guys will be put in a proper prison now," he said.

"What gave you that idea?" Haliday asked.

"The paper said they were being remanded to the U.S. Military for disposition based on their crimes, trials, and verdicts under martial law."

Haliday and Mark looked at each other. "Rob, they are going to be put to death," Haliday said.

Rob just looked at him. He was too new to martial law, nations without rule of law, post-apocalyptic disorder, and just plain scumbags doing what they wanted. He was thinking everything was back to normal.

Haliday told Rob he would contact him on the radio and fill him in on any new information as he came across it. Haliday and Mark left it at that. They headed home.

Once they arrived at home they told everyone as much information as they could. When they had talked to Lieutenant Crothall by themselves they had found out a little bit more about the start of the event.

The CRA had been working on their plans for almost 25 years. With the military slowly becoming more reliant on civilian companies for tasks supporting the military it was easier for them to infiltrate the ranks. Even positions as simple as running mess halls, maintenance of equipment or logistics control allowed them to get people put into places in key locations.

The military involvement was at higher levels and these members were counting on troops following commands in order to pull off their deception. They didn't count on a lot of troops and subordinates questioning certain orders.

If it had not been for a greater portion of military assets doing this, the country would be in total ruin. As farfetched as it had been, their plan succeeded in a manner. It brought on too much devastation and they were unable to follow through.

They actually overplayed the amount of force needed and that was what ruined their plans. Their own people could not recover from the mistakes they made. They affected more of the country than they had planned on.

Now the country was in a fight for its life. The dedication of a lot of veterans, reserves, National Guard, and active duty were the only thing keeping it intact. These patriots were taking up the load. Police officers and plain old citizens took up the fight.

"What kind of help does the military want?" Kayla asked.

"They want us to do exactly what we are doing," Haliday answered.

Blake said, "I don't understand."

"They want us to keep civil people civil and eliminate the threats," Haliday said. "We need to be the policing authority."

Everyone looked around at each other. They knew what he meant, but couldn't grasp the concept.

"They want us to go out and play mercenary?" Bev asked.

"They said go out and kill people?" Karen added.

Haliday put things as delicately as he could. He told them they didn't order the killing of people; they wouldn't do that. Would people die during the process of restoring order, yes.

It was, however, going to be an evil necessity in order to get society back on track. He explained the fragile nature of restoring order in the area.

"If we allow roving bands of people to rape, kill, pillage, and burn, then we lose the fight," Haliday said. "If we allow these criminals and scumbags to prosper, then we will lose the fight as they slowly grow in numbers. There will be a point where people will subvert to the efforts of new warlords, gang leaders or whatever you want to call them, and that will be the point which we can not return from. Desperate people will do what they need to survive and that's not always the right thing."

This inspired almost three hours of conversations within the group. As they all talked about different scenarios and options, Haliday went over to the ham radio and called Bruce.

"Hey, Roger," Bruce said. "How can I help you?"

Haliday said, "Anything new by you at all?"

"We've had a few guys come in and recon the trailer and my camp."

"Military or civilian?"

"My guess is most definitely military."

"You certain about that?"

"They all had the same boot print and they managed to avoid the signal devices I had set out."

"Sounds about right. They did the same thing here." Haliday explained to him about his encounters with the military and that even though he had more trust, he would continue to watch them closely, just in case.

Bruce told him he would try to gather as much information as he could. It was harder for him, though, as he had a smaller group and leaving was riskier.

"Just let me know whatever you can, Bruce," Haliday said.

Dawn looked at him. "How do you know they came here and checked us out?" she said.

Haliday answered, "I had Mark do an extended check of the property and he noticed the tracks."

"Why didn't you say anything?" she asked.

"No need to worry anyone."

"What if they had attacked us?"

"We'd be dead," he said. "We couldn't stand up to them."

She looked confused. He explained to her that if indeed the military wanted to take them out it would have happened already and they were more than capable.

He got up and walked over to the kitchen table. Sarah and Nancy had dinner ready. Tonight was spaghetti night with garlic bread. It smelled pretty good. Everyone sat down and started eating.

When the meal was over, everyone cleaned up. Haliday asked Bev to take the kids downstairs and watch a movie. He needed to talk to everyone.

119

Bev took the kids downstairs. David was up in the crow's nest and Alan was outside. They would be filled in later. Haliday stood up and looked around. This wasn't going to be easy.

"We have some tough choices to make here," he said.

"Exactly what do you mean?" Rich asked.

"We need to provide the military as much support as we can."

Randy asked, "What can we do?"

He went on to explain his plans. He would help Brad organize the Regional Defense Coalition. They needed to turn them into a regional law enforcement entity instead of defense force. With Chuck gone, it made even more sense.

They would need to make sure that everyone was back to understanding that rule of law had returned. People would be held accountable for their actions.

Sure, it seemed liked it was a mercenary force, but nobody was going to get anything other than what they deserved. There would be no unjust death sentences handed out.

The group would secure the immediate region, then move south to start cleaning up that area. Hopefully the military would be making contact with more groups so that they could effectively target trouble areas and would know who was doing what. One of the last things they needed was to start fighting another group of people who were trying to accomplish the same thing. That would be disastrous.

"How long do you think it will take?" Blake asked.

"I have no idea," Haliday said.

"How many of us do you need?" Mark asked.

"As few as possible," Haliday said, "because we need to make sure this place stays secured as well. I only want volunteers," he added. "I do not want anyone who has any doubts getting involved."

Mark stood up and stood next to Haliday.

Blake raised his hand and said, "Count me in."

Kayla raised her hand and Haliday told her to put it down. This started a small argument. A few of the others jumped in as well. After about 15 minutes of arguing they all came to a resolve.

Haliday and Mark would always go out. They would take along two people with them each time. They would rotate who would go. This way the cabin always had plenty of people keeping it secure.

They would gather four to five more teams from Brad's group. This would give them a total of 20 to 24 people making contact with others at any given time.

Haliday went over to the ham and called Brad. "Brad, can you come by tomorrow at noon for lunch?"

"Sure can. What's up?" Brad answered.

"We need to fill you in on what we have planned."

"OK. You want me to bring Rob?"

"Only if he leaves his panties at home."

Brad got a laugh out of that, but he also knew Haliday was serious. Rob was wavering a little bit too much on some issues. Brad would talk to him on the way there tomorrow.

Haliday pulled out a card and looked at it. He grabbed the portable ham and walked outside with it. He changed frequencies and hit the push-to-talk button and spoke into the mic.

"Lieutenant Crothall, please."

"Hold one," was all he heard back.

A few minutes passed by. "This is Lieutenant Crothall. May I ask who this is?"

"Haliday," he said.

"How can I help you, sir?"

"Well, lieutenant, it's more like we can help you, but we are going to need a few things."

"What exactly are you looking for?"

"I have Brad coming in tomorrow at noon. Can you meet us here?"

"Sure thing. Have a list ready."

"Will do. See you tomorrow," Haliday said. "Lunch is on us."

Haliday walked back in and told everyone they would have visitors tomorrow for lunch. They would start to plan the operations he had in mind.

Chapter 10

The Huey came in and landed at the small intersection of the roads by Haliday's cabin. The sergeant and lieutenant walked over to the cabin.

The sergeant looked around. "Not too bad at all," he said.

Haliday extended his hand and said, "I'm Roger. We never formally met, at least without me being an ass."

"Sergeant Edwards," the man replied.

They all walked inside the cabin where Brad was already waiting with Rob. Nobody was at the table except Haliday, Mark, Rob, Brad, the lieutenant and the sergeant.

Rich was in a nearby chair reading. Karen and Bev were cooking and Dawn was on the ham listening. Everyone else was either on security detail or downstairs. Out of sight, out of mind.

Crothall spoke first. "You have quite a nice setup here."

"It took many years to put it all together," Haliday said.

"Lot of money, too, by the looks of it," said the sergeant.

123

Haliday said, "We all pooled resources, and like I said, we have been at it for quite a few years."

Haliday's group had indeed put a good amount of money into the cabin and preps, but they also had quite a few family incomes pooled together to make it happen.

Little by little their preps grown and he saved money for the land and cabin. It had taken years to bring it all together. Without the three families contributing it would have been impossible.

Haliday had spoken with a drug representative one day at the hospital. The little blue pill was on its way and it was going to make a big splash—according to the lab techs in development and final stages of research. Haliday took the gamble and put everything into stock. He had reaped the rewards.

Soon afterward a regional manager for a big electronics chain had come into the hospital ER for treatment. Haliday spoke with the man at length. He reinvested money and quadrupled it a year later. That was the end of his trading days and the end of his luck.

Haliday had worked as much overtime as he could get for years. He worked a second job for almost five years after 9/11 to save money. That event was his final wake up call.

Everyone in the group had worked hard and made sacrifices. Six adults over the course of 15 years brought it all together. Now the effort was paying dividends.

"What do you guys have planned?" asked Crothall.

"We'll take on the job of securing our area and of helping pull the others closer together," Haliday answered.

"How so?" asked Crothall.

"Well, you want details or you want a generalization?"

"You can be vague."

"OK, we'll seek out the criminals, turn over whatever prisoners we manage to capture, and make sure the word spreads that there's a new sheriff in town."

The lieutenant looked over at Rob. "You on board with this, sir?"

"Yeah, I'm good," Rob said.

"You look concerned," Crothall noted.

"It's just that after all this destruction and death, when I saw you guys I thought it was over."

The lieutenant looked at Haliday.

Haliday said, "He'll be fine. He came through before and he can deal with it. Besides, he will be staying put and organizing the area government and people."

"You have a list of what you guys need?" Crothall asked.

"Sure do," Haliday said, sliding the paper over. "Here it is."

The lieutenant and sergeant looked over the list. They would look at each other once in awhile as they read through. It was quite a big list and not everything would be available. A few items they outright would not get.

Haliday knew the military all too well. Ask for everything you can and hope you get something out of it. Anything would be okay at this point. His group would take it.

"Can you make a copy of this for us?" asked Crothall.

Haliday looked at him. "Sure, let me run over to FedEx Office."

Rich couldn't help himself and burst out laughing. He had been listening in and kept it hidden until then.

"Go ahead and keep that one. I have another," Haliday said.

One of the small things he had thought of before was a box of carbon paper. He bought it, stuck it up on the shelf, and figured he would never need it.

He would have printed one on the computer downstairs but still wanted to keep things as quiet as possible. Handwriting the list was good enough for now.

Crothall went over it again with the sergeant who made notes on it. This was so they could put together what Haliday's group wanted.

"5.56mm, OK."

"7.62mm, OK."

"50 cal, uhm, maybe 50 rounds."

"9mm, OK."

"Forty cal, not sure."

"12-gauge, 00-buck, OK."

"M203, grenade launcher? Sorry, no."

"Smoke and teargas, OK."

"No crew-served weapons, period."

"Radios, we can spare six."

"Maps and grease pencils, OK."

There was a pause of silence.

"The rest of this gear just isn't going to happen." Both soldiers nodded.

"I noticed some injured members of your group. Do you need any medical supplies or help? Crothall asked.

"We had a doctor and nurse over to check things out already. They might actually need some supplies and help instead. Rob here can put you in touch with them when you're ready." Haliday said.

"We'll provide you with as much intel as we can, but support won't be available yet," Crothall said in finality.

Edwards added. "We can take care of prisoners for you if you contact us."

That struck a nerve with Rob. "Why don't we just kill them right then and there?"

"We're using them for labor," Edwards said.

Rob lightened up hearing that.

Karen and Bev walked over and set down a couple of pots and plates. They went to the stove and returned with a bit more food. The lieutenant and sergeant looked at it.

The lunch menu for the day was fresh tortillas, ground beef, refried beans, rehydrated tomatoes, and some cheese for burritos. They had even fried some up for chips and pulled out a jar of salsa.

"How many guys you have outside?" Haliday asked.

"The pilot and the crew chief. We told them to wait by your fire outside," Crothall said.

Rich got up, walked over to the table, and made some burritos. "I'll take them outside to the guys," he said. He wrapped them in tinfoil to keep them warm and took them out along with some hot coffee.

They finished eating quickly and then rose from the table. Haliday walked the soldiers back outside where they met up with the pilot and crew chief. They all walked to the Huey.

Crothall told them they would have another bird come by in a few hours and drop the supplies. From then on they would communicate via radio only. No more trips to visit.

Haliday and Mark walked back to the cabin as the Huey spooled up and then left. They would start planning the clean up operations as soon as they stepped back in the cabin.

*****

Bruce climbed on his ATV and took off for the Fort Custer area. He was about 10 miles away but it would take him close to half an hour through the woods and back roads.

When he got there he wasn't able to get very close. He managed about 100 yards away from the fence line before he was stopped. He turned the ATV off and raised his hands as the two soldiers approached him.

He was nervous and he had every right to be. He had a 9mm on his hip and an AR15 in a scabbard. The soldiers approached slowly as he just sat there.

He thought he would be able to get a bit closer and check things out but that was not the case. Once the soldiers arrived he really didn't know what to say to them.

The soldiers had him dismount the ATV and lay prone on the ground. They took his 9mm and a knife from him and then told him to stand up.

"What's your business here, sir?" a soldier asked.

Bruce said, "Just poking around to see what's going on."

"You have any ID, sir?"

"No, I don't."

"What's your name?"

"Bruce Mcintosh."

The soldier walked away and spoke on a radio for a few minutes, then returned. He looked over at Bruce. "Can I have your home address, sir?"

Bruce gave the soldier his home address. The soldier then asked for his social security number. Bruce hesitated at first, but then gave the soldier the information.

The soldier walked away again and returned about 10 minutes later. He told Bruce that the area was off limits and to return home. The soldier offered Bruce one of the small radios and Bruce told him he had one already.

"There'll be updates posted on the radio over the next few days," the soldier said. "Until then just stay safe."

"What did you need my info for?" Bruce asked.

"We have access to veterans' records and we checked your status."

"You guys have computers working?"

"No, we have people at the county buildings checking physical records and pulling them. Consolidating them at a safer location."

That didn't sit quite right with Bruce. Why would they be doing something like that, he wondered. Now he was wondering if he was doing the right thing by being honest.

"Sir, we plan to contact vets for assistance in the future," said the soldier when he saw the concern on Bruce's face.

Bruce was relieved at that. They handed him back his 9mm and let him return home.

Bruce told his wife and family what had happened. Next he got on the ham and called Haliday to tell him.

*****

Haliday finished speaking with Bruce. It all seemed okay to him and really just confirmed his thoughts. He knew Bruce was not in the same position as he was to help out just yet, but who knew what the future held.

He didn't expect the military to call up vets and press them into service; that was just absurd thinking. He did know, however, that the vets had certain qualities that would be useful.

128

Vets still had that sensational patriotism; they still had a high level of discipline and a high level of morals and ethics. A lot of vets practiced preparedness and were survivors. These people and those around them would be able to help restore society. More than likely this was why they would be tasked in the future, to help America make its return.

Haliday walked back over to the table. He was getting ready to sit down when he heard the Huey. Instead he wandered outside. There he saw the bird coming in slowly.

He got behind the wheel of the Ranger. Mark joined him and they met up with the soldiers unloading some boxes. They helped unload and then let the soldiers take off before finishing up.

Haliday looked down at a box. It had French writing on the side. He shifted the box around to find there was English on the other side. Canadian merchandise. English and French written on it.

He hadn't asked for this, but was thankful to receive it. It was a case of gas treatment. They could siphon gas from some abandoned vehicles and treat the gas to keep it fresh and useful.

It wasn't a lot of gear, but enough to help tremendously. There was more, too. Close to 4,000 rounds of 5.56, 500 9mm, a few hundred 7.62, 100 12-gauge rounds, 200 .40cal rounds, 25 50cal for the Barrett and a couple cases of smoke and CS teargas grenades along with the maps and radio gear.

Haliday spoke to Edwards for a few minutes. "One former NCO to another; why us?" he asked.

Edwards paused and then went on to explain. They had very few troops and they were spread very thin. Trying to handle security, aid distribution and law enforcement duties was far too cumbersome.

The troops they did have available were doing their best, but there were some very heavy pockets of resistance. Troops had already been murdered during patrols. They simply could not do it alone.

They had begged and borrowed a lot of equipment and parts to get vehicles moving again. The resource pool was limited. They had to get a grip on it as soon as possible.

Haliday nodded and shook his hand. "Good luck, Edwards."

Haliday's guys went back to the cabin and Mark had Randy and Kevin unload the Ranger. While they were doing that, Mark and Haliday walked inside to finish up with Rob and Brad.

Everyone gathered around while Haliday explained how they would try to secure the area. He pulled out a map and grease pencil.

He started circling intersections and placed an X in the circle. He drew two square boxes at two different intersections. He left these squares blank. He looked at Rob and Brad. "These roads need to be blocked off."

"How do we do that?" asked Rob.

"Chainsaws," Haliday answered. "You drop enough trees at these points and vehicle traffic won't be able to get through."

Haliday explained that by leaving two roads open with checkpoints they could partly secure the area and keep wandering gangs out.

With enough trees dropped over the roads in the areas he marked it would be very hard for vehicles to make it around the barricades. It wouldn't keep everyone out, but would make it very hard to get in with cars or trucks.

The plan would be to slowly open the roads by clearing the fallen trees when things started to return to normal. Eventually they would all be cleared. Whatever traffic existed then could move freely.

The checkpoints would be built using the trees as well. They could get the front loader from the airport working and use it to help move the logs in place.

The center of the road would be left open around 10 feet. About 50 feet in front of the checkpoint they would place a barricade that vehicles would have to drive around. They would have to use the shoulder of the road and would have to slow down. This would stop them from completely running the checkpoint at high speed. If supply trucks needed to get through they would be able to alter it later.

Haliday suggested they gather up a couple of travel trailers from the area and as many propane tanks as they could find. The folks at the checkpoints could use these as quarters.

The key would be getting enough volunteers to not only man the checkpoints, but patrol the other blockades as well. Using food should entice enough folks to volunteer.

Haliday took a red grease pencil out and looked at a piece of paper. He placed red Xs in key locations on the map. These were areas that had been identified as being dangerous. This meant that there were either gangs or groups of people in the area causing some type of trouble. These areas were key to opening and maintaining supply routes and distribution centers.

Mark looked down at the map and hung his head low. Mark's father Bill walked away and went over by the fireplace and sat down. Fresh wounds were opened.

Just a couple of miles from their farm was a red X. The loss of a wife and mother was still hurting. This lit a fire in Mark's stomach. He was burning for some payback.

The small towns they would need to secure were Cass City, Caro, Marlette, Sandusky, Brown City, and Yale. The rest in their area were already taken care of because they were closer and they had dealt with them already.

The very small townships were of no concern because the populations were spread out wide. Cass City was well within their control as well. The first place they would visit would be Caro.

"You guys know anything about Caro?" Haliday asked.

Brad answered, "My dad worked at the ethanol plant there."

"Ethanol plant?" Haliday asked.

"Yeah, you know, like gas," Brad said.

Haliday didn't know what to do. That was a huge asset. He sat there for a minute. "I have to call the lieutenant and ask about that," he said. He went over to the ham.

Sgt. Edwards answered instead of Lt. Crothall and told Haliday that they had secured the ethanol plant and not to worry about it. He told Haliday they had Caro pretty much wrapped up.

Haliday returned to the table. "Old intel. The military has it." He wondered exactly how up to date any of this intel actually was. In true military fashion, especially under the circumstances, it was expected. "What about Sandusky?"

Bill walked over from the fireplace. He looked at the map. Mark looked up at him.

Bill said, "Not much there at all but a lot of small businesses and folks supporting the local farms."

Sandusky was the next town south of them. Marlette was closer, but further south. They would be trying to simply move their southern perimeter further south. They would move from town to town as they moved south so that they could meet up with the others helping the military and join the areas together.

"It looks like we have three pockets of trouble," Haliday said.

"Any idea how many people in each group?" asked Alan.

"Looks like around thirty in this apartment complex." Haliday pointed to the map and then indicated another spot. "We have another two dozen here in the trailer park." Lastly he pointed to another apartment building and said, "This is supposed to be the worst and they have around fifty people total."

"What's the plan?" Kevin asked.

Mark answered, "We go after the trailer park first."

Haliday laid out a plan. The trailer park was the easiest target and was somewhat secluded from the other two targets. They would check that out first. They would send in a small recon team first. Once they had enough information to move in they would start the assault. If they were smart about it, it would be easier—not easy, but easier.

Gear lists were compiled and distributed. Haliday made sure that Brad's groups would have the equipment they needed. He insisted they standardized the firearms among them as much as possible.

Haliday's team all had ARs. It would be rather detrimental if they had people trying to slap AK mags into ARs and vice versa. Throw the SKSs into the mix and you could really have trouble. Uniformity was important for successful operations.

That brought up the next question. They needed to make sure they were all easily identifiable to each other. Rob suggested they use the militia's uniforms.

"No offense, Rob," Haliday said, "but I'd rather not put one on right now and get shot."

People in the area came to recognize the Russian camo pattern as being associated with the rogue militia group that had attempted to control the area and resources.

Haliday said it should be easy enough to get everyone into black clothing. All black clothing. There should be enough around to do the job. Even if it meant entering some of the neighbors' now empty houses and borrowing items.

"Borrowing" was a loosely used term now. It could be considered looting in most cases. Unfortunately, the neighbors they would borrow from were most likely dead already.

That was one of the never-ending discussions. At what point was it considered salvaging compared to looting? What level of survival justified the looting or salvaging? There was a lot of gray area there.

The plan was set and action would take place in another 48 hours. This gave everyone the chance to get the teams brought up to speed and cover the geographic layout and timetable.

Brad and Rob left and Haliday and his team started their preparations. Haliday, Mark, Dawn, and Kayla would be going out first. Haliday wasn't happy about his daughter going, but she was just as qualified as anyone and so was Dawn.

Chapter 11

For mid-December the weather was rather fair. The temperature was around 30 degrees. The previous snowfall had melted away leaving the grassy areas a mucky mess.

It was past dusk as Haliday's team moved in close to the trailer park. They held tight as Mark moved in to see what was going on. He would check things and call Haliday to fill him in on the situation.

The trailer park had been fairly upscale. Most of the homes were very-well kept and consisted of larger double-wide homes. You were hard pressed to find a typical rattrap or rusting hulk of a single-wide anywhere.

It was a small open park and literally looked entirely deserted. The only telltale sign of life was over by the clubhouse. Smoke poured out of the fireplace.

The clubhouse made an optimal retreat for this group. It had a kitchen area, large seating area, indoor pool, small gym, and plenty of room for everyone. Since it also had an outdoor pool there was a small fence around it.

Mark moved in slowly and scoped the area. He called Haliday on the radio. "Roger, I can only see a few people and it looks like they were left behind for security," he said.

Haliday sent Dawn to meet up with Mark.

Once she got there they both made sure they were well-hidden. Kayla stayed behind with Haliday, also well-hidden.

Brad's teams had placed themselves in various locations around the park. The vehicles were almost a mile away and hidden so they didn't attract attention. Brad's group had come in the Deuce and a half and a pickup truck and Haliday's group in the Tahoe. They had utilized some pole barns close by to hide the vehicles in and had moved in on foot.

The clubhouse was on the south end of the park. Haliday and Kayla moved up to where Mark and Dawn were on the east side of the park. Haliday called Brad to check his progress.

Brad had one team on each of the remaining three sides plus his own team to respond where needed. "Roger, we going in soon?" Brad asked.

"We can't right now, Brad," Haliday said. "No one is there but a few folks left to watch the place."

If they moved in, they risked getting caught inside if the remainder of the group came back. They would know something was wrong right away.

Since the group moved in a pack, they would get them all at once in the parking lot. Any members left inside they would flush out. Prisoners would be hauled away to a safe location nearby.

About two hours after waiting patiently they heard vehicles approaching. There were only three of them. One was an old Suburban, one an old Plymouth of some sort, and the third one actually looked like a Humvee.

The closer they got the more apparent it was. It was a Humvee; not a civilian H1, but an actual military turtleback Humvee. This was not looking too good right now.

Mark asked Haliday what they were going to do. Haliday told him that they had to move on with the operation. There was no way they could identify the reason these guys had a Humvee.

Especially in the short span of time they would have to catch them in the parking lot.

Haliday told everyone that he would take care of the driver of Humvee. If it was a service member he would take responsibility for what might happen to them.

The vehicles pulled into the parking lot, stopping in front of the clubhouse, and people started to exit the vehicles. Haliday paid close attention to the Humvee. "SANGB" was stenciled on the bumper. Selfridge Air National Guard Base. He could not see what unit.

The people climbing out of the Humvee didn't look remotely close to being military, active or reserve. They were fair game now. That's all that mattered.

Haliday heard someone bark out an order to get the vehicles unloaded.

He heard the same voice yell out, "Get the bitches inside and locked up!"

Haliday noticed that two females were being dragged out of the Suburban. They had their hands tied and looked quite weary. He couldn't tell how old they were, but they were fairly young. Teens or early twenties.

They were resisting, but seemed to be too weak to put up much of a fight. One of them spit on a guy who slapped her hard. If they hadn't already been assaulted, they were going to be.

Haliday told everyone to avoid the women and people around them. No collateral damage would be acceptable. These innocent women needed to be kept safe.

As they started unloading the vehicles, it was apparent they had been out looting. That was enough to prompt Haliday to start the action. In what was practically his signature opening move now he yelled out to give them a fair chance. "Police officers! Drop your weapons!"

Rob had authorized them to act as law enforcement in the region. In Rob's mind it made things appear legal. Haliday didn't need the title. He wasn't going to tolerate this, period.

The people by the clubhouse dropped their boxes of goods and grabbed for their weapons. Someone inside the clubhouse came running out and opened fire toward Haliday's group.

Haliday and his team were around 100 feet away and kept down low. Brad's groups lit up the parking lot as the hoodlums returned fire. A couple of them ran to the front door and went inside.

The two girls that were tied up dropped down on the wet, cold, mushy grass, where they huddled together. They were obviously frightened, but knew enough to stay put, which most likely saved their lives from friendly fire.

A woman ran toward the old Plymouth and swung the door open. She reached inside and grabbed a pistol. As soon as she started to raise it, one of Brad's group dropped her with several rounds, striking her chest and abdomen.

Mark and Kayla started shooting the tires of the vehicles. They flattened the Plymouth's and Suburban's. They shot at the tires of the Humvee, but it seemed to have little effect.

Three of the guys jumped into the Humvee. They started it and slammed it into reverse. A couple guys tried to run to it, but the driver slammed it into gear and floored it.

As it took off toward the road, the driver ran over one of the guys trying to reach them in hopes of escaping with them. The body tumbled underneath the Humvee as it drove away.

The run flat tires of the Humvee allowed them to get away. Nobody was sure how far away they would get, but the Humvee would be located eventually. It had taken too many hits and was leaking fluid.

Both sides were fully engaged now. The gang had taken refuge behind anything they could find, including the vehicles. They were overwhelmed tactically, but refused to give up.

Haliday was taking aim at one man when he heard a loud crashing sound. Someone had broken out one of the windows of the clubhouse. Sporadic fire came from within.

Haliday shifted toward the muzzle flashes he saw through the window. He fired a few shots toward the windows slowly and methodically. The tracers from his rifle lined up with the muzzle flashes and Haliday unleashed the rest of the magazine.

The firing from within the clubhouse stopped. As Haliday shifted back toward the gang around the vehicles and front of the clubhouse he saw a few people run for the window and door.

One of the gang members reached the window. He started to climb through and cut himself on the jagged edges of the broken glass. Once through he ran toward a room inside.

Another woman from the gang had made it to the door and managed to get inside. The man behind her who was providing cover fire wasn't as lucky. Mark cut him down with a burst of almost 10 rounds.

A lot of screaming came from those thugs that were still outside. They started throwing their weapons down and raising their hands. Almost all of them were yelling, "Don't shoot!"

Haliday called a ceasefire and after a little more than a minute all of the firing outside had stopped. Some of Brad's group started moving in slowly to gather up the group.

They were almost there when a few more shots rang out from the window. One of Brad's men took two hits center mass to his chest and went down. The rest of Brad's team near the front of the clubhouse returned fire.

Haliday fired toward the window while Mark popped a smoke grenade and tossed it inside. He followed this with a CS teargas grenade. They could hear some yelling inside, but did not see anything.

Around the back side of the clubhouse the other two teams from Brad's group were waiting. The back door flung open and three people came out coughing and gasping for fresh air. There were two men and one woman. They were ordered by Brad's teams to put their hands in the air. One man pointed a pistol and started firing. His shots were met with return fire.

The three people that came out the back door had been close together. The man who had fired and the woman died in the hail of gunfire. The last man raised his hands and pleaded for mercy.

This man was ordered to the ground. As he laid there on the ground, Brad's teams approached him. They zip-tied his hands behind his back and waited. They were not sure if anyone was still inside, but they had the door and windows covered.

Haliday, Mark, Kayla, and Dawn provided cover while Brad's group moved in again to gain control of the prisoners. They were securing everyone when they heard the shots.

There came three rapid shots first. After a moment came a single shot. Brad's group hurried up and finished securing everyone. They waited for Haliday's next command.

Haliday and Mark grabbed two of Brad's men and made their way to the clubhouse door. They switched on their flashlights and entered to clear the building.

As they were doing so, Brad's group made sure the exterior and surrounding area was safe. They grouped the prisoners together and double checked the wounded and dead.

Dawn and Kayla helped the two young women sit up and tried to calm them. They gave the girls some water and found a blanket to wrap around them. They told them everything was okay now.

Inside the clubhouse, Haliday's group was almost halfway through. They came upon a small office that had been transformed into a bedroom of sorts. Haliday and Mark entered the room.

On the floor was a mattress with a woman tied to it. She was completely naked and it was painfully obvious what they had been doing to her. She had three fatal wounds to her chest. Next to her was a man who had decided he was not going to go along with whatever was in store for him. He had murdered this poor lady in a last act of defiance before putting the pistol in his own mouth.

Haliday was sickened and angry. They moved out of the room and continued on. They next entered a small meeting room. It was clear except for a large closet.

Both Haliday and Mark were contemplating how to check it when Haliday thought he heard someone inside. He called out, "Come out slowly, hands first!"

There erupted a volley of gunfire from inside. Both Haliday and Mark sprayed the doors and walls with rounds. After they both emptied a magazine into the closet, Haliday listened.

There were shallow breaths coming from within. He looked at Mark and both of them emptied another magazine into the closet area, but closer to the floor. Haliday slowly eased open the door to find the man inside was shredded.

The rest of the clubhouse was cleared without incident. Haliday went back outside and checked on everyone. One of Brad's members was dead and two injured but not badly.

It was actually a very successful operation. Haliday looked around at the gang members. This could have been a lot worse than it was. Surprise had been the key.

The gang here had three dead inside, seven dead outside, and eight injured. Five had managed to stay safe and three had gotten away in the Humvee. There had been 26 total, not counting the poor woman inside.

The two young women Dawn and Kayla were watching over were very lucky. They had been in for a very rough ride and lucky that Haliday and his teams had happened along.

Haliday walked over to Dawn and Kayla. The two young women crouched low and looked away. They were still very afraid and Haliday's presence wasn't making it any better.

Kayla looked at Haliday. She motioned with her head and made an eye movement.

Haliday knelt down and looked at the women. "It's going to be OK; we're here to help."

One of the women looked toward him. "Are you from the government?" she asked.

Haliday almost chuckled out loud thinking about the Reagan quote; nine words to fear: 'We're from the government and we're here to help.'

Instead he answered, "No ma'am, we are working with them though, trying to help restore order. Let's get you warmed up and fed."

Brad's group went through the clubhouse and vehicles, taking out all of the food and weapons. They took anything else they thought would be needed. A few of the guys went and got the vehicles.

While Brad's guys loaded the food and weapons into the vehicles, Haliday surveyed the equipment. He took a couple of the rifles and two of the pistols. He placed them near his Tahoe along with some ammo.

He walked over to where the women were. "You folks live around here?"

One of the women explained where they were from. Haliday went over to Brad and spoke to him for a few minutes. He gathered up a box of food and headed for the Tahoe.

"Let's get you girls home," he said.

Haliday's group packed up and they all climbed in the Tahoe.

Haliday looked at his map and made some mental notes on the route. They left the trailer park and headed for their destination. They were only about 10 minutes away when they came across the Humvee.

They went to a slow crawl. Mark looked around as Haliday brought the Tahoe to a complete stop. Mark and Dawn got out and went into the nearby wood line as Haliday surveyed the small county road.

They used the woods to their advantage and worked their way up to the Humvee. The Humvee was abandoned and nothing had been left inside. There was radiator fluid all over the ground and what looked like oil as well.

Mark called Haliday and Haliday moved closer with the Tahoe. After double checking the area, Mark and Dawn got back in the Tahoe. Haliday continued on.

Mark said it first. "I wish we could have found them there."

"I hear ya," said Haliday.

His only hope was that karma would play a role and take care of those guys. In the meantime he had to finish the task at hand. About 15 minutes later he pulled into the parking lot of the apartment complex.

Mark and Dawn stayed with the Tahoe. Haliday and Kayla took the two girls up to the door. Haliday stood off to one side and Kayla the other. He had the girls wait to the side as well. There was no sense in risking a shotgun blast through the door.

Haliday knocked. There was no answer. He knocked several more times. He looked around. No one was watching. They were either gone or dead. He had suspected there might be more people around, but there weren't. Not in this building.

Then there came a soft voice at the door. "Go away."

One of the young women spoke. "Mom, it's me, Kate. Some friends brought us home."

Haliday heard the locks on the door clicking and it slowly swung open. Andrea Walters appeared and looked at Kate. She started crying and opened her arms for both of her daughters.

They all went inside. Tim Walters was on the couch and tried to get up. The girls rushed over to him. They hugged and kissed him. He wept openly. He looked over at Haliday.

Haliday went over to the couch and knelt down next to Tim. "Don't move; you don't look so hot." Haliday told Kayla to go get the first aid kit. She returned with it immediately. He then asked her to go get the equipment and supplies. She made a few small trips while Haliday checked out Tim. He cleaned him up a bit and gave him some antibiotics and Tylenol.

"Listen, you take it easy and get some rest," Haliday said.

He explained what had happened in very loose detail. He told the couple that the military was working on aid. Haliday looked around a little. He could see their struggle to survive.

He left them with a rifle and some ammunition for it along with the two pistols. He had a box of food that he left with them as well. It was quite a mix of items, but enough for now. Kayla came back in with a few pouches. She told Andrea how to cook them up. It was Haliday's famous beans and rice mixture. There was enough for three very good meals for the four of them. She handed them a small bottle of vitamins. Andrea couldn't stop crying.

Haliday went out and checked a few of the apartments that were empty. Kayla helped him grab whatever would burn and they took it all to Tim's apartment. Haliday told them to use what they could from the empty apartments for firewood.

143

Haliday went back over by the couch. Tim whispered, "Thank you."

"You're welcome," Haliday said.

Haliday went to the door. He said goodbye and the girls came over by the door and hugged him. "You girls stay safe." He walked out the door.

They hugged Kayla, who was crying a bit as well. It could have been her in the same situation.

Haliday and Kayla returned to the Tahoe and left for the trailer park.

It was almost early morning now. The sun was about to rise. Haliday pulled up and saw that Brad had everything ready to go.

"What about the prisoners?" Brad asked.

Haliday said he would call Crothall and tell him about them and then went over to the radio and called the lieutenant. They spoke for just a few minutes. Haliday returned and told Brad to put the prisoners all in a trailer. Crothall had a group on the way to take care of them. He told Brad he would wait for Crothall. Brad and his guys moved out.

Haliday sat down and waited. A lot of thoughts crossed his mind. He couldn't help but wonder how many more people would die.

Mark told him to take a break. Haliday closed his eyes for a few minutes. Not much time had elapsed when he heard the two helicopters. He walked over to a clearing and popped a can of green smoke.

Two birds came in. The Cobra stood off a bit while a Chinook landed near the smoke. The ramp in the back came down. Haliday watched the door gunners as they kept a keen eye out.

Four men exited the ramp and took up positions around the bird. Two more worked their way toward Haliday. He talked to one of them and then they all went and retrieved the prisoners.

The prisoners were double checked and then loaded on the Chinook. The soldiers boarded the bird and it soon took off, headed for Selfridge. The prisoners would be processed there.

Haliday handed one of them remaining soldiers a piece of paper that had some brief notes on it. This would show them where the Humvee was. Later in the day a team would retrieve it and airlift it back to Selfridge.

Haliday learned from one of the soldiers how the Humvee had fallen into the gang's hands. Two soldiers had taken the Humvee earlier to go retrieve a family in the area. They had convinced someone that it was a good idea. It was thought they had deserted. Unfortunately for them they had been ambushed. The Humvee had been taken and the two of them were summarily executed on the side of a road.

Haliday and his team climbed back in the Tahoe and went back to the cabin. They stopped briefly near the roadblock and talked with the folks there. Haliday was told nothing had happened, which was a good sign.

Once they got home, they got cleaned up and then sat around the kitchen table. Mark gave a brief account of what had transpired. Haliday moved off to the fireplace where he sat alone.

He was really bothered by the previous evening's events. What the gang had done to the poor woman in the clubhouse and what they had planned to do with the other two women bothered him. He was not going to let that type of behavior take root. There was no way he would allow it. People would be dealt with in a severe manner. There had to be checks and balances.

Mark walked up to him. "Mind if I sit down?" he asked.

Haliday said, "Please, have a seat."

"You OK?" he asked.

"Yeah, I'm fine," Haliday answered.

"Seems like something is bothering you."

"I know my sister is safe in Texas, but I keep thinking about my brother in Missouri and even my brother out in Oxford."

Mark looked down and then spoke. "Roger, we all know the odds right now. I'm still at a loss for what happened to my mom."

"I keep thinking about what we are seeing, how people are acting, and I keep seeing the faces of my family and friends on those poor souls we come across," Haliday said.

They both sat there for awhile. Rich came over and offered them a drink. Both Haliday and Mark politely declined asked for coffee instead. Now wasn't the time to drop their guard and relax.

Haliday sat there a while longer and just stayed warm by the fireplace. He thought of everyone—family, friends, and acquaintances. He determined that he would help end this any way he could.

He got up and called Randy and Kevin over. "You guys up for a task?"

"Sure, Uncle Roger. What can we do for you?" Kevin asked.

He gave them some flares and told them to take them out to the two roadblocks that were set up. He wrote down instructions that he wanted the folks at the roadblocks to follow in case of problems.

Haliday went over to the radio and called Brad. He talked to him a few brief minutes and explained what he was doing. Brad understood and would visit the roadblocks to help answer any questions.

Haliday went down to the basement and came up with a few supplies. They were basic food staples. These were enough to feed folks for a few days only. He was sending them to the roadblocks as well.

If he sent too much they would probably gorge themselves and run out quickly. It was nothing fancy, but enough to give the folks at the blockades two decent meals a day.

Haliday was going to make it a point to ask Crothall for some supplies for the blockades. These would be two key areas that would need defending in order to guard the small region.

The next couple of calls on the radio were to Dennis up by Camp Grayling and to Bruce over by Fort Custer. This was just to make sure everything was still on the up and up. He listened to their reports.

The final call was to Adam in the Metro Detroit area to see how he was holding up. What he heard from Adam was not very promising.

Things were getting worse each day.

Chapter 12

Bruce had told Haliday that he made only a couple of trips to check on Fort Custer. He didn't come as close as he had last time for fear of getting stopped again. What he saw was really the same thing each time. The troops were regularly patrolling the perimeter of the camp and keeping it locked down. Once in a while he saw planes come in and offload equipment.

Every once in a while there would be a vehicle or two offloaded. These were mostly Humvees and M1078 LMTVs, which was the Army's newest light utility truck replacing the old Deuce and a half. He noted there were a lot of Deuces still in use.

Bruce managed to get a glimpse of the open warehouse doors and saw pallet upon pallet of what he assumed was aid of some sort. He could not see, however, exactly what it was.

On the radio broadcasts people were asked to take the two-by-two-foot bright orange flag that was in the capsules and nail it their rooftop with the nails and washers that were included.

If they could not get to the roof they were told to place it on a vehicle or somewhere else where it would be visible. The radio announcement said it was vital that they do so. They were told this would help identify households where people were still located. The flags could be spotted by air and the coordinates marked for relief efforts.

People were asked to come outside if they heard helicopters or troops in the area. The troops would need to do a quick visual count and this seemed to be the easiest way. Along with the flag came two pre-cut pieces of tape. People who did not need aid were asked to place an X on their markers. This, too, seemed to be very odd.

After hearing different horror stories, a lot of people did not trust the government. The conspiracies abounded that these were going to be used to mark targets. That, of course, was absurd.

Dennis reported the same thing up at Grayling. The big difference up there, however, was that he had reported several convoys of vehicles, including some armor moving out to the surrounding communities.

The cities of Gaylord, Grawn, Mio, and Harrison were the points of interest for these convoys. Basically they were locations toward all points of the compass. Dennis had been in touch with quite a few people and found out that these troops were moving in and conducting recon of the areas in order to set up aid stations.

It appeared that this was the same routine across the affected area of the nation. The areas of the country still functioning were receiving people in on a daily basis but not in mass amounts.

During the first couple of weeks people stayed in place. After that they started to move toward areas that they heard could support them. Some stayed in place waiting for aid.

Moving great distances was hard. The lack of transportation impeded the ability of people to get anywhere more than 25 to 30 miles away. The risk of walking great distances and possibly finding nothing was too much. Getting help into affected areas proved fatal many times for those trying to help.

People wanting to help others would usually end up getting ambushed and whatever they had with them was always taken. Sometimes they were killed for what they had.

Haliday's area would be supported by the Selfridge group and they had some very big problems. Selfridge was on the water. They had land to the north, south, and west of them. All of these areas were very heavily populated with Detroit, Flint, and Saginaw being the main cities and each and every one of them being a problem before the event. Now they were kill zones.

There were a lot of unsavory characters that had banded together and now controlled those areas for the most part. These were going to be tough to take back.

Even though martial law had been declared long ago, no one really knew exactly how to regain control over the heavily populated areas. The thought of engaging these groups militarily was the furthest from anyone's mind, but was the most obvious solution.

Haliday took his father Rich with him to go check the roadblocks. They arrived at the first roadblock and Haliday looked around at it. He spoke to the people in charge and gave them instructions on altering the area. He told them to stagger some more log piles so approaching vehicles would have to zigzag. He also suggested a fortified fighting position off to each side of the road.

Rich suggested using a chainsaw and notching the logs. This would help prevent them from just rolling away if a vehicle struck them. He then looked around to see if any more improvements could be made.

Haliday and Rich went to check on the second roadblock. When they got there, Haliday was upset. There was only one person standing guard. The rest were inside the trailer sleeping or playing cards.

Haliday called Brad and let him know this would have to change. The group became argumentative with Haliday. He explained that if he had wanted to, he could have taken out the entire group.

"All I would have to do is sneak up on the lone guard. I could cut his throat and then approach the trailer. I'd shoot every single one of you as you came out of the trailer," he told them.

Rich said, "I would fire bomb it and let you all burn."

151

This sunk in a bit. The group realized that their complacency could be deadly. Haliday checked out the rest of the site and made the same suggestions he had previously.

When finished, they headed back to the cabin.

"When do you think we'll be able to go home?" asked Rich as they drove back.

"I'm not sure, Dad," Haliday replied, "but I don't think it's going to be any time soon."

"If you had to guess, what would you say?" Rich asked.

Haliday answered, "Dad, to be honest, I really don't know."

"You think we'll be able to at least go check on the houses?" said Rich.

Haliday explained what his thoughts were on this subject. He told him he thought they might be able to check on the houses during the summer. It might be that long before it's safe to travel that far. He also told him that he expected to be at the cabin for at least two years. They would have to grow vegetables and fruits. Hunting and fishing would have to provide meat.

"The one thing we have to consider is what we'll do for a living, Dad," he said.

"What do you mean, Roger?"

"It's not like any of us will be going back to our old jobs any time soon."

"I hadn't thought about that," Rich said.

Haliday really hadn't given it much thought either. There would be a lot of changes for those who survived. A lot of people would have to learn new trades. Most would have to adapt. There'd be a need for engineers, technical jobs, repairmen and more. However, there would be a greater need for basic laborers, people like farmers, carpenters, truck drivers, and small merchants.

He looked over at his dad. "You think I can file for unemployment?"

They both laughed. They arrived back at the cabin after just a few more minutes.

Next on the agenda was a similar operation to put a stop to, another one of the gangs. Haliday planned on going after the smaller group in the apartments for the next operation. He called Mark over so they could plan.

Mark started to study the maps. Haliday looked up and called Alan and Dawn over. "You guys are going next," he said.

"You want Nancy to go instead of Dawn this time?" Alan asked.

"That's a bad idea Alan," Haliday said.

Alan asked, "Why is that?"

"If we get in too deep, you are both at risk. I don't plan on coming back here and explaining to your kids that both their parents are gone," he answered.

Mark and he studied the maps again and finalized the plan. Haliday had taken over the paramilitary operations. Brad still ran the defensive coalition group, but the offensive actions were led by Haliday and his group.

Brad's people were brought in to help. Haliday told him that without getting rid of the gangs, it was only a matter of time before they worked their way north. That was incredibly true.

Haliday called Brad on the ham. Brad would meet him at the second roadblock and they would cover the plan for the next operation. Brad was told to bring his three team leaders.

Haliday then called Edwards and spoke to him. "How is everything going, Sergeant?" he asked.

Edwards replied, "Not well at all. We are having some major issues in the larger cities."

"What exactly is going on?" Haliday asked.

"We tried to get in and survey the cities. We had taken some trucks with aid along with us. We were lucky to get out of there," Edwards answered.

Haliday asked, "Everybody all right?"

"We had some injuries but nothing fatal. We lost the three trucks of aid we took," Edwards told him.

"That sounds pretty bad. What do you guys have planned?" Haliday asked.

There was a long pause.

Haliday had to repeat himself. He waited and there was still no answer.

Edwards finally came back on the radio. "I'll explain it in person next time we meet. We are working on a few contingencies."

Haliday and Mark looked at each other. They knew what that meant. That was bad news for the troublemakers. They had to wonder if it was even possible to take back the large cities. They did not know how many troops were available.

*****

Over at Selfridge the troops were busy loading up aid on helicopters. The same scene was being played out near Fort Custer and Camp Grayling. Across the nation it was the same routine.

The nation's railroads were being prepared as well. Dead trains were being moved from the tracks. Yards were being secured by troops. Supplies were being brought in via rail under heavy guard.

The helicopters were quite a sight. There was a mix of Hueys, Blackhawks, and Chinooks for this mission. They would be accompanied by Kiowas, Cobras, and MH6 Little Birds for security.

A lot of the helicopters were painted differently. Upon closer inspection you could see that they were foreign. These had been loaned to the United States by various governments.

On the runway was an Air Force E-3 Sentry. The AWAC, Advanced Warning and Air Control plane, stood out like a sore thumb. The big rotating radar dome gave it away.

This plane would be used to help coordinate the air traffic. With over 20 helicopters flying in close quarters it was hazardous. On top of that two F-16s would be on station around the area as well.

The birds all lifted off and headed out in formation. Those inside really had no idea how long they would be gone or how much area they would be able to cover.

It was an odd plan. Without the people being able to get to centralized locations, this was their only hope. Eventually they would have buses and other transportation to get people to camps.

The helicopters each had their own assigned area. To watch from the ground it looked like mass confusion. The E3 Sentry had carefully coordinated each bird to keep things organized.

A Huey made its way into its area. Upon seeing the bright orange marker on a home, the Huey dropped altitude. The pilot slowed down and the co-pilot marked down coordinates on a list. He wrote down the number of people he saw.

In the back of the bird the two door gunners kept watch. A third soldier took his cue from the co-pilot who told him, "Three people."

The soldier tossed out three MREs—Meals Ready to Eat. A single package of rice in a bubble wrap envelope was tossed out as well. At 300 feet off the ground the MREs would survive the fall. It was not a lot of food, but it would provide nutrients. For a lot of people it was a welcomed package.

The rural areas were far better off than the suburbs. They had their crops to rely on. Unfortunately a lot of people were not as lucky. They ate what they could, mostly corn and soybeans.

Small animals, household pets, mice, rats, farm animals, and more were all eaten. Most people hoped that nobody had resorted to cannibalism. Sadly, that option was used in some areas.

The helicopters quickly fell into a pattern. It became easier at each house. Unfortunately they were unable to reach all of the areas. The following day they pick up where they left off.

On more than one occasion the helicopters were fired upon. The door gunners would return a volley of fire and the helicopter would leave the area immediately.

In a few instances one of the attack birds would have to come in. The attack birds would lay down heavy warning fire. The soldiers made no attempt to deliver aid in these cases.

The hope was that word would spread and people would come to realize the soldiers were there to help. It would be very hard to convince some people, however.

People were not told how often aid would be delivered. They were simply told that the troops were doing what they could. They were also told that relief camps were being set up and transportation would be provided.

This by itself fueled concerns. People thought of FEMA camps and that led to more rumors. One of the biggest rumors was the use of the FEMA coffins. People had spotted these being placed on trains.

The state of the country was undeniably a big mess. People demanded more answers. Who did it? Why did they do it? What was going to happen next? They still didn't believe the information they were given.

The relief operation was going to be long and hard. Nobody knew how long it would take. Nobody knew how effective it would be. The only certainty was that more people would die before it was over.

*****

Haliday needed time to think. He put on his winter gear and went outside. He took a walk around the property checking on everything. Everything looked to be okay.

The fighting positions were all cleaned out. The group had placed some basic supplies in each position, including hand warmers, small ammo load, and an MRE. They would respond to these with full loads if they had to.

Next, Haliday checked the tree line. They had tripwires and traps set up there. After the attack on the cabin, he wanted more traps out there. The occasional animal setting off a tripwire was becoming a rarity.

They had cut some small boards into 12-by-18-inch pieces. They placed three and a half inch drywall screws in these. These were buried just below the dirt, making it hard to see the screws.

These had been placed behind trees; not just random, but trees that most people advancing on the cabin would use as cover. Fallen leaves helped to hide them.

156

Haliday had even had half a dozen punji pits put in. These were not deep, only 18 inches deep with nine-inch punji sticks buried inside. He thought anything that could slow someone down was worth trying.

One of the better improvements made were the LED lights. After most of the strobes were destroyed they set up the LEDs. These were run off a small battery bank; enough light to blind night-vision and let Haliday's group see for a few minutes.

These were some of the precautions taken to help keep the cabin safe. More importantly, they helped keep the group safe. The group knew to stay away. Haliday and Kayla were the only ones who checked on the safeguards. They did this together.

As he was walking around he saw evidence of the attack on the cabin. Trees had shredded areas where bullets had hit. Areas of the ground were noticeably disturbed. Spent shell casings were all over the ground. He would make sure that in the spring they cleaned it up. The brass would be worth something. It might even be worth reloading after being cleaned up.

He walked back to the cabin. He looked up at the crow's nest and saw David watching him. He was happy that David did this. He shouldn't have ventured out alone to begin with.

At times he wished he had a thousand barren yards in each direction. They would not have to worry about anything. Except, of course, a nice Barrett with that type of range. He walked back to the cabin area.

He went into the large pole barn and took a quick inventory of gas. All of the running around was burning it up quickly. They had roughly 250 gallons left. That wasn't enough.

He went to the cabin and called Randy and Kevin over. He said, "Take the gas cans, go out and drain any of the cars on the sides of the road. Take Blake and Kayla with you for security."

"How much do you want us to get?" Randy asked.

"Fill all ten gas cans and the vehicle you take," he answered."

"OK, we'll go now," Randy said.

"You should be able to do it within a couple of miles in any direction. Don't go south," he said.

Randy, Kevin, Kayla, and Blake went to work. They gathered the gas cans and siphon gear and took off. They were only gone about an hour. They filled the Tahoe and the 10 five-gallon gas cans. There was enough time for one more trip. They returned an hour later with more.

The gas was something they would have to keep on top of, otherwise they wouldn't be going anywhere.

Kevin asked, "What about the ethanol plant?"

"Won't do us any good," Haliday said.

"The Tahoe has an E85 emblem on the back," Kevin said.

"It's just an emblem," Haliday said. "That's not the original engine."

That would have been nice. Thousands of gallons of E85 not that far away. The military was going to make good use of that, however. That's why they had secured the facility.

The vehicles were fueled and the rest of the gas dumped into the storage tank. They next loaded their gear for the following day. Tomorrow they would meet Brad's group. Tomorrow evening they would approach the second gang.

Haliday cooked dinner that night. He made a big pot of potato soup with dumplings. A couple of fresh loaves of bread were made. It was a good, simple, and filling meal.

In the early morning, they left to meet Brad. Haliday pulled up to the roadblock. Once again, only one person was outside. Brad had not arrived there yet. Haliday was going to wait until Brad was there before addressing them.

Haliday talked to a younger kid. This kid had been standing guard at the road block by himself. Alan went down the street and stopped Brad. He had Brad's group wait with the Deuce.

Alan and Brad walked back to the roadblock.

"Hi, Roger. How are you?" Brad asked.

"I could be better," Haliday responded.

"You look a little pissed off," Brad said.

Haliday said, "I am, Brad. I told these guys before this isn't summer camp at the Y. I show up and find them all sacked out again."

Brad looked at the kid, who looked down. "You want me to try and find some new guys?" Brad asked.

Haliday looked at the kid. "What do you think?" he asked him.

"I think we can," the kid said.

Haliday walked over to the trailer and opened the door. He peeked inside. Everyone was sleeping. He reached down and grabbed a CS teargas grenade from his vest.

He pulled the pin and popped the spoon. When the CS started to come out he tossed it into the trailer. He closed the door. Within 10 seconds he heard the people inside start coughing.

As soon as the door started to open Haliday slammed it closed. He moved away quickly. In just a few more seconds the door burst open and people poured out of the trailer, coughing.

Haliday and Brad sat there watching them. The people were hacking. Tears flowed and noses were running. The people were yelling at him.

"What the hell?" one man said.

"You think that was funny?" said another.

The best one was, "You could have killed us."

Haliday walked over to the man. "Cry me a river. If you need some help doing so, go back into the trailer for some more gas."

He waited patiently until they all caught their breath. He approached each person one by one. He just looked at them. Next he walked away. He turned around and looked at the group.

"You're all lucky you are not dead," he said. "This isn't a game. You were not put out here to baby-sit. You are out here to keep your families and friends safe. You are here to make sure no harm comes to them."

One man interrupted him. "There ain't anything going on."

159

Haliday snapped. He grabbed the guy by the back of his jacket and practically dragged the man to the Tahoe. "Look at all the holes in this thing."

The man looked at the Tahoe.

"This is more than, 'Ain't nothing going on', genius," Haliday said. He walked back over to the group. "That trailer can end up looking just like that Tahoe. That CS could have been gas or explosives."

He looked over at Brad, then over at the group. "You guys need to get it together. There's no telling who might show up next."

He hoped they would pull it together. He told Brad to call the men in the Deuce and have them come to the roadblock. Brad did this and then waited.

The men arrived a few minutes later. They looked around at the group from the trailer. No one asked what happened. It was almost as if they already knew what had happened.

Haliday and Mark briefed Brad and his group on the operation for the night. They covered everything in detail and made their final preparations for the night. When everyone was ready, they moved toward their objective.

Chapter 13

The apartment complex was small. It was located adjacent to a few farms, and small stores. There were only two buildings and one building was completely empty. The other building was where the gang stayed. No one else remained.

Haliday had taken a quick look at the building. There were three entrances in the front. Three entrances in the back also. There were 24 apartments per building. It looked like the gang occupied the top floor.

There were at least 100 yards of open space on each side of the building. This complicated the operation. The lack of available cover would be hard to overcome. On the map it did not seem as bad.

Brad peered through his binoculars. He could see the center entrance on his side of the building was guarded. The left and right entrances were boarded up.

Brad called Haliday. "Roger, what's your side of the building look like?"

"Its square, made of bricks, has windows and doors," Haliday replied.

Brad was silent. He didn't know what to say.

Haliday spoke again. "Brad, I'm kidding. Left and right entrances are blocked. The center entrance has two guards."

"OK, Roger. I see the same thing on this side." Brad asked, "You have a plan yet?"

"Not yet, Brad," Haliday said, "but I'm thinking on it."

On his side, Haliday kept looking around. Even if they made it to the vehicles there was not enough cover. Launching teargas grenades was not an option either.

The people inside would only have to vacate the apartment that the grenade landed in. Trying to hit each apartment would be time consuming and ineffective. Haliday thought for a bit.

He looked around and saw a silo, and then called Brad again. "Brad, I'm going up on the silo. I'm going to take a few shots through the windows."

"But we haven't identified ourselves yet," Brad said.

Haliday said, "I'm not going to hit anyone. Just try and flush them out."

He decided they would wait until night. He would have two guys on each side of the building move in close. If they could flush the people out, his group could then identify themselves as the police.

Haliday hoped that the gang would give up. There was no telling what type of reaction they would get. Once everyone was in place, they were ready.

Now in the silo, Haliday peered though the scope. He looked carefully through the window. The people in the room were playing some type of game. It looked like Monopoly. He had to be careful.

He adjusted his angle and readied himself. The Barrett was a beast. He steadied it on the railing. The floor and curvature of the silo made it hard to use the bipod.

Everything looked good from his angle. He fired one shot. It traveled through the window. The round struck the game in the center. The cards stacked in the middle of the game flew everywhere. The people jumped away from the table.

One of the people ran from the room. The rest inside the room took cover.

Haliday said to himself, "Go directly to jail, do not pass go."

He fired once more at the table. This time he shot one of the table legs. He fired a third shot and hit another table leg. The table fell over. This was all he was going to fire right now.

The windows started to light up. The people inside were actually lighting candles.

Brad called Haliday. "I hear a lot of yelling."

"What are they saying?" he asked.

Brad said, "I can't really tell."

The entrance doors on both sides of the building flew open. There was some sporadic gun fire from within.

One of Brad's men yelled out from behind the car, "Police officers!"

The people inside yelled back, "We don't believe you!"

Haliday had not really given that any thought. Who would believe them? He would be doubtful as well.

The man by the car yelled again. "Police officers! Come out with your hands raised!"

There was more activity and more yelling.

Haliday asked the guys if they heard what was being said. One of the men behind the cars said he heard something about a mother.

Haliday was perplexed. Maybe some lady was running this gang. The gang fired some shots toward the cars. Brad's men just hunkered down. Shots came from windows and the entrance doors.

One of the men called Haliday. "The guy said it again; he said, 'Hurry up and get Ma Deuce.'"

Haliday's jaw dropped. He told the guys to get ready to run.

One of the windows shattered. It had been broken from the inside. A large barrel appeared in the window.

Haliday could not see inside. This room was dark. He told everyone to lay down suppressing fire.

Haliday's group all started firing. He told the men to run. Neither of the men listened. They refused to leave. The next sounds heard were horrific.

Thump, thump, thump, thump, thump.

It was the telltale sound of a M2 .50 caliber machine gun—known as a "Ma Deuce." There was no telling where they got it from.

The rounds tore through the cars. One of the men hiding was struck and died instantly. Haliday told everyone to fire again and told the other man to run for safety.

Another *thump, thump, thump, thump, thump.* Five more rounds were fired. The gang inside fired rifles at Haliday's group.

On the other side of the building Brad was having better luck. The two guys he put in place were able to make it to safety. The M2 was only on Haliday's side of the building.

Haliday fired a few blind shots through the window. Unfortunately, he did not hit anything. He could not see anything either. The angle he was at was a hindrance.

He ducked down low as he heard the rounds. The M2 was firing toward his position. He backed away slowly. He could hear corn spilling from the silo. He made it to the back and climbed down quickly.

He called Brad. "You hear that?"

Brad asked, "Where the hell did they get an M2?"

"I have no idea, but it's a game changer," Haliday said. "Brad, back everyone off. Stay out of sight." He called the man behind the cars. "When I say go, run your ass off."

Haliday crawled up toward Alan. "I'm going to put some smoke and CS down. I want you to use the Barrett and put rounds under the windowsill."

"Why is that?" Alan asked.

"Just do it," Haliday said, "and don't stop until I tell you to."

Alan nodded.

"Now!" Haliday said.

164

Alan started to fire rounds toward the open window. He fired just under the sill, or at least tried to. Haliday fired three CS grenades before he got one through the window.

Haliday then laid down some smoke by the entrance door. He popped five rounds over in that direction. He told the man to run and the man took off running toward him. Haliday's group covered him with fire on the remaining windows.

The M2 was silent. The return fire from the apartment was silenced now as well. Both sides were now just sitting there quietly. The man had made it from the cars and back to safety.

Haliday crawled over to him. "Damn, dude. Sorry about that." He could tell the man was visibly shaken. "You OK?"

"I think I got hit," was the man's reply.

"No. You would know if you got hit by a fifty," Haliday told him.

The man said, "I'm bleeding."

Haliday said, "It's probably shrapnel from a round exiting the vehicle."

The man felt his arm and nodded. "I think you're right."

Haliday made sure everyone pulled back.

Brad called him. "Now what do we do?"

Haliday said, "I'm thinking about it, Brad."

Thump, thump, thump, thump, thump. Five more rounds came from the Ma Deuce. These were randomly fired but came close enough.

Haliday pulled everyone further back. He thought for a few more minutes. He looked through the Barrett's night-vision scope. Everyone was staying well-hidden inside the building. He called Brad who told him it was the same way on his side of the building.

"Brad, we have to fall back and regroup," Haliday said.

"OK. Meet you at the rendezvous point."

The group convened at their pre-designated spot. Haliday asked if anyone was injured. The man from his group had some deep cuts on his arm. One man from Brad's group had been grazed on his leg.

165

Mark looked at Haliday. "I don't have a clue. They have more firepower than I thought."

"That's for damn sure," Haliday said.

"Any ideas, Roger?" Brad asked.

"I have a few. You guys really want to hear them?" Haliday replied.

"Might as well," Mark said.

Haliday went on to explain that the best bet was to wait them out and attack them on the run. He pulled the map out. "We wait for them here, here and here," he said as he pointed to areas on the map. "Eventually they will have to leave."

"Why would they leave?" asked Dawn.

"They'll want to go find more supplies," he told her, smiling.

"What are you grinning about?" she asked.

"I'm going to use you as bait."

"Bait, my ass," she scoffed.

"That's what I'm counting on."

Haliday had security watches set up. Everyone took turns. Haliday covered some plans with Mark and Brad. They were planning to leave the gang alone for the rest of the night and even the next day.

He called his group at the cabin. "We have a snag and we'll be staying out for a bit longer," he told them.

"You need some more help?" Blake asked.

"No. This time I mean it. Stay put," he told them. If they came riding in like last time, they would surely be met with a surprise. He told them why.

Mark called Edwards on the radio. He told them what they had encountered.

"Any help you can give us?" Brad asked.

Edwards said, "I wish there was. We are running thin, too. Not to mention we are trying to get on peoples' good sides. Playing cops right now won't look good."

Mark and Haliday were a bit miffed at that.

"Is Crothall around?" asked Haliday.

166

"No, sir, he's in a meeting," replied Edwards.

"At 0300 hours?"

"We have some early ops today," Edwards said.

"OK, but I want to talk to him as soon as he has a chance," Haliday said.

Haliday told Brad he wasn't very happy at the moment. Something seemed very wrong. All of a sudden everything was hush-hush. He started to get that feeling again.

He made a mental note to call Adam, Dennis, and Bruce when he got back. He wanted to see if anything in those areas had changed.

Haliday's group settled in for a bit. They found an abandoned house not too far away and used the fireplace to warm it up. Everyone took turns getting some rest and keeping watch.

In the morning they covered the plan. They were breaking up into three separate groups. Each group was assigned a specific task. The plan was to regroup after they completed the operation.

Haliday looked through the house. He didn't find what he was looking for. He went to another house next door. After knocking and looking around, he determined it, too, was empty.

Once he got inside he looked in the closets and found what he was looking for. He grabbed the items and went back to meet up with the group. He tossed the items to Dawn.

"Put these on," he said.

She looked at him and said, "Are you serious?"

"I sure am."

She shook her head adamantly. "No. I'm not going to."

"You have to or this won't work," he said.

Dawn was clearly mad. She stormed out and returned 15 minutes later. The look on her face was priceless. She was not happy at all.

"I look like a slut."

"That's the idea," said Haliday.

"These pants are too tight," she said.

"Spin around and show us," Haliday said as he broke out laughing.

She just flipped him the bird. "These shoes don't fit very well," she said, "and I would rather wear my boots."

"The shoes are important," he told her.

He explained that she had to look like she was wandering around. She had to look helpless. Wearing boots might give her away. He and his group wouldn't let anyone get that close, but, you never know.

Brad walked over. "You guys ready?"

Haliday said, "Yeah, move them out. Good luck, guys."

The three groups moved out. Brad's group would move back toward the apartment building. Haliday's group would be waiting down the main street. The third group was led by a guy named Connor.

Connors group was going to be located down a side street. They would meet the gang upon their gang's return if the plan worked. Now it was a waiting game.

Hours passed by. It was close to three in the afternoon. All three groups were getting anxious. They were all getting cold. Haliday was used to sitting and waiting. It didn't bother him.

Brad called him. "Roger, there's movement."

"OK, let me know how many and where they are heading," he answered back.

At his end, Brad watched the gang members. They cautiously checked the area. They took plenty of time to look around. A couple of them walked over to one of the cars.

They saw the body of Brad's man. One of the guys yelled back to the entrance. "We got one for sure!"

A reply came. "You see anyone else?"

"No. I don't see anyone!" the man called back.

More people came out of the apartment building. Most of them had guns. Some had them ready and others just carried them.

Brad counted. There were 12 people total. Ten were male and two were female. They climbed into two old vehicles, one being an old Woody. It looked like it had come off of a showroom floor.

The other car was an old Toyota Land Cruiser. These vehicles had obviously been taken from the original owners. The Toyota had a smaller open bed trailer hooked to it, more than likely used to transport whatever the people stole.

The two vehicles pulled out and headed toward the main street. About one mile away the gang started to slow down. In front of a donut shop they saw a woman. She had just exited the broken door.

Dawn.

She was wearing pink tennis shoes, tight jeans, a low-cut top, and a leather jacket. She had on a mismatched scarf and hat. Her blonde hair was hanging loosely from under the hat.

She turned and looked at the two vehicles. The vehicles came to a stop. She turned away from them and started walking. A bunch of catcalls came at her from the vehicles.

Dawn stopped and yelled out, "Leave me alone!" She turned and started walking away again.

"Hey, sweet thing, you need a sugar daddy?" one man yelled.

"Come on, baby-doll," yelled another.

Dawn started to cross the street. She stopped in the middle and looked right at the vehicles which were stopped now. She yelled one more time, "Go away and leave me alone you, scumbags!"

A few of the guys got out of the vehicles and started yelling back.

Dawn ran and hid behind a parked car. Haliday's group popped up from the rooftops of the buildings.

They began firing. The three guys who had gotten out of the vehicles went down instantly. The vehicles took off. Haliday's group continued firing on them.

The vehicles made a right-hand turn down a side street. They made another right-hand turn at the next intersection. Two cars were blocking the street. The vehicles started to back up.

Connor's group appeared behind them and started firing. The vehicles tried to pull forward, but the street was blocked and there was no way to drive around them.

The people in the vehicles had called for help. The apartment building was only about a quarter of a mile away. They returned fire and waited for help.

*****

Brad's group was waiting anxiously. The entrance door opened and four men came running out. They ran over to a vehicle and started getting inside.

The man guarding the entrance door dropped from a rifle round to his chest. The men getting into the car paused to look at what happened.

Brad's group opened up on these four men. His group was well-hidden and at a distance. Surprise was their advantage. Multiple rounds from their rifles helped that advantage.

Only one of the men near the car made it back to the apartment building. He had been grazed on the leg. Once he got inside somebody pulled the door closed. Shots were fired from the upstairs windows.

Brad had his men retreat. There was no sense in wasting ammo. They had accomplished what they wanted. They'd killed four men and injured at least one more.

*****

Connor's group was still trying to finish off the people in the vehicles. The two groups exchanged fire. One of Connors men ran from behind a parked car, trying to get a better position. He didn't make it.

Connor called Haliday. "We have them pinned down. They can't move, but we can't get to them, either. We have one man down."

On his end, Haliday shook his head. This made two dead and one injured in his group. He told Connor to wait while he and his group tried to move in.

Everyone in Haliday's group except for Dawn and one other man headed toward Connor's group. Dawn ducked inside a building to change while the man stood guard.

Haliday made it over to where Connor was. He sent two men up on a roof overlooking the street. One of them was Mark. Haliday yelled out for the gang to surrender.

"We got help coming!" yelled one man.

"If you're talking about the four dead guys back at the apartment building you might want to reconsider!" Haliday yelled back.

The man called his group and discovered that it was true. "We ain't giving up!" he yelled back.

Haliday gave the order to fire. Mark and the other man on the roof fired into the gang.

The gang returned fired toward the rooftop. Haliday and the rest fired also. After a few minutes Haliday called for a ceasefire. He called the guys on the roof, "You see any movement?"

"It looks like they're all dead," Mark answered.

"Cover us," Haliday said. "We're going in to check."

He along with Connor and two more men moved in slowly. They reached the vehicles, which were laden with holes. Everyone in them was dead.

He called Brad. "We have twelve bad guys dead. We also have one friendly down."

Brad said, "We have four bad guys dead, and at least one injured. We backed off for now. We don't want to mess with that Ma Deuce."

Haliday told him that everyone needed to regroup. They met at a rendezvous point close to the apartment building. They needed to get the rest of the gang some how. He was not sure how they would accomplish that.

He estimated 12 to 16 people left. That was enough to stay holed up. It was enough to secure their position.

Mark said, "Let's burn them out."

"We can't," said Haliday. "The supplies inside are too valuable."

Brad said, "Should we leave a small group and wait them out?"

171

Haliday answered, "That's too risky. We already have two dead and one injured. We can't respond quick enough if something happens to them."

Mark added, "Plus, it could be weeks."

This was quite a problem. A few more suggestions were made. None of the suggestions were viable. Haliday picked up a small radio they had taken from the old Woody the gang had used.

"Hey, is anybody in there?" Haliday asked.

"What do you want?" a woman said.

"By the authority granted unto me, by the powers to be, I hereby command you to surrender," he said.

Everyone looked at him. He just shrugged his shoulders.

The response came. "Go screw yourself, pig."

"Listen," he said, "you need to surrender."

"Why would we do that?"

"You want to live, don't you?"

There was a long pause. He waited patiently. While he was waiting, something dawned on him. While he did not stereotype people, typically people in this situation were men.

He had to wonder if there were any men inside. "It's safe out here," he said, "and we can get you to safety."

"You mean execute us," the woman said.

Haliday handed the radio to Dawn. "Talk to her."

Dawn looked bewildered. "What am I supposed to say?"

"Tell her how warm and cuddly I am. Tell her I won't hurt anyone," he said.

"Oh, you want me to lie."

"That hurt my feeling," he said.

"Emphasis on feeling, no 's' at all," Dawn said.

She clicked the mic. "Listen, we will place you under arrest. You will be transported to a federal detention camp."

"How do we know you are telling the truth?"

"You have to trust us. We tried to tell you last night," Dawn said.

172

"What's going to happen to us?" the woman asked.

Dawn looked at Haliday and handed the radio back to him. He clicked the mic. "You'll be tried and sentenced. I won't lie to you."

"OK, we're coming out."

Haliday and the group got ready. He instructed the gang to exit on his side of the building. Six women and two men came out. The men were injured.

Haliday made them walk toward him. He paid attention to the building. He did not see any movement. Once the people reached his group they were searched and zip-tied.

"Anyone left inside?" Haliday asked.

A man answered. "No. This is all of us."

"I expected six to eight more," Haliday said.

"They left us," the man replied.

"Where did they go?"

"They joined a bigger gang," the man said.

Haliday looked at Brad and Mark. That meant trouble. That meant the largest of the three gangs was now even bigger. He kept this to himself though. Neither Brad nor Mark said anything either.

Alan walked up. "I checked to make sure they are all secured and ready."

"Do you mind going with Brad and sweeping the building?" Haliday asked.

"Well, yeah, but I'll go," Alan said.

Brad took Alan and six more people and went and searched the building. Haliday called Crothall. Edwards answered instead. Edwards told him that a helicopter would be en route to pick up the prisoners.

Alan came back out of the building. "Roger, they have two full rooms of food."

Brad asked, "Can we take some?"

Haliday said, "Take a quarter of it. Leave the rest for the people around here."

173

Twenty minutes passed. Haliday heard the helicopter approach. He walked out toward a nearby field and popped a can of smoke. There was only one helicopter. It was a Blackhawk.

A couple of people had heard the helicopter. They started approaching Haliday's group. Haliday was at the ready.

One man walked up. "Are they here to help us?" he asked.

"They are here to take these prisoners away," Haliday told the man.

"Who are you guys?" the man asked.

"Just some citizens trying to keep the peace."

Two of the men from the Blackhawk came over. They escorted the prisoners into the helicopter. The two soldiers returned. "Where's the M2?" one asked.

"I'm keeping it," said Haliday.

"We have orders from Lt. Crothall to take it," the soldier told him.

"Tell Crothall that I said no. If he wants it he can ask me."

"Sir, that's U.S. Government property," the soldier remarked.

Haliday looked at the kid. "Tell Crothall I'll have a list of supplies for him. When he delivers the supplies he can have it."

The young soldier just looked at him. He turned and went back to the waiting Blackhawk. It just sat there. The young soldier came back with a radio. He handed it to Haliday.

"Haliday, this is the lieutenant," Crothall said.

"How can I help you, Lieutenant?" Haliday responded.

"We need that M2 for our operations," said Crothall.

Haliday looked at the radio. As he spoke into it he'd made a mental note of the frequency. He handed the radio back to the soldier. Brad and Alan brought the M2 out.

The two soldiers took it and loaded it onto the Blackhawk. After the Blackhawk had left, Haliday looked around. They had amassed quite a crowd.

There had to be close to 25 people standing there. A few of them were armed and that made Haliday nervous. The man who had spoken to him earlier spoke yet again.

174

"What are you guys going to do now?" he asked.

Another man walked up to Haliday and pulled out a badge. "My name is Chris. I was a police officer here. Thank you guys for the help."

"Chris, there's a bunch of food in there," Haliday said, pointing to the apartment building. "Get it distributed the best you can."

Brad had taken about one fifth of the food. The rest was left for the residents.

Haliday and Brad's groups left. Haliday told Brad he would call him later.

On the way back to the cabin Haliday asked Mark, "You getting any strange vibes lately?"

"Yes, I am," Mark said.

Something was wrong. Haliday just couldn't put it together yet. Neither could Mark. They would talk about it more at the cabin.

Chapter 14

The day after the operation, Haliday was in the kitchen making some fried cornmeal mush. He had read about it in a book, but never tried it. This was the first time.

The buckets of cornmeal were now being used for more than cornbread and muffins. He'd prepared the mixture the night before. There were a lot of curious onlookers.

The recipe was simple: six cups of hot water, two cups of yellow cornmeal, two teaspoons of salt. He added a tablespoon of sugar to sweeten it just a bit.

The ingredients were all brought to a boil, then lowered to a simmer. Once the mixture was very thick, he folded it into a large Pyrex loaf pan. The pan had been sprayed with a non-stick, butter-flavored spray.

This concoction was placed in the refrigerator overnight to set. He made two batches to make sure there was enough. In the morning he cut the loaves into one-inch thick slices.

It did not look appealing. It looked like a yellow lump of jiggling goop. He remembered reading the reaction of the author's children when they first saw it. He expected and received the same from his group.

The slices could then be fried on a griddle in butter or margarine. In this case he had used a butter substitute bought at a restaurant supply store in gallon jugs.

Once the slices were golden brown on each side he put them on a plate. He set out some maple syrup and honey, and finished cooking the rest.

The group loved it. Some used honey and some used maple syrup. Haliday actually used honey on one half and syrup on the other. He wished he could have thanked the author for the idea.

Mark helped him clean the dishes. While cleaning they talked about the recent events. Haliday sat down with his coffee and Mark sat down across the table.

"I think we're being played," said Haliday.

"I'm not sure about that," replied Mark, "but something is definitely not up to par."

"I feel like a pawn here."

"You think Crothall isn't on the up and up?"

"I'm not sure. It's just very odd. One day we can't get rid of him; the next day we can't get a hold of him." He shook his head. "Add in the frequency that we can't listen in on and it gets more odd."

"It was probably a secure frequency."

"That doesn't explain why he doesn't respond to the frequency he gave us," Haliday said.

"You have me on that one," Mark stated.

They talked about a few different scenarios. The conclusion was always the same. They were grasping at straws. They just did not know exactly what bothered them. Haliday was determined to find out.

David was sitting at the ham listening to all of the chatter. All he heard was the same thing over and over; it was simple. You could replace the names and the story was the same everywhere.

Gangs fighting gangs. Gangs taking everything from other people. People fighting each other. The cities were the worst.

178

They were either burned out, deserted, gang ridden or all of the above.

David had relayed Haliday's wish list to Edwards. Hopefully they would be able to re-supply. Haliday was not about to burn through his group's weapons supply.

*****

Bruce took another ride to check out Fort Custer. This time around he noticed a large so-called tent city. He looked around until he found one open. It had bunks inside. He spotted what looked like a wood stove.

He tried to do a quick count. His best estimate was around 2,000 bunks. He wasn't sure if these were for troops or citizens. He had heard the same radio transmission that Haliday had heard. Transportation to camps would be made available.

Bruce checked warehouses. He could see troops loading up the MREs for another drop. The helicopters were being prepped as well. It all looked normal to him.

He rode back to his trailer on his ATV and called Haliday and told him what he had seen. So far everything was okay. He would check back after two more days to see if anything changed.

*****

Dennis was keeping tabs on his area as well. Camp Grayling was a flurry of activity. Dennis reported seeing all types of equipment and crates coming in on a regular basis.

He called a few contacts he had made in the surrounding communities. Haliday had told him to find out what the troops and armor were doing.

Dennis had made contact with a man near Gaylord. The man told Dennis what he had seen. When the troops arrived there they went straight to the Gaylord Regional Airport. They secured the perimeter and added concertina wire to the existing fence. Sandbag emplacements were built around the fence line and burn barrels placed nearby.

The troops had commandeered all of the travel trailers from a local RV store. There had been 28 on the lot. These were moved to the airport and set up as their quarters.

179

The armor consisted of four M1 tanks and two older M113s, Armored Personnel Carriers. These were spread out around the compound. A few Humvees with machine guns were reserved for rapid response. The remaining trucks and vehicles remained parked. Once the compound was completely secured a few helicopters were brought in. No other movement was noted.

Almost the exact same thing took place in Harrison. The exception there was the troops used the Horseshoe Inn across from the airport as quarters.

Over in Grawn the Northwestern Michigan Fairgrounds were used. Rolls of concertina and barbed wire were set up to form a perimeter and the fair buildings were used for the troops. A makeshift heli-pad was marked off.

Oscoda County Airport was just north of Mio. Here the troops set up tents. The perimeter here was concertina as well. Just like the rest of the camps, there was little activity after they moved in.

*****

Haliday digested the information they had heard. Everyone talked about the government was doing this, or the government was doing that. Haliday stood up and looked around at everyone.

"We don't need to speculate," he said. "We need to gather more information."

"What do we do then?" Karen asked. Her daughters Dawn and Diana looked at Haliday in unison.

"We decide whether we continue the battle, or keep to ourselves," he said.

Haliday's statement brought on an argument. Everyone had a different opinion. Some of them wondered why they got involved to begin with. Some of them said they needed to keep going to help the region stabilize. Some of them flipped back and forth.

Haliday stood there and watched everyone argue. It became quite heated. After about 20 minutes he yelled out for quiet. The cabin came to a standstill of voices and opinions. He told everyone to sit down.

The energy level was extremely high. After being cooped up together for almost three months, the strain had finally gotten to everyone. It was a much needed stress release.

Haliday explained everything as delicately as he could. The EMP was none of their faults. That was beyond their control. The rest of the events were only partly in their control.

After the group had reached the cabin, Haliday could have called it quits. The couple that was captured by the militia was his fault. He could not let them take the fall for him.

Looking at a way to free them at the airport clued him in to the militia's plans. He could not bring himself to let all those people in the area suffer under the rogue militia's control.

After that it all snowballed. One thing was for certain: their presence at the cabin would have brought the militia down on them eventually, either way.

Now they were all stuck there trying to stay safe. Helping keep order in the area was one way of doing so. Just remaining at the cabin was not an option. Eventually rogue groups would start to infiltrate the area. Other people would come knocking as well. They would be unable to continue fighting them off. Going on the offensive was the best defense right now.

"We have to see this through," Mark said.

"I agree," Rich added.

Slowly, everyone came into agreement.

Haliday said, "Good, I'm glad you all agree."

"Thirty minutes ago you weren't so sure," Nancy said.

"Thirty minutes ago I was not sure about helping the military," Haliday clarified, "and I am still not sure."

"So what do you mean then?" David asked.

Haliday replied, "We keep on the offensive until we know our area is safe. After that we let Uncle Sam finish cleaning up the country."

"We all have a lot of work to do," Rich said.

With that, everyone got up. They did have a lot to do. As simple as life may seem, it required a lot more labor. A lot of little things needed to be done to keep the cabin running.

181

Kayla went outside and double checked the water tank they used for the toilet. They had to make sure it was not freezing up; otherwise they would have to use the well and they did not like doing that.

Water conservation was the key to sustainability. Not to mention running the pump required electricity they would rather reserve for other uses. The tank was rather well-insulated and large enough so that only the top few inches froze. If it got too cold it might become an issue. They had not had any issues so far.

Haliday would work on a gray water collection method to replenish the tank using old sink and shower water. Bleach would kill any fungi and bacteria. It would also help the smell.

Blake, Randy, and Kevin went out for fire wood. They restocked the inside racks and the ones on the porch. Firewood was always kept stocked. If the need arose, they could go four days without having to go to the woodpile.

Rich liked feeding the chickens. Dawn, Nancy, and Karen fed the horses and livestock. They would muck the barn and areas around the cabin to keep the odor down.

Alan and Blake grabbed the ladder. It was their turn to go clean the solar panels. Since it was a nice bright day Haliday figured it would be beneficial.

Haliday and Mark kept security watch. Nancy and Sarah kept watch over the kids and held some school sessions. Throughout the day cleaning and more small chores took place.

Bill was busy building an incubator for the eggs. Haliday just saw a conglomeration of a wooden box, a pie pan, and a light bulb and he had no idea how it worked. Bill told him it would produce chicks in around 21 days.

The extra chickens would be welcome. The upkeep of the chickens would not be. They would need to move the coop or enlarge it. Bill was the farmer. He knew what was best. His experience was greatly appreciated.

Brad had called Haliday on the ham. "Roger, you have any plans for the last gang in Sandusky?" he asked.

"I have some ideas, but nothing concrete yet," Haliday answered.

"What about a timeframe?" Brad asked.

"Brad, you and your guys take the next couple of days off. That's what we are doing."

"What about the roadblocks?"

"We'll check them for you guys," Haliday said, "and let you know if they need anything."

"Sounds good. Talk to you later," Brad said.

"Later."

It was getting close to dinnertime and Haliday decided to cook. He boiled up some wide noodles and reconstituted some freeze-dried meatballs. He added gravy and served them over the noodles with some biscuits.

Karen, Dawn, and Diana just had gravy over noodles. They were insistent that they remain as true to their vegetarian lifestyle as possible. The preps allowed them to do that.

Max, the mutant dog, waited for scraps. It got to the point where each person would leave just a tiny bit on their plates. When scraped together it was a full meal for him. Romeo, the cat, had his own preps.

Tonight they would all play games. Prior to the EMP, Haliday would scour garage sales and store closeouts for games. They had dozens stored. The games kept people thinking. It kept them sharp. More importantly, it helped keep them occupied.

He'd actually bought two of the same game. With parts more than likely missing he could get a complete game out of two. This would also leave some extra parts. He used to laugh at garage sales. He hated them. Then he stopped one day when he saw the chiminea. It had never been used and they only wanted $10 for it.

This was his awakening. When he had the time he would stop at garage sales and look for preps. He also made it a habit to stop at thrift stores. One could find loads of gear if he looked long enough.

He had found old cabinets for the pole barn. The landscape bricks he got from another garage sale; tool chests and counters from a store closeout. You could find all sorts of items.

He didn't bother with clothing or furniture, though. What was even more amazing was how many items he would find new in the boxes. A lot of unwanted or unused gifts, he assumed.

More than one item he purchased was used maybe a couple of times and that was all. The meat grinder was a great find. It was a good old-fashioned, hand-cranked, clamp on table style.

Bill was at the kitchen table looking at a sheet of paper and Dawn and Diana were talking to him. When Haliday walked over they got real quiet.

"What's going on here?" he asked.

"Nothing," Dawn said.

"Well it has to be something," Haliday shot back.

"We're going over the plan for planting the crops," Bill said.

"Why didn't you just say so?" he asked.

"Because, we didn't want you piping in," Diana said.

"What do you mean by that?"

Bill spoke up. "They told me you suffer from being too anal. You'd have fits if one row was longer than another. Stuff like that."

Haliday thought about it a moment. When he had glanced at the paper that *was* the first thing he noticed. He just started to walk away.

"See, I told you," Diana quipped.

Haliday hung his arm out like it was in a brace, just like Diana's currently was from getting her collarbone broken. He started chanting, "I can't eat meat; I can't eat meat..."

Dawn threw a pen at him.

The night was uneventful and everyone got a lot of sleep. Haliday cooked breakfast this morning as well. He made what he called German pancakes.

For each batch he used two eggs, three-quarters cup of milk, and three tablespoons of flour and blended it all together with a pinch of salt. He poured the batter on a hot griddle and formed thick blintz-like pancakes.

Another option was to pour the batter in an eight-by-eight-inch buttered baking pan and bake it at 350 degrees until golden brown on top. He had reconstituted some bananas with honey and used them as a filling. He rolled them and then drizzled a small bit of honey on top. He had sausage patties ready as well.

"Why all of the cooking lately?" Bev asked.

"I'm getting tired of breakfast burritos," he said.

The breakfast burritos were quick and easy, but they did get old after a while. He decided they needed to change up the menu. Food boredom could actually stop some people from eating enough.

Today they were going to be cleaning all of the firearms. Whether they had been used or not, they were going to be cleaned.

Haliday set up a plastic folding table. It was six-foot-long and just the right size. He laid down an old sheet on the table and the cleaning supplies were brought out. He made sure that everyone took turns cleaning the firearms. He wanted to be sure each person was familiar with each type. There would be no excuse for grabbing a gun and not knowing how to use it.

Every person was taught how to fire each one. Each person was required to fire them. The least favorite were the shotguns—especially with the women and older folks. But, nonetheless, they had to know how to handle them.

In the late afternoon Nancy called Haliday over to the ham.

He walked over.

"It's Sgt. Edwards," Nancy said.

He sat down. "What can I do for you, Sergeant?"

"We haven't heard from you in a couple of days," Edwards said.

"Gee, I haven't heard from Crothall either," Haliday replied in his typical sarcastic tone.

"He's been very busy," Edwards said.

"Yeah, so have we."

Edwards sounded like he was getting frustrated. It seemed he didn't know how to respond.

185

"You get our shopping list?" Haliday asked.

"We are working on it," Edwards said.

"Call us when it's ready. We'll let you know what's going on then."

"OK." was all Edwards said.

Mark walked over and stood there. "You have a way of pissing off people," he said to Haliday.

"I have a way of getting pissed off, too," Haliday shot back.

"Easy, I'm on your side," Mark said.

"Sorry about that," Haliday said.

But he was still ticked off. It was like a dog being turned out into a junkyard for security and then being forgotten about. Yet, the owner expected loyalty.

The day passed like many others. People had finished their chores. The kids were taught some lessons. Dinner was cooked. Those who were not on security watch were around the fireplace.

They sat and talked, sharing stories of all types. It was surprising how little you could know about the people who were the closest to you. Some of the people got some odd looks when they told their stories.

Alan was just starting to tell a story about when he sold cars when Karen, sitting at the ham, and called for Haliday.

"They need you up in the crow's nest," she said.

He bolted up the steps. When he got up to the crow's nest Kevin was pointing southeast. "I saw a flare go up, Uncle Roger. Well, it didn't go all the way up. It just kind of arced."

"Are you sure?" Haliday asked.

"I'm positive, Uncle Roger," Kevin answered.

Haliday looked through the binoculars, but could not make anything out. "Keep your eyes peeled. Let me know if you see anything else," he told him.

He went back down the steps. He picked up the ham and tried to call the roadblock. No one answered him. After the fifth attempt he called the other roadblock. They were fine.

"Listen up. Double your security and pucker up, folks," he told them, "I think the other roadblock got hit."

186

"That's just great," he heard in response.

"You guys call if you see anything at all," Haliday told them.

He went back up to the crow's nest. He listened for gunfire. The roadblock was either too far away or he had not heard any gunfire. He went back down to the ham.

"Brad, are you there?" he asked.

"Yes, I am," Brad answered.

Kevin spoke on the other radio. "Uncle Roger, I see a fire."

"Where is it at, Kevin?" Haliday asked.

"It's the roadblock," Kevin answered back.

"Brad, the roadblock got hit. The trailer is burning," Haliday said.

Brad spoke up. "You want us to go out there?"

"It's too late, Brad," Haliday said.

"I didn't hear anything on the radio. Did they send up a flare?" Brad asked.

Haliday said, "My nephew said the flare never made it airborne. He told me it arced. That tells me the person launching it was under duress. The trailer burning tells me that they were caught with their pants down."

"I'll send a couple of guys to scout it out and let you know what we find," Brad said.

Haliday said, "I wouldn't bother. But, it's your decision."

He put two extra people on security detail. The roadblock was almost five miles away. That was still too close for comfort. He had no idea where the any people were heading.

He was about to go to bed when Brad called back. "My guys didn't even get close," he said.

"What happened?" Haliday asked.

Brad said, "They got about five miles away when they ran across some cars. They turned around and they were fired on."

"They make it back OK?"

"Yeah, but scared the crap out of them," Brad told him.

"Brad, you need to tell everyone to tighten up security. You need to make sure they keep watch," Haliday said.

"Roger, I hate to ask this, but can you meet us at the roadblock in the morning?" Brad asked.

"No problem," Haliday said.

Haliday went up to see Mark. His wife Lisa was sound asleep, but Mark was still awake.

"I figured you would be coming to see me," Mark said.

Haliday whispered, "The roadblock is definitely gone. The area has been breached. I just don't know how badly though."

"What do you have planned?" Mark asked.

"We meet Brad at the roadblock in the morning," Haliday said.

He went back downstairs and decided to man the radio. He flipped through frequencies. He stopped briefly to listen in. Most of it was the same old news. The areas that were not really affected were expanding aid. It was very slow going. But, things in some areas seemed to be improving. That was a good sign— the only good sign.

He looked at his maps of the affected areas. In his best estimate, it would be a few years before the infrastructure was sound enough.

He looked out the window. It was snowing. This might come in handy. He might be able to check tracks and see where the vehicles went and how many there had been.

Morning would come soon enough and he would have his answers then.

Chapter 15

Haliday and Mark prepared to go to the roadblock. Both of them donned white camo to match the newly fallen snow. Most of the cabin was still asleep. Haliday and Mark skipped breakfast and took an extra MRE with them. Haliday still referred to them as Bag Nasties.

Mark looked over at him and chuckled. "Damn, you look like Frosty the Snowman."

"Oh, you're really funny," said Haliday. Over the past three months he had lost 30 pounds. He was still a sizeable man at six-foot-two and 220 pounds. Almost everyone in the group had lost weight. His camo was a little fluffy now.

Haliday finished tightening his gear down. Both now ready, they went outside and got in the Jeep. Haliday started the engine and they left.

The fresh snow and moonlight made it easy to navigate without using the headlights. The sun was rising slowly and soon it would be day. They were approximately half a mile away from the roadblock now.

Brad's team was not scheduled to arrive there for another 90 minutes. Haliday killed the engine and let the Jeep coast in neutral. He pulled it off to the side of the road.

He and Mark moved in on foot. They kept just inside the wood line. They moved slowly and looked for signs of the assault. They didn't find anything until they got closer to the trailer and roadblock.

They found two sets of tracks. These were only about 50 feet away from the trailer. The tracks followed the road. Whoever made them took a big chance. They were definitely not pros.

They took several minutes to finish scoping out the area. Mark covered Haliday as he moved in toward the trailer. Just like Haliday thought, he found the body of the lone sentry. His throat had been cut.

This was another sign of an amateur. Not many people knew how to pull it off. A horizontal cut would leave the victim gurgling and gasping for air. The victim may even have been able to make more sounds, depending on how deep the cut was.

Haliday looked around and could tell there had been a struggle. The blood patterns were covered by snow. However, enough had come through to show how violent it had been. He even found the flare tube.

Next, he moved toward the trailer. There was nothing much left except the frame. The rest had burned away. He counted four bodies inside.

He moved to the north side of the trailer, where he found one more body. He tried to remember how many had been there. He thought for a moment. There had been eight people total.

He dropped down to one knee and pulled out a set of binoculars. With the sun in the sky now he could see clearly in all directions. He spent about 15 minutes looking around.

He raised his arm, pointed into the air, and rotated his hand and finger to signal. This was the rally sign.

Mark moved in slowly as Haliday kept watch. One of the things at the cabin was a field manual, FM 21-60 for signaling.

Mark met up with Haliday. They both began analyze the area. Neither of them were professional trackers. They did, however; know enough to figure out what had happened.

Brad arrived with a group of three more people. He looked around and said, "Damn it. I knew I should have pulled them off the roadblock."

"It's not your fault, Brad," Haliday told him when they met.

"Any idea of what happened?" Brad asked.

"We'll give you the *Reader's Digest* version," Haliday said.

Mark added, "It's what we think happened."

He explained that two people approached the roadblock. They walked along the wood line, just inside, but enough to stay hidden. They moved in on the lone sentry.

The sentry was able to ignite the flare, but it arced instead of going skyward. He was most likely struggling at the time. One of the people that had engaged the sentry ultimately cut his throat.

The other person more than likely kept watch. The rest of the group was signaled and they moved in to the trailer. The people inside the trailer didn't stand a chance.

It looked like they tried to escape. Shots were fired from both sides. The fact that four bodies were found in the trailer led them to believe the trailer was fired upon by many people.

Two of the people were unaccounted for. Until they found them, they could not say what happened. They assumed the missing were dead. It was the most logical.

"Any idea how many of them there were?" Brad asked.

Haliday said, "At least four vehicles. I could distinguish four different types of tire tracks. A couple of sets were beefy. More than likely pickup trucks or vans. I couldn't say about the other two sets."

"What about people?" Brad said.

Mark replied, "There's no telling. There were at least eight around the trailer that were firing. It looks like another six or so had gathered over there." He pointed to a spot on the road. It had less snow. This was where the vehicles had stopped.

"Brad, it doesn't look like they came back through here," Haliday said.

"That means they found another way out or they are still inside the area," Brad responded.

In either case it posed a problem. One, four vehicles with armed individuals were running loose through the area; or two, they had caused damage in the area yet to be found. This could be stolen equipment or food. This could also mean more people killed.

Haliday said, "My guess is we find more bodies."

Mark agreed with him.

As everyone was standing there they heard the helicopters. The birds flew right over them. One bird dropped a little lower and slowed down over the roadblock. It left after just a couple of minutes.

Brad said his people would take care of the bodies. He told Haliday he would get another trailer out there with a fresh group of people. "I'll hand pick them," Brad said.

"Just make sure they know why this happened," Haliday replied.

Haliday and Mark walked back to their Jeep. They got in and drove back to the cabin.

Rich was awake and helping his wife Bev cook breakfast when they arrived back. The rest of the people were sitting around waiting patiently.

"What happened at the roadblock?" Rich asked.

"They're all dead," Haliday said.

Everyone stopped and looked at him.

Haliday gave them a brief synopsis of what had occurred. He was vague and left out the details because the kids were sitting there. The kids knew people were dying, but everyone wanted to keep the impact as low as possible right now.

"What's for breakfast, Dad?" Haliday asked.

"Bill gathered up enough eggs the past two days," Rich said, "so we are having fried eggs."

"Toast, too," Bev added.

Breakfast was served up and everyone enjoyed the fresh eggs and toast. Haliday was happy that the chickens were still healthy. Bill was doing a good job keeping them that way.

"Uncle Roger, get up here quick," Randy yelled down from the steps.

Haliday bolted up the steps to the crow's nest. He heard it before he saw it.

There was the distinct sound of a 20mm cannon along with rocket pods being fired.

*****

The helicopters had taken off on a relief flight to distribute more aid. Those inside were performing the usual mapping operations, too. They had spotted the roadblock and knew what had happened.

The night before, they had heard the radio transmission between Haliday's group and Brad's group. One bird had stopped just briefly to take a look. They then proceeded with their aid mission.

One of the OH58s had spotted vehicles slowly moving south on M-53, known as Van Dyke. The vehicles came to a stop when they spotted the helicopter. The pilot dropped a little too low to check them out.

Some of the people got out and one man fired on the bird. As soon as the man fired, so did a few more people. The helicopter backed off immediately.

The UH1 Cobra came in fast. The people fired on it as well. The Cobra was not playing any games. It just opened up on the vehicles.

The Cobra made its first pass and launched four rockets. It fired a few dozen rounds from the 20mm cannon. The bird then circled around and made another run. This time only the 20mm cannon was used.

On the third run the Cobra launched four more rockets and a hailstorm of 20mm rounds. That was it for the Cobra. It moved off and waited.

The OH58 stood off at a distance and monitored the vehicles for activity. There didn't seem to be any more aggression coming from the area.

A Huey came lumbering in slowly. Close to a quarter of a mile away it paused. The side doors slid open. Two ropes came out and touched the ground. Four soldiers rappelled down the ropes.

The soldiers moved carefully toward the vehicles. When the soldiers reached the vehicles there was gunfire. The soldiers took about 10 minutes to quell the situation.

Only a couple of people from the vehicles' group survived. The Huey came in and landed. The soldiers took the prisoners and boarded the helicopter. The bird flew back to Selfridge.

*****

Haliday told Randy to stay alert. Mark had made his way up to the crow's nest to watch and Haliday bumped into him.

"You see that?" Mark asked.

"I hope that's a rhetorical question," Haliday said.

"Of course it is," Mark shot back.

"I wonder what happened," Haliday said.

"Helicopters came in, fired bullets and rockets—" Mark began.

"You smartass," Haliday said.

Randy laughed. "You two need to stop hanging out so much. It's like you're brothers."

They all laughed. It was true. They were rubbing off on each other. Mark had become quite the smartass lately.

"Let's go call Crothall and see what he has to say," Haliday said.

He and Mark went back down into the cabin. It was practically empty. Everyone had gone outside trying to see what was going on.

As soon as they came in and spotted Haliday they started asking a million questions. Mark answered them the best he could. Haliday went over to the radio.

"Crothall, you there?" he asked.

194

Edwards answered. "Roger, we'll get back to you in a little while. We know you want to know what happened."

"I hope so," Haliday said. "That was only a few miles away."

"We know," Edwards said, "and we'll call you in a while. We need to get everything sorted out first."

Haliday had everyone arm themselves. If any of those people escaped that convoy, they might be in the area. If they were injured or just wanted to hide they might come knocking.

Haliday had Kevin call Brad on the ham. Brad said, "I heard the helicopters and gunfire. Any idea what happened?"

Kevin told him, "Not yet. We are waiting to hear from the military."

"Anything we need to do?" Brad asked.

Kevin answered, "My uncle said to make sure you tell as many people as you can. Keep heavy security."

Haliday wasn't too sure how easy it would be for Brad to find volunteers after this; the first group massacred by thugs, then thugs inside the area battling the military.

It really wasn't a battle, though. The thugs never stood a chance. The Cobra gunship made the odds overwhelming. The vehicles and people never stood a chance.

The question remained: Why in the world would you take on helicopter gunships? Those people either had to be very brave, or very stupid.

*****

Bruce took another ATV ride by Fort Custer. He stopped dead in his tracks. There was a train moving along toward the Ft. Custer National Cemetery. It wasn't the train that caught his attention.

On board the train were buses and trucks. These had all been painted flat black. There were no markings on them except for a series of numbers. One was labeled "CT-23-MI" and another was labeled "PT-32-MI."

Bruce saw two large backhoes on the train as well. He counted four small skid steers. The skid steers had forklift attachments on them. One railcar had guard booths on it.

195

The trucks and buses all looked used. It appeared they had been repurposed for this task. Of course, Bruce did not know what the task was.

The kicker was the FEMA coffins. There were railcars loaded with them. There were pallets of boxes on each railcar as well, but Bruce could not make out what they said. All he could make out was NSN: 9930-01-565-0409.

There were sealed boxcars as well. He couldn't begin to guess what was inside of them. He counted 20 boxcars. The whole train was under heavy guard.

Bruce wrote down a few notes and then went back to his trailer. He told his family what he had seen. They started to worry.

Over the course of the day he had heard the helicopters in the area. He listened on the portable radio to the messages being transmitted. They were fairly generic.

He called Haliday on the radio and told him what he had seen. Haliday in return told Bruce what he had seen earlier that morning. It was more pieces of a puzzle coming together. Still no idea what the picture would look like.

Both of them missed the days when you could flip on the TV and check a dozen news sources to find out what was happening. Or at least what people wanted you to hear. There were as many opinions as there were stations.

It had gotten too easy to edit video and sound bites. You could turn almost any event into the grandest event of all with a good editor. News was about money and politics, not the truth.

*****

It was late afternoon. Adam was looking out of a window and down at the crowd in the street. The people in this gang were not easily scared away. They knew Adam's group had supplies.

Adam's house had become easily recognizable as a prepper's home. The boarded up windows, firing ports, increased security, wood burning smoke stack, large woodpile, and more.

The gangs learned that those who were prepared had what they wanted. They would test the security of the homes. The weakest homes were hit first. As time progressed and supplies became hard to find, the gangs started to target the more secure locations. Teaming up with smaller gangs gave them more resources. It gave them more firepower.

Now with supplies almost nonexistent in the urban areas, any risk was worth taking. Losses of gang members were not only inevitable, but acceptable as well.

The more time that passed, the more creative people got. They started to figure out traps and ruses. They would try anything to get inside someone's home.

Down toward the end of the Adam's street was a smaller group. He wasn't sure how well prepared the household was. One thing he knew was that they were still holding on. That was until a few nights ago.

A woman wearing tattered clothing ran down the street. She had with her a young girl that was around 12 years old. They were screaming for help. They knocked on a few doors pleading for help.

A small group of people were coming down the street after them. The woman knocked on the door of the house Adam had been watching. After a few minutes they relented and let her enter.

For the first couple of days they seemed fine. Last night the home erupted in chaos. Adam's group had heard the screams and gunfire. They took positions upstairs.

When they noticed the home under attack they tried to help by firing on the attackers. The distance was almost 200 yards. Their line of sight was obstructed. The number of attackers was incredibly high. Adam's group did the best they could. They did manage to take out a few, but it was not enough. They could not risk going outside themselves. The home fell quickly to the attackers.

The woman who had gained their trust under the ruse of being hunted had betrayed them. She opened the door for the attackers and helped to gain control inside the home.

What had been an act of human kindness had turned into their downfall. The family was willing to share what they had with the woman and child. They had protected them. They were killed for doing so.

Adam made sure he spread the word about what he had witnessed. Even though he was not sure of the entire circumstances, he wanted people to be prepared for what may happen.

It was sad that human behavior in a matter of a few months had so utterly changed. The human body could drive the human mind to take different courses of action.

It was survival. It was in everybody. How quickly one reacted to it was a different question. Each person was wired differently. When people banded together, behavior becomes more acceptable, as people see others acting that same way. When more people act the same way they start to believe it is acceptable.

*****

Dennis was listening to radio transmissions and he was hearing the same thing Bruce had told Haliday. A train had made it in to Grayling. The cargo was basically the same as the others.

The difference in Dennis' area was that the train supplies and equipment were being unloaded and shipped out to the areas where the armor and troops had gone.

One thing was for certain: The lack of information was creating not only a mass amount of suspicion, but rumors as well. Dennis was going to try to make it to Camp Grayling. He wanted to see things first hand.

He heard a broadcast in his area asking for volunteers. They were asking for men, preferably veterans. They were not saying why. This might be his chance to find out what was happening. This might be his way in to the camp.

*****

Haliday looked over his notes. He double checked everything he had written down. He didn't have much, in all reality. He stared blankly at the papers. This had become a habit and he hated it. He wanted to know more.

Crothall called on the radio. He wanted to send Edwards out to meet Haliday. Haliday said that was fine. He would expect their visit the next day.

198

The following morning Haliday was waiting. He heard a single helicopter and walked outside and took a look. Coming in quickly was an MH6 Little Bird. The bird landed at the intersection.

Edwards came over to greet Haliday. "You ready to go?" asked Edwards.

"What do you mean?" Haliday responded.

"Crothall said we were to pick you up," Edwards told him.

"Where exactly are we going?" Haliday asked.

"Selfridge."

"I need to grab my gear," Haliday said, "and I'll meet you at the helo."

Haliday went back inside and told everyone what was going on. He told Mark to take charge of security and the rest to make sure they got the cabin chores taken care of.

Before he walked out he spoke to Kayla. "Anything happens to me, accident or not, you kill any troops you see from that point on," he said.

Kayla gave him a hug. "You'll be fine, but OK, Dad."

Haliday went back outside and over to the bird. He climbed in the back seat with Edwards. The bird lifted off and within 20 minutes they were landing at Selfridge.

Haliday eyed the base as they came in for the landing. It was the busiest he had ever seen it. There were people and equipment scattered everywhere. He expected crowds at the gates and fence, but there were very few people around the perimeter on the outside. On the inside were plenty of armed troops and vehicles.

Edwards took Haliday over to a building. Inside an office, Crothall was waiting for him. Crothall looked incredibly busy. He stood and greeted Haliday.

"I feel so important," Haliday quipped.

"You are," a voice said.

Haliday turned around.

There was a colonel at the door. He extended his hand and Haliday shook it. "I'm Colonel Jackson," he said. "Let's take a walk."

The colonel and Crothall both walked with Haliday around the building. The colonel fed Haliday typical "atta boy" BS for a few minutes, telling him how important he was to the area, before excusing himself.

They made Haliday out to be the Thumb area's savior. Haliday went along with the program until the colonel left. "Thanks for stroking me, but what's going on?" he asked.

Crothall said, "We need you to help keep the Thumb area in order. We need you to keep up what you are doing. That's pretty much it. You are the only one who has stepped up over there. We'll give you what we can and help when we can. However, we are fighting a losing battle."

"Based on what I hear you're doing fine," Haliday said.

"That's not the case, "Crothall said, "at least not everywhere."

"What happened this morning?" Haliday asked.

Crothall explained that based on activities around the major population centers they had new orders. Any aggressors were dealt with immediately.

Crothall added that anyone firing on troops or aid workers would be fired on by the military. The military had gone in and tried it the nice way and took heavy losses in some areas. This morning was an example.

Crothall and Haliday walked across a small road to another building that was being guarded by MPs. They went inside.

Crothall spoke to an MP who led them to a room with two people inside. Nothing else was in the room except for a table and a couple of chairs.

"These two people are what are left of that rogue convoy," Crothall said. "We've already interrogated them."

"It looks that way," Haliday said, noting the prisoners looked beaten, "What info did you get?"

"These two admitted to being part of the group that attacked your roadblock. They admitted to going into homes and murdering people. They stole, they raped, and they killed."

There was a knock on the door. Crothall opened it. Two MPs walked in and took the prisoners away. The prisoners didn't look remorseful at all. It almost appeared that they thought it was funny.

"Where are they going?" Haliday asked.

"With any luck, to hell," Crothall said.

Crothall took him over to another building by some barracks. Haliday didn't say a word about the gallows he had seen. He knew what was happening. Trials were quick, punishment was quicker.

They walked into the building, which was a mess hall. Crothall asked him if he was hungry.

"I could use some coffee," Haliday replied.

"There are some bagels over there," Crothall said as he pointed to a table.

Haliday walked over to the table and his jaw dropped. "Sheila?" he said to the woman there.

Sheila looked up and went around the table and gave him a hug.

"How the hell are you?" he asked.

"I'm doing good," she said.

"David is going to be tickled to death," he told her.

"He's OK?" she asked. She was emotional at this point.

Haliday gave her another hug and told her, "He's doing fine. He was injured but he's doing fine. How did you end up here?"

"I was walking to David's. I had tripped and sprained my ankle. Some of the troops going to the base helped me out, and I've been here ever since."

Crothall walked over. "You guys know each other?" he asked.

"This is my brother's fiancé," Haliday said.

"You're not going to steal our best baker are you?" Crothall asked.

"If she wants to go I am," Haliday said.

Crothall looked at her. "Go and pack your bag. We'll meet you here in two hours."

201

Sheila left the mess hall and went to pack. Crothall and Haliday walked back to Crothall's office where he pulled out some maps. They were all marked up and color coded.

He finished briefing Haliday on what was going on. Haliday planned to relay everything he was told when he got back to the cabin.

"What about our supplies?" he asked.

"We're sending out a convoy tomorrow. We'll stop at your cabin," Crothall told him.

"Sounds good. Thank you for the information."

Crothall took him back to the mess hall. Sheila joined them and then Edwards took them back to the helicopter. Thirty minutes later they were touching down near the cabin.

Haliday walked into the cabin. "Look what I found," he said.

Sheila stepped in.

David was shocked. He walked over and hugged her. He started crying. "I'm sorry," he kept repeating.

"It's OK," Sheila said. "I wouldn't have made it anyway. I got hurt."

Haliday set a bunch of papers down on the table.

"What do you have there?" Rich asked.

"I'll fill everyone in after lunch," Haliday said.

Chapter 16

Haliday was about to tell everyone what he had been told at Selfridge. He started to speak and then he stopped. "Who is up in the crow's nest?" he asked.

There was silence.

"Who is supposed to be up in the crow's nest?" Haliday asked next.

"I am," Randy said.

"Then why aren't you up there?" Haliday asked.

"Uncle Roger, I just wanted to hear what was—"

Haliday cut him off. "You just want Bubba and company to stroll on in here and help themselves?"

Randy mumbled something and then went up to the crow's nest.

Haliday looked around again. "Where's Blake?"

Kayla answered. "Where he's supposed to be."

That meant Blake was outside walking the grounds. Alan was outside as well. Until things changed, four people per shift were on security detail. Haliday was annoyed at Randy's mistake.

Haliday continued. "OK, this is what we have going on. The map of the area I'm showing you is color coded. Red indicates high threat areas, yellow for medium, and green for low. As you can all see we are in a green area.

"The Sandusky area has one big red spot left. We know that's the large group we have yet to encounter. Well, except for the breach in the road block. They were responsible. Port Huron is a mess as well. However, there's a different group of folks operating over there. They have some military support. It's a larger city, that's why. I knew someone was going to ask."

A few nods affirmed him.

"Marlette and Brown City each have one trouble spot. There are a few smaller threats as well. However, I believe once word gets out they are going to be executed they will dissolve."

"What do you mean, executed?" Karen asked.

"I'd kind of like to know that myself," Bev added.

"Who's executing people?" Rich piped in now.

Sheila spoke, "The military is."

"I thought they couldn't do that, Uncle Roger," Kevin said. "It's posse communicato, right?"

"Posse Comitatus," Haliday corrected him. "We are under total military rule right now. They are the law right now." He continued. "Now, an example is the two people who survived this morning's convoy firefight. They were already tried and hung. Things are moving that quickly."

Everyone looked at each other. No one was sure what to say.

"They were interrogated and admitted their involvement," Haliday said. "They were sentenced and the sentence carried out."

"Oh, I know how they interrogate people and so do you, Roger," David said.

Back when Roger was an MP, the military accepted the same practice of interrogation as the type heard about in the Abu

Ghraib prison in Iraq. You did what you needed to in order to extract the information.

"You guys want to go get some cheese for your whine?" Haliday said. This quieted everyone down. "I'm not going to sugarcoat things. I'm not Willy Wonka." He was starting to get a little upset. He took a moment and then continued. "Please do not interrupt me. Save your questions and comments for afterward. The military will be announcing crimes and punishments on the radio. They hope this deters people and stops them.

"The state has been divided. There are six areas. The areas were divided up by counties. The formula they used was simple; they looked at geographic area and population. We are in area four. Bad Axe is going to become the area's military control center. I do not know when it will be setup. The military will be moving into the airport there. Here's the controversial news. They are setting up camps. They intend to consolidate survivors. The camps are supposed to make it easier to distribute aid. Everyone at the camps will be expected to work. So far, I am not sure what work it is that they will be doing."

Haliday ignored the looks going around. "Those who decide not to move into a camp will have to show self-sufficiency. If they refuse, they won't receive any aid. After the initial roundup, it will be their responsibility to get to a camp. If they decide to do so at a later time, that is. They expect the process to take several weeks. There are some areas they have avoided completely. They have become war zones. Military operations have been suspended in those areas.

"Once the outer areas are secure, and order has been restored, they plan to go into the urban environments. Right now they do not have the resources to do it. People leaving the urban areas will be allowed to enter other areas. The same thing applies. They, too, will be expected to work in exchange for lodging and aid.

"They don't have any information about bringing power in. They don't have any information on how much aid they can offer. The amount of aid is limited by what other countries are contributing. The Continental United States has been divided into regions."

Bev interrupted. "I knew it. Damn FEMA camps and government control. This crap is just perfect."

Haliday laughed and said, "You'll really like the rest of what I have to say. The regions have each been assigned to what equates to a Governor. The Governors report to the President. Each state in the region will have Lieutenant Governors. Each sub region in the state will have a prefect. The prefects will work with the military and government in making sure local governments are set up throughout their areas. No further details are available on that."

"What else?" Mark asked.

Haliday looked over at Bev. She was always more involved than the rest of them when it came to conspiracies. This was going to be icing on the cake.

"They have brought in a lot of equipment and supplies," he said.

Bev said, "Like what?"

Haliday answered, "Trucks, buses, concertina and barbed wire, FEMA coffins, crates, and more."

"Damn it, I told you," Bev said loudly.

Mark spoke up again. "There are a lot of reasons for every bit of equipment they brought in."

Haliday popped a couple of aspirin in his mouth. He felt the headache coming on. This brought the conspiracy theories back around, 180 degrees.

He just let everyone talk it out. He walked over to Dawn, who was sitting next to Karen, and sat down next to Karen. "Do me a favor, will you?" he asked.

"What do you want me to do?" Karen asked.

"Over the next couple of days, talk with Sheila," he said.

Haliday didn't want to outright interrogate Sheila. Nor did he want to seem pushy. He didn't want to give her the impression he had brought her back here just to cull information from her.

This was his brother's fiancé. She was welcome, but she might not be interested in telling Haliday everything she knew. For one reason or another she might think she was not allowed.

He would be asking a lot of questions. He also knew that human behavior was also a solid form of interrogation. In general conversation people talk. Sometimes slips of the tongue can tell you a lot.

"Make sure you take note of anything she might mention about Selfridge," he said.

"OK. I'll let you know what I hear," Karen said.

He walked back over to Rich and Bev. "Mom, you always thought we would put you in a nursing home. That probably sounds better right about now, huh?"

She just looked at him. She wasn't very happy right now. Everything she had read about on the internet was coming true. She always thought Washington should have been a test bed for nuclear arms.

He walked over to David. "I need to steal Sheila for a little bit."

David protested. "Can't it wait?"

"Don't worry," Haliday said. "It won't take long."

Haliday called Mark over. He, Mark, and Sheila all went downstairs. They would not be disturbed down there.

Haliday set a notepad down on the table. "I'm glad to see you made it," he said to her.

Mark offered his hand to Sheila. "I'm Mark. I wasn't formally introduced."

Haliday asked as many questions as he could. Mark asked questions as well. After two hours they were finished. Sheila was happy it was over.

Haliday and Mark talked alone. About an hour later they decided to go meet with Brad and Rob. Haliday called them and told them he was on his way.

Haliday and Mark left the cabin. They took the Tahoe this time. Haliday wanted to make some stops along the way and fill up some gas cans.

Once they arrived at the airport they went inside. Rob and Brad were already there. Haliday walked in and said hello and then they sat down and drank some coffee.

Haliday and Mark filled them in on what Haliday had learned earlier.

Rob shifted in his seat. "Who is this so-called prefect going to be?"

"I don't know," Haliday answered.

Rob had that look on his face again.

"When the military arrives and sets up camp here, you can ask more questions," Haliday said.

This caught Rob by surprise. He had not heard that the military was moving in. Haliday avoided elaborating on that subject. In case Rob was not going to be the prefect in this area, he didn't want to stir up any animosity.

"They have convoys moving into the area tomorrow. These are aid convoys. I can't say when they will be here. I can't even say what kind of aid they will have." Haliday explained the camps to them.

Rob seemed to be okay with it.

Brad was the one who did not take it lightly. "Who determines if I'm fit to live on my own?"

"I couldn't tell you that Brad," Haliday said.

"Well, that's just great," Brad replied.

Haliday said, "Brad, for what it's worth, I doubt any of us will be scrutinized. If anything, they will want to keep us healthy and running around this place."

That made sense to Rob and Brad.

"Where do they plan on putting the camps?" Brad asked.

"That's a good question," Mark said.

Haliday looked down at a map. "The schools."

"Why there?" Rob asked.

"You have one large complex. The elementary school, the junior high, and the high school are all in the same spot," Haliday answered.

Mark added, "You can put thousands in that complex."

That was the logical choice. It was not too far from the airport either. They wouldn't need anything but a few generators to run it. The heat in the rooms was radiant electric. It would be easy to bring back online. They could get the kitchens running again as well. The ball fields and play grounds could be used for tents. Bunks and other equipment brought in would do the job nicely.

"How do they plan to get everyone there?" Rob asked.

"I can only assume they will be making broadcasts and asking people to prepare themselves. They have trucks and buses they brought in for transport," Haliday said. He then added, "I think these are questions you need to ask the military when they get here."

Rob said, "This area has a couple hundred thousand people. There's no room for them at the schools."

"I'm sure they'll be using a lot of places in the region," Mark told him.

Brad looked at Rob, "Another thing you need to remember is that at least half of the people have died already."

A lot of people kept forgetting that little bit of information. Brad asked, "Who is going to gather up the people?"

"I heard they will be seeking volunteers for work programs. Drivers and laborers. They'll reward them with extra food or something," Haliday said.

He told them that there was a program in place for people to receive new identification cards. A National ID card. The ID card would have all pertinent data on it—the person's picture, their name, date of birth, height, weight, hair and eye color, social security number, region, state, and area. This information would be listed on the card and also encoded on a chip within the ID card.

"Sounds like Big Brother has won," Brad said.

They talked just a bit longer. Brad walked them back out to the Tahoe. "This is some jacked-up crap," Brad said.

Haliday said, "Listen, Brad, I didn't say this in front of Rob, but meet me at the roadblock closest to my cabin tomorrow at 0900 hours."

"What do I tell Rob?" he asked.

"You tell him we are planning the next operation in Sandusky," Haliday answered.

"I'm not sure I like the sound of this," Brad replied.

Mark said, "Cover our ass, Brad. In case the military and government are not on the up and up."

"We have a Plan B," Haliday added.

Haliday and Mark left it at that. They knew Brad wouldn't say anything to Rob. Rob was a stand-up guy. He would cover your back. However, Haliday also knew the type.

If it really came down to it, Rob would talk. They were not going to risk telling Rob anything he did not need to know. Operational Security meant as few people involved as possible.

This was one reason that Haliday did not go into the Plan B concept back at the cabin. The group had grown and too much chitchat could ruin the plan if they had to enact it. Even though every single person knew that information was to be guarded, it was best not to let them all know just yet. This way the possibility of someone slipping did not exist.

Haliday felt bad that he had to do that, but too many pieces of the puzzle didn't quite fit right. Mark knew more about what was going on. If something happened to Haliday, Mark would be able to carry things through.

They were almost back at the cabin now. "Mark, I want to thank you," Haliday said.

"For what?" Mark asked.

"You have become a good friend and someone I can really count on. No offense, I had a lot of friends who were grunts, but you are one smart man. I'm surprised you didn't choose a different field," he said.

"I got a DUI just after basic training," Mark admitted. "We were allowed to leave base for the weekend before shipping out for advanced individual training. A few of us rented a car. We left the bar early. I had two drinks and that was enough to put me over the limit."

"Ouch, that hurts," Haliday said.

"They made me change my military occupational specialty. It was get out, cook or go infantry. I chose infantry. I was supposed to go into Military Intelligence."

"Well, regardless, thank you for being a stand-up trooper," Haliday told him.

They parked the Tahoe and went into the cabin. Haliday thought to himself, *Time to play a thousand questions*. As soon as he hung his coat up the first question came.

"What did they hear?" David asked.

"They know less than us," Mark said.

Haliday was relieved he didn't have to deal with it. He excused himself and went up to his bunk to take a nap.

Blake was on the ham radio talking to his mother. Both she and his grandmother were doing fine. It had taken weeks to get a communications schedule set up.

Trying to link the people in Belize with survivors was near impossible. There was a schedule now. They were only allowed to speak once a week for three minutes. Belize had taken in almost 12,000 people from five cruise ships. The Belizean government was making arrangements to send people home. Anyone that did not live in the U.S. would go home first. Next would be people who did not live in affected areas of the U.S. If people did live in an affected area, they would stay until notified they could come home. Although not many agreed with the policy, they knew it would be a burden for people to get them home.

There were U.S. citizens spread across the globe. Some were on business, some on vacation, and some in school. Most did not have a home to return to right now.

Bev was able to speak to her daughter Susan in Texas. Susan told Bev that a lot of aid was being shipped out of the south. The government had trains running in all directions. Susan mentioned that a lot of facilities in the area were producing as much food as they could. They were also producing parts for equipment and vehicles. Anything they thought could help was produced as quickly as possible.

Susan's son Clint worked at a Toyota plant. The plant produced Tundra and Tacoma pickup trucks. They had approximately 1,200 trucks that were ready. These were being sold to the government that was shipping them out.

There had been enough parts to produce another 700 trucks and these, too, were eventually sold to the government. With no more parts available the plant eventually shut down.

Plants that were not in affected areas started closing. There was no need for a lot of products. In many cases they relied on parts from within the affected areas. The unemployment was another issue to deal with.

Areas along the coasts increased fishing. The fish was processed and sent into the interior. Cattle were processed and meat was turned into jerky or freeze-dried. The same was done with other livestock.

Bev had not heard from her son Greg in Missouri. She held out hope they were okay. She also came to the realization that she may never see them again. Her grandchildren down there all had young children of their own. Survival was questionable.

Across the nation almost every single family had been affected. There were mothers, fathers, sons, daughters, brothers, and sisters who were geographically separated, and now their families were touched forever.

Haliday woke from his nap. He had missed dinner. He wasn't hungry anyway. Instead he grabbed a glass of iced tea. He yawned and looked around.

It was time to plan the next operation. This operation was going to take some finesse. It was a much larger group. He told Brad they would need more help; at least 12 more.

He looked around. "Where is everyone?"

Alan answered. "Karen, Nancy, Sheila, and Dawn are downstairs playing cards. Randy, Kevin, Blake, and Kayla are all doing laundry. Mark, David, and Bill are on security. Sarah is playing games with the kids. Lisa, Rich, and Bev are already sleeping."

"Oh, okay," was all Haliday said. "Alan, anything new on the radio?"

"I talked with Adam a little bit," Alan said.

"What did he have to say?"

"It's looking pretty bad for him. He's not sure how long they can last. There's a large group hanging around his house," Alan replied.

"I wish there was something we could do to help him," Haliday told him.

"Me, too," Alan said. "I hope they can hold on."

Chapter 17

Elsewhere in Michigan, other things were happening as well. A man named Jimmy had made it out of Detroit. It was rough going as he moved along with just his shopping cart. Eventually he found a large garden wagon. It was 24-by-48 inches and had side rails 12 inches tall.

He transferred everything he had in his possession onto the cart. The cart was heavily loaded. Items kept shifting and falling off. Jimmy took out a big wad of para-cord that he kept with him.

Jimmy laid it out on the ground. He made a grid pattern with pieces that he cut from the cord. Every four inches he tied it off in a knot. When he was done he had a makeshift cargo net.

He laid the cargo net over his gear and tied it down. This worked quite well. Any food he had was well-hidden under the pile of ragged clothes, a few old pots, and other items.

When he had left on his trek, he wasn't sure where he should go. He just knew he had to get out of the city when he had left. Canada sounded good to him. He didn't know why.

Instead of trying to cross in Detroit he chose to work his way toward Port Huron. He did this for many reasons. The tunnel crossing had flooded and there were no pumps to keep out the small trickles of water.

The bridge was still intact. This would have taken him through Windsor. Windsor was far smaller than Detroit, but still heavily populated. Again, he chose Port Huron.

As he had moved closer to Port Huron the realization that it was a mistake took root. Port Huron was almost as bad as Detroit. Jimmy changed direction.

He found himself heading north. As he moved along he ate whatever he could find. In one park he emptied out a couple of bird feeders.

The feed was a mix of shelled pumpkin seeds, sunflower kernels, peanuts, dried cherries, and tree nut pieces. It wasn't the best but was loaded with nutrients. It was enough to keep him going.

At other times he had to rely on small rodents or birds if he could catch them. He had become very proficient with a slingshot. Pigeons and seagulls were eaten often.

Even the bird population started dwindling, especially with the winter close at hand. Jimmy was getting more desperate as he moved on. An inner voice kept pushing him.

He made it as far north as Sandusky. Once he arrived there he looked for a place to settle down for the harsh winter. He found himself looking at a small theater. He went inside and looked around.

The concession stand had been looted early on. Almost everything had been taken. The only things left were a couple boxes of popcorn and oil packets underneath the popcorn machine. He was soon able to figure out how to pop it.

He took refuge in a projector room. He used his knife to cut open a large portion of the theater seats. He used the foam to line the walls of the projection room. This provided insulation. Along with his sleeping bag, it would keep him warm enough to survive.

*****

Adam looked out of the window. His group kept a constant eye on the house down the street. So far the gang had stayed down there, but he wasn't sure how long that would last.

His group had provoked the gang by firing on them. The attempt to help the other household had failed. Worse yet, it drew even more attention to Adam's house.

The gang had watched Adam and his group. They knew they would have to fight hard to get anything from Adam's house. It was the reason they chose the other house first.

Eventually that luck would not hold. The home they invaded only had so many resources. The gang would eventually use them all. When that point in time came, they would want more. They would need more.

Adam wasn't sure if his group could hold them off. He started to make plans to bug out. If it came down to leaving in order to survive, then his group would leave.

There were a lot of scenarios that could play out. Adam's group started reviewing all of their contingency plans. They worked on modifying them as well.

*****

The truck had two Humvees riding along with it, including a Deuce. They pulled into Haliday's driveway. Haliday walked outside and met them. There were several crates on the back of the Deuce.

Haliday called Randy, Kevin, and Blake over.

The passenger in the Deuce climbed out. "Anything with an H on it is yours, sir," the man said.

"OK, thank you," Haliday said.

Haliday directed the three boys to get the supplies unloaded. The process only took them 10 minutes. The supplies they received were typical of the previous supplies they were given.

Haliday noted the rank on the man's uniform. "Where are you heading now, Specialist?"

"The airport," the specialist responded.

"Drive safe. Watch out for rush hour," Haliday said.

The specialist climbed up in the Deuce and the three vehicles left. Haliday had heard the transmission on the radio. They would be rejoining another 20 vehicles heading to the airport.

He looked down at his watch. It was almost time to go meet Brad. He asked if anyone wanted to go. Diana said she might like to go. "OK, who else?" he asked.

Karen and Bev wanted to go.

"Gear up, meet me in the truck," he said.

Haliday went out to the shed and took a quick inventory of the supplies that were brought in. It was just enough to replenish what they had expended in the previous two operations.

He walked over to the Tahoe and started laughing. Diana was having a hard time maneuvering into the Tahoe with her brace on. He would check with the doctor later to see if it was okay to take it off.

They arrived at the roadblock to see Brad. Haliday laughed again watching Diana trying to get out. He would have suggested she stay behind, but it was nice for everyone to get out of the cabin.

Brad glanced at her. "You must be tired of that brace by now."

"It's very annoying," Diana said.

Haliday walked over and hung his AR on it. "But it sure comes in handy," he said.

Diana just looked at him. "Jerk."

Haliday took the AR off Diana's brace and walked back over to Brad. "Let's go talk, Brad."

"OK."

Haliday and Brad walked a little way down the road. Haliday explained to him what he wanted him to do. "Brad, identify some people you can trust; at least a couple of dozen."

"What about Rob?" Brad said.

"No. Keep him out of the loop on this one."

"What do you want us to do?"

"I want as many of you as possible to each hide a gun and some ammo," said Haliday. "Don't tell anyone. Then I want as many of you as possible to get on the work details. See if you can get a couple of volunteers to join the camps when they open."

"You don't trust the government?" Brad asked.

"You do?"

They both chuckled a bit. "I just like to make sure there's an even playing field," Haliday added. "If we have people inside, it serves a lot of different purposes. For one, food supplies last just a little bit longer. The volunteers will be eating on the government's dime.

"Secondly, we get some raw intel from inside the camp. We might want to use a few women in there, too. Troops tend to be a little loose-lipped around women. They tend to underestimate a woman's abilities. Third, if things go south we know the operation. We will have people in place and know how they operate. That's probably the most important."

"You don't expect to take them on in that case do you?" Brad asked?

"Hell no. It would be suicide," Haliday said.

"Then why?"

Haliday said, "To buy some time. Let us get the hell out of here."

"I guess that makes sense."

"If—and I mean if it goes bad—then we will cut ties and get everyone out as soon as we know it's going south."

Haliday explained that it was all just a precaution. It was just a contingency plan. If everything was okay, they would all be fine. If it wasn't okay, they would move to another location if possible.

They both walked back to the trailer by the roadblock.

"Are these guys paying attention?" Haliday said as he pointed to the group on blockade duty.

One of the men spoke up. "We sure are,"

"How so?" Haliday asked.

"We pull six-hour shifts. There are four of us on and four off. So far it has worked out fine," the man said.

Haliday looked down at the tracks in the snow. He noticed there had been quite a few vehicles that passed by earlier. As he looked around he noted some stakes placed in the ground. These were painted orange.

Haliday said, "Who put these here?"

"The military did," said one man.

"Did they say what they were for?"

The man said, "Guard booth is what they told us."

"They say anything else about it?" Haliday asked.

The man said, "We were told they would be using our blockades as checkpoints. The other roads they would block even further. This would control entry and exit to the region."

Haliday thought to himself, *that's one little bit of information Crothall left out.* The look on Brad's face told him that Brad understood how important it was to have a Plan B now.

Haliday and Brad covered the strategy plan for the next operation. This was the larger group in Sandusky they still had to contend with. He asked Brad to bring along as many people as he could.

He told Brad they would meet again in two days. This would be when they would go in and try to get rid of the last gang in Sandusky. The government had been broadcasting warnings. Hopefully people were hearing them.

"Brad, are you there?" came a squawk on the radio.

Brad answered back, "I'm here, Rob."

"Are you on your way back?" Rob asked.

"I'm leaving here in just a few minutes," Brad answered.

"Good. We have some problems I need help with. The military is out of control," Rob said.

"What do you mean Rob?" Haliday asked.

"They are moving military equipment around, some soldiers are walking around the town, there's things that look like tanks, they want to use buildings, all kinds of stuff," Rob said.

Haliday looked at Brad. "I'll go with you," he said.

"Sounds like a good idea," Brad said.

Haliday looked at Brad and said, "What did he expect. A truck full of Easy Bake ovens and cake batter?"

Haliday rallied everyone together. They got in the Tahoe and followed Brad to the airport. On the way there Haliday called the cabin and told them he would be back later.

When everyone arrived at the airport, it was a mess. Tempers were flaring. The townspeople were yelling at the military. The military had taken up a defensive posture.

Haliday and Brad walked over to Rob, who was arguing with a lieutenant that no one had met before. This guy was a butter bar, a second lieutenant, very fresh. Next to the him was a sergeant. Haliday asked the sergeant to step aside and talk to him for a minute.

"What's going on here, Sergeant?" Haliday asked.

"Who are you?"

"Haliday."

"Oh, OK. Sorry, sir," said the sergeant.

"So, what do we have here?" Haliday repeated.

"Well, that guy over there," he said, pointing to Rob, "said we need to leave. He said he is not going to allow us to take over the airport and supplies here."

"Who told you to take over the supplies?" Haliday asked.

"Colonel Jackson," the sergeant said.

"What else is going on here?"

"These people are all upset because we didn't bring any aid."

"What exactly are you here to do?" Haliday asked.

"Secure the airport and set it up as an aid station and operations base," the sergeant answered.

Haliday told him to follow him. They approached the lieutenant and Rob. Brad was standing there as well.

Rob looked over at Haliday. "Did you know what was happening?" he asked.

"Relax, Rob. We'll get it worked out," Haliday told him.

The lieutenant looked at Haliday, who stared right back at him. Neither of them said anything for a long moment.

Finally the sergeant spoke up. "Sir, this is Roger Haliday."

The lieutenant extended his hand. Haliday shook it.

"Let's all go inside where it's warmer," said Haliday.

They all walked in to the admin building and in to the office and sat down.

Haliday spoke first. "This is how it's going to go down. The military is going to take over the airport for their operations. They can move in troops and equipment as they see fit. It only makes sense they use the airport and runway. The townspeople sacrificed a lot for the supplies that are on hand. These supplies will remain in their control. If they have to move them out of here they will. They will not be handled by the military, period. What else?"

The lieutenant said, "We will need some volunteers to work here. They'll be bunked and fed."

"That's fair enough," Haliday said.

"When the camps are up and running, those in the camps will be bunked and fed in exchange for work," the lieutenant added.

"What kind of work would that be?" Brad asked.

"I don't have the details yet," replied the lieutenant.

"Well, when you do, we'll decide what happens then," Haliday told him.

"Exactly who is going to have authority around here?" Rob asked.

"The military, under control of the government," the lieutenant said.

"That doesn't bode well. I thought they were setting up a new government," Rob remarked.

A sense of tenseness thickened in the room

"We are, but it takes time," the sergeant answered this time.

"And what about the aid you were supposed to bring?" Haliday asked.

The conversation was starting to heat up again. Rob was taking it all personally. Haliday had noticed that Rob had changed over the past month. He was becoming a loose gun.

"Rob, step outside for a minute with me," Haliday told him.

Rob and Haliday stepped outside for a few minutes to talk.

"Rob, what's going on lately?"

"What do you mean what's going on? It's easy for you," he told Haliday. "You run around here. You have trucks, food, everything you need. I go in to check on people and find them dead. Every day goes by and more people are dead. You have no idea what it's like. You sit there on your high horse, Mr. Big Shot. Mr. I-Can-Survive-Anything."

Haliday just looked at him. "Rob, are you forgetting how you got here? Are you forgetting how a lot of these people got here? Have you forgotten the sacrifices my family and I made for this place? You think I don't have family and friends that have died? You don't think I worry about those who may still be alive? You have got to be kidding me, Rob."

Rob looked at him. "I'm sorry, Roger. I'm at my breaking point."

"Rob, you need to understand that we can't save everyone. Right now there has to be a leader. That leader will have tough choices to make."

"I'm not sure I can do it, Roger."

"You'll have to figure it out quickly, Rob," Haliday told him.

He and Rob and walked back into the office and sat down. The conversation continued with only a few more small details to wrap up. When they were done Haliday and his group left.

The military would be setting up their perimeter at the airport and moving in equipment and supplies. From that point on the airport became their base.

Rob and Brad's people moved the supplies. They consolidated what was left and placed it all in the co-op. The amount of supplies that were left was dwindling. The sooner the aid arrived, the better.

Haliday made a right turn and took a different road than he normally took. He drove down the road and stopped at a small intersection and got out of the Tahoe.

He looked down at the snow on the road. There was a set of tracks that were very familiar. A single Humvee had come through there. He walked back to the Tahoe.

"What's wrong?" Bev asked.

"Nothing yet," Haliday said.

He let the Tahoe follow the tracks. They led up to the west side of his property. He stopped the Tahoe; he could see where the Humvee had stopped.

The snow was melted around the areas where the tires had been. The engine area was melted, too. Haliday double checked the area. It had indeed been just one vehicle.

He told Bev and Karen to step out of the Tahoe and keep watch. He needed to go into the trees and check things out. He followed two sets of footprints. They led into the woods.

He noted that the prints had the same treads. They were no doubt military in nature. He saw an area where they stopped. On the ground was another sign. There were prints from knee guards.

He followed the prints around. They stopped at various locations where Haliday's group had set up traps. More than likely the trouble spots had been mapped out.

He returned to the Tahoe. Bev and Karen climbed in as well.

"What did you see?" Karen asked.

"It seems the military has been keeping an eye on us," Haliday said.

"What do you think that means?" Diana asked.

"It means we are perceived as either a threat or someone wants to know more about us," he told her.

They drove back to the cabin. Once inside Haliday told Mark what he had seen. The two of them worked on plans to move the traps as soon as possible.

Haliday hoped for more snow. A fresh dusting would help hide the tracks. On the other hand, if they made a big enough mess, it would also make it hard to tell where the new traps were.

The next day everyone would be outside relocating the traps. The operation would have to wait another day. Haliday would make sure the cabin and his group was safe first. He called Brad and told him they had a delay. He didn't tell him why.

He was positive that all of the ham radio traffic was being monitored. He was going to set up a code system that he and Brad could use. He knew it was something he should have done that much sooner.

At this point they knew almost everything about Haliday's group anyway. Any future movements or activities he would keep secret. Thinking back in time, he had made quite a few operational security mistakes.

Haliday went into the kitchen again. Sarah and Kayla were cooking. Tonight's meal would be Mexican lasagna. Layered tortillas, beans, onions, tomatoes, and cheese. Fresh lettuce would have been nice. They did have homemade sour cream, though.

Karen walked up. "You have a minute?" she asked him.

"Sure, what do you need?" he answered.

"A little help with some supplies downstairs."

Haliday followed her down the steps. "What do we need?"

"Nothing, but I wanted to tell you in private," she said. "Earlier when I was talking to Sheila, she mentioned something odd."

"What was it?"

"She mentioned something about Crothall being busy."

"No offense, but that makes sense," he said

"No, she made it sound like he had two areas he worked for," she said.

"How is that?"

"Crothall was talking to Edwards and said something about juggling two operations at once. He would be happy when it was just one," she said.

He nodded. "Anything else?"

"She said Crothall stopped talking when he heard her out in the hall."

"OK, I'll ask her about it. That's pretty important."

They went back upstairs and to the kitchen. After dinner Haliday asked Sheila to talk a bit. They went over to the fireplace. Mark joined them.

"You heard Crothall talk about two operations, I understand?" Haliday asked.

"Yes. How did you know?" Sheila asked.

"That's not important. I need to know as much as you can tell me," he said.

She explained in detail what she had heard between Crothall and Edwards. Haliday and Mark listened intently. Both took notes. After Sheila was finished they asked her more questions about what they heard.

None of what it made sense. If they were to understand it correctly, it would appear that Crothall, Edwards, and many others were part of the CRA—the Constitutional Restoration Army.

If that was the case, then the CRA was using some serious psychological operations and had people convinced the government was still in control, while in all reality the CRA was.

Sheila was excused and she got up and left.

Haliday looked over at Mark. "I don't know about you, but my head is spinning."

Mark said, "Mine, too."

"The last gang in Sandusky is still a major concern," Haliday said.

"I know. Let's finish that op, and then hold back until we find out what's going on."

"I agree."

Haliday called for Randy, Kevin, Kayla, and Blake. The four of them came over and Haliday had them follow him down the stairs.

They sat around a table and Haliday went over the plans for the operation. Everyone was paying close attention except for Randy. He kept losing interest. Haliday decided he would speak to him after the meeting.

After three hours, Haliday and Mark were finished briefing them. Everyone except for Randy was excused.

"What's wrong, Uncle Roger?"

Haliday looked at him. "Randy, you need to have your head in the game. Tomorrow night it's going to be worse than you can imagine. Worse than anything we have seen yet."

"I know, Uncle Roger," Randy said.

"Other people are going to be counting on you," Mark added.

"I got it, I got it," Randy said.

They went upstairs and went to sleep for the night.

Chapter 18

After breakfast everyone was busy with moving the traps and disguising them. The animals were fed and the rest of the chores were taken care of as well.

The rest of the day was spent preparing and checking the equipment for the operation. Tonight they were going to be taking the Tahoe and a Jeep, the one they had taken away from the rogue militia when the cabin was attacked.

Haliday went by and checked each and every person. Mark followed and he, too, checked each and every person. They were ready to go. They loaded up into the vehicles and left.

They met with Brad and the people that he'd brought with him.

Haliday did a head count. "Brad, I counted seventeen people total. Where's the rest?"

Brad looked at the group. "Roger," he said, "a lot of people didn't want to volunteer."

"Why not?"

Brad said, "Most of them said they didn't have to. They said now that the military and the government are here, that it's not necessary."

"They what?" Haliday said.

Brad looked at him. "Roger, a lot of people think that now that the government is here they don't have to do anything. I tried to tell them that it wasn't that easy. A lot of them didn't want to listen."

"Do they realize they have to work in the camps or for the government in order to receive assistance?" Haliday asked.

"They don't seem to think that's the way it will be. One of the problems is Rob," Brad answered.

"What the hell is Rob doing?"

Brad said, "He's pretty much telling people exactly that. He's telling them things will be much better now that the government is bringing in aid."

"Basically, he drank the Kool-Aid, right?"

"Yep."

"Great. Just great," Haliday said.

Mark said, "Let's get going, guys."

The group went over the assault plan one last time. Since there were no questions, they moved out. They left the Deuce parked where it was. It was far too loud. The gang would hear it coming.

As the group was heading toward the apartment complex they spotted a small amount of smoke. They drove by the smoking remains of the town theater. Practically nothing but ash and twisted metal remained.

Haliday drove his Tahoe as close to the apartments as he could. Mark drove the Jeep up close as well. This complex had 12 buildings. The gang, however, had chosen a building that was by itself.

Haliday looked at it through binoculars. "You have got to be kidding me," he said.

"What's wrong, Dad?" Kayla asked.

He handed the binoculars to her.

She took a long look and said, "Oh my goodness."

The radio crackled. "Roger, are you seeing this?" Mark asked over it.

"I sure am," Haliday answered.

"What the hell are we going to do?" Mark asked.

"Grab Brad and meet me by the Jeep."

Haliday, Mark, and Brad all met by the Jeep. All three had the same look on their faces. The gang had heavily fortified their building. They either knew what was coming or someone inside had experience. The gang had placed a security emplacement at the front and back door of the building. Each emplacement was manned by two individuals with rifles.

The windows on the lower level were boarded up. The gang had placed junk piles under each window. The junk piles had all sorts of metal protruding from them. No one would be able to access the windows or get through them easily.

The windows on the upper floors were boarded as well. These had firing ports cut into them. The windows on each end had a large port to be used for observation. The group had no doubt that they had been spotted.

This gang even went as far as to protect their vehicles. They had pushed broken down cars into a row. These cars actually blocked the gang's working vehicles. They could exit the building low and make it to their vehicles while being protected.

Haliday had no idea what, or who, was inside that building. Right now they were running different scenarios past each other. Simply ordering the gang out was not going to work.

They decided that this would require a serious amount of planning. Haliday and Brad headed back to their positions. They told everyone on the radio to pull back.

Haliday was 100 feet from his group when he heard the first shot. This was followed by two more. He ducked down low and ran toward his group. A series of shots erupted from both sides.

"Who the hell fired?" Haliday asked.

"Dad, it's Randy," Kayla said as she pointed to a clump of bushes.

Haliday looked closely and saw his nephew balled up behind the clump of bushes. He couldn't tell if Randy had been shot or was just scared. He yelled out, "Randy, are you OK?"

"I'm shot, Uncle Roger," Randy said.

"What the hell was he doing, Kayla?" Haliday asked.

Kayla replied, "He said he could sneak up closer and get a good shot at the guys by the door. I told him no. He kept arguing with me. I kept telling him no."

There were still shots being fired from both sides. Mark and Brad were calling on the radio trying to find out what happened. Haliday told them to hold on and hold their fire.

"Dad, I was talking to you on the radio, and Randy took off. I tried to call him back," Kayla added.

"It's not your fault, kiddo. Don't worry about it," Haliday said.

Haliday called everyone and told them what happened. He told them to hold their fire until he could come up with a plan. He had to think for a minute.

He called Kevin over. "Look, here's the plan. I'm going to blanket the area with smoke. The group is going to lay down suppressive fire. You and I will have to run out and get him."

"OK, Uncle Roger," Kevin said.

Haliday told everyone the plan and then started laying down smoke. As soon as he did the gang fired on the area.

Randy screamed out. "I'm hit again! Help me!"

Haliday laid down some more smoke.

Gunfire erupted everywhere. Blake, who was next to Haliday, grabbed his vest, causing Haliday to fall backwards. Blake and Kevin ran out to where Randy was.

Haliday popped some more smoke and fired toward the building. Everyone emptied magazine after magazine into the building and the security emplacements by the door.

Kevin and Blake dragged Randy back to safety. Haliday went and checked on Randy. He had been hit once in the chest and once in the leg.

Haliday tore open Randy's jacket and shirt and found the chest wound. He knew by Randy's breathing that it had hit his lung. Randy had a sucking chest wound. Haliday told Kevin to go get a first aid kit.

Blake was standing there. "Sorry, Mr. Haliday. I just figured I was quicker than you."

"It's OK, Blake. You are, and thank you. Go see if they need help over there," he said as he pointed to a few other people.

Kevin ran and grabbed the kit and raced back to Haliday.

"Randy, what were you thinking?" Kevin said.

Randy was barely able to speak. He tried to mouth some words, but could not. Haliday took out an Asherman Chest Seal—an ACS—and wiped down Randy's chest, then applied the ACS.

Randy was able to breathe noticeably better. Haliday taped off the ACS some more. Haliday tore open Randy's pant leg. He looked up at Kevin.

Kevin looked at Randy. "What were you thinking, man?"

Randy was barely able to say, "I just wanted to make my brother and my uncle proud of me."

Kevin said, "I'm proud of you, brother."

Haliday put a compression bandage on Randy's leg. He looked at Randy. "I'm proud of you, too, Randy. You did good. You helped us break in there."

Randy said, "Really?"

"Yeah. They are coming out now. That's why the firing stopped," Haliday said.

Randy's eyes blinked slowly. In just a few moments he closed them for the last time. Haliday slammed his fist on the ground and yelled. Kevin started crying. The femoral artery had been severed; the blood loss was too great.

Kevin was still kneeling by his brother when Kayla came over and knelt down by her cousins. She bent over and kissed Randy's forehead. She, too, started crying.

Haliday got up and walked over to the Tahoe. Tears ran down his face. He just stood there for a few minutes.

Blake came over. "Mr. Haliday, Mark is calling for you."

"I know, Blake."

Blake went back to the group.

Haliday called Mark. "Mark, you heard, right?"

"I'm sorry, Roger. I really am. What do you want to do?"

"I'm staying. Anyone who wants to leave can go ahead. I am not asking you guys to do this," Haliday said.

"What do you have planned?" Mark asked.

"I'm going to go over to the south side of this building, and I'm going to put one hundred rounds of fifty-cal into it."

"Roger, you think that's going to do any good?"

"Mark, if I can take out the doors and windows, then I can put smoke, CS teargas, and flares in there. I'll burn the bastards out. I don't care," he bit out.

Mark was going to try to reason with Haliday, but he knew that would be a losing battle. He called Brad on the radio. "Brad, load up your men and head home."

"Negative," Brad said. "We're here for the long haul. What's your plan, Roger?"

Haliday wiped his face off. "I want a volunteer to come with me and load magazines. I am going to continue with a sustained rate of fire. No pauses. I'm going to let them sit and wonder as long as I can. What I want you guys to do is exactly the same thing. I want one shot at a time fired into the windows and at the emplacements as well. One round every ten seconds until it's go time. I'll be firing one round every minute. When it's go time we'll open up on them. We'll launch as much smoke and teargas as we can at them. Like I said, they can all burn."

The group was divided into two separate groups. One group would cover the front of the building, one would cover the back. Haliday would be firing on the back.

Each group made sure they had good positions. Haliday insisted they stay as safe as they possibly could. This assault was more of a mental attack.

234

Each person was assigned a letter of the alphabet. The idea was simple: someone would yell out "A" and fire their round. The guy who was "B" would count to 10 and do the same thing.

Each person would be firing a round approximately every two minutes. Haliday would be firing a round a minute. He would be trying to take out hardware points on the windows and doors.

Everyone took a small break. They had the opportunity to get something to eat, drink, and use the bathroom. It was 2:30 a.m. by now, and it was time to start the assault.

Mark launched a couple of teargas grenades from his 37mm launcher toward an emplacement. It did not have the effect he wanted. The people inside must have had gasmasks.

Haliday had the Barrett's bipod rest on the hood of the Tahoe. He fired the first round into the door handle. The door swung open just a little. He watched as the door closed. He fired another round into the door, about 4fourfeet up and a foot from the door handle. He watched the door swing open a little bit.

The rest of the group started their slow, methodical firing. The gang returned fire. After a couple of minutes the gang stopped firing, obviously trying to figure out what was going on.

Haliday's next shot was at one of the observation ports. There was no way he could tell if he hit anyone or not. He was just trying to make their lives hell. His next shot one minute later was where he approximated a door hinge would be.

His group kept up the firing schedule. After 45 minutes the gang inside started firing back in rapid succession. They did this for only five minutes before they stopped. Haliday's group just kept their slow, methodical rate of fire going.

One of the plywood window coverings fell down. When Haliday saw people put it back up, he fired six shots into the area rapidly. The plywood fell back down and stayed down.

Haliday told the guys to fire into the window if they saw the plywood go back up. He concentrated on the door now. After another four shots it literally fell off its hinges. No one inside attempted to put it back up.

On the opposite side of the building another window cover had fallen under the unremitting, methodical gunfire. Haliday's group was starting to take a toll on the gang inside. They were wearing thin.

The gang members inside were literally going crazy. No matter which apartment or room they went into, rounds came into the building. They were losing mental control.

The gang members started yelling and arguing back and forth. When the door popped open, they suffered their first death inside. The next death came when the window cover fell. There were multiple injuries inside, too.

The pure drone of shot after shot was driving them crazy. The heavy return firing was meant to dissuade Haliday's group from continuing their assault. It didn't work.

The gang had stolen a huge amount of food and equipment; however, ammunition was at a premium. They were getting low. They were not sure how many attacks they could hold off.

One of the gang members took a look out of a window portal right when Mark was ready to fire.

Mark took the gang member out with the shot.

The gang now had three dead.

Originally, there were over 50 people that had joined the gang. Some members had left on their own and others had been kicked out. The group was down to 40. They now had three dead and six injured leaving 31 people able to fight.

The sun was starting to rise. Haliday was out of rounds for the Barrett now. He was preparing the 37mm on his AR. He popped a teargas cartridge into it. He took aim at the window.

He gave the command and everyone in his group opened up.

The gang members inside started to panic. Seeing this, the leader spoke to a few people and quietly worked his way to the lower level.

Haliday fired the teargas, but missed. He fired another round and missed again. He attempted one more time and missed as well. The only benefit was that the canisters were on the ground and a small amount of teargas made it into the open windows.

Haliday fired a smoke grenade at the window. This one went right through the opening.

"Fourth times the charm," he heard someone say.

"Yeah, too bad its just smoke," he answered back.

He popped a few more smoke grenades toward the building. Mark launched a few from his side of the building as well.

These, along with the amount of gunfire, rattled the gang.

They continued arguing back and forth and asking their leader what they should do. They couldn't find him.

The leader, along with four other people, was readying themselves to escape.

The small group of five had worked toward the door. When the smoke covered their exit, they ran to one of the cars. They managed to get inside and get it started. They took off.

Mark called Haliday and told him the men were escaping. Haliday took three of his men with him and they jumped into the Tahoe and took off after these guys. He wanted payback.

The gang started threading their way through the streets with Haliday charging was after them. The gang took a turn and headed down a street where the leader had to lock up the brakes. Stalled cars at the end blocked their path.

The leader tried to wedge his car through, but could not make it. He started to back up and turn around.

Haliday pulled up toward the end of the short street and blocked it. He and his three men got out and laid down fire.

The gang had gotten out and was now using their car for cover. They could not escape down the street. They would have been gunned down for sure.

Haliday kept yelling at them to give up.

The gang refused.

The firing continued. A couple of Haliday's group had made their way with Brad's Jeep toward the building. Two of them climbed up onto the roof using a fire escape ladder in the back.

One of the men with Haliday tried to run to another position to get a better angle. The gang fired on him. He didn't stand a chance and dropped immediately.

In a matter of moments a second story window shattered onto the ground below, followed by a chair tumbling down onto the concrete. Haliday was surprised and took aim to fire at the window.

Haliday saw a pistol aimed down at the car and saw the muzzle flashes from the barrel. The gang reeled around and looked up. All of a sudden the men on the rooftop fired down on them as well.

The entire group was decimated. None of them had survived. Haliday received an "All clear" from his men on the roof.

Jimmy heard a voice yell out.

"You up there! Come on out with your hands up!"

From his window, Jimmy loaded his pistol magazines. He heard the voice from outside a couple more times.

"Come on out! You're safe!"

Jimmy sat there for a minute. He yelled out the broken window, "OK, I'm coming down!"

Jimmy went down the stairs and exited the building with his hands in the air. He still had his pistol in his coat pocket. He had loaded magazines as well. He walked out into the street.

Haliday walked up to him with an AR15 at low ready. He looked Jimmy over. "Put your hands down, but don't get stupid."

Jimmy lowered his hands. "Who are you guys?"

"Just a small janitorial squad, you could say," Haliday told him.

Jimmy looked at him with an odd expression on his face.

"We're cleaning up the scumbags in the region," Haliday said.

Jimmy nodded once to indicate he understood.

"My name is Roger Haliday." He lowered his rifle and extended his hand.

Jimmy was surprised. Here he was, looking like the lowest form of life on earth after his personal trials to survive, and this complete stranger was offering his hand. "James Kent, sir."

"Don't call me sir. I was an NCO and worked for a living," Haliday said.

A few more people gathered around. A couple still had rifles at the ready.

"Thank you, by the way," Haliday said.

"You're welcome, and I prefer Jimmy," Jimmy answered.

The rest of the people in Haliday's group told Jimmy thank you as well. Jimmy felt good. He had made an impact and helped these people.

"No offense, Jimmy, but you look like something that just came out of a dog's ass," Haliday said.

Jimmy looked down at the ground.

"Raise your head, soldier," Haliday said. He had noticed Jimmy's dog tags hanging outside of his shirt.

Jimmy looked up at Haliday.

"You did a hell of a job. I can't begin to understand what you have been through. I apologize, Jimmy," Haliday said.

He told Jimmy to follow him. They went over to the Tahoe.

Jimmy recognized the SUV. This was the one leading the Deuce he had seen earlier.

"We still have some work to do, over at the apartment complex. The rest of this group actually," Haliday said.

"Why would that be, sir?" Jimmy asked.

"Call me Roger, please," Haliday said.

Jimmy looked at him.

Haliday said, "We don't want you to get involved. This is our business. But when we are done, we would like to give you some supplies for helping us out."

At first Jimmy protested. He insisted that he would be okay. Haliday told him that he would not take no for an answer. Jimmy relented after 10 minutes of arguing. He wasn't sure if he liked Haliday, but he already respected him.

Jimmy asked if he could retrieve his supplies. Haliday said to go ahead and sent two men to help him. They returned with Jimmy's belongings. Haliday eyed what little Jimmy had.

Jimmy said, "They burned down the theater where I was staying. I lost almost everything."

239

"We saw it smoldering earlier. Don't worry about it, Jimmy. I'm going to make sure you get what you need," Haliday said.

Haliday tried to start the Tahoe. It wouldn't start. Nothing happened when he turned the key. He got out and looked it over. There were quite a few bullet holes in it. Haliday popped the hood and looked at it.

Jimmy poked his head under the hood as well. "You have a Leatherman, and some tape?" he asked.

Haliday handed Jimmy a Leatherman tool and dug out some duct tape.

Jimmy worked on a few wires for a couple of minutes. "Go try it now."

"OK, will do," said Haliday.

Haliday climbed behind the wheel and turned the key. The Tahoe started right away. "Get in, Jimmy."

Haliday's group drove back to the apartment building to finish the operation.

After a couple of hours it was over. Haliday's group had continued to fire on those who were left. After an hour of convincing, the rest of the gang finally gave up.

Haliday's group had cleared the building and made arrangements for the prisoners and wounded to be picked up.

Jimmy walked up to him. "That was some seriously mess up crap, sir."

He started to speak again and Haliday held his index finger up. "Hold on, Jimmy," he said and then walked away.

Jimmy was caught off-guard. He turned around to find Brad was standing there.

Brad said, "No offense, Jimmy. He needs a few minutes. He just lost his nephew last night."

Jimmy watched as Haliday walked over to his nephew's covered body.

Haliday knelt down beside him. Kayla and Kevin walked over and knelt down, too. All three had tears in their eyes. Mark met Haliday and placed a hand on his shoulder.

"Go ahead on, Roger," he said. "We'll bring him home. Take the Jeep and we'll use the Tahoe."

Haliday stood up and thanked Mark. Kayla and Kevin joined him and then went and sat in the Jeep.

Haliday got on the radio and talked to Crothall. When he was finished, he walked over to Jimmy, who was still standing there. "Jimmy, I have a proposition for you."

"What's that?" Jimmy asked.

Haliday said, "The military is about to start distributing aid. They have some bases and outposts set up. They need some good mechanics."

Jimmy said, "I don't know."

Haliday said, "Jimmy, you deserve the chance. They'll provide you with shelter and food in exchange for work. You'll earn pay as well. I don't know how much, or even what, but it'll be something."

"Where at, sir?"

"Selfridge or the outpost in Bad Axe."

"Where will you be?"

"Bad Axe area, Jimmy."

"That's where I'll go," Jimmy answered.

Haliday called Brad over and explained what was going on. He told Brad to let Jimmy get some clothes out of the apartments along with anything else he needed.

"I'd take you myself, Jimmy," Haliday said, looking toward his nephew's body, "but I have something to do."

"Thank you, sir."

Haliday shook his hand and looked him in the eye. "Jimmy, you've been through all types of hell. You survived what most people could not. You persevered. When you were down, you rose up and came through for us. It's me who should be thanking you. Thank you, Jimmy."

Haliday started walking away, and then turned and looked back at Jimmy still standing next to Brad. "Be proud of yourself, son; you've not only earned it, you deserve it." He turned and walked away.

Chapter 19

Haliday, Kayla, and Kevin walked through the door. Rich was sitting at the kitchen table waiting.

Bev came walking over. "Where's the rest?" she asked.

Haliday said, "They're on the way home, Mom. Have a seat."

"What's going on?"

Sarah walked up and looked at her brother Kevin. She could tell immediately that he'd had been crying. She started to cry. He hugged her. Bev started to tear up as well.

Alan and David were on security detail. The rest of the group had made their way to the kitchen area.

Haliday looked at everyone. They all knew what was coming next. "Mark and Blake are bringing Randy home."

"How bad is it?" Bev asked.

"I'm sorry, Mom," Haliday answered.

Everyone was tearing up at the words. This was now their second loss. They heard the Tahoe pull up.

Mark and Blake walked in and Mark walked over to Haliday. "Roger, where do you want us to put Randy?"

"Let me get some clean clothes and stuff. I'll meet you guys in the pole barn. We'll clean and dress him in those," Haliday said.

David and Alan were relieved by Dawn and Karen. Rich told them what had happened. Mark's father, Bill, went outside and into the pole barn. He started the old backhoe.

He took the backhoe down to the corner of the property. He paused for a few minutes and looked at his wife Linda's grave. He then started digging the grave for Randy.

The top six inches of soil was cold and hard. Bill struggled, even with the backhoe. After he broke through, the digging was a little easier. He managed to get a five-foot-deep hole dug.

Haliday and Mark brought Randy down wrapped in a blanket. Haliday got down in the hole and laid Randy down inside it. Mark helped Haliday climb out.

Haliday, Bill, Mark, and Blake covered Randy. They mounded the dirt of the grave. Haliday looked up in the direction of the cabin and waved the group coming out down to the grave site.

Bev had brought the Bible down and Haliday read the same passages he had read for Linda. Everyone except Sarah, Kevin, and Haliday walked back to the cabin.

Haliday hugged them both and told him how sorry he was. He looked down at the grave for a few somber moments, and then walked back up to the cabin. Kevin and Sarah stayed for almost two hours before they came back up to the cabin.

Haliday showered and changed and then sat by the fireplace. He was quiet the rest of the day. He had left a note by the ham. When his sister called, he would need to be the one to tell her what had happened.

She would be heartbroken. Any mother would be. Haliday thought it over and over. He wished he had never taken on the role of cleaning up the area for the military.

He tried to justify it. He told himself it was either take the fight to them or defend the home once again. He told himself he

244

should have let the military do it. He told himself a lot of things. It was a harsh lesson in reality.

He sat alone in the chair by the fireplace. He drifted off to sleep and awoke almost every hour. He thought about Randy, the event, the country, and would then drift off to sleep again.

Around six in the morning, Mark's wife, Lisa, woke Haliday up. "You're wanted on the radio," she said.

"OK, thank you." He got up and stretched. He was pretty stiff from sleeping in the chair. He noticed it was a bit cooler in the cabin. He threw a couple of logs on the fire place and then threw some wood in the wood burner as well.

He walked over to the radio.

Blake was sitting there. "It's Dennis."

"Dennis, it's me, Roger. What's going on?" Haliday said, taking a seat.

"Sorry to hear about your nephew."

"Thank you."

Dennis said, "I'm heading into town for a meeting. They are going to discuss the camps, ask for volunteers. Explain what's going on and everything."

"OK, good. Can you ask a few questions?"

"What would that be?"

Haliday said, "Ask them about the form of government and who is in charge right now. Then ask them about the aid distribution and how often it will be handed out. See if you can find out if they have groups conducting police activities or paramilitary activities in the area."

"Is there anything else?" Dennis asked.

"See what type of work they want the volunteers to do. Ask them about U.S. currency and if it's worth anything. Hell, ask them anything you can think of," Haliday told him.

"OK, I'll let you know what I find out and get back to you later this afternoon."

Haliday got up and walked into the kitchen. Diana was in there trying to get herself a bowl of oatmeal. The brace made it

245

difficult. It didn't help that the oatmeal was too thick this morning.

He walked over and helped her. "You want some bananas in it?"

"No, honey," she said.

He looked at her with a smirk on his face. "I didn't think you cared."

"Bee honey, I don't eat bee honey," Diana said.

He laughed. "Yeah, yeah, yeah."

The bananas were packed with honey on them, but he'd forgot that detail. He finished up fixing her oatmeal.

He walked over to Dawn where she was sitting down at the table eating. "Go ahead and help her take that brace off later," he said.

"OK, I will," Dawn said.

Rich came in. "Good morning everyone," he said.

"Good morning, Dad," Haliday said.

Over the next 15 minutes everyone else woke up and came down for breakfast. The conversation was filled with nothing but small talk. After breakfast they all went about their daily chores and routines.

Haliday went outside to the pole barn. He spent some time not doing much more than tinkering around with things. He was just trying to occupy himself. Kayla came in.

"Aunt Susan is on the radio, Dad," she said.

Haliday walked back with her to the cabin with his arm around her shoulder. "This is going to be hard, kiddo."

"I know, Dad."

"I don't know what to tell her," he admitted.

Kayla said, "Just tell her the truth."

Haliday made it to the radio. He sat down and took a deep breath. He looked around. Rich, Bev, Kayla, Kevin, and Sarah were the only ones there. Everyone else had given them their privacy.

"Susan, it's Roger."

"Hey, little brother. What's new?" Susan said.

"Susan, I don't know how to tell you this... I hate to have to say this, but we lost Randy yesterday," he said.

There were a couple moments of silence. "I don't understand," Susan finally said.

He explained that they were in the midst of the operation and Randy had tried to get closer so that the group could gain an advantage. He told her that this last group was well-trained and had the advantage. He explained that they were ready to back off, but Randy could not get out fast enough; the gang had started firing. Randy was able to buy the rest of them more time.

He told her they did the best they could.

Susan did not really respond.

He got up and put Kevin on the radio.

After that, Sarah, Bev, and Rich talked to her for a couple of minutes.

After the radio call, Haliday sat back down by the fireplace.

Mark came up to him. "You know the, odds Roger."

"Yeah, and we've both lost to those odds haven't we?"

Kayla walked over. "Dad, it's the radio again."

Haliday got up once again and went over to the radio. "Roger here."

Sgt. Edwards was on this time. "Sorry to hear about your nephew," he said.

"Thank you. How can I help you guys?" Haliday asked.

"There's a meeting at the airport tomorrow at 0700 hours. Can you be there?"

"Sure thing," Haliday answered.

After the call, Haliday told Mark he could go; everyone else would be staying behind. There would be no chances taken. He was not going to lose anyone else right now.

He was just about to get up when he heard Dennis over the radio. "Roger, it's Dennis."

"Dennis, what do you have?" Haliday asked.

247

Dennis responded with, "Not a lot. They were very vague in answering questions. But hear me out and I'll tell you what I have heard."

Dennis told him that the government structure was the same as the one Haliday had been told. However, the prefects were all being brought in from the outside. No one local was being chosen.

Next, he told him about the currency. The government claimed to have records of bank accounts and that was it. They said they were working on a plan to distribute currency in an effective manner. That was all they said.

What Dennis said next was very surprising. The government would be laying claim to any and all assets not directly claimed by people or their next of kin within a one year period.

That was odd. That was a lot of money, cars, homes, and land—not to mention all of the various equipment, contents or whatever else was left.

The government said it would need the assets to recoup all of the funds that were needed in the recovery efforts. To Haliday it sounded like the Big Brother conspiracy.

The people were told that volunteers would be housed at the camps. They would be paid in credits that would eventually be redeemed for currency. What specific tasks they would perform was left out of the equation. When someone asked what jobs were open they were told, mechanics, electricians, cooks, laborers, and other basic jobs. Nothing specific was mentioned. They were told specifics would be discussed when people were designated to the different work teams.

Some people would be relocated to other camps in order to properly distribute labor during the relief efforts. These people would be compensated for their property. Returning would not be allowed. The government said the logistics were too difficult to handle that.

Distribution points were being readied. Initially, aid would last until early spring. After that the distribution centers would be closed and only those in the camps would continue to receive aid after that.

Everyone was expected to use the shuttles and government transportation to go to a camp. They would receive their new government IDs. They said they were going to set a date. You would have to do it by that date.

"Roger, that's about all I heard," Dennis said.

Haliday was surprised by another voice on the radio.

"Same here at Fort Custer," Bruce said.

"Nice to hear from you, Bruce," Haliday said.

"Roger, just so you know, I'm not going back anytime soon. I don't trust them at all," Bruce added.

"I agree, it sounds quite odd. I would think things might be handled differently," Haliday told him.

Dennis said, "I have not decided yet. We might be able to make it to the spring here. I think that's what we might do."

"OK, guys. Keep in touch. Let me know if you see or hear anything different," Haliday said.

He had serious doubts now. He'd need to see what was going on tomorrow at the airport. After that he might be changing his tune.

He checked his watch. He had an early morning shift for security from four a.m. to six a.m. He decided to go to bed early, so he said goodnight and went up to his bunk.

When he woke up he got dressed and went up to the crow's nest and relieved his brother Alan. Alan didn't say much. He just went down and went to bed. Haliday almost took it personally.

It was close to six a.m. when he heard a vehicle off in the distance. With few vehicles on the road and no ambient noise, it was easy to hear things. The noise was to the west of him.

Mark pulled up in the Tahoe and Haliday went up and climbed in.

When they pulled up to the gate, Haliday said, "Hang a right Mark."

Mark took a right-hand turn and drove down the road until Haliday told him to take another right.

At the next intersection Mark took yet another right-hand turn. He stopped the Tahoe next to a Humvee. The Humvee was empty.

Haliday said, "Hold on a minute Mark."

He got out of the Tahoe and walked over to the Humvee. He pulled out a knife and gouged the tread of the rear tire and took off a large chunk of it. He got back in the Tahoe and told Mark to head to the airport.

"What do you think they are up to?" Mark asked.

"I honestly don't know."

"They have to think we are up to something."

"Well, I agree, but I couldn't tell you what," Haliday agreed.

They pulled up to the gate at the airport. The gate was heavily secured. Two soldiers approached the Tahoe. Two more soldiers kept weapons trained on Haliday and Mark.

One soldier approached Mark. "IDs, please," he said.

Mark looked at Haliday, then back at the soldier and said, "No."

"No National ID, no entry," the soldier said.

Haliday bent forward and looked at the soldier to see that he was an E-2, a private. "Where do we get a National ID?" he asked.

"Inside the admin building."

"Where is the admin building, Private?"

The soldier pointed in to the compound at the admin building. Mark and Haliday were both familiar with it.

"Can I ask you a question, Private?" Haliday said.

"Yes, sir, go ahead," the soldier replied.

"How can we go in and get our National ID if we need a National ID to enter in the first place?"

The soldier stood quiet for a moment as he thought about it. He looked at Haliday and Mark and then told them to hold on a minute. He walked over to a radio and spoke to someone inside for a minute.

He walked back over to the Tahoe. "OK, we need you to leave your weapons with us. Then proceed to the admin building," the soldier said.

Mark and Haliday looked at each other again.

"We're leaving, Private," Mark said. He put the Tahoe in reverse and started backing up. He backed up and pulled off to the side. A Humvee pulled up to the gate as they sat there.

Haliday watched the Humvee pull in and park near the admin building. He told Mark to head back to the cabin. Mark was about to pull onto the road when one of the soldiers walked over to the Tahoe.

"Sgt. Edwards wants to see you guys," the soldier said.

Mark put the Tahoe in drive and then pulled up next to the admin building. He and Haliday got out and started up a short set of steps.

A soldier was at the door. "ID, please," he said.

Haliday was about to go ballistic when Edwards walked up.

"They're OK, soldier," Edwards said. "Why don't you two follow me?" he added.

Haliday and Mark followed.

They went into a conference room. Already seated inside were Brad and Rob. Both had an ID clipped to their clothing. Haliday looked at Edwards and noted he had one as well.

"First thing we need to do is get you two a ID cards," Edwards said.

"Not going to happen any time soon, Sergeant," Haliday said.

"Look, Roger, everyone is going to get one eventually," Edwards told him.

"Then I'll wait until eventually gets here," Haliday said.

The two of them just stared at each other for a couple of minutes, each one waiting for the other to give. Haliday just looked at Edwards, canted his head, and spread his arms in a *what?* gesture.

"You are an insufferable son of a bitch," Edwards said.

"Now that that point is settled, let's get down to business," Haliday said.

251

Edwards said, "The prefect for this area will arrive in about one week."

Rob looked over at Edwards. "What do you mean? I thought I was going to be the prefect."

"The government thought it would be best to bring in an outsider; someone with a fresh view and no ties to the area. To make sure everything is as fair as possible," Edwards replied.

"What the hell do you mean *fair*?" Rob asked.

Edwards said, "To make sure the community all gets a fair share of resources."

"Sounds like bullshit to me," Rob said.

Brad asked, "What is your definition of fair?"

Edwards was obviously feeling extremely uncomfortable right now. He was the messenger and was about to be shot.

Haliday said, "I'm rather curious as well."

"Look," Edwards said, "we have to make sure there's no hoarding, no gouging, and that everyone gets what he needs."

"Exactly how long is this *fair* going to last?" Rob asked.

"Well, however long it takes to get the infrastructure back in place," Edwards replied.

"So let us get this straight: We raise crops, and you take and distribute them as you see fit?" Rob asked.

"You'll get paid for time," Edwards said.

"Paid what?" Brad asked.

"You'll get pay and rations like everyone else," Edwards said.

"And the profits?" Brad asked.

Edwards was squirming now. He said, "There won't be any profiting until the infrastructure is sound."

Haliday stood up. "Let's go Mark."

Mark stood up.

"Where you going?" Edwards asked.

"We are not going to sit here and listen to this crap," Haliday said.

Brad stood up as well. Rob stood next. Both tossed their ID cards on to the table.

252

"You guys are blowing this out of proportion," Edwards said.

Haliday walked over and stood six inches from Edwards' face. "Listen here, shithead. You do whatever the hell you want with the people who volunteer," he said pointedly. "You do whatever the hell you want with their land if they surrender it to you. You lay claim to whatever abandoned property and equipment you want to. But you even begin to think about taking anything from anyone who doesn't want you to or you will be among the first to find out what a bad idea it was."

He, Mark, Brad, and Rob all walked out and went over to the Tahoe. A few of the soldiers were watching them. Haliday quietly reached down and took his rifle off of safe. Mark had already done so.

Rob said, "You know that's a death wish, right?"

"Sure is, but I won't go down without a fight," Haliday said.

Edwards walked outside and went over by a Humvee and talked to one of the soldiers next to it.

Haliday walked that way, stopped, and looked at the rear tire. He held his hand out and said, "Here."

The soldier held his hand out.

Haliday dropped a chunk of tire tread in it. He looked at Edwards and said, "We can't win, but we can make it hard on a few of you. Keep them away."

Edwards said, "Haliday, you have it all wrong."

Haliday didn't even pause to listen. He kept walking away. He told Brad and Rob to get in their Bronco and follow him. In minutes they left the airport.

Haliday took a few turns on the city streets. He spotted an old shoe store and pulled over. He, Mark, Rob, and Brad all went inside.

There were shoes all over the place. Haliday looked around. "No Jordans or LeBron James left here," he said.

"Who owns this store anyway?" Mark asked.

"Johnson, but he died. So did his wife," Brad said.

"So according to Edwards, this will all become government property. That is if no next of kin claims it within a year," Mark said.

Rob said, "Their relatives might."

"Not a chance in hell," Haliday said.

"I agree," Brad said.

The four of them sat around and talked for almost two hours. The biggest topic of discussion was the fact that the government was hell bent on turning the country into a socialistic state—much like the USSR had been.

"Comrade Citizen, thank you for your wheat production. The collective will be stronger with it," Haliday said.

They all chuckled. Each and every one of them wanted to help others, but there was a fine line between helping and handouts. Fair trade meant exactly that: Fair *trade*.

If someone did not have an item to trade, then labor would most likely earn them what they wanted. Wheat for corn, apples for fish, beef for chicken, food for clothing, work for any of the above. It was how the country started. It was the American way.

The toughest part came next. They had to figure out how they would all be able to survive and make it through. Any hope of government help was just shattered.

Rob said, "You think we made a mistake?"

Brad said, "Not to sound like a cliché, but I'd rather die a free man than allow the government to own me."

Haliday said, "I'm not certain the government is going to make it. There's a lot of crap going on that we don't know about yet. I don't think we made a mistake yet, but we have some more work ahead of us, guys."

He handed Brad a book and explained how to use it for code. The radio would now be monitored by the military. The military and government would not be very happy with them now.

Brad and Rob stayed for a few minutes to talk after Haliday and Mark left to go back to the cabin. When they arrived, they filled the group in on what had transpired.

Chapter 20

Haliday's head was pounding. He had a migraine. It had been a few days since the meeting with Rob and Brad at the airport. Crothall had made attempts to contact him on the radio, but he had ignored them.

He kept in contact with Brad, who was feeding him as much information about the airport and government as possible. A few of the townspeople were discontent with the government's objective. On the other hand, some could not wait to volunteer.

The general mood of everyone else in the cabin was dim. Practically everything that had happened since the EMP seemed to have been for nothing.

The injuries—and more importantly, the loss—of loved ones were far more devastating now. Haliday second-guessed every decision he had made. He wasn't sure what to do next. He gathered everybody around for a meeting.

"Listen up, everybody. We are going to have to figure out what direction we are going to take," he said. "By that, I mean we need to understand the government's objective and how we fit in with that."

Rich asked, "Do you have anything in mind?"

"No, I don't," Haliday said, "but this is going to be a decision we all make together. We'll talk about it more at a later time. I want all of you to think it through first. Right now we need to secure as much fuel as possible. I want every single gas container we have available to be filled. This includes the underground tank."

"Are we leaving?" Bev asked.

"No, we just need to be ready to though. We also need to prep a trailer with supplies, just in case," Haliday added.

He was about to continue when Alan called down from the crow's nest. "We have company on the way!"

"Who is it?" Haliday asked.

"Looks like the military and they have some black buses with them," Alan said.

Haliday said, "Everyone gear up and grab your weapons. Get the kids down into the basement. Diana, you keep an eye on them. Sheila, help Diana."

Haliday grabbed his rifle and went outside. He could hear the vehicles coming down the road. He turned around to look for Mark to see that he was on his way up to the crow's nest with the Barrett sniper rifle. He had the M24 up there as well.

Everyone in Haliday's group scrambled to take up a defensive position. They were all in place by the time the vehicles pulled up to the cabin's gate. Haliday had his rifle at low ready.

Slowly approached the vehicles. There were three Humvees, two Deuce and half trucks, and two old school buses painted black.

Haliday could see inside the buses and saw people in civilian clothes. He made a swift study of the convoy and noted that the gun turrets on the Humvees were scanning back and forth. Troops had dismounted the vehicles and were all standing on guard.

Haliday just stood where he was. *This dance again, huh*, he thought to himself. He lowered his rifle and let it hang there.

Two soldiers walked up to him. Haliday did a head count as they approached.

He counted 11 soldiers. The Deuce's and the buses had other people inside of them; drivers and helpers, he assumed. They were wearing gray pants and had black parkas on, six total. None were armed.

The two soldiers were now standing in front of Haliday. As soon as one of them started to talk, Haliday held his finger to his mouth. "Shh." He looked to the sky.

He waited just a minute and heard the helicopter. He looked back down at the soldiers and said, "I wouldn't feel right without knowing you had my buddy in the Cobra close by."

The two soldiers looked at each other as if they had expected the smartass comment. One of them said, "Sir, we are here to offer all of you transportation to the camps."

"No thank you," Haliday said.

"Sir, you have to show us that you capable of living out here or you have to come with us."

Haliday looked at him and said, "Do you know who Sam Elliot is?"

"An actor," was the reply.

Haliday said, "Then you'll understand this saying: 'You must be a special kind of stupid.'"

The soldier became flustered.

Haliday could tell the young man was getting mad. The soldier opened his mouth to speak, but he cut him off before he could utter a single word. "You can't even be serious. You can't tell me that after looking around here you even have that question in your head."

"We're under orders to list an address with a quick inventory of the household's number of people and their supplies," the soldier said.

Haliday saw the clipboard in the soldier's hand. "I'll fill your form out, save you some time."

The soldier handed him the clipboard.

Haliday wrote a few things down and handed the clipboard back to him.

The soldier looked at it and said, "You really are an ass."

He showed it to the other soldier with him. It read, "Roger's cabin, lots of people, enough stuff to live, go away now."

The second soldier chuckled, then turned and just walked back toward the small convoy. "Let's go."

The first soldier just eyed Haliday a bit. After a moment, he turned and rejoined the convoy as well.

As the soldiers mounted their vehicles, Haliday looked at the windows on the buses. He was horrified by what he saw. The images reminded him of concentration camp pictures he had seen in his history classes.

The people were unkempt. Their faces were hollow and their eyes seemed lifeless. It was a haunting image. The convoy pulled away and left the area.

Haliday just stood there.

He was still looking down the road as the vehicles drove away.

Kayla walked up next to him. "What's wrong, Dad?"

He turned and looked at her. "Did you see the people on the buses?"

"No, Dad. Why?"

"They were different than the people we've encountered so far."

"I don't understand, Dad."

He said, "These people were knocking on death's door. They were emaciated. I've never seen anything like it on our own soil. I still can't believe it. I can't even begin to imagine what they have been through."

The people that he had seen were indeed different. These people were from the more urban areas of the region. They didn't have the farms to rely on for any wheat or corn or storage of other crops. Their scavenging skills were put to the test, but they had been unable to provide enough sustenance for themselves and their families. In some cases they relied on what they had at home, which was not enough.

In other cases they moved from one location to another trying to seek food and supplies. They had survived as long as they could. The camps were their last chance to live. Haliday could not fault them for that.

He and Kayla walked back up to the cabin. He told everyone to go ahead and return to their meeting. "That's exactly why we need to get ready to leave," he told them all. "I can tell you this much. We don't stand a snowball's chance in hell against them. If they decide to waltz in here, we are done for sure."

"Where the hell are we going to go?" Karen asked.

"I'm not sure. We don't have a Plan B yet. I'm open for suggestions," he added.

Rich said, "What about going home?"

Mark said, "I don't think that's a good idea. If the military doesn't have control of the major cities, your houses are more dangerous."

"I thought they had the suburbs under control," David said.

"No, not even close," Mark said.

Bev asked, 'So we're screwed?"

Haliday's head was about to explode now. He didn't have the answers the group wanted. He didn't have a plan to keep them safe. He had underestimated the government's response to a major SHTF event.

Here they were, in their bug out location, having to consider moving. This was far from optimal. There was nowhere they could go. Other than setting up tents somewhere, they could not think of any other options.

They all agreed on one thing, however; they would avoid a fight with the military at all costs. They would not allow the government to ambush them, draw them into a fight at the cabin or anything else. They would retreat if it came down to it.

Mark asked Haliday, "Did you find it odd that they pulled up right to the cabin?"

"I did."

"You know they intended to do that right?"

"Yeah, I know. I think it's their turn to play mind games with us."

Blake walked up and said, "Brad's on the radio for you Roger."

Mark said to Haliday, "Stay put, old man. I'll get it."

Haliday thought about that comment. At 46 years old, he was indeed an old man under these circumstances. If he was still in the service he would be riding a desk. He was taking a beating physically and mentally. Had he known how physically demanding it really was he would have put more effort into a steady physical fitness routine that was more demanding.

Mark sat down at the radio. "Brad, it's Mark."

Brad said, "Hi, Mark. I'm just using the open frequency because the information I have is general knowledge. Or, at least it will be soon."

"What do you have?"

"The roadblocks are now under military control."

"They moved in troops?" Mark asked.

"They did more than that."

"I'm all ears."

Brad went on to explain everything. The military had brought in troops to replace the volunteers at the roadblock. The troops used the trailers the first day they had taken over. On the second day, the trailers were moved off to the side of the road. Each of the two roadblocks received an armored guard booth complete with a large metal gate arm.

The troops left the logs in place on the approaches from the south. The northern approaches then received the same type of log barriers. There were two Humvees at each roadblock. These had been up-armored and had M2s in the turrets. Brad wasn't sure how many troops were stationed at each roadblock, but it didn't matter.

It was certain that they were well-armed. More than likely they had M203 grenade launchers, M249 machine guns, and M136 AT4 Anti-Armor weapons, which were portable, shoulder fired rocket launchers. They would certainly be able to control any of the traffic that went in or out of the area. They would effectively be able to resist any attempts to attack the booths.

Brad said that two more checkpoints had been added to the west. This allowed access to the Saginaw and Bay City areas. These roadblocks were out of Haliday and Brad's area.

The remaining roads had all been blocked. Essentially this separated the upper Thumb area. As control of the southern areas was gained, the roadblocks would either be moved or eliminated.

In either case, the Thumb could act independently. The area was rich for crops. The woods were sparse, but provided more than enough wood for fireplaces and wood burning stoves. They had the small airport and a few other small runways in the area. For helicopters it was ideal. They even had water resources surrounding the entire region except for the southern border.

This had been why Haliday originally selected the area. It was close enough to reach rather quickly. It was far enough away to eliminate the hordes of people in the large cities. The area also provided all of the resources they would need.

"That's all kinds of good news, Brad," Mark said.

"It gets better, Mark."

"How is that?"

"You have to have the National ID card to move between the check points."

"It just keeps getting better," Mark said.

"Actually, you have to have the ID card, period. If you get stopped anywhere, you must show it," Brad said.

"OK, thanks for calling, Brad. I'll tell Roger," Mark said.

"One more thing, Mark; we plan to get our IDs just to avoid any of the BS," Brad added.

"I agree it's a good idea; I just have to convince Roger and the rest of the group," Mark said. "Have a good night, Brad."

*****

261

While Haliday was contemplating his plans, Adam was doing the same thing. The thugs outside of his home had his group worried. The group of thugs looked liked it had increased in size. Adam's best count now put the gang at around 40 people.

He hadn't seen anyone else on his street in the past few days. His group split the security watches into 12-hour shifts. Anyone who was trained and could use a fire arm was expected to help stand guard.

His group had changed shifts at seven p.m. The off-going shift ate dinner and relaxed before going to bed at nine p.m. One of the group members fed the wood burner stove. They had two more days' worth of wood in the attached garage.

Adam looked outside at the woodpile. The homes in the area were too close for comfort. Retrieving more wood was going to be a dangerous job. As he studied the woodpile and the surrounding landscape, he could not help but to curse under his breath. There were a lot of areas from which they could be attacked.

The neighbors' homes, sheds, and bushes all provided great concealment. If the thugs had any sense, they would be waiting in those areas. Based on the ruse they used to get into the neighbor's house down the street, he assumed this is what they had planned.

In his area, the radio announcements had told people to move toward central pick up locations. Most of these were common intersections. In the suburbs, it would be too hard to go house to house right now. They were told that once officials had enough volunteers, house to house operations would commence. They did not have the required amount of manpower right now.

Adam was hoping that maybe the thugs would give in. He hoped maybe they would take the opportunity to move into the camps. There, they could probably set up shop, almost like a prison gang.

Now there was a thought. He figured some type of group would try and rule the camps somehow, but the military and government would probably put a stop to it. On the other hand, if prisons were truly an example, they might *not* put a stop to it.

That idea was farfetched. This group was living like royalty. They stole jewelry, cash, silver, gold, and anything of value. The food and supplies they took sustained them.

Adam was still deep in thought when one of his group members called him over. He went over to a window and took a quick look. It looked like five people were making their way toward Adam's house.

They were moving slowly and seeking cover as they approached. They all appeared armed with rifles. Occasionally the men would stop and talk amongst themselves. They split into different directions.

Adam told everyone to keep an eye out and report what they saw.

The group of men started moving even slower now, stopping often.

Once in a while Adam caught a glimpse of a flashlight. The light didn't move though. Adam tried to figure it out. They would move, then stop, and he would see a glimpse of the light.

"They're mapping the area," Adam's brother told him.

"Why not do it during the daylight?" Adam asked.

"Because if they did it during the daylight, it would be far more obvious as to what they were doing. We would see them with paper and pens."

Adam and his group watched the men recon Adam's house over the next few hours. When the men were done, they returned to the house down the street.

Adam went down to his office where his ham was located. He pulled out a large sheet of paper and pinned it to a nearby bulletin board. He looked it over.

He called his brother and a few others over to his office. They all looked at the paper. As part of Adam's bug in plan, he too had mapped out the area surrounding his house.

He knew the size of the houses around him. He also knew the size of the sheds and any other permanent objects around him. He had a rough idea of the height of the objects and the distances.

When he had started mapping the objects, he'd used a range finder from his golf bag. He just explained to his neighbors that he was playing with his new golf toy. He would relay the distances to his wife using his Bluetooth headset and she would write the information down.

What they needed to do now was to analyze the small map and look for the obvious points of aggression. If things worked out okay, they could use their knowledge as an advantage.

"Let's see if we can get some more wood in here," Adam said.

"You think it's safe?" Adams's brother Ronald, asked.

"We didn't see anyone else out there. We should be OK to get some people out and grab another days worth," Adam said.

The woodpile was in the back of the yard. The neighbors always complained about it. The pile was large enough to supply Adam for six months. This would get them through any winter periods. The neighbors always said he had too much. They said he only needed a face cord. He could always have more delivered. They said it was an eyesore and that it detracted from the value of their homes. They didn't know the intended use. He always just shrugged it off and told them he liked fires in his fireplace.

He didn't have room for any more and didn't store much in his garage prior to the EMP. Storing that much in a garage would allow too many rodents to invade his home.

He got a group together and they made their move. In a matter of only 10 minutes they managed 30 pieces of wood. This was good enough for now and was all the risk they were willing to take at the moment.

Adam decided he would work on the problem in the morning. He was tired and having a problem thinking rationally. In the morning, he would give Roger Haliday a call and see if he had any ideas.

Adam went to bed and made a mental list of what he needed to do. He finally managed to doze off.

When he woke up in the morning he ate breakfast and then called Haliday.

"Roger, it's Adam," he said.

"Adam, it's good to hear from you. How are you holding out?" Haliday said.

Adam replied, "We're not doing very well at the moment. The gang that's down the street is starting to give us problems. I'm pretty sure they plan to come at us soon."

"You don't sound too confident in being able to fend them off."

"I'm not. They have some pretty good vantage points. We knew staying here was a risk. We didn't expect this large of a group to come at us. Have any ideas?" Adam asked.

"Adam, I probably could not tell you anything you don't already know. Keep the high ground, keep concealment and cover, and try to keep the element of surprise," Haliday said.

"I figured as much, but thank you."

"What exactly are they up to?"

Adam said, "Last night they mapped out the area. We have it mapped out, too, not that it will do any good."

"Have you thought about catching them in a crossfire?"

"What do you mean?"

"I don't know your layout or anything, but here is an idea. It's a long shot. Maybe try and get some shooters out in the houses nearby. Once the shooting starts they can fire from their vantage points," Haliday said.

"That's an idea, but how are the guys going to get back to safety? Or what if the gang turns on them?"

"Scratch that idea, Adam. I'm at a loss here. Sorry," Haliday said.

Adam said, "We thought of bugging out, but there are too many of us. We couldn't move enough supplies, and wouldn't know where to go."

"Wish I could help, but we're in the same boat. The situation here is getting tense. We no longer have the support of the military or government. We might have to bug out ourselves."

"Seems like we are both in a bind."

Haliday said, "Adam, I'm going to give you my address in Shelby Township. You are more than welcome to use the house.

It might be a better option than where you are. If you can make it to the Bad Axe airport, then we can try and get you set-up around here. I know it's a long shot, but we'll help as much as we can."

Adam asked, "The last time you spoke to the military, did they mention how long it would take to secure the cities?"

"Last I heard, they weren't even close."

"Thank you, Roger. Good luck to you." Adam said.

"Good luck to you, too, Adam."

Adam sat back in his chair and thought about things. His group had some tough decisions to make. Unfortunately, he didn't have much time to make those decisions.

He checked the windows and looked around outside. He could see the gang moving around. He also noticed that it was starting to snow. It was a heavy snowfall and the first major snowfall of the year.

Adam talked to everyone in his group. Right now they had to stay put and put up their best fight.

They spent the day making preparations around the house.

Chapter 21

The next day, Haliday checked in with Adam. Adam's luck was holding out. The gang had yet to make a move on his house. It had been three days since they mapped the area. Once in a while Adam's group noticed a few people doing walk-by reconnaissance.

Haliday went out and started the Tahoe and pulled it up to the cabin. His parents, Rich and Bev, got in along with his brother, Alan, Alan's wife Marie, and their two children. Haliday's nephew Kevin also joined them.

They rode into Bad Axe and went to the airport. They checked in and filled out all of the paperwork for their new national IDs. After the military checked everything out, their pictures were taken and IDs issued.

Haliday took the group back to the cabin and then Mark took the next group over for their IDs.

By the end of the day, everyone had their new IDs. No one was thrilled at all.

Haliday held his up and looked it over. It was hard plastic, an eighth of an inch thick, with a computer chip embedded inside. The ID had the typical information printed on it. It looked like it would be hard to forge. Everyone was given a lanyard and told to wear it around his neck. He went and sat down by the fireplace.

Bev said, "Why is yours red?"

He looked at the ID card. "Let me see yours."

She handed her ID card to him and he saw that hers was blue in color. Everyone else pulled theirs out. Mark and Lisa's were red as well. The remaining people all had blue.

Mark said, "The red has to indicate veterans. The three of us are the only vets here."

Haliday had recalled what Bruce told him a few weeks earlier. The military and government would be asking veterans for help. It seemed odd that they segregated them with different colored ID cards. On the other hand, they could quickly identify threats.

This only instilled more conspiracy talk.

Bev was always the most outspoken person in the group. She said, "It's that bitch Feinstein. She has it out for veterans. All of her 'they are all mentally ill talk' and crap."

Although Bev did not know it, Feinstein had been in Washington during the event and never made it past two weeks. She had been caught up in the whole mess as the parties fought for control of the country.

Most of the senators and congressmen had actually been caught up in the fighting and mess. Less than 20 percent of them were still alive. The fight in Washington had been intense.

Haliday looked the card over. He wondered what the chip had on it. He wondered if he could wipe the data clean by running a magnet over it. He thought about that for a moment.

He looked at the refrigerator and saw a magnet on the front of it. He looked down at the ID card again. He decided against it at this time. The last thing he needed would be to get detained somewhere while the rest of his group was allowed to leave.

He walked over to the ham and called Bruce near Fort Custer. "Bruce, any good news?"

268

Bruce said, "Nothing really. They are moving some people into the camps."

"Anything else?" Haliday asked.

"I was stopped while out on one of my recon drives. They told me I had to get the National ID card. They said next time I didn't have one I would be detained."

"Detained for what?" Haliday asked.

"Violation of some national law. They just spit out all kinds of BS I didn't care to listen to. Then, they gave me directions on reporting to Custer for the ID."

Haliday said, "I thought you weren't going near the place again?"

My curiosity got the best of me. "Roger, you still peeing in their Wheaties?"

"Yes, I am, which brings up my next question. Are you going to get the IDs?"

"Nope. I talked to my wife, father, and mother in-law. They all said we can just hang out here and stay off the grid," Bruce said.

"We went ahead and got them. But they have my number now. Not too happy with me. I don't think I'm getting a Christmas card next year. I don't want to draw you into any of the BS I might get into, so I'll just check in once in a while. You take care, Bruce, and good luck."

"You, too, Roger."

Haliday called Dennis near Grayling. "Dennis, are you listening?"

"I'm here, Roger," Dennis answered back.

"Anything on your end?"

"Nothing much. Just the same as everywhere else, I suppose. We went and got the ID cards. We are a little closer to town though, so it's riskier for us to travel without them. From what I hear, we have quite a few of the checkpoints around here as well. Each day it seems like they are getting more of the armor and equipment from the MATES running. I've also seen some convoys heading south. Trucks and armor. Rumor has it that they are heading for Grand Rapids, Lansing, Ann Arbor, and Detroit. That's just rumor, though."

"That's quite a bit of information, Dennis. Thank you," Haliday said.

"No problem. I'll keep in touch with you guys if anything new pops up. Oh, one last thing. The military is saying that close to eighty percent of the population has died."

"Eighty percent?"

"Yes. That's in the affected areas. I guess they said the total population is now just forty-five to sixty percent of what it used to be."

"OK, thanks," Haliday said.

He grabbed his head and leaned back in the chair at the end of the call. He bumped Dawn who was standing there listening. He looked around and noticed Mark, Bev, Karen, Blake, and Kayla standing there, too.

Dawn asked, "Do you think it's really that many people?"

"I hope not," Haliday said.

"That's a lot of people Dad," Kayla added.

"It sure is," he said.

"It could be worse," Karen said.

"It's going to be," he said.

"Why is that?" Dawn asked.

A few more people gathered around to listen at this point. Rich actually answered the question. He explained that with most of the industries working on just-in-time manufacturing schedules, there were no stockpiles like there used to be. The food manufacturing was no exception. Food was either frozen or stored for processing at later dates. The food could still be used providing the storage mechanisms were not affected.

With that in mind, the lack of being able to process and transport food would affect the entire country. The entire country was dependent on itself. To add insult to injury, companies without work would start laying-off people. Without work and money, the financial system would collapse. For all

270

intents and purposes, it already had. Therefore, the cycle of death would continue.

"Well, now that we have that great news to digest, why don't we top it off with some dinner?" Haliday said.

He stood by the window of the kitchen as he helped with dinner. There was fresh snow falling. They already had eight inches on the ground from the previous snowfall a few days ago.

It looked like they would have about a foot of snow on the ground by morning. Michigan was a northern state, but surprisingly, the past few winters had been mild with little snowfall.

Soon everyone was sitting around eating dinner. It was spaghetti night. The dinner was easy to make, nutritious, and most of all, filling. All of the conversation was small talk.

Haliday asked, "Bill, how are the animals doing?"

"So far so good," Bill said. "The only problem is feed. We might need to butcher another cow to help conserve food."

Haliday nodded.

He was clueless when it came to the horses and the livestock. He relied heavily on Bill and Mark to take charge of the livestock and Dawn and Diana to take care of the horses. The rest of the group just followed their directions.

Haliday's least favorite jobs were mucking the stalls and cleaning the chicken coop. Everyone in the group had to contribute equally and everyone did their share. Whenever he had a lot on his mind, he went out to the pole barn. He would throw a log or two in the wood stove out there and fiddle around with things. He went out to the barn after dinner.

He was always trying to fix anything that was broken, invent new booby-traps or just tinker to pass time. It helped clear his mind and allowed him to think.

Bill came out to the barn soon after. He checked the chickens and walked over to Haliday. "I see you have some ice fishing gear," he said, nodding to what Haliday was working on.

Haliday laughed and said, "Yeah, don't know much about it though."

"Your dad never took you fishing?" Bill said.

Haliday said, "Oh no, we have gone plenty of times. Lake Erie, Belle Isle on the Detroit River, Drummond Island, a lot of places. I just never really went ice fishing. Is it the same?"

"Fundamentally so, Roger. But there are some differences. That old tractor work?" Bill asked as he pointed to an old Ford tractor nearby.

"It started when we got here. I'm sure it still does." He looked at Bill and said, "Bill, I have to be honest. I don't know anything about some of this stuff. I can fish, but ice fishing is new to me. But I bought the stuff because I thought we could use it." He gestured to the tractor. "I bought the tractor thinking we would farm. I can't even begin to tell you the first thing about raising crops, more or less even planting a single seed. We bought a lot of stuff here not really knowing how the hell to use it."

Bill sat down on a stool by him. "Roger, you put together a hell of a retreat here over the years. I find it hard to believe you guys don't know what you're doing."

"I can't take sole credit for it. This was something that everyone sacrificed for. We all put in a lot of time and effort. We all did a lot of research. We were reading books, looking on the internet, watching a variety of TV shows and more."

Bill said, "Roger, I've noticed on thing about your group. They have one common goal, but different approaches. Your father is good with mechanical skills. Your mother is good with medical skills. I noticed Karen is quite an organizer.

Dawn and Diana have the horse knowledge and farming ability. Everyone has skills. I find it hard to believe you guys didn't plan it that way."

"That was the intent, Bill."

"Well then, it sounds like you guys know what you're doing. So, what's really on your mind, Roger?"

"I guess I'm just worried about everyone," Haliday finally said.

"What do you mean?"

"Bill, Mark is your son. You're a smart man as well. You have to know that things are going to get worse over the next couple of months."

"Don't you think we'll be safe here?"

"I wish I could say we will be. But with the government and military having a set agenda," Haliday said, "I'm not so sure about that."

"Won't they just leave us alone?"

"Not a chance."

"Why not?"

Haliday explained in length what he thought. "Bill, they have an agenda. A lot of things are going to happen that just don't fit in with typical rescue and aid efforts. If you think about it, it's an agenda that will alter the country as we know it. Basically everything we know will have changed. That includes freedom.

"They want to seize the assets of those who have died and have no next of kin to claim those assets. The family has one year?" Haliday shook his head. "That pretty much guarantees the government will get whatever it is the people had. The Federal cash reserves, paired with what they seize, could practically pay off the U.S. debt. Then the sale of land and assets to whomever they choose adds to the coffers. There's no telling what they will sell, and to whom.

"If you think about it, industry here could practically be foreign-owned and operated. It would almost be like handing the world our resources and having the world rule us. Who knows; maybe that's the plan. Taking the stock and produce that everyone grows and raises and redistributing it seems a little leftist to me. They claim when the country is stabilized, then— and only then—will the people be able to earn profits from their efforts.

"Who will determine when the country reaches that point? Will it be one year? Will it be two years? Will it be three, four or even more? Or will they say that the effort allows the country to run more efficiently and it will be that way forever? Don't even get me started on firearms. Take those away in a situation like this and the government wins. The tyrannical takeover of the country could be upon us. On the other hand, we may be leading up to a revolutionary war if they continue with their agenda. The lack of control of the big cities leads to yet another problem. Sooner or later something has to happen. Either the people are going to end up coming this way, or somehow control has to be restored in them.

"The big cities have loads of resources themselves. I mean, even just basics. Who knows what type of supplies is warehoused. Medical, building, mechanical, you name it, there has to be a load of it out there. The government will seize it for the good of the country. The country needs it all, too. It's a real mess out there. That is what really worries me."

He cleared his throat. "Eventually that pile of garbage is going to grow. Once that pile of trash is big enough, it'll flow this way. I'm not sure how well we could continue to repel people who are dead-set on taking what we have. That is what worries me the most. This group has made its share of sacrifices. I don't think we need to make any more. However, there's too much uncertainty."

Bill was looking down at the ground now. He knew all too well what was meant by sacrifice as he remembered his wife Linda. He looked back at Haliday. "We'll be fine, Roger. As long as we continue to fight for our beliefs, we win."

Haliday nodded. "Let's go inside and see what the rest of the group is up to."

They walked back into the cabin.

The kids had all been put to bed. The adults were all sitting around the fireplace talking. Bill walked over and joined them.

Haliday went to the ham and picked up the mic. "Hey, Adam, this is Roger," he said. He repeated the call two more times, but there was no response.

He decided he would try again in another hour. He admitted to himself that he was worried. Adam had told him that the increase in gang activity was climbing each day. Adam expected an attack at any time.

Haliday wanted to see if there was any other news out there. He planned to call Bruce, Dennis and then Brad. Almost on cue, he heard from Brad.

"What's new, Brad?" he asked.

Brad said, "Roger, we have all kinds of equipment being brought in. They brought some more buses, more trucks, a few pieces of armor and a bunch of stuff on pallets."

"What kind of armor?"

"They have four-wheels; they say Military Police on them, and they have three of them. They also have an eight-wheeled Stryker," Brad answered.

"Those are M1117s."

The M1117s were four-wheeled armored vehicles made for light fighting. They were more heavily armored than up-armored Humvees, but not as heavily armored as light or heavy tanks.

The Stryker was a somewhat similar vehicle; however, it had eight wheels, better armor, and better gun systems. These would be formidable against anything the townspeople or any gang could throw at them.

"No idea about what's on the pallets?" Haliday asked.

"No idea at all."

"What about asking the volunteers they are using?"

"No one who has volunteered has come back out of the compound. Neither have any of the people moving to the camps," Brad said.

"That's a little bit odd, Brad. You hear from anyone at all?"

"Not a single person. If anyone goes in for an ID, they are taken directly to the admin building and then brought back out."

"Well, if you hear anything else, let me know."

"Oh yeah, they have people working on the school, turning it into a camp. But we figured that much," Brad added.

"OK, Brad, thanks for the information," Haliday said.

After that call, he called Adam again. There was still no answer from Adam's group. Haliday's stomach turned. He was confident that Adam's group was in trouble.

"Are you there, Bruce?" Haliday asked.

"Yeah, I'm here," Bruce responded.

"You don't sound too happy right now."

"We went and got our ID cards. They interrogated the hell out of me, my wife, my father, and my mother in-law," Bruce said.

"That made you that angry?"

"No, the sons of bitches separated us from our daughters and interrogated them. A ten- and twelve-year-old," Bruce said.

"What the hell prompted that?"

"I guess my little scouting trips to look in on them. We weren't going to go get the ID cards, but then we thought about what you said, about moving around."

"Damn. Sorry, man," Haliday said.

"Anyway, they know all about our trailer, and our preps. Nothing I can do about it now anyway. I heard what Brad said, and we got a bunch of the same stuff in here. A lot more though. I think we have maybe four or five times as much."

"OK, thanks again, Bruce," Haliday said.

Dennis piped up next. "We went and got the IDs, too. So much for sticking it to The Man," he said as he laughed. "But damn, interrogating little girls. What the hell is wrong with them?"

"I have no idea, but I would be pissed too," Haliday said.

"We have not had anything but some cargo planes come in. Nothing was off-loaded except pallets of who knows what. This stuff was all put on trucks and sent out to the other camps."

"So, it's pretty much the same routine all around the state then it sounds like."

"Not really. The camps here are bustling with people. Over the last two days, people are leaving in the morning and returning in the evening. I have no idea what they are doing yet. I haven't had the opportunity to talk to any of them yet."

"Can you let me know as soon as you find out?" Haliday said.

"I sure will."

"OK, thanks, Dennis. Talk to you later."

Haliday thought about the information he had just heard. The questioning of Bruce and his family, especially the young girls, really irritated him. He had never heard of that in a civilized nation.

The next item that bothered him was why the volunteers had not been allowed to leave the camps in his area. He had to question whether they were camps or prisons. It could be he was overreacting.

There was of course, the obvious question: What were the volunteers up by Camp Grayling doing? He was anxious to learn about that.

He clicked the mic and tried Adam's group one more time. "Adam, you guys there?"

There was still no answer.

He left a note by the radio. He wanted to be awakened if Adam called. Until then, he settled into bed for the night.

Adam's group was in a fight for their lives.

Chapter 22

In the late evening while on watch, Adam had looked out the window and saw the gang approaching. He alerted everyone in his house, who then scrambled to take up defensive positions. The group had fought off attackers before, but not a crowd of this size.

Adam watched the gang's movement carefully. The gang first sent five people toward the house. These five people then split up and went separate directions, surrounding the house.

After 30 minutes, another group of people from the gang converged on the house. This group had 10 people in it. The spotters in Adam's group kept a close eye on the gang members' positions. A few of the gang members were walking around from position to position.

The mood started to get tense in Adam's house, getting fidgety.

The gang made yet another move.

Twenty more gang members came down the street. There were now a total of 35 of them surrounding Adam's house. The gang members moved from position to position, trying to confuse Adam's spotters. It was night now, with no daylight left.

The spotters keeping watch used markers and wrote on the walls what they had observed. More accurately, they wrote down the number of people in their assigned target areas.

This information was relayed to other members in the house who would be able to fire on the target areas. Some of them had assigned areas but could not really see the areas that well. Unfortunately, they would have to wait for movement before they could fire.

One interesting item was that the gang had brought along some type of homemade battering ram. This was placed by one of the stalled out cars on the street in front of Adam's house.

Adam heard some shouting come from the gang outside. They were demanding that Adam's group surrender. They told Adam's group that if they all just came out and gave up, they would be safe.

No one from Adam's group responded. They all sat quietly and waited. Adam told them not to fire until they were fired upon. He held out just a small amount of hope that the gang would go away. He heard one man from the gang shout at the house.

"You need to come out and give up! If you come out now, we'll let you go!" He was the gang leader.

Adam knew that wasn't going to happen. These guys were not going to let anyone walk out and leave, for fear of those people coming back for retaliation or to reclaim their food and supplies.

"Listen up in there! I'm not going to wait all day. You guys have about ten minutes to decide. I'm warning you guys, it'll get real ugly for you. I'm a retired Green Beret! A leg!"

Adam glanced out of the window and got a quick peek of the man. This guy was in his mid-thirties, maybe six-foot-tall, 180 pounds. He had a knit hat on and Carhartt pants with a black jacket.

The man waited for a few minutes, then walked over to a car and sat on the hood.

One of Adam's group walked over to Adam and said, "You think that guy's telling the truth?"

Adam said, "I doubt it. He didn't look old enough to be retired. Even after only twenty years of service, this guy still looks too young. From what I understand Green Beret's prefer Operators or Special Forces. Not to mention if you called one a 'leg'—which is slang for a grunt or infantryman—non-airborne, I think you'd get your ass beat. Besides, this guy's tactics are amateur at best."

Adam told the man in his group to go and pass the word. The man quickly made it through the house and told everyone.

Adam had noticed the weapons the gang had when they had approached. They had a lot of AR15s and shotguns. He could not tell what type of pistols they had, and he noticed not everyone had a pistol visible.

"OK in there! You guys all had your chance!" the man shouted.

Adam's group was nervous now. The people in the gang moved around a bit more. They seemed to all be settled in now. Adam told his group to stay ready.

The gang fired a few shots at the house. Adam's group did not return fire yet. The shots fired at them were random, maybe 50 rounds total.

Luckily, no one in Adam's group was hit. The rounds fired from the gang caused a little bit of damage to the house, but most of it was confined to the windows.

The gang fired another volley of shots at the house.

Adam's group did not return fire.

The gang had no idea why not.

Adam's group looked around the house at the broken windows and holes in the walls.

The gang leader shouted, "You guys in there get a taste of what's coming your way? You guys had enough yet?"

Adam gave the signal and his group opened up on the gang. The group members knew the layout of the surrounding houses and obstacles. They had dialed in their sights for these locations. The gang was not caught off-guard, but they didn't expect

Adam's group to fire until the gang fired once again. The gang had relaxed their positions slightly. This proved to be a fatal mistake for many of the gang members. The fact that Adam's group had laid out the target areas compounded the gang's trouble.

Two of the gang members had taken up a position behind one of the neighbor's cars. The men were concentrating on the front of Adam's house, primarily the front door and windows.

What they did not realize was that a small bathroom window, on the second floor of Adam's house provided the perfect trajectory for the rifle fire that took both their lives. They never saw the muzzle flashes from the side of the house.

The rifleman in Adam's house had taken a bead on the first man. After his first shot, which struck the man in the head, the rifleman shifted slightly and fired three shots into the second man.

A couple of the gang members nearby, however, did see those muzzle flashes. Once they zeroed-in on the window and confirmed the muzzle flashes, they fired on the window.

By this time the man firing from inside the house had already ducked down and given up on using the window for further firing. It had been a long shot that worked, but working twice was a risk he wasn't going to take right now.

The only other window on that side of the house was the bathroom on the first floor. The small size of the window and its location did not provide enough coverage, or enough of an advantage, to be used.

Adam's house backed up to another house that was only 50 yards away. In between this house and his was an assortment of obstacles. He had a shed in the back and so did the neighbors around him.

The neighbor behind him had a hot tub on their deck. There was another gang member behind it. A rifleman in Adam's group who was up on the second floor was able to fire on the man.

The man took a hit to the shoulder and ducked down as the round shattered his shoulder blade. He just stayed down under cover. The rounds penetrated the hot tub, but caused nothing more than leaks from the water that had been left in it. The water sprinkled over him as he lay there, leaving him cold and wet. He was still able to use his right arm and shoulder his rifle. He readied himself to rise up and return some fire.

Close by the hot tub was the neighbor's shed. Two gang members shouted over to their friend that they would provide some cover fire, and then started firing toward Adam's.

The man behind the hot tub got up and ran toward the shed. As soon as he stepped off the deck he slipped on the snow and fell down. He rolled over and started to get back up.

Shots rang out from another window at Adam's.

The man was struck more than seven times. The two men behind the shed screamed and continued to fire at the house. Their friend died after just a few moments. Both lungs and his aorta artery had been pierced.

The side of Adam's house where the attached garage was located was a blind spot. The gang could advance from this side fairly easily if they moved carefully enough. Once they reached that point, they could then move toward the front or the back of the house. Either direction would provide them the opportunity to enter the house. Anyone inside the house would have to expose himself through the windows if they wanted to fire on the gang members. This would then allow the gang to effectively return fire.

At the front of the house the gang was embedded behind various stalled automobiles. Some of them had also taken up positions in the homes across the street.

When Adam's group fired on the gang, they managed to kill one and wound three others. Beyond belief, one of the gang members was standing up next to a car. He was hit several times in the torso and fell into the street. Another had been shot in the foot while he was kneeling behind a car. He was still able to move and reposition himself. He moved closer to the car for more safety.

One woman who was with the gang had been behind a car and had fired toward the second floor of Adam's house.

Adam's group returned fire on her position.

The glass from the car windows shattered, covering her face and eyes with small pieces of glass. Her eyes became scratched and bloody, temporarily blinding her.

A third gang member who was hiding in one of the houses across the street was hit when he turned on a flashlight and revealed his position. A round had grazed his head, splitting his scalp open.

Inside Adam's house, one man had been firing on the gang. His rifle and arm had been exposed through a broken window. He took a round to his right forearm, shattering both the ulna and radius bones.

He could no longer hold his rifle, nor could he use his arm. He only had his left arm available and had to resort to using a pistol. He was told to withdraw from the window position and wait in case the house was breached.

Another man in Adam's group had caught a ricochet in his upper shoulder. The round had penetrated the skin and remained just below the skin's surface. He was still able to continue in the fight.

Adam's group continued to return fire. They had good coverage of their assigned target areas, but that was all. The gang had managed to find areas that Adam's group could not cover.

Adam made his way through the house. He stopped and checked on everyone. The mood in the house was solemn. This particular fight gave them all an uneasy feeling. He tried to reassure everyone, to tell them that everything would be okay. The group knew better. They knew the outcome would not be as pleasant as Adam expected.

The gang stopped firing. Adam's group stopped firing shortly afterwards.

The leader yelled out, "This isn't going to end well for you people in there! We'll give you one more chance to leave!"

Adam's group just waited. As they looked around, they could see the shattered glass from the windows. There were several hundred bullet holes in the walls. It was a miracle no one had been killed yet.

The gang leader yelled out one more time. "That's it! That was your last chance! Now you get an ass whooping!"

Some of the gang members shifted positions, prompting Adam's group to fire on them. Once Adam's group fired, the gang fired back. They continued to fire back and forth.

The gang leader ordered a group of six people to move in along the side of the garage. He instructed them to take their homemade battering ram with them.

It took two people to carry the battering ram. It weighed a little over 100 pounds. This conglomeration would prove to be a good match against a door.

The smaller group worked their way toward the garage. They had been down the street a short distance. Staying in blind spots, they safely made it to alongside the garage. Once they got there they simply waited.

The gang stopped firing once again. During the last melee of shooting a few more gang members had been hit and one of Adam's group was hit. This was Adam's first fatality. Two others in his group were injured as well.

The man in his group who died was struck in the eye by a piece of buckshot. It entered his brain, causing him to convulse violently before finally succumbing to the injury.

The two others received moderate injuries. One was an upper chest wound that nicked the lung to a woman. She was able to cover the wound and tape down the bandage.

The other injury in Adam's group was another arm injury. One of the men had been firing from an upstairs window and had been hit in the left upper arm. He was still able to shoulder his rifle and fire.

Fortunately for Adam, they had been selective in their group's effort to recruit. No one with very young children was allowed to join. The youngest person in the group was now 19 years old.

This had been a decision that the group had made as a whole. It had always been on their minds as to what would happen to small children in a firefight such as this.

As the gang and Adam's group continued to exchange gunfire, the gang's pace of fire slowed down. He could hear someone outside shouting orders, but barely hear what was actually being said. He assumed they would be making another push to get in or get them to surrender. His home was littered with spent shell casings and the bandages were now starting to pile up as well.

Many of the group was starting to get hit by pieces of the house itself and from rounds penetrating the home. The home was vinyl sided and had offered little protection against the bullets. Adam had never invested in armoring the walls. The group thought that bugging in, with a lot of firepower, would be sufficient. Now they second-guessed that decision.

Adam went upstairs to assess the situation, going from room to room checking in on everyone and asking if they had enough ammunition.

Everyone had plenty for the moment. Adam was about to go back down to the first floor when he heard a loud crash on the front door. He raced down the stairs to see what had happened.

The small group outside the house with the battering ram used it to strike the door. The door didn't give much. The battering ram was not working like the gang expected. Two members of the gang tried the battering ram once more.

Adam heard another loud crash as the ram struck the door again. The door barely moved, but he noticed the integrity of the door changing. He had installed a metal door and frame. It had been suggested as one of the best security doors on the market. After he installed the door, he made a few modifications around the frame.

He had surrounded the frame with one-by-six oak boards, screwed into the doorjamb and surrounding wall studs. Next, he installed three brackets on each side of the door, also attached to wall studs. The brackets held three wooden bars in place. Each one was an actual two-by-six, not the typical trimmed down dimensional lumber common in the big box home lumber and hardware stores.

Adam looked up at the small balcony in the foyer. Two of his group members had taken up a position there and were now looking down into the foyer. Adam raced to the back of house.

286

He slipped on the dining room floor and fell. He looked over at the patio door wall. They had boarded this up and placed obstacles in front of it outside to help defend it.

The windows on the back of the house allowed Adam's group to keep an eye out for attackers and assist in repelling the attackers from the back of the house.

He heard a loud crash at the front door. This one sounded much different than the first crashes. He rose to his feet. He heard his group shouting, saying that the gang members were all making a rush for the house.

The gunfire erupted as furious as ever. A few of the gang members threw Molotov cocktails at the home where they shattered on the vinyl siding. The gasoline started to burn, but fortunately the flames burned out.

Adam heard one last crash at the front door. The door could no longer hold and started to give way. By this time his brother had come near the kitchen to help him. They flipped the kitchen table onto its side and took cover behind it.

Another loud crash was heard and the front door swung open. Adam, his brother, and the two men on the foyer balcony overlooking the door all started to fire, but no one entered the house yet.

Some of the gang members across the street fired at the door. One by one, three cans of smoke were thrown through the door. The gang members had evidently acquired them during their other attacks.

The smoke was heavy and filled the foyer. It drifted upwards toward the balcony as well. The living room next to the foyer rapidly filled with smoke. Adam and his group took no chances and began to fire toward the open door once again.

One of the gang members managed to crawl in on his stomach without being seriously wounded. Once inside, he blindly pointed a shotgun and fired round after round until it was empty. He then pulled out a pistol and started firing randomly around the area.

Adam's brother was struck by a round in his upper thigh. As he attempted to take aim at the smoke filled area, he was then hit in the chest and fell backwards.

One more gang member entered the doorway. He threw more smoke canisters into the house and the entire front of the house was filled with smoke.

Two men from Adam's group had been in the living room and had to retreat. They retreated to a small hallway close by that led to a couple of bedrooms and the first floor bathroom. This was a major mistake. The battering ram came through the living room window, opening a large hole.

One more strike from the ram widened the hole. The two men on the upper balcony and Adam tried to fend off the attackers. There was so much confusion that two more of the gang made it inside the home.

The rest of the gang outside of the house was firing nonstop. The walls were easily penetrated. Pictures on the walls fell. Furniture was riddled with bullets and splinters flew in every direction. Decorative vases broke and fell to the floor. The inside of the house was total chaos. The gang members inside kept firing as well. One of Adam's members in the hallway took a hit through his right temple, killing him instantly.

As the smoke started to clear, more gang members made it into the house. They used pistols, rifles, and shotguns to fire on Adam's group, who fought hard to repel them.

Six members of his group from the second floor made their way to the foyer balcony and blitzed the entire foyer area with rounds. Two of them ran down the stairs. As soon as they reached the bottom of the stairs they were met with gunfire. One man went down instantly. The second man dropped low to the floor and kept firing back.

In a matter of a few minutes the rush of Adam's group continued. As the shots continued to be traded back and forth, another Molotov cocktail came through the front window.

Adam could not believe the gang was going to burn the house down. This meant burning all of the food and supplies the gang was desperately trying to take. One in his group grabbed a fire extinguisher from the corner of the kitchen and put out the flames before they were able to spread.

More members from upstairs made it to the first floor. They fought intensely against the gang members inside the home. They finally managed to repel them.

The gang members outside all retreated. Adam's group did their best to fire on them as the gang ran to safety.

The carnage left throughout the house was horrifying.

Adam's group managed to get the front door closed and they used the two-by-six planks to wedge it in place. They took the kitchen table and lodged it in front of the living room window. These were only temporary measures.

Adam looked around at the members of his group. He then looked around at the dead and wounded. He walked back over to the dining room and dropped down to his knees next to his brother's body.

He closed his brother's eyes and kissed him on the forehead. He got back up and looked around again. There were a lot tears in the group. Everyone was either related to or knew someone who had died.

He walked through the house. He counted the number of injuries and the number of dead. His group had sustained a total of seven deaths, and 12 injuries. Some injuries were minor and some were severe. He was overwhelmed. He sat down and gathered his thoughts for a moment. There were six dead gang members in the foyer and living room.

A few of his group members moved the kitchen table blocking the breached window. They pushed the gang's dead bodies through the opening and then placed the table back.

The gang outside had not faired much better. They incurred 15 deaths and another 15 injuries. They still had almost 20 members who went unscathed. Adam's group had only nine.

Neither side was firing now. Both sides were licking their wounds.

The gang leader shouted out to Adam, "This ain't over! We'll be back, you bastards!"

The gang members carefully retreated back to the house they had invaded the week before.

For some odd reason, Adam's group didn't fire on them as they retreated. There was very little fight left.

Adam sat on a step to the staircase. His wife walked over to him.

"Honey, we need to decide on what we're going to do," she said.

"I don't know what to do," Adam replied.

She said, "I'll talk to the group and see if they have any ideas."

"I love you, honey," he said.

His wife made her way through the house and spoke with the group's members. She was getting an idea for what to do. She was also gauging the group's state of mental welfare, which was very low.

Adam went into his bedroom and retrieved a blanket. He laid it down next to his brother's body. Another man came over and helped him wrap his brother in the blanket. His brother's wife stood there sobbing.

Part of the group wrapped up the remaining bodies. The rest of the group tended to those who were injured. When they were finished, Adam spoke with everyone to see if they had any ideas.

"Listen up, everyone," he said. "We were wrong to think we could hold out here. They have far more people then we do. I don't think we can sustain another attack."

Most of the group knew he was right. With all of the damage to the house, coupled with the blind spots and the gangs' manpower, they knew it would be their last fight.

One man said, "What do we do, Adam? Where can we go?"

Adam reached into his pocket. He pulled out a small piece of paper. He walked over to the ham radio and called Haliday.

"Roger, are you out there?"

"Adam, this is Kayla, his daughter. Do you need him? He's sleeping," Kayla said.

"Please," is all Adam said.

In the Haliday cabin tucked away in the falling snow, Kayla went and woke Haliday up. He went down the stairs and over to the ham.

"Adam, what's wrong?" he asked.

"Roger, I don't even know where to begin," Adam said.

Haliday could tell by the tone of his voice that something serious had happened. Adam had helped out his neighborhood during the early days of the event. He had even helped Haliday's brother, Alan, get in touch with him.

"Adam, whatever you need, brother, you tell me and I'll do my best to help."

"Your offer still stand on your house?" Adam asked.

"Hell yeah. You head to that intersection. Once you get there I will give you the address. If the house is empty, you go right ahead and use it. If it's occupied for some reason, we'll get you out here, unless you want to come out here directly."

"The house should be fine, Roger. If it does have someone in it, I'll call you."

"OK. When you get there, I'll give you some more info that will lead you to a cache. It's not much, but it'll help you guys out. You have the folks come get me on the radio if you need anything," Haliday said.

"Roger, thank you."

At his bullet-ridden home with dead and injured, Adam looked at all of the anxious faces. He could see they were all scared. He was scared as well. Now they had some work to do in a short amount of time.

He went over to the door that led to the garage. He slowly opened it with a pistol at the ready in his right hand. Behind him was another group member with a shotgun.

They entered the garage and swept the area to make sure it was clear of any gang members. Once satisfied it was empty, the group began working to get things ready to bug out.

Chapter 23

Haliday had his own issues to handle in his areas. However, across the state, and even the country, more was happening as civilization continued to fall apart. The government was finally mobilizing.

Over at Selfridge a convoy was ready to leave. The soldiers were checking ammo loads, vehicle rigging, personal gear, and some were praying.

The mission at hand was to go straight into downtown Detroit and right into the Federal building. At that point, they would secure the building and fortify it to be used as the state's headquarters.

Lansing had been the first choice, but after careful review, they decided Detroit would be better. The decision was based solely on political thinking.

Michigan's government was centrally located in Lansing. For the most part, the ruling Federal government did not want any state or local entities involved.

The feds kept telling everyone that with too many political factors involved, aid and the restoration of the country's stability would falter.

It made sense to a lot of people, but it also threw up red flags. Big Brother would be controlling any and all aspects of life in the post-apocalyptic United States.

The security at the main gate opened it up and then watched as the convoy pulled out. There were 12 vehicles with 60 combat-ready troops inside them.

A direct route to the old McNamara building would take them east on I-94 and right into the downtown area. The trip should take no more than 90 minutes at a slow, controlled pace.

When the convoy was close to the Federal building, two MH-6 Little Bird helicopters would deliver eight additional troops to the rooftop of the building. Unfortunately they would have to rappel in. There was no helipad on the roof.

With the troops assaulting from the top and ground levels, they hoped it would be an easy operation. The small underground parking area would be the biggest threat to the assaulting troops.

It had many mechanical rooms and concrete walls to be used as fortified hides. Smoke, gas, and stun grenades would be heavily used in there.

The lead vehicle was an MRAP, a Mine Resistant Ambush Protected vehicle. It didn't resemble any typical vehicle. Haliday called them big boy Tonka Toys. They worked just fine, however.

There was little to worry about on the freeway as they made their approach. The biggest obstacle was maneuvering around the stalled vehicles. The troops had with them a much larger MRAP variation that was used for recovery of smaller military vehicles. Attached to the front of it was a large appendage that resembled a snow plow on steroids.

If a vehicle was in their way, this vehicle moved forward and pushed it out of the way. None of the troops would have to risk exposing themselves to potential hostile threats.

Just inside the border of Detroit, the troops ran across a makeshift roadblock. They stopped almost an eighth of a mile away from it. The troops took up positions to guard their flanks and rear. The convoy commander was watching the activity around the roadblock with binoculars. He estimated approximately 10 people at the roadblock itself. He counted four more, two on each bank of the freeway keeping guard as well.

The exit ramp was completely blocked. The vehicles had been placed into positions to make it nearly impossible for anyone to pass. Right in the center of it they had two vehicles parked nose to nose.

The convoy commander guessed they would roll these out of the way and allow others to pass after extracting some type of toll. Just as he was about to ask for a volunteer he saw two men waving a white rag approaching his position. He heard rifles and machine guns being cycled through to ensure they were ready to fire.

The two men from the roadblock approached.

The convoy commander watched them. He looked for more movement in the area and spotted two more locations to the convoy's rear.

The two men reached him. Both were dressed in ordinary clothing and looked like average Joes from the neighborhood. Nothing about their appearance stood out.

He looked them up and down and said, "How can we help you gentlemen?"

One of the men replied, "You can pay the toll to pass our checkpoint."

"You obviously don't understand. We are the government, Unites States troops," the commander replied.

"And that means what right now?" the man asked.

The commander said, "That means we are passing through; no toll, no crap from you, no ifs, ands, or buts."

The men just stood there looking at each other.

The commander spoke up again. "You folks need to move the barricade and let us pass. This is your only chance."

The two men glanced at each other and laughed. They obviously thought it was funny. "Look here, General, it's half of the food you have with you or you don't pass," one said. "We have snipers ready to fire on you guys."

A loudspeaker rumbled to life and a stoic voice was heard. "This is the United States military. Place your weapons down and abandon the barricade."

The voice repeated the command three times. After the third time, the voice on the loudspeaker added an additional sentence. "You have five minutes to comply before action is taken."

The two men from the barricade just looked at the commander. One asked, "You take us for some kind of stupid?"

"Not at all," came the commander's reply.

"You must. You don't think we know you're yanking our chain? You are not going to fire on us. We're United States citizens. On the other hand, it's your job to help us, so kick up the food," the man said.

The commander was obviously annoyed. He gave a signal and the loudspeaker came to life again. "We will fire on all hostile positions," it blared. "Leave now if you do not wish to engage."

The two men turned around and started walking back toward the barricade. The man who had speaking all along shouted back to the commander. "Sit there all day, moron!"

"One minute remaining," the loud speaker said.

The two men held up their hands and flipped off the convoy commander.

The commander shouted out a few orders. The troops all adjusted their positions.

It was a mere 15 seconds until the deadline when an AH-64 Apache helicopter gunship swooped in low. It hovered only 100 feet above the convoy.

With a deafening roar, the helicopter's 30mm chain gun came to life. The rounds struck the two vehicles being used to block the center of the road.

The convoy commander watched the men at the barricade take off running for the safety of other vehicles nearby.

Two telltale swooshes were heard as the pilot unleashed two hellfire missiles. These struck the two vehicles, demolishing both of them in a fraction of a second.

None of the opposing force fired on the convoy. The heavier MRAP moved forward. It pushed the remaining pieces of the vehicle out of the way.

The troops had mounted their vehicles and the convoy slowly drove through the now abandoned barricade. The commander looked to his right as they passed by.

He saw the two men huddling down next to a vehicle. He placed his index and middle fingers against his temple and snapped off an old-fashioned Boy Scout salute.

The two men just looked on as the convoy passed.

The commander looked over at his driver and asked, "Did they really think they were going to get what they wanted?"

The driver looked back at the commander. "Sir, there are all variations of stupid in the world these days."

The commander said, "You are one hundred percent correct. It used to be you needed waders for the gene pool, and now you don't get your feet wet wearing flip-flops."

They both laughed as the convoy moved closer to the Federal building. They didn't encounter anyone else until they reached the downtown area.

Most of the people they saw were apparently out scavenging. They would see them with a few items here and there, but not loaded up as if they were moving to other locations for refuge. There were, however, very few people.

They paused at one intersection where a younger teenage boy was rooting through piles of garbage. The commander looked ahead to the boy who was nearly emaciated.

The commander could not help but feel sorry for the kid. In front of the commander's vehicle the gunner ducked down into the MRAP. When he emerged, the commander noticed two small, brown packages in the gunner's hands. These were MREs. The gunner tossed them to the boy.

The boy scooped them up and hurried off. The MREs would most likely provide the boy with more calories than he had eaten in the entire past week.

The commander smiled. At least there was still some humanity left among them. They didn't encounter very many people. The weather was most likely responsible for that.

It was bitter cold out. There were snow flurries and it was only 15 degrees outside. The smell of burning wood was prevalent in the air. Fires to keep survivors warm.

Another odor that caught their sense of smell was that of burned-out buildings. They could see where entire buildings had been torched. The windows were melted or broken out from the heat, and the charred wood exterior moldings and black scorch marks rose up from the openings.

Oddly enough one building was still smoldering. The fire that had consumed it had taken place only a day before. The commander could not make out the sign on the front of it. The only word he could see was "Textiles."

They were less than a block away now. The convoy stopped. A group of eight soldiers readied themselves. They worked their way toward the Federal building, scouting the area as they went along.

The soldiers took plenty of time to map out all of the potential trouble spots. The few people that did see them ran inside and hid. They did not know what was going on; they just knew they didn't want to be involved.

The soldiers took up positions around the Federal building. They could see where a couple of windows were broken out on the fourth floor on each side of the building. They spotted people in the windows and it was obvious that they had been seen as well. The soldiers called on the radio and another group of eight troops approached.

The second group broke up into four two-man teams. These teams each took one side of the building. They were designated as marksmen.

The remaining troops and vehicles moved in closer still. They took up various positions around the building as close as they could get. There were several large parking lots nearby that did not provide much cover. The building had large concrete bollards placed around the perimeter. There was a large iron gate leading to the underground parking lot which was closed.

The two MH-6 Little Birds came in quickly, one at a time. Each bird had four troops standing on the skids. The bird hovered briefly and the troops rappelled down a short rope and onto the rooftop.

These troops secured the roof top immediately. They moved to the stairwells where they found the doors locked. A couple of soldiers attempted to shoulder open a door but failed. The doors were heavily sealed. After a few attempts they heard some gunshots from inside. The soldiers backed off and regrouped.

They yelled toward the stairwell, "U.S. Army! Cease firing!" They repeated this numerous times until the firing stopped.

They heard a woman's voice yell through the door. "There ain't no Army anymore!"

One of the soldiers on the roof replied, "Ma'am, yes there is, and we are securing this building. Open the door and come out with your hands raised!"

Another volley of shots rang out from within. These shots were useless since the heavy steel doors were impenetrable to her small arms fire.

"Go ahead and have your people look around outside and you'll see the military vehicles!" the soldier yelled back.

They waited there for a bit to see if she would answer.

On the other side of that door, the woman talked with a man that was with her and this man ran down the stairs to talk to the others occupying the building.

This group that had taken over the Federal building had chosen one of the best locations in the city. The only other building that offered more protection was the Federal Reserve of Chicago, Detroit Branch.

The group of people inside the building had formed together within weeks of the initial power outage. One man had worked for the Federal Protective Service and was able to gain access to the building. As time passed he became an outcast. The group had welcomed in people who had total disregard for any law or order. As more time passed, the activities became more criminal.

The former fed fled one day when he tried to stop the group from killing a few people and they turned on him. By pure luck he managed to escape. He never went back to the Federal building.

The man that had been in the stairwell with the woman was now on the fourth floor. He found the leader of his group, Jake, who was looking out the window and analyzing things down below.

"Jake, they're on the roof, trying to get in," the man said.

"Try to hold them off. I need some time to think," Jake answered back.

The man said, "OK, we'll try."

The man made his way back to the stairwell and climbed up to the top. He was winded when he got there, but still relayed the information.

The woman said, "What do you think he's trying to figure out?"

"I think maybe the stuff in the parking garage."

"We're in trouble if that's the case," she said.

Meanwhile, the officer in charge of the assault studied his options. He wanted to get some troops into the underground parking garage. He came up with a plan and asked for a small volunteer.

A female sergeant came forward. The officer pointed out some areas on the drawings he had. The sergeant would attempt to gain access through a small utilities access shaft. This, however, would only get her into the garage.

Once she got there she could scout out the garage and report on her findings. If she could get the outside access opened, the troops could move in and it would give them control of the roof and basement.

The sergeant worked her way through the utility access shaft. After 15 minutes she had managed to reach the garage. There was an access panel leading into it, which she found locked. She was able to get a small pinhole camera poked through the panel vents and slowly moved it around to capture as much video as she could.

The space was tight and she was unable to see what was on the monitor. The video feed was recorded so she could take it back and let the commander review it.

Working her way backwards took much longer. It was nearly 45 minutes before she was climbing back out of the access shaft.

She handed the camera unit over to the commander. He took the unit and started playing the video back as a few others looked on.

He paused and stared. "Sergeant, did you see this?"

She replied, "No, sir. It was too tight of a fit so I just recorded it."

He handed the unit to her. She played the video back and just about halfway through it she, too, paused the recording. She turned her head and vomited.

Another sergeant who had also been watching started heaving as well. The commander took the video unit back and mumbled something unintelligible.

In one corner of the garage there was a stack of bodies. It wasn't the carnage that bothered them. Nor was it the rats feasting on the flesh.

You could tell immediately that the bodies had been harvested for food. There were definite signs of human action where cuts of meat had deliberately been removed. The fact that this group had resorted to cannibalism was what had sickened everyone. Not even four months had passed and people were eating each other.

The commander notified his squad leaders to prepare the troops. The tolerance they would show to these people would be very limited. They would be given one chance.

The loud speaker on the MRAP blared away. The people inside were told to drop their weapons and exit the building. They were told the military knew of the crimes that had been committed.

They did not mention the cannibalism. That would have told the people inside that they had access to the garage and they wanted that kept secret. They did not receive a response from the people inside.

301

The people inside decided they had nothing to lose. They figured instead of prison they would fight until the bitter end. They, too, prepared for the fight which would start shortly.

The sergeant worked her way back into the access shaft and managed to maneuver the camera and small monitor around so she could see what was happening.

The commander signaled for the assault to start. The troops started firing on the open window positions. The suppressing fire allowed a demolition team to make it to the iron gate of the parking lot. Once they arrived, they quickly placed explosive charges on the lock and hinges of the gate. They retreated and then took cover. The detonation severed the lock and hinges and the gate fell flat onto the pavement.

Two of the convoy vehicles darted into the lot. The demolition team went directly to the small door next to the garage door and readied it for explosives.

The team on the roof approached both stairwells. They heard shots being fired from within. Still, the rounds did not penetrate the doors.

The sergeant was able to see that no one was in the garage at the moment and she gave an all-clear signal. Simultaneously, the rooftop troops and the demolition team at the garage set off their charges. They tossed in some flash-bang grenades, and then entered the stairwell with their rifles at the ready.

One woman inside was startled, but began raising her pistol. She was shot immediately.

The man that had been with her had already started descending the stairs, deciding he would rather run than fight. He ducked out onto the fifth floor and hid in an office.

The second stairwell was breached with more difficulty. The flash-bangs did not have the desired effect and the soldiers received return fire. One soldier pulled the pin on a fragmentation grenade and lobbed it into the stairwell. The grenade exploded and the soldiers heard screaming.

Of the two hostiles in the stairwell, one died immediately. The other lay there bleeding from his head and neck. The soldiers entered the stairwell and they found him. They removed his weapons and left him there. They called on the radio and gave the man's location so a medic could work his way there when it was safe. However, the man died just minutes after being left.

The door to the garage was completely blown off its hinges. The troops threw in flash-bang and smoke grenades. The sergeant watching on the camera told them the area was all clear.

The troops spilled into the garage. One man ran over to the access shaft and used a pair of bolt cutters to cut the lock off. The sergeant was relieved to get out of there.

The soldiers spotted the pile of harvested bodies. The effect on video was one thing, but to see it in person was another. This angered the troops.

The garage was clear and all they needed to do now was to enter the building itself. The demolition team ran up to the door and set the charges. They blew the door open, but before they could throw in the grenades a cloud of gunfire erupted from the opening. One soldier was struck in the abdomen and legs.

The soldiers fired into the open doorway. This bought them a few seconds while two fragmentation grenades were tossed inside.

The concrete entryway deflected the fragments as they bounced everywhere, shredding the hostiles who were inside waiting for the troops. The soldiers fired on them as they entered, making sure the threat was eliminated.

The remaining hostiles were all on the fourth floor. They fired on the soldiers through the open windows. The soldiers had few opportunities to move closer. The marksman teams were well in position now. They started to use the hostile fire to zero-in on the threats and return the fire. They were not sure if they were really hitting their intended targets.

The commander ordered them to open fire using the machine guns. They concentrated their fire on the open windows. The windows to the left and right of those shattered as rounds struck them.

The people inside were not intent on surrendering at all and returned fire as well. Unfortunately for them, they were severely outgunned. They retreated toward the center of the building and away from the windows.

The soldiers outside were able to move in closer. They repositioned their vehicles to help support their assault. The momentum was on their side.

The soldiers on the roof started working their way down floor by floor. Each floor was empty. They locked the stairwell doors to prevent anyone from entering the floors they'd just cleared.

The soldiers in the garage started working their way upward. They did not meet any resistance until they reached the third floor when two men came down from the fourth floor and tried to pin them down.

The two men exchanged fire with the soldiers. The soldiers donned protective masks and tossed CS teargas grenades at them. Once the men started choking and retreating. The soldiers cut them down.

When the assault team from the roof reached the fifth floor they could hear the gunfire on the floor below them. They felt rounds hit the floor beneath them, but none penetrated the concrete sandwiched between them. The fifth floor was nearly cleared. The soldiers were entering the final office when they spotted a man hiding. They ordered him to stand up.

As the man stood up, he grabbed the desk top to balance himself. He inadvertently grabbed a stapler sitting on the corner of the desk.

One soldier entering the office spotted the object, and not knowing what it was, fired on the man. He fell down across the desk top. The troops checked his lifeless body, and then secured the floor.

Both assault teams were now ready to converge upon the fourth floor. There were four dead, five injured and 21 people left on the fourth floor ready to fight the military.

The commander ordered CS grenades to be launched from grenade launchers into the open fourth floor windows. The soldiers fired their launchers.

The fourth floor was riddled with almost 20 CS gas grenades. The doors to the floor were blown open and the troops entered the floor. A half-dozen people in the group of hostiles had gasmasks and were able to escape the effects of the gas grenades. They returned fire on the assaulting soldiers.

The soldiers took a few hits and luckily incurred only a few injuries, none of which were life threatening. They retreated to the stairwells. Once there they threw in more gas and flash-bang grenades. After the flash-bangs went off, they darted back onto the floor.

The soldiers did not waste any opportunity to fire. Any movement they saw was fired on. With plenty of magazines for their rifles, three round bursts were the soldiers' preferred choice.

The commander had ordered the soldiers positioned outside of the building to hold their fire. He did not want to risk any friendly-fire incidents. Only the marksman could fire if they were sure of their target.

With so much gas and smoke from the flash-bangs still lingering it took longer than expected to mop up the operation. The soldiers finished without any additional casualties to their ranks. The outcome for the hostiles inside the building was very different. Only eight injured people would make it out of there. They would be taken into custody, tried, convicted, and sentenced to death.

The assault drew quite a few onlookers. Several people approached the soldiers outside of the building. Most of them thanked the soldiers for taking action against the people inside.

The commander learned from the onlookers that the group inside was terrorizing people in the area. They stole whatever food and supplies they found. They raped and killed without conviction.

The commander didn't tell anyone of the cannibalism. The crimes committed already were heinous enough. He didn't want to alarm anyone else in the area. He assumed that people already knew it was happening.

The troops did not waste any time. They cleared all of the bodies out of the building. One of the trucks in the convoy had FEMA caskets on it. The troops were able to place three and four bodies in the large caskets. These would then be disposed of at the mobile crematories back on Selfridge.

The doors and windows were all checked to make sure the building was secured. Signs that had been brought with the troops were put up declaring the building to be under government control and not to trespass.

A large white board was placed on the front of the building. The troops would use this to disseminate information to any people in the area.

The onlookers started asking about aid. The commander didn't have the answer to that. He told the people they were there to secure the building and prepare it for operation. He was careful to let the troops know not to engage the people in detailed conversation. He also let them know not to distribute any aid to them yet.

As much as they all wanted to help these people right then, they had to finish their operation. Worrying about droves of people showing up and hindering their efforts would be counterproductive.

The troops moved in their equipment and supplies. They had brought in sheets of plywood and were able to get the windows sealed up from the weather. The rest of the day was spent setting up their operations center and securing the area. They also had another task that was being performed by four soldiers.

Those four soldiers were going from office to office and removing the hard drives from the computers. They did this in the data center as well, removing them from the servers.

Although the EMP had destroyed the computers, the plates themselves could be removed from the defunct hard drives, remounted in new units, and the data recovered. The hard drives were placed in rugged, black, foam-lined containers and taken to the roof. Once on the roof a helicopter came in and the crew chief lowered a cable and hoisted the boxes into the bird.

These hard drives contained data on the area's active duty troops, reserves, veterans, militia groups, activists and more. The government had plans for everyone.

The hard drives were flown back to Selfridge. A few of the trucks, including the one with the bodies, made their way back to Selfridge, too. Only 20 of the troops, including their casualties, returned with them. The rest stayed to guard the building.

Now that the Federal building was secured, it would eventually become the stronghold during the move to retake the city and restore order. The troops did not know it, but this particular operation would be one of their easiest.

Chapter 24

Adam had an older Chevy Suburban in his garage. It wasn't anything special to look at it, but it ran, even after the EMP. This would be the primary bug out vehicle they would use.

On top of the Suburban was mounted a rack system. Adam got the idea from work trucks. It was originally designed to accommodate ladders and extended over the hood to provide additional space.

He had installed a small planking system that would serve as the floor of the rack and some short side rails. Along with a few small structural changes he had made, the system allowed him to transport 15 plastic totes without having to strap them down.

The totes were common plastic totes purchased at a local super center for just a few bucks each. The group loaded these with as much food as they could and then duck taped down the plastic lids. After loading the food totes, the group made sure they loaded as much ammunition into the vehicle as they could. The rear seats were removed to accommodate the injured. They had two more vehicles to prepare.

The second vehicle in the garage had belonged to Adam's brother. This was a four-door pickup with a shorter bed and cap. The rear seating area was used for more food and equipment storage. The bed was loaded with a mattress for passengers.

The third vehicle was outside in the backyard. This vehicle was an older Jeep Comanche. Getting this one loaded with equipment or food would be difficult, so they opted to use it for passengers only.

Adam called for everyone to gather around. They had one last task to perform. All of the dead were gathered and placed in the living room. They held a short service and said their goodbyes.

The group finished their preparations and loaded all of the injured into the vehicles. As they did this, Adam walked around the first floor of the house and filled some small plastic milk jugs with gasoline.

He and another man went into the living room and placed the remainder of the firewood that was in the home around the bodies and soaked everything with more gasoline. It may have seemed disrespectful and crude, but none of the survivors wanted any of their loved ones to become meals. It was a disgusting fact, but people were cannibalizing each other.

The time had come to bug out. Five people ran out to the Comanche sitting in the backyard. Two jumped in the cab and three in the back. Two more people ran out from the house and opened the gate. They all had a small amount of gear with them.

The Comanche pulled out onto the street toward the house filled with bandits. There was a short exchange of gunfire between those in the vehicle and a couple of observers the gang had posted.

As this exchange was occurring, the garage door at Adam's house was opened and the remaining two vehicles pulled out onto the street and turned to the main road. As soon as these were out of the garage, the Comanche started backing up.

The people in the back of the Comanche provided enough cover fire so that the others could escape. The three vehicles all made it to the main road and then started on their journey.

The gang had won. The leader approached Adam's home with caution. They surrounded the house and checked it out. Once they felt safe enough they went inside.

Suddenly the leader yelled loudly for everyone to get out. The gang members that had entered Adam's house all ran for the doors. They had barely gotten outside when the flames started.

The fire had been started by using a cigarette and paperclip, something that Haliday had used many times before. The smell of gas had alerted the leader, thus causing him to panic. The flames spread quickly throughout the home. The makeshift funeral pyre in the living room went up in a massive ball of flames. As the small plastic containers of gas melted, the gas inside of them spilled everywhere, causing more fire.

Adam and his group didn't bother to look back. There was no point. The entire house was engulfed in flames. Their dead were now safe, and the gang would not get any of the prized supplies Adam's group had left behind.

The members of Adam's group had taken sleeping blankets with them to keep warm. The injured were also covered with these. The people in the back of the Comanche took turns keeping warm with theirs or providing security.

It was early morning and the sun would break in a just over an hour. The small convoy avoided anything that looked like trouble. They were halfway to their destination when they ran into a small bit of trouble. On one of the roads, they encountered a small roadblock.

Those keeping guard at the roadblock were mostly asleep. One man spotted the approaching convoy and called out to the others. They awoke and scrambled to take up fighting positions.

Adam stopped the vehicle and put it in reverse. The people near the roadblock fired in his direction. The people in the Comanche jumped out and returned fire.

As soon as Adam's Suburban and the pickup got turned around they sped off. The Comanche turned around as well and the men shooting jumped into the back. It too sped off. Luckily no one was hurt.

Adam was spent, both physically and emotionally. He slowed to a crawl and struggled to read the street signs. His wife told him that they had made it to the intersection. The area was a typical, small, suburban neighborhood.

Adam looked around and spotted a fenced off area. A sign on the fence identified it as a landscape company. Two people from the Comanche quickly checked it out and then the three vehicles pulled in through the open gate.

They sat there for a few minutes. Adam reached down and grabbed his ham radio. He called Haliday. He waited a few minutes for him to get to the radio.

Haliday said, "Adam, it's Roger. How you doing?"

"We made it to the intersection. Actually an area close by."

"Any more trouble?"

"Not really. Just a small barricade, but not much trouble. They fired on us, but no one got hurt," Adam said.

"Is the area safe?"

"Actually, it doesn't look like much is going on. This spot might be OK for a while."

"You think you can make it there if I talk you through it?"

At his cabin, Haliday listened to Adam, envisioning his predicament. He didn't want to risk giving out the address. He figured the intersection he told Adam about before was close enough. He could walk him right to his house using some visual clues.

Hopefully by doing so, anyone else listening in would not try to locate them, start trouble, and try to steal what little supplies Adam and his group had left.

"I think we can handle it. I'll send in a recon team first," Adam said.

"What's it look like where you are?" Haliday asked.

There was a pause while Adam looked around. "A lot of woodchips."

Haliday had to think for a minute. It finally came to him. The landscape yard. The more he thought about the woodchips, the more he realized that they would provide plenty of fuel for a fire pit or fireplace. It surprised him no one had thought about that.

"OK, Adam, here's what you do," Haliday told him.

He gave Adam a set of instructions that would take him directly to Haliday's house less than half a mile away. If Adam was comfortable with it, he was welcome to use it.

Adam said, "I'll call you back as soon as we check it out."

Haliday sat back in his chair at the ham, hoping for the best of Adam.

Adam asked for two volunteers. A man and his wife stepped up. Both were in their forties, physically fit, had never had any kids, and were well trained. They had taken multiple survival courses and seminars.

The couple took the directions and moved out. They didn't have a specific address. Haliday had said they would be able to figure it out immediately, under the current circumstances.

The couple moved slowly down the street. They paused and looked at a house that had smoke coming from a pipe stack on the roof. They could smell the wood burner working on a few small logs.

The man looked at the house across the street and chuckled a bit. The mailbox didn't have a name on it. Just the house numbers, but it was a unique design. It was shaped like a .45 caliber pistol. You opened the barrel and placed the mail inside. Along the top were the words *Molon labe*. Translated from Greek it meant, "Come and get them."

The couple eyed the house and approached slowly. The closer they got, the more they were sure it was Haliday's. The covered windows, multiple locks, even the warning sign in the yard that read, "Due to the high cost of ammo, no warning shots will be fired." Yes, this indeed was the place. It looked empty. They would make sure it was.

The front door was closed. They worked their way to the back and found the patio door wide open. They carefully entered the house.

Once inside they turned on the flashlights mounted to their rifles. They swept the rooms as they entered them. The house was completely empty. It was evident that it had been thoroughly ransacked.

There was not a single cupboard or closet that was not opened. The furniture was overturned, the pictures torn off the walls—it was a total mess. The good news was that no one was living there.

The woman told her husband she would go get the rest of the group. She went outside and made her way back to the group waiting in the vehicles. She spotted curtains moving on the house where they had seen the smoke. She made note of this.

When she arrived back at the group she told Adam what they had found. Adam was concerned with the house across the street and called Haliday.

"Roger, what do you make of them?" Adam asked.

"I'm surprised they made it. But they won't bother you. They keep to their own," Haliday said.

"You sure about that?"

Haliday's tone was understanding. He knew that Adam had every right to be concerned. They had just been through hell and could not afford to go through it again. Not right now, at least. "Adam," he said, "you'll be fine. Trust me."

Adam considered this for a minute. Haliday had just given them his home to use. Who in their right mind would do that? He had no reason to doubt Haliday. He got his group ready to move.

The man in the house opened the garage door after figuring out how to take down Haliday's safeguards. The Suburban and pickup pulled in. The Comanche drove around to the backyard and parked up against the patio deck.

The group quickly moved inside and set up a security detail. A few of the people quickly organized the master bedroom to use for their injured. The rest of house they placed back in order as well as they could. It was not a large house, but right now it was better than what they had.

Adam called Haliday again and thanked him profusely.

"Roger, I can't thank you enough," he said.

Haliday told him how to get the solar panels and 12-volt outlets working if the equipment was still there. Adam went down into the crawlspace and noted that it was partly flooded, but the battery bank was above the water level.

The batteries were missing, obviously stolen, and would need to be replaced. Adam figured it would be an easy enough task with the number of dead vehicles left in the area. He checked the solar panel to find it was still intact. No one had bothered to take it, which surprised him. He looked at all of the water in the crawlspace. His wife made her way to him and looked at it.

"If we filter it, it'll be fine for our use," she said.

He nodded. "That was exactly what I was thinking. There has to be about two thousand gallons here." They went back up into the house.

They spent the rest of the day tending to the injured and getting the house situated. They had to work on heat. It was still too cold out.

The next morning Adam went outside. It was eerie. There were no visible signs of people except for across the street. Adam had to take a chance. He slung his rifle on his back and cautiously approached the house.

A man came out onto the wooden porch. He had his own rifle pointed at Adam.

"Stop right there. Don't come any closer," the man said.

The man was in his late sixties, with a long gray beard and a thin build. Another man came out as well, carrying a pistol. He looked like a younger version of the old man.

Adam glanced briefly at the mailboxes by the road. The one at this house said Fox. The one next door said the exact same thing. Father and son, living next to each other.

"I don't mean any harm," Adam said looking back to them.

"What are you guys doing over there? the old man asked.

Adam said, "A friend said we could use his house."

"I'm supposed to believe that?"

Adam told the man he was going to grab a radio. He slowly reached in his pocket and pulled out a portable ham. He called for Haliday and then told the old man Haliday was on the net.

"Now what makes you think I'm that stupid?" the old man asked.

Adam spoke into the radio. He slowly approached the old man and placed the radio at the old man's feet.

"There, you can ask him yourself," he said.

The old man hesitated, and then picked up the ham. He looked at it doubtfully. He fingered the transmit button and then pushed it.

"OK, tell me something only my neighbor would know," he said brusquely.

Haliday said, "Your name is Fox; it's on both mailboxes for you and your son."

The old man said, "Big deal. That don't mean anything."

Haliday said, "I used to own a party rental company. I always cleaned the moonwalks and other inflatables in my yard."

The old man said, "Big deal. That could have been known to a lot of these people."

There was a pause while Haliday thought for a minute. "OK," he said, "this is something that only you and I know."

"Go ahead then."

Haliday said, "The day we moved out there was a crowd. People died. When I looked up at you watching us, you put your head down. You wanted to help, but you didn't want to blow your own operational security."

The old man put his rifle down. He knew then that it was indeed Roger Haliday. They never said more than hello to each other in all the years they'd lived there, but still he knew it was Haliday.

He looked down at Adam. "Why don't you come inside and we can talk a few minutes?"

Adam waved off a few members of his group that had been watching and went inside the old man's home. Adam told him what had happened. He asked the old man if the area was safe.

"We get a few small gangs time and again, but nothing we can't handle," the old man told him.

Adam looked around. The old man looked thin, tired, and hungry. The son looked the same. He wondered how they had lasted. An older woman walked in with coffee. Adam's eyes lit up.

She had been in the small kitchen when they had walked in. The kitchen looked barren. Adam thought to himself, *that might just be the trick*.

They kept little to no food around. Barely ate enough to subsist, so their appearance alone was not threatening. Anyone searching their home would not find the family's cache.

He assumed the three of them were not only lucky, but very smart as well. He had to applaud them. They did one of the best jobs at keeping up the ruse he had seen.

"How are you guys set over there?" the old man asked.

"We can hold our own for now, but need to get some heat," Adam said.

The old man pointed. "Go a mile down the road and you'll see a heating and cooling shop. They'll have the piping to connect that wood burner in Roger's garage. Should have everything you need."

Adam smiled. The old man had kept a close eye on Haliday for sure. He made a mental note to have a few people go get the supplies they needed for the wood burner. "Anyone else in the area we need to worry about?"

"Not really. A few more prepper groups, but no one is on the move."

"I still can't believe you guys don't have large gangs roaming around," Adam noted.

"We did. It was awful around here for a lot of people. A lot of folks moved out to Selfridge, toward family, or who knows where. A lot of folks were killed," the old man explained.

Adam didn't doubt the man's story. The one thing he could not grasp was that this location was really no further from Detroit than his own home had been.

As if reading Adam's mind, the old man said, "I know it seems odd. We've been listening to the ham like everyone else.

This is how we see it; the military doesn't need to protect the people out in the sticks. Those people are hard to get to and can stand on their own I guess. The big cities and close suburbs are long gone and will be for a very long time. So, it looks like they created a gray area. An area between the cities and the sticks. They patrolled these areas and killed off as many of the gangs as they could. Keep the cities and the sticks separated."

"The military patrols around here?" Adam asked.

"Yes they do. In a sense, I mean. Have been for a couple of months now."

Adam could not believe what he heard. How could it be? he wondered. He never heard anything about it.

"Anything south of M-59 is fair game right now. Anything north is too risky for the gangs. The military sees a large group moving and they just roll in and massacre them."

"How do you know this?"

"I have another son. He's in the service. That's all I can say and I have said too much," the old man said, standing up.

Adam took it as his cue to leave.

The old man walked him to the door and said goodbye, and good luck. Adam went back to Haliday's house.

He tried to digest what he had heard. He told the group about it. They all had questions but no one had answers. Adam then remembered the wood burner.

He and two volunteers took the Comanche out. On the way he thought about the old man's words. The more he thought about it, the more it made sense.

Let the cities crumble. Let the agricultural areas survive by placing a buffer between them and the population. Then, assist the people in the farmlands to keep safe.

After due time, you would have a viable area to grow food and raise livestock. The masses in the city who couldn't survive would be weeded out. Those of criminal elements were eliminated. By this means the government had basically decided to commit genocide. They were reshaping the country by reshaping the makeup of the population.

Adam could not believe it. No one in his group could.

After a hard day's work they had the wood burner installed. It wasn't the prettiest job, but it would work just fine. They spent the next few days gathering wood.

There was plenty around in the surrounding wooded areas, plus they had a ton of woodchips from the landscape yard. They would be able to stay warm through the winter and into spring.

They calculated their food preps. They had around three months' worth. Mostly freeze-dried and dehydrated; a lot of beans and a lot of rice.

Adam called Haliday, who offered up a small cache. Adam told him, "No thank you."

He would rather that be kept secret as a last resort. Haliday told him if he needed it, just give the word.

He explained to Haliday what the neighbor had said. Haliday didn't doubt it either and admitted to being blindsided by the information. But then again, he had heard about the government infighting. Maybe they were still at it.

A week had passed since Adam's group had moved to Haliday's. They had not encountered any trouble. Only once had they spotted a military patrol in the area.

The patrol consisted of an MRAP and two Humvees, both appeared heavily armed. Adam's group paid no attention to them. They wanted to be left alone and didn't want any trouble.

Settled in for the rest of the winter, Adam's group worked on contingency plans. Whether or not they stayed or moved elsewhere again, they would need to make arrangements to grow food and prepare for the following winter.

They had no idea what the future would hold. It would be a long, cold winter and they would be hungry. Spring was a couple of months away. Hopefully it would bring a brighter future.

Chapter 25

Over near Fort Custer, Bruce was in his trailer reading a book. He had not ventured out after the last incident when his family went in for ID cards. They had decided that they would forego any future trips outside of their camp. The only reason to stray out of their area would be for hunting.

Bruce put his book down and looked outside the window of the trailer. His wife was outside getting some firewood. He thought about life before the EMP.

After high school he had entered the Army. He had decided that one tour of active duty was enough. At the time he was not interested in changing his Military Occupational Specialty, which he would need to do to advance in rank.

His MOS didn't prepare him for much in the civilian world so he picked up various jobs as time passed. He eventually met his wife and then landed a decent job.

He'd worked as a troubleshooter for an automotive supplier. His forte was troubleshooting issues with the electrical harnesses produced by the company he worked for.

He eventually had his two girls and moved up the company ranks as a line foreman. Life was pretty good for him and the family. He had always prepped in one way or another and now had the chance to enhance his preps. His father and mother in-law hadn't joined in, but did contribute money toward the cause. His father did help build out the trailer and prepare the camp, however.

The economy started to slide downward and the auto industry took a major hit. Bruce went to work one day to find his locker contents and personal belongings boxed up. The company gave no notice. They just shut down one day and moved production to China. The company knew what they had planned, but they had never given the workers any notice.

Bruce found himself looking for a new job during the worst economic crisis he had ever seen. The housing market dropped. The foreclosure rate skyrocketed. People were losing their jobs everywhere.

Bruce sold his home for barely enough to cover what he owed and downsized. The only job he was able to find he hated, but soon learned to embrace. He landed a fulltime job with a property management company. He traveled the area, going from building to building fixing things—doors, cabinets, lighting, and more.

The one benefit was the amount of materials he found to use in his preps. As the buildings were remodeled or repairs were made, he would recycle items. When companies moved out of their spaces they often left behind a load of good equipment.

Before he would throw items in the dumpster, he would think about possible uses for them. He was allowed to take whatever he wanted for his personal use. He did this for the two years prior to the EMP. He was able to gather the materials to build his shed, including wood, cement, windows, paint, even hardware. His trailer was retrofitted with recycled materials as well.

The wood stove was a demo left behind from a business that closed down. The insulation under his trailer was from another area that was demolished.

As he thought about it all, he looked at his wife once more. This time he noticed the difference in her face. She had lost nearly 25 pounds. Except for his children, they had all lost weight.

When she came inside she saw a look of concern on his face.

She asked, "What's wrong, honey?"

"I'm thinking about food storage," he answered back.

"What about it?"

"Let's do an inventory and see exactly what we have. I think maybe we can increase our calorie intake. I think we are being too careful."

She looked at him and said, "It's not like we couldn't stand to lose a few pounds."

"But we might need to keep up our energy levels," he shot back.

"Bruce, I think you're worrying too much. We haven't lost any weight in the past month, which means we have leveled out our diets. We are all healthy; no colds, no sickness, no weakness. We're just fine," she told him.

He thought about it for a moment and decided she was right. Just to put himself at ease, he decided to run through the supply list anyway.

He walked through the trailer, checked all of their caches and calculated their remaining stores. They would make it just over a year without having to gather anything except water.

Nothing extremely gourmet, and fresh game meat would be a bonus, but they would make it unless some misfortune came about. Like most preppers, they had a lot of beans and rice.

One of the biggest problems they would have to overcome would be boredom. His group was small, money was spent wisely, and luxuries like Haliday's group had were nonexistent in his camp.

He, too, had taken advantage of a lot of garage sales. He concentrated on used books for enjoyment and for educating his children. They were expected to be home schooled five days a week.

The book education was augmented with basics; knife sharpening, fire starting, putting up shelters, and other survival skills to help them in case things got worse.

Other entertainment consisted mostly of card games for the adults and a large supply of board games for both the adults and children. They played a different game each night to help break up the monotony.

Cabin fever would be hard to battle. They had become used to the modern life. Television, radio, iTunes, tablets, video games, text messages, the internet, and more.

All of it was gone in the blink of an eye. It would be years before it all came back, and that was if it ever did come back. There was no way to tell.

Bruce and his family hunkered down for a long, cold winter. They like many others wondered what the next couple of months and spring would bring into their lives.

*****

Over by Camp Grayling, Dennis was in a slightly different position. The area was a flurry of activity for the military, but not really for anyone else.

They had stopped taking volunteers for work details and now only accepted people into the FEMA camps. Dennis had missed out on the chance to get in and see what was going on firsthand.

He looked around his small house. He had enough firewood to keep warm during the winter and could cut down a few more trees if he needed to.

The food situation was more of a concern than anything else. They had stocked up for the typical winter they usually endured, but they had miscalculated how long their current stocks would last.

Dennis had forgotten that during the week they were always able to make a trip into town for fresh milk, meat, or any other items they were running low on.

He took an inventory of everything they had and then started on a rationing plan in order to stretch their supplies. He worked on the plan for three days.

Some time in mid-April they would run out of food. He had no idea of how much aid would be available or if there would be any at all.

He took a walk out to his garage and looked around. He would need to take action in order to survive. He looked at everything in the garage. With some ingenuity, some hard work, and a lot of luck he could repurpose a lot of items and use them to assist him in getting food.

He spotted an older seine net he had used years ago for smelt fishing. He thought about that. They would wade out into the water, net down low, sweep in an arc and walk up onto the beach.

A couple of days of freshwater smelt fishing each spring often produced more smelt than he ever wanted. Usually a barrel full.

He would take them home and host a big smelt fry for him and the neighbors. That usually used up half of the barrel.

The rest he would cut diagonally from the top of the head down to fin, removing the head and guts. They were then smoked and put away for him to snack on during the year.

This spring, just after the ice thaw, he would be out smelting for sure. He would take as much as he possibly could and use every single one. While most guys used dip nets, he found the seine net to work much faster.

Spring was too far off now. He needed food now.

He looked over in a corner and spotted some old t-posts. A thought crossed his mind. He decided to take some of the t-posts, anchor them in the small river nearby, and attach the seine net.

If he had any luck, he would be able to snag some fish this way. He made plans to take the gear down to the river and give it a try.

The t-posts, a couple of cinder blocks on each side, and that should do the trick. He would try it for a few days, then pull the net out and let it dry. No sense in taking a risk and letting it get damaged by letting it sit out too long.

He had regular ice fishing gear, too. The auger was a manual version, so he didn't have to worry about lugging a gas motor around.

The unfortunate thing was that many more people would be out there ice fishing as well. Instead of the occasional ice fishing trip, people would constantly be out there.

He had some wire and wooden stakes, so setting up snare traps was also on the list of things to do. Anything with meat on it would be welcomed.

He sat down and looked at the wall. He saw the case for his bow hanging up. Next to that was a quiver case full of arrows.

When he originally decided to go hunt deer, it was already too late. The deer population had dwindled rapidly after the first few weeks following the EMP. The game population in general had rapidly declined. People over-hunted within weeks. Everyone had families and mouths to feed.

The game that was left was scarce. The animals learned quickly that man was an enemy. They moved away from populated areas. He'd heard stories of hunters coming back empty handed after days of hunting. He also heard stories of some hunters never making it back. He decided that hunting was not an option. He would make do with what he had and try the fishing and trapping.

Just before he left the garage he looked on a nearby counter. There were packets of seeds they'd purchased on closeout. The thought of fresh corn and vegetables was appealing. The hard fact that it would be almost eight months before they could harvest any of it was depressing.

Dennis walked back into his house and sat down by the fire. He talked to his family and together they finished laying out their plans. He would keep in touch with Haliday and Bruce during the upcoming months, sharing information, sharing hope, and praying they would survive until spring.

Praying that they would survive the troubled times.

*****

The Bad Axe airport slowly became busier than normal. The airstrip was still being used to ferry in supplies for surrounding FEMA camps.

The FEMA camps nearby had also reached capacity. They had more than enough volunteers to work at the jobs that had been offered to the people.

326

The remaining people were given menial, repetitive tasks to perform in order to earn their keep. In return, they were given shelter and food.

The food that was cooked was very basic. Bags of rice and beans were brought in, along with spices to add to them. They were used in over 70 percent of the dishes cooked.

Breakfast consisted of oatmeal or cereal grains with reconstituted powdered milk. Lunch was merely a ration bar, similar to a granola bar. Dinners were mostly stews and soups with bread.

Meats were rarely included in the meals served within the camps. The military and acting government officials ate along with the people; however, it was rumored they enjoyed special treats in the privacy of their quarters.

Rob was still bordering on giving in. He started to work more closely with the area prefect. Rob was consulted on numerous occasions concerning the general area.

He was asked questions about the farming and fishing industries in the area, the general make up of the population, any locations for specialized industries, electronics, mechanical manufacturing and more.

One thing Rob discovered, though, was that his stockpile of paper products from his small store had come in handy. He was glad they had been stored at his home in the pole barn.

He would be using them to barter for a variety of items to include some food, gas, ammunition, and even hard currency like silver and gold.

He made sure that his dealings would be kept quiet and by doing this it prevented him from actually caving in altogether. He didn't want them to force him to end his trading empire.

The acting government didn't trust him that much and the information he was given was limited. The military kept a close eye on him.

Rob wasn't sure what the rest of the winter would bring for him. He was certain, however, that he and his family would be able to make it until spring. Of course, that would depend on how much worse things would get.

Brad kept completely out of sight and out of mind. He still led the regional law enforcement group, but they kept their operations separate from military control. The only dealings they had with them were when they had to turn over prisoners. Brad did have his ears open and had a lot of people listening in so he could gather information on what was transpiring.

Brad and Haliday had plans to keep in touch and continue to sort through everything that was going on. They would share information and keep it to themselves.

The region looked like it would be quite secure. There were only a few small trouble areas with very small groups causing problems. These would be easy to mop up.

The military and acting government started to ramp up their efforts in the area. Everything they did was kept quiet. There was no transparency in their operations. This fueled the conspiracy theories.

The camps were filling up with more and more people each day. The cold weather would be claiming more lives of those unable to seek out the assistance that was being offered.

The urban areas were more of an issue for the military than originally thought. There still existed mass gangs and groups who were determined to run the cities as they saw fit. Any operations inside these areas would be met with hostility. Groups inside these areas that chose to live by a rule of law would find themselves in dire need of aid to defend their lives.

*****

Haliday sat at the fireplace deep in thought. Most of the group had gathered around. They had quickly learned that once Haliday was in thought, a group discussion soon followed.

He didn't say anything for quite a while. The rest of them made small talk and waited. He sat there even longer than usual as he thought of the past few months.

There was no sense in revisiting the past. A lot had happened, mistakes were made, lives were lost. Dwelling on it would only bring people's morale down.

What they needed to do was concentrate on planning for the future. There was an enormous amount of work to be done. Mere survival at this point was really a fulltime job. If things didn't change for the better it would become a career.

Rich spoke first. "Roger, where do we go from here?"

"We review our plans, again and again, and then we review them again," Haliday said.

328

He explained what most of them already knew. The government was extremely questionable right now. The government agenda was extremely unclear. In some aspects it seemed like a dictatorship; in others a rebuilding attempt.

Some of the immediate concerns were fuel. Eventually the stores of fuel they had would run out or go bad. If there were no means of replenishing those stores, survival would be harder.

There was only a limited amount of fuel left in the surrounding vehicles that had been abandoned and access to the gas stations underground tanks was limited as well. Without fuel treatment, it would clog fuel injectors and carburetors anyway.

They would need to resort to using the horses for plowing, planting, and cultivating the fields. With a fairly large group, there would have to be a lot of crops planted. They would also need extra produce for trade.

They had the seeds—that was the easy part. Making sure the crops were properly taken care of would heavily rely on Bill's knowledge. Mark grew up on the farm with his dad and together they would be able to direct the group's efforts.

The hardest part to figure out was whether or not the government would actually confiscate the crops, and if not, how to keep them secure from everyone else.

They had access to plenty of wood, so heating and cooking fuel was readily available. It would be a matter of making sure it was cut, seasoned and rotated.

Electricity was a luxury. When gas ran out, the generator would be useless. The solar power would not provide as much energy as they needed. Refrigeration would become a thing of the past unless they made changes to their power usage.

In order to save power, they planned to stop using the luxury items that very few others enjoyed right now. The computer, TV, and small sound system they had protected in order to survive the EMP would have to sit idle.

If they lost the ability to refrigerate food it would mean any fresh meat would have to be smoked, turned into jerky or packed in salt to preserve. They could only slaughter smaller amounts to prevent waste.

Water was abundant and they would be able to treat it effectively for drinking and cooking. Showers would need to be limited in order to prevent waste.

The group had a very large stock of ammunition. Keeping that level up would depend solely on just how much more trouble they encountered. There would be no more hunting the bad guys. Aggressors could come in the form of individuals, small to large groups, or even the government. They would have to decide when fighting—or if fighting—was no longer an option.

This was all contingent upon what the country and the acting government was doing. That was the million dollar question. What exactly was it they were doing? What exactly were their plans? Would they succeed?

The government was still battling groups across the affected areas. They were still struggling to bring in aid. Restoring the country would be a difficult task. Cities were still burning. Gangs were still roving, raping, killing, pillaging, and ruling urban areas. Removing them was not as easy as the government had originally thought.

Haliday went on and on and everyone listened. He expected loads of questions, but received very few. Everyone understood the gravity of the situation.

Having cut ties with the government and military for now afforded them fewer options. With all of this in mind they finished the discussion on the future and their plans.

He looked around one last time and stood up. "We have made it this far and we can make it through the rest of what's to come."

They all stood up to either assume their security duties or go off to bed. When morning came it would not only be the start of a new day, but also the start of yet another unknown future.

Haliday took some time to himself to think it all through again. The EMP event itself, the government infighting, the current military operations, his own group's efforts and more.

There were still a lot of unanswered questions. There were still a lot of unknown events to arise. The one thing he knew for certain was that the rest of this winter, and then spring, would bring about more change.

In fact, the next few months would answer a lot of questions. Who was in charge? What really happened? What was the government and military agenda? How many more people would die, and what would survivors do?

Would power be restored soon? Would more help arrive? Answers he did not know, but answers, Haliday hoped, would bring a brighter future.

Afterword:

Fiction is never truly just fiction. We can never really invent anything without the influence of what already exists. As we move around in our daily routines, we encounter many different things that influence what we perceive.

We see colors that are derived from other colors. We enter buildings that are based on other architectural styles. We even ride in vehicles that take design cues from others, or eat new foods that are mixed from different cultural tastes.

While most of this occurs innocently and without intent, we do have one problem. As tragic man-made events occur around the world, people learn from those events and use them to further their own agendas. They seek to make a bigger impact. They seek to increase the terror, the pain, and the suffering.

Wars are fought over land, money, religion, and more. They are fought with thousands of people, thousands of vehicles, and hundreds of aircraft and ships, yet they start with only one bullet fired.

We never know when an event may occur. We don't know where it may happen. We don't know how long it will last, or who it will affect and how. We can, however, know one thing. We can know that being prepared can help us get through it.

About the author:

Matthew D. Mark continues to reside in Michigan with his daughter Kayla. Still working in the security field after a career in the military and law enforcement, he also continues to write.

His works now include Dark Days Rough Roads, Dark Days Troubled Times, and he is currently working on the sequel to complete the series. He has drafted a short story compilation to be titled and released at a later date, which includes 4 different short stories.

Matthew continues to enjoy his hobbies, family and outdoor activities and remains a firearms enthusiast. He has also enjoyed the opportunity to speak to some various groups on the subject of preparedness.

Watch for the sequel

32930715R00189